I0572258

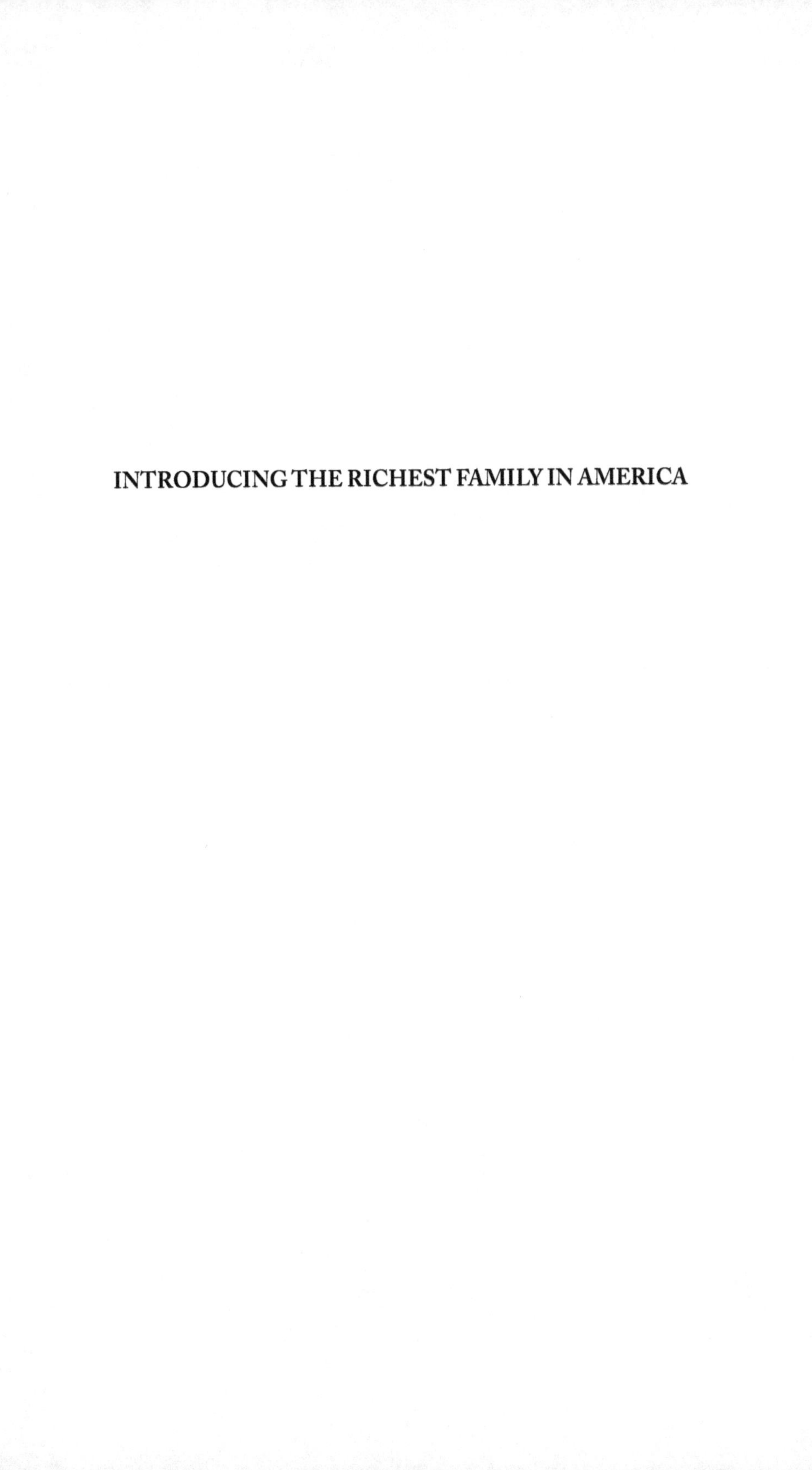

INTRODUCING THE RICHEST FAMILY IN AMERICA

Introducing the Richest Family in America

A Novel by David Drum

BURNING BOOKS PRESS
LOS ANGELES

ISBN # 978-0-9845646-0-6

Library of Congress PCN # 2010906471

First Edition

BURNING BOOKS PRESS
LOS ANGELES

WWW.INTRODUCINGTHERICHEST.COM

"Beware of what you Desire Most, For You shall Have it."

-- Old American Proverb

1. Enter the Prince

The minute the vice president of legal affairs returned from walking the pigs, he wiped off his soft brown cowboy boots and hunkered down to business.

Vice President Simon Butterknut slipped off the jacket of his blue Armani suit. He plucked out his golden cuff links. He rolled the French cuffs of his starched white shirt up to his elbows. For good measure, Vice President Simon Butterknut loosened his rich silk tie to take some of the tension off his moist, vice-presidential neck. Then he leaned back in his wide-bottomed oak swivel chair, put his boots on the desk, and rang his secretary Beatrice Van Bunkle for coffee.

The square-jawed lawyer, who slightly resembled the actor Jack Nicholson, snorted and shook his head like a dog shaking off rainwater.

Walking the pigs, he had worked up a sweat. The raging bull in his brain was now pawing the ground, preparing to charge a lazily-sleeping matador. He would show his father-in-law, old Commodore Commode.

Simon was at last working like a good corporate lawyer—setting up secret meetings, anticipating objections, making cryptic notes to himself, and blowing smoke at everyone around him. The vice president of legal affairs was spinning a complicated spider web of corporate deceit and flies would be humming into the grid before long. Where was his coffee? Had any other son-in-law of a major private company ever hatched such a scheme? Taking flight on the heady gas of his daydreams, Simon felt his broad-shouldered body practically rising into the air, his teeming brain taking flight on parchment wings. In his mind's eye he again became the flying Icarus of commerce, lurching ever higher toward the brightest, richest star in the corporate sky!

Simon Butterknut had formulated a plan to change the way business was done at the Commode Company, a stodgy old manufacturing firm which already generated an embarrassing amount of profit. A Prince of a plan! If every painstakingly-arranged domino toppled onto the next, Simon would be recognized for who he was. On that happy day he would receive the accolades he deserved as one of the company's most farsighted men. In Simon's grand scheme to revamp the Commode Company down to its roots, it was irrelevant to him that the business was doing fine just the way it was.

Around company headquarters, it irritated Simon that his smooth fraternity boy charm worked wonders on everyone except his father-in-law and boss, practical, plodding old Commodore Commode. Simon suspected that the old capitalist didn't think much of him, even though he gave him one of the most important jobs in the company. In a more distant time, of course, a younger Simon had swept away Commodore's daughter, the former Petunia Rockefeller-Commode, rumored to be the wealthiest girl at Stanford.

Although he was a transparently ambitious prig who wore a tie even to the grocery store, Simon's fast talk and overly friendly fraternity boy manner somehow mitigated his uptight appearance and made him seem worldly to young rich Stanford girls like Petunia Commode. After he weaseled his way into Petunia's life as a tutor, the ambitious young law student laid elaborate plans to charm her pants off with his big mouth, his flashy little Corvette, and his glib Omega Pi charm.

Simon's scheme worked like a charm. Petunia was at first amused and then entranced by his fast, constant patter. In the end, Simon not only married Petunia Commode, he accepted an executive position with her father's 130-year-old company, too. Embedded as he already was in their enormously-profitable family business, like a tick on the hindquarters of a dog, it was not necessary to observe that the ends justified the means.

Legal Affairs hadn't even been a real department until Simon began his struggle to add more employees, and build his department up. Over the years, Simon had pushed and suggested and rationalized and argued and managed to hire more than a dozen more lawyers to people his corporate fiefdom, which now occupied most of the second floor of Commode Company headquarters.

It didn't bother Simon that his staff had less to do than he did, and that the other lawyers sat at their desks most of the day, pretending to work, sending out for coffee, and keeping their heads down.

❧

Simon's personal odyssey began with *The Prince*. He kept Machiavelli's pungent little self-help book in the top, right-hand drawer of his desk. Simon had kept a copy close by ever since his first year of law school, when a scowling old law professor sarcastically remarked that the book contained everything a young lawyer would ever need to know about office politics. Simon often consulted the spicy little volume. One afternoon Simon fell asleep with his face buried in *The Prince*, and had a prophetic dream.

In the dream, Simon became a Prince. Returning from a series of pitched battles where he established his excellence in combat for all to see, the Prince entered the old castle in sweaty battle garments, only mildly surprised that he could fly. Was that applause in the next room? The Prince lay down his shield, his dagger, his sword, his winged battle helmet. Without a glance at his Rolex Daytona he floated effortlessly up to a golden raised podium to the masculine thunder of loud, hearty, whistling applause.

Microphones and cameras materialized: all pivoted toward the Prince. Simon grandly surveyed the multitude of loudly-shouting admirers spread out before him. Grasping the podium with both hands, Simon looked out over a sea of cameras and microphones, took a deep breath, and realized that he was finally going to get the recognition he deserved.

That day Simon awoke with a start, Miss Van Bunkle tapping like a woodpecker at his office door. Still drooling a bit from his nap, the vice president of legal affairs jerked up his head with a few lines of Machiavelli imprinted on the side of his face. Glancing at his Rolex Yacht-master, and drying his mouth with a monogrammed handkerchief, the Prince hurried into the conference room with an imaginary triumph in his heart and strange new ideas festering in his head.

From that Friday afternoon on, Simon worked to connect the reality of his life with the heady flush of victory and fame he had experienced as a premonition in the dream. The sweet smell of all that was promised propelled Simon forward into more and more ethically dubious territory. The Prince, for Simon now thought of himself as the Prince, saw himself as a sure-footed alpha goat, scrambling and battling his way up corporate mountain to the craggy pinnacle of fame itself.

It helped that Simon was the only one in the company who knew Commodore's most closely guarded secret. Almost by accident, he discovered that the old billionaire had a fling with an Asian girl a few months before he and Milly were married. It was nothing, as such things go, but the old billionaire nursed a secret obsession with the beautiful Chinese girl who was the first woman to pull him into bed. Indeed, Simon knew that Commodore fantasized about her for years while having dutiful sex with his late wife, Milly.

Was it only a coincidence that Simon stumbled upon this bit of information a few hours after his Friday afternoon dream? Right after work he waded into Happy Hour at the Binderback Hotel. Simon sidled up next to a beefy, thick-lipped Mediterranean woman in a long black dress and black lipstick who was staring glumly at herself in the mirror over the bar. Simon sat down, made a few playful comments about her black fingernails and the ankh charm around her neck, and then struck up a conversation. The woman in black turned out to be Commodore's personal grief counselor. She was having a bad day and needed to talk to someone about her work.

After the woman in black hinted that she had some juicy personal information about the wealthiest man in Montecito, Simon became fascinated by everything she said. The Prince stepped up the patter, plied her with Manhattans. After several drinks, the loose-lipped grief counselor put one leg on the floor and suggestively rubbed her hip against him, like a hippopotamus in heat. At three drinks she already resembled the big-breasted Italian actress, Sophia Loren. When Simon cracked a wicked Jack Nicholson smile and playfully slipped his hand up her dress, the Happy Hour mating dance began.

"What *are* you doing?" she laughed. "You're somebody *famous*, aren't you?"

As the mating dance whirled towards a climax, the Prince laughingly herded the tipsy grief counselor through the lobby and into the elevator, peppering her with innocuous questions about Commodore. The grief counselor pretended to be surprised when Simon unlocked the door to the corporate suite, smiled a wicked smile, and gently pulled her inside.

In his darkest brooding moments, Simon pictured himself as The Bastard Prince, the unacknowledged rightful heir to the golden throne. Locked in constant combat with everyone around the King, he plotted his way through the murky night, keeping only his own counsel, as fitted a hero destined for great things. He was a corporate gladiator clad only in simple Armani, Gucci briefcase in hand, guided through battle after battle by only a modestly glowing Rolex on his wrist. Aye, as he conspired with the world the Bastard Prince became even more crafty, clawing his way farther and farther up the organizational chart with only animal cunning, sharp wordplay, and an increasingly clever and complicated scheme. Slashing and burning his way to the throne! Out-thinking his clueless opponents! Pulling a blanket over the eyes of the corporate sheep! Driving deep the dagger from behind! The Bastard Prince knew it was only a matter of time before the hard-shelled old king would roll off his throne, land on his back like a helpless beetle, and expose his private parts to the sky. And ever since Simon's prophetic dream, passages from *The Prince* popped into his head at the strangest moments.

Simon sometimes felt like he had a crafty old Italian co-conspirator leading him up the long, winding, rock-strewn stairway to heaven.

But it is necessary that the Prince should know how to color his nature well, and how to be a great hypocrite and dissembler. For men are so simple, and yield so much to immediate necessity, that the deceiver will never lack dupes.

—Machiavelli, from *The Prince*

Simon Butterknut was at that moment in an enviable position. His filthy rich wife was more or less wrapped around his finger. He knocked down a salary that would have embarrassed even some lawyers. Petunia received a handsome allowance which rang into the Butterknut family coffers like clockwork twelve times a year. And Simon and Petunia spent much of their time gloating over Petunia's growing stock portfolio, the vacation houses, the fleet of cars, as well as the miscellaneous properties earmarked for Petunia (and therefore for Simon) that Commodore and his late wife had not yet assigned to the trust. Simon's large gray stone mansion with the Italian slate roof was the envy of all the other lawyers in the firm. The latest addition was Simon's huge personal gymnasium at the lower rear story of the mansion, a birthday surprise from Petunia and her mother. But that was another story. If Simon remained a prig who wore a tie to the grocery store, he had acquired all the trappings of a rich, successful man. He had a walk-in closet full of Armani suits, and an expensive hand-tooled cabinet to hold his precious collection of Rolex watches. The mansion's garages were filled with the virtual rainbow of businesslike Mercedes sedans that Petunia had given him for various birthdays and anniversaries. It impressed the vice president's staff that he drove a different-colored Mercedes to work each day of the week, and on special occasions slipped them cases of good wine and expensive Cuban cigars. Although Simon had no real friends, it was enough that all the other lawyers envied the life he led among the crème de la crème of Montecito.

The Prince had long ago hypnotized Petunia with his high-octane patter. With persistent gentle bullying Simon had molded his pig-loving wife into an intellectual copy of himself. But Petunia also loved her animals—sometimes, Simon suspected, even more than she actually loved him.

For their honeymoon, it was his animal-loving wife's idea to take a long, stomach-churning flight over the ocean and go on a wild animal-watching safari in the wilds of Africa, a honeymoon Simon barely survived. In Africa, his portly new wife thrilled to the sight of shifting, quickly-trotting herds of exotic animals, and the late-night cries of carrion-devouring hyenas. Simon remembered mainly the rickety cot on which he tried to make love to his wife. He remembered the truly huge African mosquitoes which easily penetrated the mosquito nets over his cot but never seemed to bother Petunia. Simon could also not forget the dozens of shirtless black Africans who sullenly carried their bags, and were forever relieving themselves at night behind his tent.

Neither could he forget the sarcastic remarks he couldn't quite overhear from the unshaven, tobacco-chewing South African guides, and the clouds of unbelievably foul-smelling dust kicked up by their guide's mud-spattered Range Rover as he led their much newer Range Rover after pack after pack of frightened, skittering wild animals.

After three weeks in the heart of Africa, covered with mosquito bites and suffering from a persistent diarrhea, Simon tried to forget what became one long extended trip to the men's room on the nightmare flight back home.

Under the influence of local hero Ronald Reagan, who had a ranch down the road, Petunia impulsively built a stable behind their new mansion and filled it with expensive quarter horses. Suddenly their friends all were fancy pants cowboys on million dollar horses, forever complaining about welfare and taxes. Simon didn't enjoy bouncing around after Petunia on the saddle of a horse, but he did enjoy wearing the Western outfit and especially the cowboy boots that Petunia gave him, which added almost two inches to his height. For a time they maintained a popular arena for local horse shows, near Petunia's stables. Then one afternoon Petunia's horse stepped on a wasp nest which one of the gardeners knocked off the blacksmith's horse trailer. Her horse rocketed and twisted into the air, threw her off, and left her bruised and humiliated. Petunia angrily burned her riding outfits along with most of Simon's western clothes. His signature cowboy boots were all that remained from this phase of their marriage.

The day the horses were shipped out to the dog food factory, whinnying loudly as a long caravan of horse trailers passed their house, Petunia's mother dropped off an unexpected gift—a small black purebred Chinese pot-bellied pig with a collar of her mother's fragrant gardenias around its neck.

Petunia soon adored the knee-high little pig, which followed her around the mansion like a perky little dog. The outrageously expensive little creatures became Petunia's next great obsession. As she acquired more and more pigs, Petunia built them a special enclosure behind their mansion, which over time grew larger and more elaborate.

What was basically an enormous pig sty now included a large fresh water lake which took up almost a quarter of their property. The lake was the exclusive property of the pigs, who were encouraged to jump into the water to keep cool.

In the center of the lake was an island covered with expensive custom-built pig houses, and flanked by tall palm trees. South American parrots had been established in the palm trees and trained to flap their wings and warn the little pigs of approaching danger. Petunia named her idyllic little enclave Pig Island, and it cost a fortune.

Although he was nominally in charge of the family finances, money streamed like a raging river through Simon's fingers. There was always some house or building to remodel, some payment or insurance premium to meet, some lavish anniversary gift for one of the relatives to put on the joint credit cards, some new car to buy or to service, or one more thing that he or Petunia or the veterinarians or the architects or the contractors or the realtors needed right away.

Although they floated through their lives on an virtual river of money, neither Simon nor Petunia had much impulse control. Simon and his wife enjoyed a lifestyle which would have been the envy of many an Arabian prince, but it was a lifestyle that he could barely support even with Petunia's allowance. If his tight-fisted old father-in-law ever learned the state of his family's finances, Simon feared, the penny-pinching old capitalist would surely think him a fool.

Simon sensed in his gut that his father-in-law didn't like him. The old billionaire rarely invited the vice president of legal affairs into his office for a chat, or consulted him on even the simplest business maneuvers, much less the annual financial giveaway known as "union negotiations."

The old capitalist never took Simon to lunch or dinner without Petunia along. He had never once invited Simon for a one-on-one game of golf on his beloved personal golf course, although Simon knew that Commodore had played golf with almost every other employee at the firm. And on one occasion, which was now permanently seared into the Prince's brain, Commodore hinted that maybe the vice president of legal affairs wasn't much of a catch for his darling Petunia.

Being brainlessly competitive, Simon desperately wanted to show his superiority to the old man. But at the office, Commodore shot down every one of the Prince's best ideas. Even the way the old billionaire pretended not to ignore him was humiliating to Simon.

For one thing, the Prince desperately wanted the third floor corner office overlooking State Street with a view of the Pacific Ocean. It was right down the hall from Commodore's office, and near the nerve center of the business. Simon wanted to be able to throw open the double office windows and see the ocean over the rooftops of Santa Barbara, like a Sicilian prince surveying his coastal kingdom. He was sure the view would inspire the other lawyers when they came into his office. But Commodore stubbornly refused to even discuss the idea with Old Bernie Tyler, an avuncular old toad who actually wore a green eyeshade to work and probably hadn't even opened the window of his third floor office in ten years.

When Simon approached Bernie on his own, offering flattery and Cuban cigars, the cantankerous old accountant gruffly waved Simon out of his office. When Simon slipped behind Bernie's back and suggested to Commodore that he take over the old pencil-pusher's quarters, Commodore told him Bernie was only a few years from retirement, and to let the old toad squat in the office as long as he wanted.

No amount of harping or hectoring could penetrate Commodore's stubborn resolve on what Simon had framed as the corner office struggle. The old billionaire didn't even seem to care that the Prince wanted Bernie Tyler's office now.

Commodore had also churlishly blocked Simon's single best idea for raising the legal staff's morale. More than a year before, Simon ordered catered country French lunches on Friday for the legal affairs department—generously including the pretty young secretaries and even one of the paralegals. The company could easily afford it. The catered lunches were a morale-booster. Loosened up by the French wine, black bread and blood sausages, the secretaries had taken to making eyes at their pontificating bosses. Several of the second and third vice presidents had slipped over to the corporate suite at the Binderback Hotel with their secretaries. Simon had received hearty compliments and high-fives from every one of them after they came back to the office and pompously announced they had given their hard-working little girls the rest of the afternoon off.

But one fateful Friday, without even giving Simon a heads up, Commodore barged into the legal affairs department a half hour or so after lunch was served. Commodore angrily pushed Miss Turlington off the lap of one of his second vice presidents, and then permanently cancelled the catered lunches.

When the huffing and puffing old capitalist called Simon into his office, he curtly let Simon know that he wanted him to stop his staff from fraternizing with the secretaries once and for all. Furthermore, he ordered Simon to go home and have lunch with Petunia every day, in order to set a better example for his staff.

Ever since that day, Simon and Petunia ate lunch together at the mansion. After lunch they lazily strolled out toward Pig Island, romantically holding hands. At the appropriate time, the pig whisperers would magically appear with four or five well-groomed little pigs on leashes, all snorting to go. Simon and Petunia would take the leashes and walked their pack of waddling, grunting little miniature pigs around the bark-covered path that circled the lake and then back over the wooden footbridge that linked the path with Pig Island.

Although Simon swore to Petunia that he adored her little animals, he sometimes wished that a few dozen of the little pigs would run away. Petunia spent too much of her time on Pig Island. She stubbornly refused to have her sows neutered. Consequently, the pig population exploded. Veterinarians and birthing specialists and groomers and animal dietitians and hoof-trimmers and animal exercise specialists moved in and out of Petunia's pig sties almost daily. At least one of the sows was always having a baby, and Petunia had to be present to help the delicate little purebred sows give birth. Or some other little pig was having trouble holding down its lunch. Or the younger pigs needed vaccinations against this or that new pig disease, or it was time to trim the hooves of the older boars, and Petunia needed to be there.

As the Pig Island herd grew larger and the herd more valuable, Petunia began to fear her valuable animals might be targeted in some sort of bizarre terrorist attack. After 9/11, she installed an elaborate alarm system. Petunia also hired an army of large, tattooed former professional wrestlers as night security people, to protect her little pigs at night.

That very day, after walking the pigs, a somewhat distracted Prince had hurried back to the office, sat down, and quietly flicked a nugget of pig poop off his right boot.

Miss Von Bunkle had left the cover letters for the family board meeting on his desk. After he polished up his boots, the Prince went over the letters like a hawk, pen in hand, searching for typographic errors.

If all went as planned at the board meeting, the Prince would show the company how to screw the U.S. government out of billions of dollars of tax money, and help them lay off every lazy, over-paid employee they had by moving the company's factories to China. Simon had only to convince Commodore to move the plants overseas. Once the plants were moved to China, Simon knew, the old man would lose touch with the business, as he had already done with the plants in Cleveland. With the old man dithering away his declining years on the golf course, the Prince could take the reins of the company in of his hands. Simon's smiling face would appear on business magazines and in newspapers. Perhaps Simon would even be offered a fancy TV show like Donald Trump, or run for political office, like Mike Bloomberg or Ross Perot.

All over America, he knew, executives were happily selling out their countrymen and moving to China, making themselves look like geniuses by simultaneously cutting labor costs and inflating profits. But the Prince's hints about moving the factories overseas had been ignored by the old man.

Commodore's eyes glazed over when Simon brought in his personal copy of the *Wall Street Journal* and tried to interest the old man what other giant corporations like General Electric and Wal-Mart were doing to improve their profitability in this way. And of course the old capitalist's brusque dismissals made Simon even more aware that he didn't yet have any actual power at the company yet. Blushing with humiliation after each rebuttal, the Prince angrily left the office resolving to try to win the day again.

The Prince knew that his plans would have to jell fast and completely, so that the old man couldn't change his mind like he always did when he mulled things over.

One obstacle was that Old Commodore fancied himself a good patriotic American, since he had served for a couple of years in the U.S. Navy, and was forever reminiscing about his military days. Even with the lure of additional profits, Simon presumed the old capitalist would have a knee-jerk reaction against moving his family's business out of the United States. It would take some serious manipulation to bring the stubborn old capitalist around. And since the stubborn old rooster had rebuffed his best ideas so many times before, the Bastard Prince reasoned that the only way to crack open a few eggs in the corporate henhouse was to creep through the back door of the coop in the middle of the night, surprising and impregnating sleeping hens.

The Commode Company had been set up as a family corporation. All three children had one seat on the board and one vote, as did Commodore himself. Simon needed allies and he would find them. The Prince knew he could have his way with Petunia, who was dumb as a post when it came to business. Simon's brother-in-law the Doctor was a natural ally, since he too had a wife in the palm of his hand. Greedy as a hog, but claiming to be an internationalist since he studied plastic surgery for a few months in Brazil, the Doctor could be folded into the plan as soon as he saw there was something in it for him.

❧

Simon set down his china cup of coffee. As he rose to his feet to go to the men's room, he assertively slammed both boots to the floor, a gesture which said *Let's get on with it.*

Almost immediately a snippet of Machiavelli popped into Simon's brain.

> It has never happened that a new prince has disarmed his subjects; on the contrary rather, if he has found them unarmed, he has armed them, and in that way he has made them as it were his own, and made those faithful who before were suspect.

> —Machiavelli, *The Prince*

Of course, there was an irritating fly in the ointment—the family embarrassment, Philip "Filly" Commode. Petunia's little brother was beneath contempt as far as Simon was concerned. As usual, the little fairy had not confirmed his attendance at the board meeting, which was annoying to Simon. Little Filly barely bothered to show up late at every family board meeting, forever complaining about how busy he was. And every year, Simon could count on Philip's bitchy remarks about the length of Simon's presentations. These remarks became more irritating every year.

The Prince despised the little faggot, who among his other irritating habits had recently dyed his hair a disgusting shade of red. The little fairy led an idle life of spending other people's money, tooting up the houses of the rich and famous. Although Philip Commode appeared to be successful, the Prince suspected his interior design business was heavily subsidized by Commodore's money.

Simon still carried a resentment over the artsy-fartsy decorating job his brother-in-law did on his home gymnasium. Simon suspected his fruited-up home gymnasium made him the butt of cruel jokes in the legal affairs department.

His mother-in-law herself, he found out later, had asked Philip to decorate the gym. Simon dared not criticize a thing.

The home gymnasium was supposed to be a birthday surprise for Simon although it was difficult to ignore the contractors swaggering in and out of what had been the servants' quarters at the rear of their mansion carrying workout equipment.

Probably for spite, the little faggot was inspired to put frilly little brown plaid Early American skirts around each piece of gym equipment, like so many fruity little dust ruffles around the bottom of an antique bed.

At the surprise birthday party for Simon four years before, the gymnasium was unveiled for the first time. Simon could almost feel the other vice presidents snickering behind their hands when Filly grandly led them all into the gymnasium and flicked on the artsy-fartsy faux California Gold Rush era crystal chandeliers.

Simon despised the look on Filly's face as he swished around the gymnasium, talking about feng shui and reveling in the comments about the color-coordinated skirts and how well they fit into the warm traditional feel of his sister's very traditional house.

And when the little fruitcake pranced up to the brown-skirted sports refrigerator to show the other lawyers that he had thoughtfully filled it with Simon's favorite brand of gourmet beer, the smell of old money radiated off the red-headed little faggot like the stench of entitlement itself.

❦

"There's a lady here to see you, Mr. Butterknut," Miss Van Bunkle warbled over the intercom. Simon glanced at his Rolex Daytona. The future was now.

"Send the little lady in, pronto," Simon snorted. He slid his cowboy boots off the desk, pulled himself together, and prepared for his rendezvous with destiny.

As more Machiavelli popped into his brain, the Prince again slammed down both boots with an assertive *bang*.

We have said how necessary it is for a prince to lay solid foundations for his power, as without such he would inevitably be ruined. The main foundations which all states must have, whether new, or old, or mixed, are good laws and good armies. And there can be no good laws where there are not good armies.

—Machiavelli, *The Prince*

The beautiful Chinese woman he cozied up to at the international trade show had finally arrived. Once a famous lady golfer, Long Drive Loo had empty factories in Shanghai. If it could be arranged, the Prince hoped for some sexual chemistry between the old capitalist and the brash, manipulative, overtly flirtatious Miss Loo.

Long Drive Loo strode into Simon's office with a confident smile on her face. The Prince stumbled around the desk to greet her. The Asian beauty in the red golf outfit cocked her head to one side, ripped off a golf glove, and extended a small, muscular hand that was warm as a piece of fresh toast.

"Where nice man?" She cawed.

Among the other causes of evil that will befall a prince who is destitute of a proper military force is, that it will cause him to be scorned; which is one of those disgraces against which a prince ought to guard, as we shall demonstrate further on.

—Machiavelli, *The Prince*

2. Enter the Billionaire

Somewhat earlier that morning, just a few blocks from his office, Commodore Commode stepped out of the town car and began his morning walk.

Although his company was now headquartered in the little beach town of Santa Barbara, where winters were hardly brisk, Commodore wore a proper overcoat and scarf to work as his father and grandfather had done in Cleveland.

On the sidewalks of Santa Barbara, the old billionaire blended easily into the casual morning foot traffic in the breezy little California beach town. Vacationing couples in Hawaiian shirts slipped past with paper cups full of Starbuck's coffee. Yawning vendors unlocked their shops. Nobody noticed the slowly-walking older gentleman in the tweed overcoat and billowing scarf.

The patriarch of his family, and many times a billionaire, the old capitalist took extraordinary pains to keep a low profile. By choice, he was an invisible man in the business world. His company was not listed on any stock exchange, he didn't sit on any other company's board of directors, and his name didn't pop up in any Wall Street journalist's Rolodex. He thought of himself as an ordinary man who just happened to run a prosperous manufacturing business. Indeed, he had a phobia against any form of unseemly public recognition.

Few people knew that Commodore Commode was the richest man in the United States, with a greater fortune than Donald Trump, Bill Gates, Ted Turner or any of the other showy, high profile business billionaires put together. Commodore had been born into more money than he could ever possibly spend, but he was obsessively ethical and completely honest. At times, the family's enormous wealth almost seemed to embarrass him. He was not in touch with show-your-ass America where success meant being recognized by thousands of people you didn't want to know, and where crass trumped class as regularly as dandelions went to seed in the spring.

This modest, simple gentleman was trying to get used to being a widower. He was still not entirely comfortable with the idea that he might well spend the rest of his life alone.

An energizing breeze riffled through the palm trees. Wind off the ocean put Commodore in the mood for a few extra blocks of walking. In the distance, he heard the faint roar of surf rhythmically crashing. He found himself on a street that ran along the beach, near a huge old avocado tree under whose spreading branches homeless people sometimes congregated.

As the old capitalist passed the old avocado tree, three dubious-looking tramps shuffled forward. The unfortunate wretches were harmless, he knew, and a bit pathetic. Commodore didn't wish to hear their sad stories, but he could help them get their morning cup of coffee. The old billionaire kept a few quarters in his overcoat pockets, to give away on these occasions.

"I made light bulbs for General Electric until they moved my plant to Mexico," a scratched-up man a tank top said, holding out his hand.

"Some Mexican's got my job, unless they up and moved the plant again."

"My old job's in Sri Lanka—they got kids working for a buck and a half a week with no safety equipment, making little plastic thingamajigs for Wal-Mart," a badly sunburned woman explained, struggling to articulate her betrayal. "We used to make that stuff right here to a good wage."

Without hearing much of what they said, Commodore gave them all quarters. He wistfully remembered feeding ducks as a very young boy. His Austrian nanny often took him to the park not far from the lake and encouraged him to feed the Mallards circling hungrily in the dark brown Cuyahoga River.

"Fifty fucking *cents*?" the last and most belligerent of the bums shouted. "What kind of bullshit is *this*?"

Commodore was not accustomed to being addressed in this manner. He faced the last of the bums, a defiant gentleman in a tattered three-piece suit and blue plastic flip-flop beach sandals. Cocked at a slight angle over his nose was a pair of designer glasses held together with duct tape, and behind the eyeglasses two eyes were rolling wildly.

"MBA with honors from Wharton, third head derivatives buyer at Lehman Brothers for six years, blow off my house in Connecticut, and you give me *quarters*!" the former investment banker shouted, proudly flinging down the coins.

"Sell me out, give all my bosses a bonus, off shore what's left of my company to Bangalore? Hire new employees who barely speak English? You ever try to talk to Bangalore on the *telephone*?" he demanded.

Commodore did not engage with the angry, trembling stranger. He gave the man all the coins he had in his pocket and turned away. Then he heard the former investment banker hurl the handful of coins to the sidewalk.

Commodore heard the man jumping furiously up and down on the coins, flip-flops flapping, as if to pound Commodore's small gift into the ground.

"Goddamn *quarters*?" he cried. "Give me back my *country*!"

The old billionaire glimpsed a meaner and more desperate world, one that was quite different than the world he knew. As he walked away, this emotional exchange left him feeling uncomfortable and mildly embarrassed.

The old capitalist experienced relief at the sight of Commode Company headquarters. His company's elegant, unmarked Mission style headquarters was located in what once had been Santa Barbara's finest luxury hotel. Although the ivy-covered building was no longer open to the public, Commodore retained the hotel's elegantly-attired saluting doormen. Their crisp white and gold uniforms and epaulets reminded him of his more heroic days in the U.S. Navy.

As Commodore approached, the uniformed doormen snapped to attention and saluted military-style. With an efficient military flourish, the doormen flung open the double brass and glass doors for the captain of their ship, Commodore Commode.

Stepping inside, the old capitalist realized that the broccoli and goat cheese omelet his chef had prepared for breakfast was spewing gas into his digestive tract. Even after the walk, Commodore felt bloated and uncomfortable as he lumbered across the lobby and stepped into the waiting elevator.

The old elevator was a slow-moving contraption of hammered brass and copper. Its interior was embossed with images of soaring California condors and Joshua trees. The last Art Nouveau elevator ever made in the United States, the elevator had been constructed for a luxury resort hotel in Death Valley. Commodore's son Philip had picked it out of an auction house catalog when he was thirteen years old, already a design prodigy with opinions about everything.

Commodore thought his son's interest in this might be a first step toward Philip's taking an interest in the company. But his only son turned out to be less interested in the family business than in interior design. Of Commodore's expectations for his son, only the lumbering Art Nouveau elevator remained.

The brass elevator gates racketed slowly shut. Commodore spread his legs and braced himself, anticipating the usual takeoff towards the top floor. The old capitalist expelled gas in a long, loud, forceful burst.

"Goat cheese," Commodore barked.

The elevator man nodded, took a deep breath, showed his teeth, and stared straight ahead, as expressionless as a guard at Buckingham Palace.

Ever since his late wife Milly switched him to a high fiber diet to protect his heart, the old capitalist had experienced frequent attacks of gas. His children and his employees never complained. The old billionaire assumed that nobody else but his deceased wife was personally offended by the pungent. high fiber flatulence he periodically released into the air.

In the stuffy old elevator, the scent of his own body secretly thrilled him. He believed that his flatulence had a distinctively stout, manly smell. This was true. Commodore was stout. He was also a man. As the exotic fumes of his animal self drifted up through his tweed overcoat and scarf, permeating the elevator like the aroma of a fat, wet cigar, the old billionaire began to daydream...

❦

Commodore Cornelius Commode, III, inherited a family business which generated an extraordinary amount of money. Although running the family business was not his first choice of occupations, Commodore was very good at it. Like his industrious Austrian ancestors, he was humble and cautious enough to avoid impulsive financial mistakes.

The only male of his generation to carry on the family name, Commodore had grown up surrounded by servants in a stately old Victorian mansion in Cleveland, Ohio. The Cleveland mansion had been his family's homeplace for more than a hundred years.

The summer after his senior year in high school, against the wishes of his mother who thought it demeaning and dangerous, he insisted in working on the manufacturing line of one the family's factories. Young Commodore gloried in being a regular guy on the assembly line, eating a sack lunch with the boys, and getting his hands dirty. But after one summer on the line his father abruptly pulled him into the main office on the second floor, and told him his mother would not permit her son to work on the factory floor again.

Commodore escaped his family's expectations only once more in his life, when he impulsively joined the U.S. Navy near the end of the Korean War. In Asia, he fell madly in love with a Chinese girl despite his formal engagement to Milly Rockefeller. But elegant dependable Milly was waiting for him with a knowing smile, two glasses of champagne, and a gardenia in her hair when his ship returned to San Francisco. Commodore married her at the end of a proper engagement, as he had promised to do.

It was perhaps inevitable that he would oversee a manufacturing business begun by his great great great grandfather, the eccentric Austrian-American immigrant and onetime utopian socialist, Nicholas "Red Nick" Commode. Red Nick's business churned out stream of simple but durable products, fixtures in the bathrooms of many American homes.

Headquartered in the heart of America, over time the Commode Company had grown into a complex of five large interlocking factories, each manufacturing parts and components for the family's bathroom products which were well known and respected in the trade.

Commodore's ancestors were old-fashioned and prudent enough to sell their products for what they were worth, that is, what they cost to make plus a modest markup. Even then this was considered bad marketing, but for the Commode family it had been good business. Competitor after competitor fell by the wayside, victims of their own high prices and shortsighted greed. This left Commodore's family a fat rich goose of a business, forever generating golden eggs.

Commodore had never considered changing the way the company did business. Publicly-owned American companies made a big show of constantly revamping themselves, he knew, all the better to raise executive salaries. But the Commode Company had never found it necessary to call in the consultants from McKinsey, to change its focus, to reinvent itself, to restate its earnings, to focus on quality first, to pursue excellence, to reverse directions, to restructure its divisions, or even to acquire, divest, or diversify. With Commodore's steady hand on the rudder, the business was steady as she goes.

The company's Cleveland employees were decently paid, adequately productive, and happy enough with their union contracts. However, Commodore didn't think much about the workers since his company's headquarters was no longer located in a few modest offices on the second floor of the huge old red brick manufacturing plant in Cleveland, still the heart of the largest factory complex in town.

Commodore and Milly Commode were old money. They grew up with the understanding that it just wasn't proper to flaunt the extent of their wealth. Neither Commodore nor Milly wanted the children to surrender to what they saw as the tacky allure of high profile fame in America.

They saw the lower echelons of American society as a sort of unseemly flea circus hopping with sexually-active young Hollywood actors and actresses, doped-up professional athletes, smoke-blowing book and bangle salesmen, dissembling politicians, get-rich-quick artists, shamelessly crowing businessmen, and other dubious celebrities. Commodore and Milly wished to raise their family happily untouched by celebrity, scandal, tabloid gossip, or any of the noisier American forms of fame.

❧

"It's the penthouse, sir," the elevator man whispered out of the side of his mouth. Commodore awoke from his daydream to the sound of a tiny bell pinging. The elevator door was open. The old billionaire stepped out of the musky elevator into the fresh cool air of his third floor office reception area.

His young secretary, Miss Gander, rose to greet him in a prim blue suit. She handed him the usual stack of correspondence from the plants. The old capitalist grunted, nodded, scooped up the local newspaper, strode into his office, and closed the door.

Commodore took off his overcoat and scarf and hung them carefully on an old brass coat rack that had belonged to his great grandfather. Next to the coat rack were the golf clubs he'd brought in to practice his putting, since the annual golf tournament was coming up and he needed to make a good show. On his desk Miss Gander had left a steaming cup of hot Earl Grey tea, a pitcher of cream, and a few little Tyrolean mints to help him start his day.

The old capitalist sat down, popped a tiny mint into his mouth, and set aside the paperwork. For some reason he picked up the family portrait he kept on his desk. and experienced a moment of quiet longing.

The family portrait had been taken near the gazebo in Milly's English garden. In the photo, Commodore and Milly were seated on a small stone bench, a distinguished older couple, dutifully holding hands. His former wife looked like a frail, antique angel, with her slender body and pale skin, staring up at him with obedient eyes.

Standing directly behind them were the children—Petunia, Philip, and Clementine. The girls looked respectable enough, but Commodore had always thought Philip looked a little too grossly Bohemian with his nose in the air and that long red scarf he insisted on wearing flung back rakishly over his shoulder like some kind of French revolutionary. Commodore didn't actually notice his two sons-in-law just a step behind their wives, flanking them like two awkward book ends. Both of his handsome son-in-laws looked uncomfortable in their wedding tuxedos. Both had their hands crossed over their groins, and exhibited hauntingly artificial smiles.

Milly had insisted the family use the famously grumpy little society photographer Peter Ruffino-Goldberg. Commodore vaguely recalled the pushy, bearded, arm-waving little gnome in an oversized beret, supervising a virtual army of assistants.

In a flash he remembered Milly bringing the silver-framed photograph into his office and proudly placing it next to the telephone on his desk the day before she died.

Then, out of the blue, Miss Gander knocked four times on the door to Commodore's inner sanctum. The old billionaire set the picture down, somewhat irritated. He hadn't even had time to open the paper.

"Who is it?" the old billionaire demanded.

3. Enter the Children

Milly told everyone that their children took after Commodore's side of the family. In contrast to the Rockefellers, who were tall and somewhat lean, the Commodes came into the world built more like solid little fire hydrants. Each of the children was born with Commodore's relatively square, stocky body, and like their father they had rather short arms and legs, and a little less neck than usual between the head and the shoulders.

All three children grew up in the blinking of an eye. The girls attended Stanford; one married a doctor and the other one married a lawyer. After a slow start in life, Commodore's son now ran his own business.

Commodore's oldest daughter, Petunia, had married a broad-shouldered corporate lawyer who seemed to spend more time working out in his personal gymnasium than he did sitting in the office. Unfortunately, as soon as Commodore offered him a position, it took the young lawyer no time at all to become puffed up with his own self-importance.

Around the office, Petunia's husband developed a disturbing tendency to poke out his chest and brag like a carnival barker after he had won some meaningless little victory or other. This inner office chest-pounding annoyed Commodore to no end. To make it worse, Simon was compulsively competitive. His son-in-law never stopped aggressively and continuously pushing for personal perks like catered meals for his hideously overstaffed legal department, or a corner office uncomfortably close to Commodore's own. It annoyed the old billionaire to see the vice president of legal affairs jockeying madly for position and influence at company staff meetings when it wasn't necessary to jockey at all.

Commodore had long ago realized that his son-in-law was one of those unfortunate men who felt himself locked in continuous combat with every other male in the room. Sadly, Commodore thought, his son-in-law was exactly the kind of man who bullied his way to the top of the corporate world— shortsighted, greedy, and self-promoting, carrying an ethical balance sheet devoid of either humility or scruples. Every day of the year, American corporations were being run toward the rocks by such men, the old capitalist felt. Although he did keep Simon employed at a decent salary, the old capitalist was leery of giving him much responsibility. Around the office, he avoided his fast-talking son-in-law as much as possible.

Yet every time Commodore tried to tell his late wife Milly how he felt about Simon, she reminded him that Simon was taking good care of their Petunia. And Petunia did seem happy with her vice president, her sprawling country estate, and her growing menagerie of disgusting little animals.

Commodore's second child, self-centered Clementine, had married a slender, intense plastic surgeon she also met at Stanford.

The Doctor, as he now insisted on being called, was not a low profile addition to the family. Commodore thought the Doctor was little too eager to get his face before the public. Milly had tactfully questioned Clementine about some of Clipster's more outrageous television commercials, but Clementine had assured her it was a normal part of the medical business since the Doctor specialized in high end plastic surgery with a small but growing celebrity clientele.

It was not easy to miss his son-in-law's incessant late-night commercials, all of which began with a darkly roiling screen and the sound of plaintive violins.

"UNHAPPY? THINK YOU MIGHT A LITTLE WORK DONE?" CAME THE SULTRY FEMALE VOICE.

CUT TO AN EXTERIOR OF THE DOCTOR IS IN OUTPATIENT SURGICAL CENTER IN MONTECITO (A VENTURE RELUCTANTLY FINANCED BY COMMODORE).

"THERE IS ONLY ONE PLASTIC SURGEON DISCREET AND SKILLFUL ENOUGH EVEN FOR THE MOST FAMOUS OF CELEBRITIES AND HELPING EVERY DISCRIMINATING WOMAN OR MAN WHO JUST WANTS TO LOOK AND FEEL YOUNG. HELP IS HERE! HELLO! THE BEST-KNOWN PLASTIC SURGEON ON THE WEST COAST PRACTICES RIGHT HERE IN SANTA BARBARA," COOS THE INVISIBLE FEMALE.

AS THE ANXIOUS VIOLINS CONTINUE, STAINLESS STEEL DOORS DRAMATICALLY BURST OPEN AND R. BARON CLIPSTER, M.D., MAJESTICALLY STRIDES INTO THE OPERATING ROOM. SHOT FROM A LOW ANGLE TO MAKE HIM LOOK EIGHT FEET TALL, CLIPSTER WEARS BLUE OPERATING SCRUBS. AN OVERSIZED STETHOSCOPE DANGLING FROM HIS NECK. CLIPSTER SCREWS IN HIS MONOCLE AND SMILES BENIGNLY AS HIS NAME FLASHES THREE TIMES AT THE BOTTOM OF THE SCREEN, IN ORANGE NEON.

"THE DOCTOR IS IN!" WHISPERS THE FEMALE VOICE. MEDIEVAL CHANTS BEGIN AS CLIPSTER SLOWLY LIFTS HIS BEAUTIFULLY-MANICURED HANDS (WITHOUT THE EXPENSIVE WEDDING RING CLEMENTINE BOUGHT HIM, MILLY ONCE OBSERVED).

A BEAUTIFUL NURSE WITH ENORMOUS BREASTS SLIPS SURGICAL GLOVES ON THE DOCTOR'S HANDS, THEN STEPS BEHIND HIM TO REVERENTLY FASTEN HIS SURGICAL MASK.

IN CLOSE-UP, CLIPSTER'S EYES DART AROUND THE OPERATING ROOM LIKE A MEDICAL GUNSLINGER SCANNING THE HORIZON FOR INDIANS.

SUDDENLY, STAINLESS STEEL DOORS BURST OPEN, AND A PATIENT COVERED BY A SHEET IS WHEELED IN ON A GURNEY. THE DOCTOR TURNS TOWARD THE GURNEY AS THE HEAVENS BLAZE WITH SURGICAL LIGHT AND THE MEDIEVAL CHANTING ABRUPTLY STOPS.

"THE DOCTOR IS IN!" THE FEMALE VOICE WHISPERS AS THE NURSE PLACES A SCALPEL IN HIS HAND.

THE CAMERA CUTS TO A DRAMATIC CLOSE-UP OF CLIPSTER'S MASKED FACE, AS IF SEEN BY A PATIENT SUDDENLY WAKING UP DURING A NOSE JOB.

"NOSES SCULPTED IN HEAVEN, THANKS TO THE DOCTOR!" WHISPERS THE VOICE.

CUT TO AN "AFTER" PICTURE OF A BEAUTIFUL RICH WOMAN LOOKING IN A 3-WAY BEDROOM MIRROR, TRYING TO WIGGLE A GORGEOUS LITTLE BUTTON NOSE SO PERFECT IT APPEARS TO BE MADE OF PLASTIC. HER HANDSOME SLIM RICH GRAY-HAIRED HUSBAND APPROACHES HER FROM BEHIND, AND HUGS HER AFFECTIONATELY.

CUT TO THE MASKED DOCTOR, SHOT FROM BELOW, WORKING AWAY LIKE A TORMENTED RENAISSANCE SCULPTOR ON SOMETHING WHICH APPEARS TO BE LODGED INSIDE THE CAMERA..

"PERFECTLY ROUND AND FIRM BREASTS, THANKS TO THE DOCTOR!"

CUT TO A GORGEOUS DOLLY PARTON LOOK-ALIKE IN A TIGHT SWEATER WALKING OUT OF THE DOCTOR IS IN SURGICAL CENTER. HANDSOME YOUNG CONSTRUCTION MEN POP OUT OF A MANHOLE, WAVE THEIR HARD HATS IN GOOD-HUMORED ADMIRATION, AND LOUDLY WHISTLE.

CUT TO THE MASKED DOCTOR, SCALPEL IN HAND, WORKING FURIOUSLY AWAY.

"HAS YOUR BUTT BEGUN TO SAG LIKE AN OLD BAG OF BEANS? HELLO! THE DOCTOR IS IN!" WHISPERS THE OFF-CAMERA FEMALE.

CUT TO A GRAY-HAIRED WOMAN IN A SKIMPY BRAZILIAN THONG, WHO BENDS OVER TO OFFER A TRAY OF MARTINIS TO HER BEAUTIFUL YOUNG GUESTS SEATED AROUND THE POOL.

TO THE SOUND OF FLAMENCO GUITARS, THE WOMAN SMILES BACK OVER HER SHOULDER AT THE CAMERA AND WIGGLES HER SURGICALLY-ENHANCED BUTT FROM SIDE TO SIDE.

CUT TO THE DOCTOR'S SLENDER, INTENSE FACE. CLIPSTER WHIPS OFF HIS SURGICAL MASK. HE DABS HIS FOREHEAD AND SMILES BENIGNLY AS HIS 800 NUMBER FLASHES OFF AND ON, IN BRIGHT NEON YELLOW.

"NEED A LITTLE WORK DONE BEHIND THE SCENES? HELLO! THE DOCTOR IS IN!" WHISPERS THE SULTRY FEMALE VOICE. "VISIT THE DOCTOR IS IN OUTPATIENT SURGICAL CENTER IN MONTECITO TODAY."

The old billionaire had lost count of how many times he had seen Clipster's commercials, but it was several dozen too many.

Clipster had even mined the foyer of his and Clementine's home. The ubiquitous commercials erupted from TV monitors the minute you entered their house. For her part, Clementine insisted that the commercials were working. According to Clementine, the Doctor was forever turning business away.

Still wearing his surgical outfit, and screwing in his monocle with a twist of his fingers, Clipster would slip into their table at the Montecito Country Club and immediately pull out the business cards. The Doctor told anybody who would listen that it was his medical mission in life to make beautiful women even more beautiful, and older men more attractive to their wives, and incidentally to younger women.

Then suddenly, like an expensive sports car moving into high gear, the doctor would start dropping names—bragging about how had done "a little touch-up work" on this or that celebrity, either in Santa Barbara or in the branch office he maintained at additional expense to Commodore in Beverly Hills. Although the old capitalist suspected that some of the celebrities would have preferred that the Doctor keep their names confidential, he dropped their first names all over the country club. Michael Jackson's name came up frequently at that time, as did some of the other one-name celebrities like Liz, Jack, and Cher. Commodore had heard The Doctor drop the same names a hundred times, but Clementine never seemed to tire of hearing them, or of repeating them again and again, as if to assure herself she was in the best possible company with her own surgically-altered face and body.

Their only son Philip had been Milly's favorite child, the only one of the children who could always make Milly laugh. Milly delighted in Philip's mimicry of the more pretentious ladies in her bridge clubs.

And Milly roared at the clever way Philip imitated the walk and talk of the clumsy, uptight prep school boyfriends his sisters occasionally brought home from private school.

Like his mother, Philip was strung tight as a mandolin. Like his mother, Philip suffered from anxiety and panic attacks. Like his mother, Philip dealt with his demons by staying busy almost all the time.

As a young man Philip flitted around the world like a lonely mosquito, attending the world's best art and design schools, always exhibiting extraordinary potential, but usually withdrawing from school behind a smoke cloud of what his father believed were half-baked complaints. For years, Philip drifted. Complaining loudly to his mother on interminable long-distance calls as he went, Philip studied in London, Amsterdam, Paris, Copenhagen, and West Berlin. Finally, in Barcelona, where he met his good friend Diego, Philip finally stayed in one place long enough to complete an art school degree.

Philip lived differently than the girls. While the son-in-laws drove ostentatious cars, Filly and his platonic friend Diego tooted to work in electric hybrids, bicycles, or modest little red Vespa motor scooters. Environmentally-conscious Filly had solar panels on his roof and windmills on the hills of his estate. He landscaped with native plants, and collected rainwater in barrels. His gardeners placed stylish little compost bins at intervals around the grounds to recycle the lawn trash and trimmings. Milly had been impressed by Philip's unusual house and environmentally-friendly lifestyle, even the community gardens, which had been ahead of their time. Philip's unusual house had been featured in several magazines. But there were things about his son which Commodore was forever at a loss to understand.

Philip Commode Design employed a great number of strikingly handsome young male assistants. Slender, limp-wristed young men of every color answered Philip's phones with witty, upbeat remarks. The handsome young men trotted back and forth with Philip on visits to the country's great estates, carrying portfolios, sketches, fabric samples, color charts, and catalogs. They seemed to love nothing so much as pacing around this or that mansion, measuring couches and windows and walls, and shooting snapshots with their phones. Lately, Philip's assistants had taken to wearing what was almost a uniform of ridiculous tight black pants and loose, ruffled red silk shirts that made them all look like some cross between a flamenco dancer and a ballerina. But the better class of women preferred to do business with stylish men and Philip was certainly stylish, Milly had told him. Milly insisted that all of Philip's employees and friends were stylish, too.

Commodore was at a loss to understand this. The last time Commodore made his way through the bicycles parked outside Philip's office, he noticed Philip's entire front office had been repainted a peculiar shade of red. And inside, some of his employees actually appeared to be dancing.

The old capitalist also didn't understand the ubiquitous Diego, Philip's platonic friend and alleged business partner. The scion of a wealthy Spanish bullfighting family, the handsome Spaniard seemed to spend most of his time traveling. Commodore didn't have a clue about what to make of Diego, although he knew Milly had simply adored him.

Even Commodore observed that both girls spent fortunes on clothes that only made them look slightly ridiculous. But his well-tailored son, with his perfectly-cut pants and tailored jackets, could always attract admiring glances from both men and women the minute he stepped into a room.

And as for carrying on the family business, Commodore no longer expected anything of Philip. He had long ago lost hope that Philip would even get married, much less father a child who might someday take an interest in the business.

When he was in art school, Philip would occasionally bring home a sullen, hollow-eyed girl who didn't seem to like herself or anybody else either. Two of the girls were said to be famous model in Europe. But no matter what praise Commodore and Milly heaped upon this or that girl, they never saw one of Filly's scowling, chain-smoking girlfriends again. Philip was just a confirmed old bachelor now, Milly cheerfully assured him before she died. She confidently predicted that their son would someday do something of importance in the world.

Commodore did miss hyperactive Milly, who put together an unending string of family vacations which basically held the family together until the year she died.

Like many successful businessmen, Commodore had allowed his wife to manage everything that wasn't connected with the business. The old capitalist regularly deferred to Milly's ideas about their homes, their parties, their vacations, and anything to do with the children.

A high-strung woman who jogged three miles around the estate every morning to ward off panic attacks, Milly had been obsessive about the proper rearing of their children. Milly had selected their nannies, their private schools, their tutors, given them generous allowances, shopped with them, had lunch with them regularly, made sure they remembered each other's birthdays, and so on.

Every year before she died Milly locked herself in her study, planning family vacations to more or less the same places every year.

The family summered near Martha's Vineyard, where Milly had inherited a summer home on the ocean. Winter vacations were spent in the Palm Beach mansion acquired by Commodore's ambitious great grandmother, who had clawed out a niche for the family in East Coast society. Occasionally, Milly penciled in a week or two in the Cayman Islands, to allow Commodore and the family an occasional cruise on his beloved if chronically under used yacht.

While planning vacations, Milly sometimes discussed the possibility of staying in the penthouses they owned in Central Park, the small islands the family owned off South America and Spain, or even the older properties Commodore's family had acquired in various parts of Europe. These vacations never happened. Another place Milly never got around to visiting was Commodore's family's Victorian mansion in Cleveland which had been more or less boarded up for years.

At Milly's funeral, several well-powdered divorcees had sidled up to Commodore, smelling of expensive perfume and dabbing their eyes. They offered uncomfortably lavish condolences, hugs and wet kisses.

At the graveside, a couple of very young ladies with tears streaming from their eyes actually slipped him perfumed business cards engraved with their pictures as well as their names and telephone numbers. This was mildly unsettling.

After countless sessions with his relentlessly probing grief counselor, Commodore had more or less worked through his loss. He had begun playing more golf, this year making a determined effort to improve his game. After a decent interval, he had even gone out on a couple of dates, but the coyly desperate society women he dutifully dated hardly compared to Milly.

Although Commodore missed the order his wife brought to their life, their relationship had not been of the passionate sort. Theirs had been the practical sort of marriage common in the union of two great fortunes. Commodore was from one of Cleveland's oldest and most respected families. And of course, Milly was a Rockefeller, from the Ohio branch of the family, once removed, but not so far removed that she didn't enter the marriage with a considerable fortune of her own.

Although Milly had a flamboyant streak, she insisted on things done properly with the children. As the girls approached puberty, Milly was especially fearful of the private schools of the Midwest, and especially Ohio's aging private schools which were all rumored to be in rapid decline. One of Milly's greatest fears was that some fast-talking cad from one of Cleveland's unseemly families would try to marry one of the girls for her money. Milly sent the girls to private schools in California, not far from the Ronald Reagan Ranch, where every student's family had to be listed for at least two generations in the *Social Register*. She sent Philip to a private school in the same part of California.

Commodore recalled that young Philip left for school in the middle of a snowstorm. Commodore remembered shaking hands with a heartbreakingly elegant young man in a tweed overcoat, scarf and hat, who was trying bravely not to cry. The minute Philip's nanny opened the door, a gust of cold snow swirled into the foyer. and covered Milly with snow. Milly locked herself in her bedroom and wept for three days.

Milly was soon flying out to California every weekend to visit one child or another. Milly had to fly out and accompany the children back to Cleveland on the airplane for holidays because she was afraid they might fraternize with some of the questionable boys from public school.

The girls were already begging Milly to move to California. Opinionated Philip did not want the family to move away from the homeplace in Cleveland, although Commodore never understood why.

❧

Relocating company headquarters to California was surprisingly easy. Leaving Cleveland's red brick factories behind, Commodore purchased an old luxury hotel in Santa Barbara, remodeled it to suit his purposes, and moved the essential people to California. Although he sometimes missed the biting cold of Cleveland's winters, and the exhilarating flush of spring, Commodore eventually grew comfortable with Santa Barbara's breezy small town ambience of beaches and palm trees. His wife seemed happier there, and Commodore grew accustomed to the temperate weather where he could at least play golf all year long.

Commodore purchased one of California's last remaining Spanish land grant estates from lawyers representing the quarreling, sickly heirs of Don Chiclet de Barajas-Montecito. Much of the three thousand acre estate was within the city limits of tony little Montecito, one of the most exclusive cities in California. Milly chose their acreage in Montecito. Before they moved, Commodore built Milly the towering 72-room mansion she wanted at No. 1 Swizzle Stick Road.

Milly modeled her home on the Southern plantation, Tara, from the movie *Gone with the Wind*. With encouragement from Philip, Milly even purchased some the actual furniture used in the movie from the movie studio, and worked it into the interior of the house. On one of her grander days, Milly named their mansion "Commodora" and had the name inscribed in ornamental wrought iron over the entrance to their estate.

Commodora's long curving driveway was flanked by purple blooming Jacaranda trees. From their limbs dripped tasteful tendrils of an unusual variety of Spanish moss, giving the approach to the house a romantic Deep South look. Near the front entrance a circular driveway looped around a charmed circle containing more than a hundred of Milly's well-trimmed gardenia bushes.

Behind the mansion, just off Milly's bedroom patio, lay her carefully-groomed English garden. Beyond the garden lay Commodore's private golf course, the pony stables, and the clay tennis courts. Closer to the house were the croquet and badminton areas, the greenhouse, and the indoor and outdoor pools and all the rest of it.

At Philip's suggestion, Commodora's pressed-tin ceilings were festooned with antique crystal chandeliers. Pictures of dead relatives from both sides of the family had been scattered about Commodore's study and the library. There was a surprising amount of Louis XIV furniture worked into the house itself, particularly in Philip's suite of bedrooms. Even the servants' quarters displayed the precocious young master's rococo touches.

After Milly's first party, Commodora was the talk of Montecito. Guests stepped out of limousines and town cars under six imposing white Corinthian columns which fronted the façade of their three-story estate. The entry hall was as big as a house. To the right, where they received guests, was Milly's showpiece, which Philip had already christened the Grand Ballroom. High above the dance floor, in the center of a high arched ceiling in hammered gold leaf interlaced with Mediterranean tile, hung a stunning 124-candle crystal candelabrum filled before every party with scented candles from Paris.

At the coming out party for Petunia, ropes of fragrant gardenias were strung across the ceiling of the Grand Ballroom. Petunia made a grand entrance, of course. So many people attended you could barely see the popular singer Johnny Mathis backed by the Henry Mancini Orchestra on a raised stage on the far side of the ballroom.

At every party, resplendent Milly welcomed her guests in a floor-length white satin gown. She wore most of her diamonds and a pair of long white satin gloves which could have been worn by Scarlett O'Hara herself.

"Welcome," she would dryly laugh, with a sweep of her arm toward the Grand Ballroom, "to Commodora."

"Milly! It's magnificent!" the matrons squealed, clasping their hands and jumping up and down.

"I love it!" "I want one!"

Women and their husbands entered the Grand Ballroom with unsuppressed delight and just a twinge of envy, Commodore noticed. The compliments Milly received at every party pleased his wife to no end.

Ground was broken on the golf course even before Milly's architects finalized the plans for the mansion. The day they moved in, Commodore walked the professional quality private 18-hole golf course on the estate grounds with Milly and his faithful valet, R.G. Spartan. The golf course smelled of freshly-cut grass, birds sang in the trees, and Milly, Spartan and Commodore all pronounced it entirely grand.

As soon as they moved into Commodora, one or another of the children was forever popping in from prep school for a weekend of shopping, pony riding, swimming, or socializing.

For the first few years, it seemed like every weekend still another private school limousine was picking up or dropping off one or another little Commode, and a group of their perfectly-groomed little friends.

Commodore often often glanced out of the window of his study to see Milly giving a group of uniformed children a tour of the English garden. Many Saturdays, Commodore awoke to the sound of pony hooves on the riding path, of croquet balls being tapped across the lawn, or the shrieks of well-groomed little children holding their noses and politely jumping into one of the pools.

When Petunia and Clementine came out as debutantes at the Montecito Country Club, Philip actually helped design each of his sister's spectacular and unusual ball gowns. To his mother's everlasting delight, Petunia and Clementine's gowns were the talk of Montecito.

Neither of the girls was academically inclined, but Milly absolutely insisted they both attend Stanford. At Stanford University, Petunia unexplainably set her head on getting into law school. Petunia became quite close to her broad-shouldered, fast-talking tutor, at about the same time that Clementine became enamoured of one of his friends, a medical student. One weekend, Petunia and Clementine brought their boyfriends home for dinner and impulsively announced their double engagement.

When Commodore discovered that Petunia's ebullient young fiancé had racked up significant unpaid debts, he had his lawyers draw up a pre-nuptial agreement that the law student signed without a second thought. When Commodore learned that Clementine's fiance also had no signigicant resources, his attorney drew up a second pre-nuptial agreement.

Petunia's husband was given a secure job, and Commodore quietly paid off the medical student's loans, and funded a long, lazy residency in Brazil. When Clementine whispered to Milly that she wanted to come home to Montecito, Commodore bought his son-in-law an established plastic surgery practice in Santa Barbara and challenged the ambitious young doctor to make it grow.

❧

As the swallows return to Capistrano, the children had all returned to Montecito. Milly quietly encouraged their return. From time to time, Commodore wondered if the children might be better off living somewhere else, and not quite so entangled with each other, but he knew without asking that Milly vehemently disagreed.

Each child was given acreage along Swizzle Stick Road. Architects were hired and homes were built. The only condition Milly imposed on the kids was that they take vacations with the rest of the family.

Petunia and her lawyer came first, with a squat, two story 57-room mansion at No. 2 Swizzle Stick Road. Their home was a classic of imported gray stone and brick with a slate roof, mimicking the English country style of the Biltmore Estate. Clementine went ultramodern with a double domed, metal-skinned home, at No. 3 Swizzle Stick Road, which her architect hailed as a deconstruction of the Taj Majal. No. 4 Swizzle Stick Road was Philip's small faux French Gothic castle, entered via a small drawbridge over a moat of bright green water brimming with lotus plants and reeds. At night a group of small brown singing frogs—a native species, Philip proudly claimed—croaked discreetly in the water. Philip's castle was also occupied by his platonic friend, Diego, when he happened to be in town.

The family lived in what was said to be the best neighborhood in the United States. Oprah Winfrey's mansion was right down the road. Their neighbors were all rich as kings. Some were Hollywood types or professional sports stars or computer moguls or business tycoons. The others were scions of rich old California and East Coast families, trust fund babies who worked hard at living well.

Nestled among the mansions of Swizzle Stick Road it was not difficult for Commodore to think of himself as more or less a regular guy.

Three mornings every week, as regular as clockwork, Commodore hacked his way around the front or back nine with his faithful valet, the uncomplaining Englishman R.G. Spartan. One cool winter morning, as Commodore happily hacked his way around the back nine with his deferential valet, the thought struck him that if only he could find a wife who loved to play golf as passionately as he did, his life might just be heaven itself.

4. The Doctor Is In

Like many smart ambitious men and women who sail through medical school, Baron R. "Barrie" Clipster, M.D., was hotly competitive by nature and coldly materialistic by training. He had been taught to work fast and hard in medical school, to keep his knives and surgical instruments sharp and sterile at all times, and to bill for everything as soon as possible after the surgery.

The Doctor did as he was taught, and a good deal more, but it was never quite enough to keep the Doctor's worry wolf away. The worry wolf was not kept at bay by the fact that the Doctor worked constantly to establish an image of himself among the well-heeled citizens of Santa Barbara and Beverly Hills as a physician who was always working.

Of course, the Doctor did cut a distinctly singular figure. As his admen recommended, the Doctor wore his royal blue surgical scrubs to every party and wedding to which he and Clementine were invited, happily accepting invitations even when Clemmie was out of town.

The Doctor knew it was important to meet the local crème de la crème in the comfort of their own homes, and of course to discreetly slip them business cards so they could effortlessly contact the Doctor who was forever working. This one-on-one marketing strategy had paid off, more or less, for he got new clients. But as the Doctor worked more and more, raising his rates at every conceivable opportunity, he and Clementine only spent more money.

On the face of it, an enormous volume of business ran through The Doctor Is In, Inc., his medical corporation. But the outrageous bills his girls express-mailed to his clients the day after their surgeries were never quite enough. His work never quite seemed to generate quite enough money when all his expenses including his staff salaries, his few personal perks, his business expenses, his offices and staff in Montecito and Beverly Hills, his weekends in Las Vegas, his airplane and speedboat maintenance, the racehorses he and Clemmie had bought, his television advertising budget, his generous gifts and freebies to a few of the girls at the office, and his staggeringly expensive malpractice premiums were factored in.

The Doctor had billed almost $80,000 that very morning, respectable money for less than three hours work. His girls had already prepared bills to go out in the next day's mail. Yet the minute his surgically-altered clients paid up, the Doctor knew, the money would waltz right back out the door.

One of that morning's noses entered on the rather sour face of the scion of an old San Luis Obispo cattle-ranching family, Miss. B.P. Punter. The somewhat bovine Miss Punter presented with a huge honker he'd nearly cut in half, a bloody mess of cartilage and flesh that he hoped would heal into something like the sketch his facial sculpting artists prepared.

The second surgery was a minor nostril adjustment for buxom little "Boo Boo" Furlow, a Dolly Parton look-alike, formerly of Cleveland and now of the Chicago Furlows.

Perky little Boo Boo had her personal pilot fly her back to Chicago an hour after the surgery, as the Doctor advised her not to do. Of course, the patient blithely ignored his advice, as almost all of the very rich were prone to do. Boo Boo wanted to be back in Chicago with a flesh-colored bandage over her nose before her husband returned from the commodities exchange with a couple million dollars of soybean futures contracts and a half-eaten Snicker's bar in his hip pocket.

The Doctor had already sculpted Boo Boo twice before— only a small amount of artful sculpting was required each time, since Boo Boo was already beautiful as a Barbie doll. When she returned to Montecito for the lifting of the bandages, in four to six weeks, the Doctor hoped the result would be a small perfect nose made even smaller and more perfect on the invisibly aging corn oil heiress.

The Doctor's beautiful noses didn't last forever, of course. No plastic surgeon's work ever really lasted, he thought philosophically. Rearranged cartilage wasn't bone, and it couldn't hold the shape he gave it permanently. That was one of his profession's dirty little secrets, along with big new breasts that became hard as bowling balls, eye work that left beautiful new eyelids not quite able to close at night, cellulite and wrinkles which were blasted, lasered or Botoxed away only to reappear again, hairlines that would not stop receding away from individually-placed rows of hair implants, and ears, butts, bellies and foreheads that would simply not remain pinned or stapled back into their most flattering position.

Early in his career, the Doctor wondered if perhaps he was displeasing God by trying to alter nature's handiwork. He had been raised by Bible-thumping Baptist evangelicals, after all, and he could not quite forget the sermons he'd been forced to sit through every week until he slipped away to college. But the Doctor long ago rationalized away these misgivings, since planned obsolescence was the American way.

And of course, the Doctor had married a woman who was now a walking example of all the good things that could be accomplished with high end plastic surgery. Even around the office, his female staff also proudly displayed the huge breasts, high cheekbones, and tiny button noses he had given them in lieu of bonuses at the end of the year in one of his two impressively equipped on-site operating rooms.

But behind its glitzy facade, the Doctor's medical corporation was losing more and more money every year, and it wasn't all losses for tax purposes. Given his upbringing in an environment of dour, waste not, want not thrift, this humiliating, money-hemorrhaging state of affairs was a thorn in the Doctor's side, one he lamely tried to remedy by spending more money on advertising.

The power of advertising had been explained to him in medical school by a cynical old gynecologist with a handlebar moustache and a deceptive twinkle in his eye. And as soon as he went into practice, the Doctor began to buy TV commercials. Quickly he saw for himself advertising's power to create demand, and to mold a flattering image. Before long, the Doctor fell in love with the image of himself which his ads created, the image of a consummate medical professional who was constantly working. So many people had seen his commercials on late-night cable TV that the hard-working

Doctor was often recognized on the streets of Santa Barbara and sometimes even hailed on the street in Beverly Hills.

Although the results were never quite what his admen projected, the Doctor continued to advertise heavily, hoping against hope that revenues would overtake expenses. Only a few more tummy tucks, Botox parties, or vaginal rejuvenations per month would put him into the black, he reasoned. But the additional patient "hits" promised by his fast-talking admen didn't materialize as fast as the bills for the additional flights of television spots they continuously urged him to run. Despite an occasional sniping remark from his accountant or some obviously jealous colleague, the Doctor held to his business plan and called for more and more commercials.

Still, after the two nose jobs, the doctor had several hours to kill that afternoon. Doctor despised not being busy during business hours and his worry wolf began howling.

The minute the Doctor swiveled back in his comfortable leather office chair and propped his feet up on his desk with a medical journal in his hands, the shrill voice in his head reminded him that he was competing with a lot of other doctors who would kill for his clientele. The Doctor sometimes imagined he could hear the distant clatter of rubber-soled shoes as a hungry herd of new white-coated plastic surgeons passed their boards and leaped into practice. The hungriest among them were up to their ears in debt, he knew, and thundering up Celebrity Road to try to lure away his best clients. Many nights the Doctor would actually bolt from bed in a cold sweat. In his dreams he became Frankenstein's monster, pursued through the woods by shouting, white-coated medical students carrying oversize surgical instruments, placards, and flaming torches.

That afternoon, The Doctor's self-pitying professional funk was disturbed by only one puzzling phone call. It was his brother-in-law Simon, breathing heavily into the phone.

"Tomorrow's the day, Clippy," Simon whispered. "Under the gazebo. We made a deal. Remember?"

"Frankly, no," the Doctor sniffed. "I don't have the vaguest notion what you're talking about."

The Doctor did half-remember some promise he'd made to Simon at Petunia's birthday party. But the Doctor hadn't written down the date and whatever it was slipped his mind. Simon's secretary left two messages yesterday but the Doctor hadn't bothered to read them, since they were obviously not celebrity-related.

"You don't remember what we talked about under the gazebo?" Simon demanded. Always the lawyer, Nutty could have been badgering a reluctant witness on the witness stand.

"You don't remember tomorrow, you assured me it's a definite yes, we'll take my airplane?"

"My dear Simon," the Doctor wearily began. "First of all, I had two extremely difficult surgeries this morning. Do you know how much back-to-back surgeries take out of a physician? Frankly, I'm exhausted. I can barely keep my eyes open. Don't expect me to focus on ... you."

The Doctor opened the medical journal, and looked over an advertisement for silicone inserts featuring two bespectacled large-breasted girls.

"Clippy, we have a god damned personal god damned *agreement!*" Simon hissed.

"Check your calendar!" Simon hissed. "My secretary left two messages yesterday! You gave me your word!"

"As a professional with the highest ethical standards, of course, my word is my bond," said the Doctor, closing the magazine. He still did not remember the conversation.

Finally, with effort, the Doctor recalled Simon droning on and on about something, a scene in his mother-in-law's garden. But even though it more or less involved him, the Doctor hadn't really been listening. In a flash he remembered Simon rattling on and on as they stood under a grape arbor or perhaps the gazebo covered with wisteria in his mother-in-law's English garden. Focusing intently, the Doctor remembered only two dangerous-looking black bumblebees humming to and fro over the rim of his second martini.

"What's the problem, Clippy," Simon said. "You've got an airplane! Your office is closed tomorrow. It's Friday."

"Celebrities get nominated for things like Academy Awards, Emmys, and Country Music Awards every day of the week. Then, at the last minute, they look in the mirror and realize they need a little work done," the Doctor began, as if explaining the basics of sandwich-making to a child.

"Just suppose that an actress whose face is known to every person in America calls my office, and asks Doctor to double her lower lip size tomorrow," the Doctor said, a note of professional urgency creeping into his voice. "If that celebrity demands immediate help from a medical professional, that physician absolutely has a duty to open the office and give her everything she wants the minute she wants it. As a physician, Nutty, I took a sacred oath to help people," the Doctor sniffed.

The Doctor was beating around the bush because he was reluctant to admit his office would be closed the next day, and that he wasn't very busy at the moment. His office was almost always closed on Fridays, Saturdays, and Sundays. Even around family, however, the Doctor was reluctant to disturb the image his commercials had painstaking crafted, the image of an A-list doctor who was always working. The truth was, the Doctor had worked on only one Friday since he opened the office, an early morning hair transplant operation for a small celebrity in his early 30s who still passing as a child.

The Doctor knew in his heart that a last-minute call was not likely, but he hung onto the hope that somebody who was somebody's personal manager might still call within the next hour or so. He felt he absolutely had to keep his options open until five o'clock. If you got twelve hours' notice from a celebrity, he sniffed to himself, you were lucky.

"Clippy, this involves you. We've got to do this tomorrow," Simon said. There was an uncomfortable silence.

"I'll have to run it past Clementine," the Doctor finally said.

"Since when do you ask your wife if you can use your own airplane?" Simon practically shouted.

"Clemmie locked the hangars last month, Nutty. There was a little incident with a few of the office girls. Clementine only needs to know where I'm going, who's accompanying me, and when I'm coming back," the Doctor explained.

"You don't *know* where we're going!" Simon shouted. "Tell her you're going with me! We'll be back tomorrow! God damn it, this trip is supposed to be confidential!"

"All right but I can't confirm this until six this evening at the earliest," said the Doctor. "Call me at home. There's a fair statistical probability we can go."

"A fair what?" Simon said.

"Call me at home after six o'clock."

After he hung up, the Doctor sat in his private office for the rest of the afternoon, nervously reading magazines under the Clipster family coat of arms. At five o'clock, the Doctor announced over the office intercom that the office would be closed tomorrow, have a nice weekend, and left his girls to lock up the office.

On the way home, ramming the accelerator pedal of his Porsche Boxster to the floorboard, the Doctor roared past his personal airstrip without even glancing at it. The hangar that housed his jet was locked. This thought put him even deeper into a funk. His old fraternity brother didn't realize he had stirred up an emotional storm inside the Doctor, with his questions about what the Doctor actually controlled, whose airplanes, etc. Were those actually the Doctor's airplanes locked in the hangars, if Clementine held title to them and now even kept the keys in one of her purses? Was the building at the far end of their driveway really his mansion? Legally, of course, the answer was no. Everything they had was in Clementine's name, even the medical buildings. The Doctor tried to put all of this out of his mind.

The locking up of the airplane began with the Doctor's last practically innocent weekend scoot to Las Vegas with a case of Chivas Regal and two of the office girls. The Doctor was surprised to see Clementine show up at the airstrip in her little white Alpha Romeo on a Sunday afternoon, just in time to meet his returning plane. It turned out she had flown in early from Milan. Clementine's haughty announcement in front of the girls that she would lock up his airplanes whether he liked it or not was extremely galling to Doctor. It probably embarrassed the office girls as they staggered out of the jet, blushing and shielding their sensitive skin from the sun.

Nosing his Porsche up the last stretch of driveway, the Doctor lifted his hand to ward off the reflected glare of the late afternoon sun. His metal-skinned mansion positively burned with reflected sunlight. This time of year, sun also reflected mercilessly off the stainless steel and brushed aluminum trees that flanked his mansion's driveway. The Doctor zigged and zagged down his angular driveway, squinting all the way.

Despite the heavily-tinted windshield of his Porsche Boxster and his artfully-tinted monocle, it was impossible at this time of day to look directly at his own metal-skinned house which was topped by two brilliant, blinding awkwardly-leaning towers of reflected solar fire. The Doctor kept his eyes on the side of the road. He knew well enough that the mansion he couldn't bear to look at resembled nothing so much as two flaming metal breasts bursting out of the earth without the benefit of a decent brassiere.

In the early days of his practice, the idea of two deconstructed breasts atop his personal home had made him chuckle with delight. It had given him great pleasure when Clementine slyly pointed this out to visitors.

However, in the Doctor's current frame of mind, his award-winning residence looked less like a fashionable riff on the Taj Mahal than some wild architectural joke, a mad collaboration between a coked-out young architect determined to make the world notice his eccentric genius, and his trendy, insecure, obsessively fashion-conscious wife.

As he shielded his eyes, the Doctor imagined Clementine waiting for him upstairs in her master bedroom, which took up nearly half the house. Her multi-level suite of bedrooms lay up a curving stairway in the right tower, which loomed over the left tower where his small home office, the library, and a few less important rooms were located.

As the Doctor cruised to a stop, he descended even further into his petulant funk. Sunlight off the twin titanium towers only reminded the doctor that he hadn't done a decent breast enhancement for almost two weeks.

What was the matter with the local women? He had seen them at the country club in their swimming suits and their tennis outfits—every woman in the club needed work!

Market research done by his advertising agency told him that the majority of women between 18 and 65 in Santa Barbara were being exposed to at least three of his commercials per week. Yet his business was hardly increasing. Was it an identity problem, or a branding problem? His admen told him they stayed awake at night, trying to get it right, and the Doctor himself was baffled. Would the slump in his work yield to more carefully targeted advertising and increased frequency on certain cable channels, as his admen continually suggested?

The Doctor unsnapped his soft pigskin driving gloves and tossed them into the glove box of his surgical steel Porsche Boxster, then swung open the door.

Like an agile grasshopper he carefully unfolded his lanky legs from the cockpit of his beautifully polished sports car. Leaving the keys in the ignition for the parking valet, he pulled himself to his full height. Then the Doctor hurried up the angular sidewalk to his lavish, haute moderne mansion at No. 3 Swizzle Stick Road.

At that moment he noticed two of Clemmie's maids, Lupe and Conchita, hurrying toward him with bags of designer clothing in their hands. Adjusting his monocle, the Doctor felt his blood pressure rise. Clementine was giving away clothes again.

Clementine spent a small fortune to being home those clothes, the Doctor knew. His wife now shopped more than nine months a year, traveling back and forth to almost every fashion show in the world. And once again, Clemmie was giving away what was probably a couple hundred thousand dollars of designer clothing. A few items were in the original packaging and had never been worn, The Doctor noticed. When Clemmie was home for any length of time, the doctor's wife spent a lot of time cleaning out her many closets, all the better to fill them again with new clothes. Only her twenty-six pairs of Blano Mahlniks were exempt from these periodic purges.

In front of the Clipster mansion, the little maids hopped off the bus in Saks Fifth Avenue or Prada. Cooks showed up to work in strangely fitting Gucci, Valentino, or Christian Dior originals. Even the gardeners and pool cleaners came to work in scarves and accessories by Clementine.

The thought of servants arriving to work in designer clothing for a day of rinsing out toilets, skimming the pool, gardening or mixing drinks aggravated the Doctor, who came from a line of money-conscious skinflints who had barely saved enough money to pay for Stanford and his first two years in medical school.

Since his marriage to Clementine Commode, to which his parents had somehow not been invited, the Doctor had made an effort to forget his parents and every wrong idea he had been taught about saving money.

Following Clementine's lead, the Doctor had learned to guiltlessly squander large amounts of money on himself. However, the Doctor could simply not escape his early financial training when it came to other people, even his own wife. Try as he might, he resented his wife's continual designer clothing giveaways. Of course, he dared not express these feelings since much of what Clementine spent was Old Commodore's money. Clemmie would throw her successful father back in his face again and again if he criticized her lifestyle in even the very smallest way.

For all the financial angst the Doctor experienced at that moment, the expensive designer clothing in the arms of the Mexican maids could have been his own. Although his festering resentments were frighteningly close to the surface, the Doctor forced a smile as the happy little maids waddled toward him.

"*Buenas tias*," said the Doctor, adjusting his monocle with a squint, and majestically nodding.

"Mas beautiful ropas from la Senora Beautiful!" little Lupe laughed, happily hugging an overflowing Saks Fifth Avenue garment bag.

Conchita lifted high her two large paper bags from Bloomingdale's New York, smiling as if she were the happiest little maid in the world.

"Good fortune for you!" cooed the Doctor, trying to smile around his clenched teeth.

The Doctor was supposed to be happy for them, he knew. He knew his role as the benevolent *patron*. But happiness was not the emotion which rose to his throat as the maids scurried past him with their new clothes.

As if on cue, the lawn sprinklers rose up like a school of jumping fish, and blasted them all with a watery fizz.

The Doctor walked angrily through the fizz toward his front door, house keys in hand. Suddenly, up rose the real source of his anger. Why hadn't he done more than two noses that day? Two miserable noses?

The Doctor was probably the best-known plastic surgeon in Southern California, but he was still not working to his full potential!

That his talents were being under-utilized frosted the Doctor as he unlocked his huge front door. Their impressive front door was 12-feet tall, a specially commissioned work of brushed copper and brass inlaid with an artist's abstract rendition of the Clipster family crest. The artist, he recalled, sent Clementine a bill for more than $175,000.

Walking through the door usually made the Doctor feel rich and powerful, but today for some reason it made him felt like a visiting dwarf. Thank God, the Doctor told himself, thank God, thank God, I've married into money. And thank

God for Commodore's money because Clemmie's clothing buys and giveaways were ripping through the dough.

The Doctor slammed the door with the firm metallic "chonk" that usually reminded him of closing the door to his well-built little Porsche. But today, the sound reminded Doctor of his first unsure days at medical school—slamming the remains of his hideously hacked-up female corpse, "Lucy," back into the freezer after breast enhancement lab.

The foyer television sets were silent! The Doctor's hackles rose as he realized that Clementine had again switched off the motion-activated device that tripped a display of his commercials in the foyer. Once again, he realized with a snort, the commercials he and his admen so carefully plotted and shot did not begin playing the minute he slammed the door.

"The Doctor is in!" Doctor Clipster sternly announced.

He looked expectantly around the cavernous entry hallway. The two life-sized lacquered tigers flanking the stairway to Clemmie's rooms seemed to leer at him in silence.

"Clemmie!" he cried. "The Doctor is in!"

For the first few years of their marriage, Clementine had met him at the door as faithfully as a well-trained dog. In the sensual tropical heat of Brazil, she had positively dripped with passion as she met her bitchy, slender, upwardly-mobile plastic surgeon at the door.

In their first years on Swizzle Stick Road, when the Doctor returned from the clinic, Clemmie would come excitedly running down the stairs in a designer gown with no underpants. Together they'd run hand-in-hand up the onyx stairway to her bedroom in the tallest tower, switch on her rotating bed, and he'd chase Clemmie back and forth across the room until she let him catch her.

When he slipped off her clothes, he'd whisper how beautiful she had become, and how much more beautiful certain procedures could make her, something she never tired of hearing. When Clementine had gotten her fill of compliments and promises, she'd rip off his scrubs and make love to the Doctor like a snarling whippet in heat.

It was a continuing mystery to the Doctor why their relationship changed. He still didn't quite believe it. More often than not, he'd return home to find his wife far from her rotating bed—an affable old St. Bernard with a half-empty brandy jug around her neck, no longer particularly eager to see him, and no longer wagging her tail. These days his wife seemed only energized by leaving town to shop for clothes and jewelry to put on that magnificent figure and face he and his colleagues had given her, one surgery at a time.

Clementine's surgically-altered face and body raised certain issues. For one thing, the more beautiful Clemmie became, the better she looked in clothes. The better she looked in clothes, the more clothes she bought, the more she went out of town, and the more compliments she expected when she returned.

The Doctor had seen this same narcissistic fascination with appearances among many of his well-off clientele. Some ability to emphasize with other people was lost as his clients became more and more flawlessly attractive, awakening more and more narcissism, the Doctor had observed. Vanity had become the handmaiden of beauty. And more and more, Clementine seemed to love her clothes and herself more than she loved her Doctor. Because of this, perhaps, it bothered him when she gave her expensive garments away. It felt to the Doctor as if a piece of their relationship was being discarded, too.

In the ringingly quiet foyer, the Doctor suddenly imagined he heard the sound of two beautiful, intelligent, happily-skipping little girls, his imaginary daughters. His two imaginary daughters were always happy the Doctor was in. They skipped happily down the hallway toward him, one after the other, long blonde hair flopping up and down over the shoulders of their neatly-pressed private school uniforms.

"My Doctor is in!" the youngest imaginary daughter screamed, jumping up and down.

"My Doctor is in, too!" the other cried.

The children were a fantasy, of course. In the beginning, he and Clementine had talked of children, and had undergone extensive genetic counseling. His urologist told him he had a low to normal sperm count, perfectly adequate for reproduction, and Clementine's gynecologist swore she was completely fertile. It was theoretically possible that they could have children, as the Doctor had always secretly wanted. But even after his phalloplasty, they were hardly even having sex. The thought had struck him that children would interfere with Clementine's jet set lifestyle, more and more of which was being conducted offstage. Just last week the Doctor noticed one of her Jack Russell terriers trotting around with an empty plastic wheel of birth control pills in its mouth. The Doctor had not dared confront Clementine regarding what the dog carried into his personal bedroom and dropped quietly on the floor next to his bedroom slippers.

The Doctor's imaginary daughters scampered out of sight behind a pressed tin sculpture as the little maid from Honduras stumbled into the entryway. In her ridiculous uniform, Clemmie's personal maid looked like a short, brown, broad-shouldered visitor from another planet. She did not speak. The little maid only pointed outside.

Like the other servants, she wore one of the bizarre uniforms Clementine purchased in London two years ago, at an art and livery fashion show at the West End of London. After Clementine returned home, the Doctor recalled, she lined up the servants in their uniforms to show him what she'd done.

The Doctor immediately hated the tight, silvery, broad-shouldered uniforms. For one thing, looking at the uniforms almost made his eyes hurt. He didn't like the high stiff collars, the exaggerated shoulders, or the badge-like holograms placed over each servant's heart. To his eye, they made the servants look like extras from the set of "Star Trek." But Clementine loved the bright, eye-catching uniforms, and of course her brother Philip assured her they were a perfect match for the house. Even after the Doctor hinted broadly at his displeasure, once even boldly comparing the servants to silverfish moving from room to room, Clementine had stubbornly retained the uniforms. Not only that, as if to spite him, Clementine flew the buck-toothed little British designer back to Montecito to refurbish the uniforms every year.

Still pointing, Clemmie's uniformed little maid appeared to be adrift in deep space. The Doctor noticed that her uniform's pointed shoulders were askew. The little maid had been drinking with Clementine, the Doctor suspected.

Clementine was forever enticing the servants to have a drink with her, and then another, because she didn't like to drink alone. The Doctor took a deep breath, screwed in his monocle, and walked outside.

He found Clementine in the Sahara Desert Oasis. It was one of several ersatz "environments" the landscape architects placed around the grounds to keep Clementine from getting bored. This particular patio, covered with pure white sand, was surrounded by a ring of aluminum faux palm trees. The centerpiece of the Sahara environment was a tall double waterfall. Water tumbled down a long ramp of plastic boulders and rocks toward the Doctor.

Clementine lay on a low-slung, jewel-encrusted Egyptian lounge chair which had been signed by the famous artist, Salvador Dali. The lounge chair had been positioned under an extra large beach umbrella to ward away the sun. Droplets of chlorinated water hung in the air.

Clementine wore a new white bathing suit, a large floppy white sun hat, and matching sunglasses. She held an empty martini glass in her hand, as indolent as Cleopatra herself. She rolled over in the lounge chair toward her dogs without looking at the Doctor, and tried to clap her hands.

Three obedient little Jack Russell terriers sprang to attention in the sand. Staggering back and forth on their hind legs, they excitedly tried to nip the waterfall's chlorinated fizz. The doctor knew this comical if slightly pathetic performance would only stop when the dogs were exhausted, or when Clementine commanded them to stop, and offered them something to drink. The little terriers had already developed a taste for gin.

The minute he noticed one of the dancing terriers relieving itself on the jewel-encrusted leg of the lounge chair, the Doctor raised one eyebrow and dislodged his monocle.

"Clemmie darling," said the Doctor, addressing his wife's back and butt in his best professional voice. "Aren't we lovely this afternoon?"

Clementine looked back over her shoulder, her mouth slightly open, as if awakening from a dream. Her face was so tight she could no longer actually smile, although she made something of an effort. Clementine managed only a sort of grotesque grimace, pulling back her unnaturally large red lips from her unnaturally white teeth. The Doctor knew Clementine meant this to be a smile, but the overall effect was slightly grotesque and he wished she wouldn't do it. Unfortunately, the Doctor had no idea how to broach this particular topic with his wife, or any other. If Clemmie didn't ever try to smile, he advised her in his mind, she would be forever beautiful. But the Doctor didn't dare suggest anything of the sort to Clementine, since she reacted strongly to even his most tactful and benign criticism.

"Dogger home from offish?" she said, rattling the ice cubes in her empty glass.

"As a matter of fact, thank you, I had two extremely difficult surgeries today," said the Doctor. "I don't know how I make it through those surgeries. And now wouldn't you know it—Simon has asked for my assistance."

Clementine turned her attention to the dancing Jack Russell terriers, which immediately began barking at the Doctor.

"Babish," Clementine said to the dogs. "Shit down for Dogger."

The well-trained little dogs sat down in perfect formation, expectantly panting.

Old Muldoon quickly trotted out of the mansion like a rotund silverfish, silver tray in hand. Martinis rocked and tottered back and forth on the tray. Today, perhaps because he was working the Sahara Oasis, Old Muldoon wore an ornate headscarf in the Middle Eastern fashion. From the look of his turban and the front of his silver uniform, the Doctor observed, he was probably soused too.

Old Muldoon bowed a little too grandly, and then lowered the silver tray with one hand for Clemmie to exchange her empty glass for a drink, as he had been trained to do. Next, old Muldoon placed one fresh Martini in the sand in front of each of the motionless little dogs. With a grand flourish, he offered the last remaining drink to the Doctor, who picked it neatly off the moving tray with his nimble surgeon's fingers. After a deferential nod to all of them, old Muldoon adjusted his headscarf and shuffled darkly away through the sand.

"Drinkie one, drinkie two, drinkie new," Clemmie said to the dogs, snapping her fingers at the panting little terriers.

To Clementine's delight, the dogs obediently lowered their muzzles and began snorting and lapping furiously.

"Shit, doctor," Clementine said, patting the arm of the chair next to her as she might have patted it for a child.

The Doctor obediently sat down. The Doctor wasn't particularly comfortable with his hemorrhoids on the jewel-encrusted arm of the lounge chair. However, he leaned forward and gamely forced a smile.

"You are so perfectly exquisitely beautiful," the Doctor smiled, squeezing Clementine's arm benignly. "*Exquisitely beautiful.*"

After a moment he added, "By the way, Clemmie, could you let me have the keys to the little jet tomorrow morning? I've been asked to run some sort of errand with Simon. We'll be back tomorrow way before bedtime."

Clementine tried to smile. The Doctor smiled warmly in return and caressed her arm.

"I'll get the keys right now," she said. "Baron."

Clementine never let the Doctor forget that turning him into a titled Scottish Baron had cost a fortune. It started with a perfectly innocent lie. Foolishly trying to impress her on their first date, the Doctor told Clementine he was descended from Scottish royalty. One of his blustery old uncles had made this grand statement with a wink and a nod to a few of the more impressionable children at a Clipster family reunion. The Doctor's alleged link to royalty fascinated Clemmie, and she bragged about it to everyone in the sorority house. Then her mother wanted more information for their engagement announcement to be placed in the local newspaper. When Clementine pressed him for specifics, the young medical student's life became a nightmare.

The Doctor located his red-nosed old uncle in the Mission District of San Francisco, where he was living the high life with two stray Dalmatians and a cardboard box.

The inebriated old gasbag could not remember telling the horrified young medical student that the family was descended from nobility. So the jig was up. In a fit of honesty that he was sure would cost him his fiancé, the Doctor finally came clean to Clementine. To his surprise she simply refused to accept the truth. As he watched in amazement, Clementine began to shell out money with the assurance and determination of someone whose every dream had been made to come true.

A shadowy fixer was located somewhere in the bowels of Scotland who promised to "secure a new royal title forthwith." The old shyster claimed to have unearthed a very authentic Clipster family crest, but he demanded a hefty fee to transfer a Scottish title to America. After Clementine shelled out a second truly exorbitant fee, the old crook claimed there were "complications"—more than a hundred Scottish Clipsters still alive, and every one of them entitled to an additional compensation according to Scottish tradition. In the end, the young medical student was aghast at how much money the old crook extracted from Clementine.

But the young bathroom fixtures heiress gave her medical student a copy of the official Clipster coat of arms a couple of weeks before they were married, and R. Baron "Barrie" Clipster, M.D., had his first real taste of the miracles that could be achieved with money.

If the crest looked like a pair of rusty scissors over a dog dish, the Doctor instantly realized that adding a royal title to his credentials gave him a little something extra with which to impress a high-end celebrity clientele. When Clementine's younger brother decorated his office, young Philip insisted on mounting an embossed blowup of the crest in a huge, hand-carved oak frame which had once embraced a Leroy Neiman.

"Are you actually a Baron?" patients would ask after they noticed the coat of arms displayed on his office wall. It was so large it could not possibly be missed even by the more nearsighted patients.

The Doctor would nod curtly, adjusting the monocle he had taken to wearing in Brazil. And another favorable first impression was made.

At the moment, Clemmie's three Jack Russell terriers lay on their backs in the sand. Two of them were kicking their tiny paws into the air. The Doctor knew it wouldn't be long before one or more dogs developed a serious case of diarrhea.

Clementine got up, wrinkled her nose, adjusted her sun hat, and nodded haughtily to the Doctor. Clementine released a tiny fart as she turned toward the house. She sloshed away under her floppy white hat without saying a word. The dogs sniffed the air, whined, and began crawling away after her.

Again the Doctor was alone. He sat down in Clementine's lounge chair, fingering his stethoscope and inhaling the chlorinated breeze.

"The Doctor is in!" one of his imaginary daughters cried, poking her head out from behind the trunk of a faux palm.

Both daughters began skimming lightly across the sand toward him, wearing school uniforms and saddle oxfords, their blonde hair flopping up and down. Of course they adored him like a god.

"The Doctor is home!" one cried, throwing up her arms.

"The Doctor is in!" the other corrected.

Circling the lounge chair, the Doctor's imaginary little girls leapt like graceful fauns, and then froze in the air. He admired their exuberant physicality. Doctor dearly loved his two perfect little daughters, who were unbelievably intelligent. The girls would be off to school in a flash but of course now they longed to spend their every waking hour with The Doctor.

The girls disappeared in a puff of smoke as the Doctor's cell phone rang, a James Bond movie ring tone.

"So you got the plane?" Simon demanded. "We've got to leave at five o'clock."

The Doctor recognized the hissing voice of his old fraternity brother. Simon's cell phone signal seemed to be crackling and fading, as usual. Poor Nutty was forever struggling with his cell phone reception.

"Of course I got the plane," the Doctor said, angrily releasing his monocle. "But isn't five o'clock rather early."

Unless he had to fly south to meet a celebrity in the Beverly Hills office, he didn't normally get up that early. Clementine's breakfast cook didn't even come to work until eight o'clock.

For a moment the Doctor wondered about his old fraternity brother. He recognized the voice of a man under great stress, like so many of the overworked senior plastic surgeons he had assisted in the operating room during his residency. From the distant past, the Doctor recalled masked figures with wildly flashing eyes and scalpels in both hands, men liable to make and cover up a serious mistake or two in judgment while in the process of getting fabulously wealthy.

"Just *be there*, Clippy," Simon hissed, and hung up.

The sun was setting in the west. Slogging across the sand under a headscarf came the dutiful figure of old Muldoon. The butler from outer space adroitly stopped and handed Doctor the keys to his airplane. Then Muldoon bowed at the waist, extended a silver tray on a shimmering silver arm, and elegantly offered Doctor a fresh martini.

5. A Secret Journey

Early the next morning the Doctor awoke much too early and drove to the airport. His Porsche's headlights flashed on the stiff, scowling figure of Simon Butterknut pacing back and forth in front of a black Mercedes. Simon wore a brown Armani business suit and overcoat, dressed for action. As the Doctor stopped the car, Simon immediately began pointing at his watch, one of his prized Rolexes, no doubt. Simon hurried forward as the Doctor quietly slipped out of his Porsche and tried to suppress a yawn.

The Doctor wore the blue silk scrubs which had long ago become his everyday outfit. Over his heart was the Clipster coat of arms, and over that the monogram "The Doctor Is In" in a sweeping arc of blazing gold thread. Inside his right scrub pants pocket was a special hidden compartment which the Doctor instructed the maids to fill with business cards the minute they came back from the dry cleaners. When worn with the oversized stethoscope and his signature monocle, the Doctor knew, he was easily picked out of a crowd.

The Doctor also knew well enough from his days in Brazil that women of a certain age and even some men found the medical look and particularly the oversized stethoscope sexually appealing.

"So what's up, Nutty?" he asked, unlocking the hangar.

The Doctor cleverly sensed that his old fraternity brother, a schemer from the word go, was working yet another hidden agenda.

"A journey to the east," Simon said. "Think of it as dialing for dollars, Clippy, just like old times with the girls."

"Just like old times," the Doctor smiled.

This was an inside joke between the two former fraternity brothers. The Doctor understood the financial implications immediately. After strapping himself into the plane, Simon cracked open his black hand-tooled Gucci briefcase. The Doctor heard his old fraternity brother clumsily break open a bottle of prescription medication and pour himself a handful of airsickness pills.

Through his monocle the Doctor observed his old fraternity brother quietly washing each pill down with a sip of a Starbuck's large double latte he had apparently picked up for himself on the way to the airport. It was impossible not to notice that his old fraternity brother had not thought to bring along even a small double latte for the Doctor.

Still, the Doctor felt a conspiratorial thrill in the pit of his gastrointestinal tract. As he adjusted his monocle under the flight helmet, the sleek little jet banked like a soaring sea gull over the twinkling mansions of Montecito and turned east.

The granite slopes of the Los Padres Mountains popped out of the darkness like a row of small grey lower teeth. The Doctor's jet rose over tree-covered mountains as far below them, in the morning light, a giant black condor glided toward its nest atop a tall craggy mountaintop with some kind of dead animal in its claws. Neither Nutty nor Clippy noticed the large black carrion-eating bird.

"We're dialing for dollars again," the Prince whispered, clutching his arm.

"Ah-ha," said the Doctor, clasping his stethoscope.

So Simon had a plan. Something big was afoot to get his old fraternity brother into an airplane. The Doctor knew that Simon—whom he still affectionately called "Nutty," his Omega Pi nickname—was secretly terrified of flying. Even Nutty's wife didn't realize that every time Simon had hopped into a jet for family vacations to Cape Cod or Palm Beach, her handsome, muscular husband spent most of the trip in the plane's tiny washroom, sometimes even heaving up the industrial strength airsickness pills the Doctor secretly prescribed for him before they went aboard.

❧

So long ago, at Stanford—where Simon affectionately dubbed the Doctor "Clippy"—they'd been two comically overextended fraternity brothers, so far in debt they were the running gags of Omega Pi. The two fraternity brothers regarded each other suspiciously at first, since they were both ambitious young men transparently focused on securing their future by marrying one the wealthy sorority girls who roamed the Stanford campus like herds of beautiful, well-dressed, bleating sheep.

Clippy was romancing a wealthy Alpha Beta whose roommate, Petunia Commode, was rumored to be the richest girl in Stanford. One night after sex, Clippy's date confided with a bitchy snicker that Sister Petunia, who was not known for her academic prowess, actually had fantasies of going to law school. Did Brother Clippy know a law student who needed a few extra dollars, to tutor Petunia for the exam?

Clippy passed the word to the only law student he knew, his fast-talking fraternity brother, Nutty, who became his instant best friend. And Simon hit the jackpot with Petunia Commode. Later on, returning the favor, Nutty tipped him off that Petunia Commode had an equally available sister, a mildly neurotic sophomore named Clementine. Clementine wanted to talk to a medical student to discuss plastic surgery on what she thought was her horribly misshapen nose. Although the Doctor had more or less set his sights on pediatrics, he changed his specialty to plastic surgery the night he met Clementine Commode. The wide-eyed heiress seemed to hang on every word of every medical procedure he explained.

❧

Don Dumper, plants manager, stepped forward to greet them at the corporate airport in Cleveland. Dumper was clearly a Commode Company man, as transparently honest as the day was long.

As they shook hands, the Doctor observed a certain lack of fashion consciousness in the man. Dumper's belly protruded far over his belt in the mid-western manner, the Doctor noticed, giving him the look of a man who was eight months pregnant. Under his off-the-rack tweed coat, a stiff, ketchup-stained clip-on tie rolled out over his modest paunch.

The rather plainly-dressed manager was an excellent candidate for liposuction, the Doctor noted. If he had the right health insurance, the doctor would also recommend a little eye work on those baggy, tired-looking Middle American eyes. On the way to the car, the Doctor made a mental note to give the lumbering middle manager some pertinent medical advice and a business card on the way back to the plane.

"I hope you're not having any real serious medical problems, Mr. Butterknut," Dumper said, with sympathetic eyes. "Even Old Mr. Commode never brought along his own doctor when he inspected the plants."

"For God's sake—I'm not sick! This is Commodore Commode's son-in-law! He and his wife have a seat on the company board of directors!" the Prince snapped. "We didn't come here to joke around."

Dumper reacted as if he had been slapped in the face. After they climbed into the back seat of Dumper's late model Ford Taurus, Dumper quietly took the wheel and sped away without another word.

In the main office, Commode Company secretaries and supervisors talked on the phone or scurried around, carrying piles of paper. Ascending a metal stairway to the second story of the plant, the Doctor took note of the prominent row of pictures of Commodore's ancestors beginning with the devilishly frowning Nicholas Commode. Every one of those stout, dour Victorian business tycoons needed extensive work.

Dumper led them into a second floor conference room whose windows overlooked the factory floor and then dimmed the lights.

"What you're seeing is the pride of the Commode Company right now," Dumper said. "You fellows seeing the fastest finishing line in the United States. Mr. Commode personally approved the installation of this just last year."

Out the window, far below them, lay the factory floor. Borne on a long black conveyor belt, tiny white half-finished Commode Company toilets passed quickly below them like a string of gleaming white Chiclets. As the line jerked to a stop for a couple of seconds, a huge machine that looked like a mechanical preying mantis branded each white toilet with the black Commode Company logo just inside the front of the bowl. As the mechanical insect withdrew, two small sweating, cursing middle-aged workers on the seat-bolting crew struggled to screw on a plastic toilet seat in the same period of time. They finished up just as the line started up again, with an angry hiss of steam and a jerk of the conveyor belt, repeating the whole process again.

"Are these guys cooking with gas, or what?" Dumper asked expectantly. Simon did not reply.

The manager took them to another of the five plants where plastic toilet lids were being manufactured in great quantities and pallets stacked up to the ceiling.

"Is that the odor of silicone?" the Doctor sniffed, recognizing a familiar smell.

"Yes it is," Dumper said. "You got a great nose."

"Thank you, but you're not the first to notice that," the Doctor smiled modestly, stroking his nose. "I'm also very familiar with the material from my own work."

In the middle of inspecting still another plant, where the remote-control and oversized custom toilets were produced, the Prince lifted his diamond-studded Rolex Yachtmaster and stared pointedly at Dumper.

"Let's go back to your office right now," Simon snarled.

On the way to Dumper's office, the Doctor fingered his stash of business cards. His critical surgeon's eye observed a number of secretaries waddling from desk to desk in the outer office. The ladies were broad in the beam in Cleveland, the Doctor noticed. But those big Northern European rear ends could be dramatically reshaped with some of the better new techniques. If he had a bit more time, he might gather a group of secretaries and conduct a brief lecture on tumescent liposuction, a procedure so gentle most of the women whose butts and thighs were slimmed could walk normally after only a few days of rest.

The Doctor was already distributing business cards when Simon called him back into Dumper's office and closed the door. The plant manager's office was so small there was barely room enough for Nutty and Clippy to squeeze into chairs on the opposite side of his desk. A faded black and white 8 x 10 picture of Dumper and a much younger Commodore hung on the wall. On the desk were framed pictures of Dumper's roly-poly wife and matching children.

"So we've sped up the lines to pretty much maximum potential, on all three shifts, just like Mr. Commode and you fellas in the main office asked us to do. These old union guys all earn those big productivity bonuses now," Dumper said. "You saw them working."

"These employees are *unionized?*" sniffed the Doctor, who like most over-paid professionals disliked unions.

"Yes sir," Dumper nodded. "The union's been here since Mr. Nicholas Commode. You probably know the Commode Company was one of the first union shops in the United States. Our median wage is $43 an hour now, for the real old hands, plus benefits, whatever the union negotiates," Dumper earnestly explained.

"I must tell you that the very best minds in the medical profession believe unions are a trap for the working man, and I tend to agree with my enlightened colleagues," scowled the Doctor, ominously fingering his stethoscope. "The solution we in the medical profession bring forward is to provide first-rate professional service at the maximum reimbursement government, insurance companies, and certain wealthy individuals can afford to pay. In our most successful medical practices, of course, the solution is not to unionize, but rather to incorporate. Do your good work, send off your billing statements, take your tax write-offs and let the free market work its magic. You and your colleagues here in Cleveland might think about that before you bring in a union."

"Well, doc, union guys do all the work in all five factories here," Dumper said. "You saw our guys working their butts off, I guess. The guys don't want these jobs to move overseas."

"That's exactly what I'm here to discuss," Simon said, pushing aside Dumper's family pictures and cracking open his briefcase.

The Prince pushed a contract across the desk, and handed Dumper a wide-bodies Mont Blanc pen.

Dumper held the contract in both hands and began to read it under the florescent lamp. His hands and lips appeared to be trembling as he read.

"As plant manager you'll be in the catbird seat when we relocate. You get a five hundred thousand dollar bonus to keep the lid on with the guys when we pull out, and another five hundred thousand when we move to China," the Prince said.

Dumper's eyes widened and he blinked a couple of times. "You're offering me a million dollars?"

"You'll make a million dollars cold and you'll get an all expenses paid vacation to China, but that's only for starters," the Prince said, smiling a wicked smile.

"China?" Dumper said, leaning back, blowing air through his lips, and shaking his head. "China? Me? Us? Moving? I still got kids in school."

"It's only a formality but we need your signature right away," Simon said, tapping the contract.

On the way back to the airport, the Doctor sat in the front seat next to Dumper, as he had discreetly insisted on doing. The Doctor slipped two business cards into Dumper's top pocket, behind the plastic pencil protector, and patted Dumper's chest benignly. The Doctor smiled his warmest smile.

Dumper looked suspiciously at the Doctor, obviously startled at being patted on the chest by a smiling medical professional believed to have perhaps the best bedside manner in Montecito and Beverly Hills.

"In California, Don, you don't just have to be a celebrity to get plastic surgery. The common man is stepping up to the plate, if you know what I mean," cooed the Doctor, patting his chest again.

Dumper stared straight ahead and kept both hands on the wheel.

"You might ask, where does a man interested in this sort of thing start? Obviously, there's liposuction," the Doctor said, gently patting Dumper's belly. "And of course the Doctor is in for a little eye work. When you get that big bonus, why not let Doctor sculpt those baggy eyelids and make you look ten years younger? My wealthier male clients tell me that the eye work and liposuction combo makes them even more sexy and irresistible to younger women."

Dumper smiled politely. The Doctor believed he had perked the plant manager's interest. He made a mental note to have his girls follow up with a phone call at the appropriate time.

Somewhere over Arizona, Nutty used an airsickness bag. The Doctor put the jet on automatic pilot to check his messages. A text message in Doctor's private mailbox! Often personal managers of celebrities used this method to demand a particular preliminary date for surgery. But no, the Doctor found only a brittle little squib from Clementine, asking him to pick up two fifths of Johnny Walker Red and a large bag of gourmet dog food at the vet's before he came back to the house.

As the shadowy maw of the Grand Canyon passed beneath them, Nutty passionately grabbed his arm.

"We'll move everything overseas, the machinery, the assembly lines, everything," the Prince confided. "But get this,

Clippy. Here's the kicker. The minute the plants go to China, you and I become independently rich!"

"Rich?" the Doctor sniffed, suddenly attentive.

"How about a check for a hundred fifty million dollars?" The Prince asked, his eyes shining. "Does that sound good?"

"Yes, frankly," the Doctor replied.

"When the board of directors approves moving the plants, you and I each get a cashier's check for $150 million. It's a finder's fee—get this—paid by the Chinese government!" the Prince said. "Their government actually pays us a finder's fee for moving our plants to China!"

As he looked out the side window, the Doctor tactfully ignored the slight odor of vomit on Nutty's breath. The sun began to bury its head in the far end of the Grand Canyon.

"We deposit the checks into our personal bank accounts in the Cayman Islands, we pay zero taxes, Clippy."

"I don't have a bank account in the Cayman Islands," the Doctor sniffed in the gathering darkness.

"Clippy, I set up your account. We're set. My hundred fifty million goes in first. Bang! Your hundred fifty million goes in next. Bang! And here's the rub—it's your personal account! It's all your money! Even if she knew about it, Clementine wouldn't be able to touch a dime."

"I like it," cried the Doctor "Count me in."

6. Enter a Mysterious Lady

It was the day of the Montecito Country Club's Celebrity Pro-Am Golf Tournament. As Commodore's driver loaded his golf clubs into the trunk of the town car, the old capitalist was cranky and slightly worried. There would be celebrities at the club's biggest event of the year, of course, and even an over-the-hill pro golfer or two, along with his and Milly's dearest friends and acquaintances from the country club. Having been the butt of a certain amount of snide gossip for the past two years, the old billionaire dearly wanted to make a decent showing.

Every year, the Von Turkles acted like they were doing him a favor, pairing him with some semi-regular from "Hollywood Squares." Playing golf with celebrities was an honor, the Von Turkles fervently believed. Commodore's Hollywood square partners were charming enough in front of the cameras, but neither of his celebrity partners was able to actually play golf. Their last place finishes were publicly posted in the main clubhouse for everyone in the club to see.

Commodore privately pinned the blame on his celebrity partner's inability to focus on anything but being photographed. Two years ago, Commodore was paired with Dr. Burnell F. "Catfish" Washington, an ageless black ventriloquist whose large and easily-removed false teeth (he put his teeth on his hand and they talked back to him) and his background as a dentist were his claim to fame. Dr. Washington's talking false teeth were a separate personality apparently known to the public and the other Hollywood Squares as "Mr. Choppers."

Commodore was surprised the first time his golf partner's dentures jumped from his mouth into his hand before a squatting television tabloid photographer. He was even more amazed when the teeth appeared to begin talking. Catfish turned to Commodore with a twinkle in his eye. He looked at the dentures, and clacked them together.

"I think my old mean golf partner don't like Mr. Choppers," the clacking dentures appeared to say.

When the camera swung to Commodore for a reaction shot, his golf game immediately disintegrated.

And last year's celebrity partner, the corpulent country western singer Little Winnie Winkler complained all day long that not nearly enough press was following her around. Perky Little Winnie flew all the way out from Nashville for this, she snorted to Commodore, referring to herself in the third person.

More than once, while taking far more than her share of their golf cart, Little Winnie tried any number of perky little ruses to attract the attention of passing photographers but they all seemed headed somewhere else.

"My golf partner is complaining about my game!" Little Winnie wailed and whistled.

Blushing and looking away so as not to be photographed, Commodore despised perky Little Winnie's pathetic ploys for attention. Finally he asked her not to make a fool of herself on the golf course, and stiffly requested that she keep what was left of her mind on the game. She didn't speak another word to Commodore for the rest of the match. However, at the 18th hole, where the laziest photographers lay in wait, Commodore was sure his partner deliberately eight-putted the last hole with her putter upside down to attract attention to herself, and also to embarrass and spite him.

It mortified him that the tournament's scores remained prominently posted in the clubhouse for almost two months after the event. No one said anything directly to his face, but Commodore saw the way his old golfing partners and their wives avoided his eyes and suddenly became silent as he entered the clubhouse in the weeks following the tournament. Commodore was certain that his last place finish had been discussed at length, and that he had been made the butt of unseemly jokes when he was not around.

This year, the old capitalist hoped, things would be different. In the weeks leading up to the tournament, Commodore practiced obsessively. He kept a set of clubs in the office and spent an hour every afternoon putting golf balls into a plastic cup. Golf pros came out to the mansion to give him lessons three times a week. Commodore was so horrified at the prospect of being humiliated a third time that a couple of nights he was actually unable to sleep. The old billionaire actually rang his valet, lit the course, and played golf until the sun rose.

Commodore also hoped for sort of assistance from his son-in-law, Simon. Although Simon never expressed much interest in golf before, this year he volunteered to sit on the tournament's steering committee. Commodore was delighted, of course. He gave Simon as much time off as he needed to attend committee meetings, and made a larger donation than usual to the charitable event. As the tournament approached, Commodore secretly hoped Simon might try to get him a decent partner. It didn't seem proper to Commodore to use his influence with Simon. But Commodore did pointedly mention that he could not bear to be paired with still another shamefully preoccupied celebrity who would stop everything to mug for photographers right in the middle of a game.

Both his sons-in-law would be at the tournament, Commodore knew, but neither would be playing golf. Clementine's husband would be hanging around the clubhouse in one of those ridiculous surgical outfits, kissing up to the celebrities and passing out business cards. Simon would be strutting around the clubhouse with his chest stuck out, the only man at the tournament in a business suit and tie. But none of Simon's strutting and blowing mattered, Commodore thought, if he had somehow helped to pair Commodore with a suitable partner. As the old billionaire stepped out of the town car, he experienced lingering doubts about his son-in-law's ability to come through in the clutch.

※

Arches of pink balloons shifted quietly in the breeze at the entrance to the clubhouse. Bug-eyed photographers squatted beside the door with their cameras, hungrily awaiting celebrities. As his clubs were unloaded, Commodore put on his plaid golf cap and walked toward the Von Turkles.

The immaculately graying older couple held hands next to a table full of name tags, discreetly awaiting the arrival of celebrities. The Von Turkles were flagrant name droppers, Commodore knew. Under their snooty facades it was obvious enough that they were the worst sort of celebrity hounds. They organized the tournament for the sole purpose of cozying up to the celebrities, whose first names they tossed around the clubhouse for almost the entire year.

"Mr. Commodore Commode has arrived," Mrs. Von Turkle warbled to her husband.

She slapped a name tag over Commodore's heart, and absentmindedly air-kissed the old billionaire. Like an anxious poodle she was already glancing furtively up the driveway for the limos of approaching celebrities.

"We simply could not arrange a celebrity match for you this year, Commodore," said Mrs. Von Turkle, passing him along to her husband. "I'm so sorry."

"I can assure you we had many long conversations on this very topic with your son-in-law," old Von Turkle said. Smiling his sad sympathetic smile, old Von Turkle sadly shook his jowls at the bad news.

Just inside the clubhouse, Simon waited in a ridiculous oversized cardboard cowboy hat. The hat and attached pink balloon looked particularly ridiculous over Simon's business suit. But Commodore's son-in-law lit up like a light bulb and boomed a hearty welcome as he approached. Next to Simon stood an attractive Asian woman in a red golf outfit. Beneath a wedge of straight black hair, she turned a pretty face to Commodore and smiled a bewitching, Mati Hari smile.

"Commodore, this is your golf partner for the day, Miss Long Drive Loo," Simon said. The Prince leaned toward Commodore and smiled a wicked smile.

"Miss Loo is a former professional golfer," he whispered to Commodore. "She just flew in from China."

The Chinese woman bowed politely. This modest gesture of respect made an impression on Commodore. All his life he had been surrounded by brassy American club women who wouldn't bow to any man for love or money.

Miss Loo removed one of her golf gloves, and extended a moist muscular hand. The old billionaire saw an unmistakable flash of competitive fire in her eyes.

"We make good golf partner," she said.

"I dearly hope so," Commodore replied.

Simon vanished. Miss Loo clapped her hands.

An Asian caddie in a red shirt appeared out of nowhere with a rattling bag of golf clubs over his shoulder. Miss Loo clapped her hands a second time. A second red-shirted Asian caddie hurried out of nowhere, carrying Commodore's clubs. Club rules specified caddies although of course the golfers used golf carts. Right off the bat, Commodore was impressed by the stout military bearing of Miss Loo's red-shirted men, who seemed always to be standing rigidly at attention.

Miss Loo strode to the first tee and hit a strong, spectacular drive that caught the attention of every man in the crowd. After Commodore's modest drive, they stepped into their golf cart and glided noiselessly away, followed by their two trotting red-shirted caddies.

The surprisingly talkative Miss Loo had yet to master the English language. Still, she managed to relate to him that, some time before, she had been the first Chinese golf pro to compete in American golf tournaments. She had once won the biggest women's golf tournament in the United States, she said, and it made her famous for three months in China.

"What business you?" Miss Loo asked as their cart sped up the second fairway.

"Little family business," Commodore said.

"Family business best," Miss Loo agreed.

On the third tee, Miss Loo hit a third spectacular drive. Matched with a competitor of this caliber, Commodore bore down as much as he possibly could, in an effort to not embarrass himself on the greens. He could not help but notice that Miss Loo had a splendid little figure. Her calves tightened like violin strings as she teed off with a sexy twist of her derriere and a dramatic swish of her red silk golf skirt.

As the game progressed, Commodore came to admire Miss Loo's blunt, slashing style. He worked hard to accustom himself to her somewhat clumsy efforts at making conversation.

On the fifth fairway, Miss Loo expertly pitched her ball onto the green, within two feet of the flag before turning to Commodore.

"What family business you?" Miss Loo asked.

"We have a few little factories here in the United States," said Commodore, wading gamely into a sand trap after his ball. "We have a line of bathroom products."

"How many factory?" Miss Loo asked, batting her eyes as Commodore struggled to knock his ball out of the sand trap. "Three factory, four factory, five factory?"

"Yes!" Commodore replied.

The questions about his business were asked in what Commodore felt was a rather direct and strangely flirtatious way. This was flattering, of course, since every woman he had ever known went to sleep when he talked business. But Miss Loo's interest proved to be more than flattering. It gave Commodore's self-confidence a lift and inspired him to play somewhat smarter golf. To keep up with this exhilarating woman, he felt, he had to play some of the best golf of his life. He actually achieved par on three holes in a row.

Commodore watched Miss Loo attempt a tricky, uphill 22-foot putt from the far edge of a long, uneven green. Miss Loo hunched over the ball, lazily swinging her muscular butt back and forth like a hen preparing to lay eggs.

Suddenly the golf ball cracked off the tip of her putter, rolled in a long lovely upward curve up and across the green and back down again, caught the far side of the hole and rolled around the lip of the cup five or six times like a long French kiss before falling in for a birdie.

My God!" Commodore exclaimed, taking off his Scotch plaid golf cap. "That was beautiful."

Miss Loo modestly bowed. Commodore squatted down next to Miss Loo to check out the lay of the green and passed a rather large amount of gas. Miss Loo, smiling sweetly, seemed to nod her approval.

"My family five empty factories in Shanghai, easy ship to U.S.," she sang, somewhat discordantly as they sat in the cart.

"You don't say," Commodore said.

A rattling sound behind them signaled the approach of the huffing, puffing caddies. As Miss Loo prepared to tee off, the two Asian caddies took off their red golf hats and put them over their hearts, sweating profusely. This display of Eastern discipline impressed Commodore, since it vaguely reminded him of his days in the Navy.

※

Coronets sounded from the loudspeaker atop the clubhouse, marking time for the champagne brunch. Golf carts festooned with pink balloons glided away from the clubhouse, carrying gourmet box lunches and bottles of iced champagne. All over the course, clean-cut young men and women set up a folding tables and chairs, popped open beach umbrellas, and unpacked box lunches for the competitors.

Commodore and Miss Loo ate in the intimate shade of an undulating white mushroom-shaped umbrella. Miss Loo picked at her lunch with plastic utensils as the young people behind them struggled to open a bottle of champagne.

"My family five factories empty," Miss Loo remarked, out of the blue. "Long time ago, make tank for Chinese army—five factory many tank," she explained. "No tank now. My family big, nice uncle, aunts, nieces, nephews, cousins, many relative. One husband, dead," she added.

With a loud pop, the kids opened the champagne. Two pretty young blondes held the overflowing bottle in both hands like a wild thing.

The blonde kids hurried toward Commodore as fizzling bubbles spilled onto the fairway and finally into the plastic glasses he and Miss Loo both held out for champagne.

"Goodness," Commodore lifted one eyebrow.

He and Miss Loo touched plastic champagne glasses. As he sipped champagne, the old billionaire heard even more of Miss Loo's personal information.

"Husband run over by tank, die on factory floor, no doctor help, very sad," she said, wiggling her nose and signaling for more champagne.

"I'm sorry to hear that," Commodore said.

As Miss Loo's insistence, they touched glasses again. Then Miss Loo leaned toward Commodore and confided that when she was a girl, a fortune teller in Nanking told her that she would someday fall in love with a handsome businessman from a foreign country who would rescue her family from financial ruin.

"You don't say," Commodore said.

As the coronets sounded to resume play, Miss Loo tossed her empty plastic champagne glass back over her shoulder, and bared her teeth in a look that was practically erotic.

"Maybe my family, your family," Miss Loo said, rising to tee off. This particular remark came out of nowhere and was inexplicable to Commodore. But Miss Loo smacked another 300-foot drive that rang like a bell.

Despite two or three embarrassing putts and what seemed like an eternity in the rough off the tenth hole, Commodore played his best golf in years. As they finished the course, their combined score was 6 below par.

"Beautiful," said Commodore. "Good show."

To Commodore's surprise, he and Miss Loo won the tournament. When the Van Turkles announced their victory to the crowd, Miss Loo took Commodore's hand and marched up to the bandstand. As the Montecito high school marching band played "Hail to the Chief" under an arch of swaying pink balloons, Miss Loo bounded onto the stage, snatched the oversized trophy from Mrs. Von Turkle, handed it to Commodore, and turned to face the crowd. A young man from the local paper stepped forward to take their picture.

"Long Drive winner! Old man winner today too!" yowled Miss Loo, pumping her fist in the air. The photographer caught the old billionaire in the red golf outfit sheepishly holding the trophy for the exuberantly fist-pumping Miss Loo.

Commodore escorted Miss Loo through the crowded lobby of the country club to her car. Everyone in the room seemed to be smiling at them, as if they had just been married, or received an Academy Award. To Commodore, of course, the attention was mildly distressing. But Miss Loo's white limousine was waiting at the clubhouse door. Miss Loo pecked him on the cheek and left him holding their trophy.

"We partner now," Miss Loo whispered in his ear. My family win, you family win, too. Understand?" she smiled.

Commodore Commode did not.

7. A Glimpse Of The Sea

As **Commodore Commode climbed** into the back seat of his town car, he was surprised to see that his driver had donned a business suit, and wore an oversize cardboard cowboy hat, topped by a small pink balloon. Then he realized that Simon had presumptuously taken the driver's seat of his town car. Simon threw his arm over the back of the seat and practically leered at Commodore.

"Did I come through for you in the clutch, or what?" Simon asked, pushing the cardboard hat back over his forehead like a cowhand in a beer commercial.

Commodore was grateful to Simon for pairing him with a delightful partner. The victory was pleasant and satisfying. On the other hand, Simon had obviously spent too much time socializing with the other volunteers at the open bar. His son–in-law was actually smirking. Simon displayed an improper lack of gravity about the tournament and Commodore himself which irritated the old billionaire, who found Simon's giddiness positively juvenile.

Simon stretched both hands over the front seat, palms out, forcing Commodore to lean politely forward and give him a high-five, a completely unnecessary proletarian gesture.

"What happened to my driver?" Commodore asked.

Although he tried to relax, the old billionaire was not happy. Simon's presence was already dissolving Commodore's dreamy good mood. Even more than usual, Simon's patter was annoying. The old billionaire could handle Simon at work, where he was just another employee in a stuffed shirt, firing off memos that were easy to ignore. But here he was, presumptuously taking the driver's seat of Commodore's town car, and as anxious as a puppy for praise and recognition.

"You didn't thank me for my assistance," Simon pouted.

"Yes, of course. Thank you, Simon."

"It wasn't easy to roll the Van Turkles, if you know what I mean," Simon said, lewdly winking. "Mrs. Van Turkle was sure you'd want a celebrity. When I talked my way around her at the last minute, old Van Turkle didn't want to make any changes to the card. You can be grateful your boy Simon learned how to work a room in law school."

"Thank you again, Simon."

Commodore began to regret he'd asked his son-in-law for help. Simon would be bragging about this all over the legal affairs department. The secretaries would be gossiping. Commodore winced at the thought of so many lawyers and secretaries privy to some of his private business.

Simon smiled a wicked smile. "And how did you like that sexy little partner I got you?"

Commodore stared at Simon with rapidly mounting irritation.

"The lady was quite charming," Commodore stated, waving his hand for Simon to start the car. "And thank you for your help for the last time."

"You're a single man now, Commodore," Simon said, lifting his eyebrows with a lascivious twinkle in his eyes. "She's a beautiful widow. And it's probably been years—"

"Be silent, Simon. What you are suggesting is not proper," Commodore said.

Horns began to honk loudly behind Commodore's town car, which had not yet moved.

Looking out the window, Commodore noticed old Van Turkle staring at him from the clubhouse window, tapping politely on the pane. The old basset hound shook his jowls at Commodore, a gesture of disapproval. Mrs. Van Turkle's face appeared next to the face of her husband, a well-groomed poodle framed in a halo of stiff white hair. Showing her small white teeth, Mrs. Van Turkle also began gesturing. Looking to the rear, Commodore realized the Hollywood Squares limousine was trying to pull up to the clubhouse entrance.

The Van Turkles burst through the clubhouse doors together, prepared to make a scene.

Mrs. Van Turkle hurried toward the celebrity limousine. Old Van Turkle walked glumly toward Commodore, his jowls shaking from side to side, a grim enforcer in a golf hat.

"Simon!" Commodore shouted. "For God's sake, go!"

Simon started the car. Removing his hat and pulling away, Simon kept his head down, as contrite as a puppy that had just peed on his master's shoe.

After the stress and excitement of the day, Commodore was grateful for the silence on the way home. Climbing a hill and rounding a curve on the way back to Montecito, Commodore glanced out the window to see the ocean gleaming brightly away between two low hills.

The Pacific Ocean at that moment resembled an enormous gold lame bedspread extending from the beaches of Santa Barbara to the end of the earth. As the sun disappeared in the west behind a bank of red clouds, up rose fingers of golden light like a fan before the face of a mysterious lady.

Commodore suddenly recalled a similar sunset on the wind-swept deck of the USS *Felicity*. As San Diego harbor shrunk away behind him, and the wind toyed with his hair, the young sailor felt himself a warrior for America, ready to fight the Communist menace anywhere it reared its ugly head. Clutching the ship's iron railing, exhilarated by the sea air, the young sailor witnessed a sunset over the ocean grander than anything he had ever seen in his life. This spectacle stirred up every particle of romance in his practical young warrior's heart. Although the Korean War would be over before the USS *Felicity* dropped anchor on the other side of the Pacific, the young sailor felt simultaneously humbled, exhiliarated, and frightened by his important patriotic adventure.

In the back seat of his town car, awash in memories, all that was left of that young sailor grasped his chest and connected with the wild, seductive sirens of the sea.

8. An Unexpected Gift

That night Commodore took dinner on the small patio off his suite of bedrooms, overlooking Milly's English flower garden. Milly's heirloom roses had begun to bloom, Commodore noticed. This would have excited Milly. She would have had the servants bring in arrangements of roses for the dinner table.

Commodore's chef prepared a nice meal—a small salad, lamb chops, small servings of baby spring vegetables, and a small glass of good red wine. But the old billionaire only picked at his food, eating slowly, sighing, and passing gas occasionally as he tried to calm down from the excitement of his day.

The scent of roses wafted in from the garden. For some reason, Commodore remembered the smell of crushed flowers that he associated with his golf partner, Long Drive Loo. Not only was Miss Loo reasonably attractive, as Simon had crudely pointed out, she had also pushed him to play the best golf of his entire life. For Miss Loo's assistance in rescuing his badly-damaged reputation he was deeply grateful.

Not only that, she had left him holding their trophy. Commodore wondered if it would be proper to send the delightful Chinese lady a small token of his appreciation. Asians were forever sending gifts, he knew. He and Milly had been friends with the Ben Lee Wings, a nice couple from Taiwan in the import-export business who lived at the far end of Swizzle Stick Road. Wanda Wing loved Milly's parties. Every time Commodore turned around, she was modestly presenting Milly with some little gift or other, which of course Milly reciprocated in due course.

"Mr. Commode... Mr. Commode, sir."

Commodore recognized the archly affected British accent of his longtime valet, R.G. Spartan. Clearing his throat, the old valet waited for permission to enter the patio from the other side of the French doors. The old valet held something in his hands which appeared to be releasing a small shower of colorful yellow sparks.

"Come in, R.G."

With great dignity the old valet strode majestically onto the patio, carrying something a bit larger than a grapefruit. It flung off sparks, like an electric hot potato. Whatever it was, it was neatly wrapped up in Chinese red paper. It was festooned with more than a dozen short, fizzling and popping Chinese sparklers. The puzzled old valet handled the artfully-wrapped package as if it were something that might explode. He grimaced a little as he danced around with the package.

"I believe it's some sort of gift, sir," said the dancing old valet. "A heavy-set Asian gentleman in a trench coat dropped it off a moment ago."

"Well, then put it down," Commodore said.

"It certainly attracts the attention, sir, whatever it is," the valet said, as he placed the sputtering package on the table.

"The packaging is unusual."

The old valet quietly plucked off the sparklers. He backed away from the table as Commodore opened the package.

Under the outer wrapping of red paper was a lacquered round box somewhat bigger than a softball. The little round box was artfully inlaid with pictures of jet planes taking off and landing. Inside that was a second Chinese box of white lacquer inlaid with polished brass images of what appeared to be factories and ocean tankers which was even more beautiful than the first. Inside that was a third box in a black lacquer case which was inlaid with a single small carved ivory fish. And nestled inside that, in a nest of soft white silk, was a gold-plated golf ball. As the sparklers fizzled out and were quietly set aside, R.G. glimpsed what appeared to be an impression of two small, red lips on the face of the golf ball.

Commodore asked R.G. to read him the meticulously folded note he found in the package.

DEAR ROMANTIC BIG BUSINESSMAN FRIEND,

REMEMBERING HAPPILY OUR LOVELY GOLF GAME, AND OUR BEAUTIFUL VICTORY OF ONE DAY AND OUR SMALL TALKING. THIS GIFT NOT FROM ME, TO YOU. FROM MY FAMILY, YOUR FAMILY

— MISS LONG DRIVE LOO

Lifting one eyebrow, the old valet read the note aloud. He solemnly refolded the note while Commodore inspected the gold-plated golf ball.

Mr. Commodore seemed somewhat fascinated by the mark of two red lips on the golf ball. However, to R.G., this seemed inappropriately erotic.

"Bring stationary. I'll write the lady a thank-you note immediately," the old billionaire snapped.

"Of course, sir." Spartan turned to go.

"And bring me those gift catalogs from the library. We'll pick out a little something nice to send her in return," he said, gesturing with the golf ball.

"Very good sir."

The golden golf ball seemed to leap out of Commodore's hand and onto the marble floor of the patio. The lipstick-covered golf ball bounced in high slow arcs through the French doors and into the house, following the old valet into the library as if it had a mind of its own.

9. A Dark Star Rising

Over the next few weeks Commodore warmed a bit toward Simon, whom he came to regard as not quite so much a fool. Looking back, Commodore couldn't quite remember exactly how Simon became so involved with the exchange of gifts. Somehow, seeming to foresee everything, his son-in-law had proved himself extraordinarily useful.

A couple of days after Miss Loo's first gift arrived at the mansion, for instance, Simon asked if he could bring in a couple of distinguished Asian Studies professors from the University into Commodore's office to analyze her gift's significance. The two professor's interpretations were a revelation to the old billionaire.

When the two professors entered Commodore's office, they bowed deeply. One of the professors wore the long, Poncho Villa moustache often seen in Asian action movies. The older and smaller of the two had a permanent smile which seemed pasted into the center of his white, poorly-trimmed beard. Both professors wore traditional silk clothing.

"Golden golf ball sign of great respect in China. Even more than Japanese, Chinese people love golf! Gift of golf ball—from great golf champion?" the smaller professor exclaimed, clasping his hands in delight under his beard. "Very fortunate omen."

The second professor asked Commodore the date and time of his birth. He snorted, frowned, and stroked his moustache as he punched some numbers into a hand-held computer.

"Ah ha!" the larger professor cried."You fortunate man— lady golf champion sign of Rat and you very compatible Monkey astrological sign."

"Rat and Monkey? In year of dragon? With golf ball first gift? Good fortune!" the old professor cried.

After the professors left, Simon placed on Commodore's desk a thick file containing what appeared to be a very complete rundown on Miss Loo. Simon apparently had the foresight to hire a private investigator to check out Miss Loo's background, which appeared to be impeccable.

As he looked over the file, Commodore noted that Miss Loo's family owned several large industrial building in Shanghai. Her family actually resided in an old imperial dynasty palace. The family even had an interest in a golf course not far from downtown Shanghai which was utilized exclusively by high-ranking members of the Chinese business and government elite. That Miss Loo's family had an interest in a golf course rather delighted Commodore.

Also in the file were stacks of old newspaper clippings, detailing the golf tournaments Miss Loo won in China, and also the big women's professional tournament she won in the United States which made her a national hero in China when she returned.

"She's rich, she's beautiful, she's athletic, she's clever, and she sent you a very significant gift," Simon announced, bolting into the office as Commodore was looking over the information in the file. "What else do I need to say?"

As the gifts multiplied, Simon seemed positively psychic about the gifts sent by Miss Loo. He had sensible information to present, and made sensible suggestions at appropriate times about gifts to be sent in return.

Over the next two weeks, the old billionaire and the lady from China madly exchanged gifts.

In return for the delightful golden golf ball, the old billionaire sent Miss Loo a leather-and-mink trimmed one-of-a-kind designer golf bag. She sent him a pair of soft pigskin leather golf shoes and a golf belt signed by the most famous athletic wear designer in Hong Kong. He sent her diamond-studded lambskin golf gloves from Tiffany's. She sent him a platinum wristwatch signed by Tiger Woods that played the "Wild World of Sports" theme song on the hour. And so it went, gifts flying in and out the door.

R.G. Spartan quietly observed that Mr. Commode was quite delighted by the little game of gift exchange. Mr. Commode was doing nothing improper with Miss Loo, of course, the old valet observed, although there was some obvious foolishness and an apparent adolescent fascination. As a way to get acquainted, it was a bit whimsical, and certainly unusual, but all quite proper as such things went.

Still, Spartan observed, the old billionaire did not seem to have quite fallen in love with the mysterious lady. The old valet believed that love was a will-o'-the-wisp composed mostly of fantasies and misperceptions about the beloved which in a matter of months vanished in the wind.

More precisely, it seemed to the old valet, Mr. Commode was a lonely widower caught up in the heady exhilaration of sending and receiving exotic material objects from a beautiful and somewhat mysterious woman in a distant romantic land. However, the old valet also noticed that each of Miss Loo's clumsily-worded perfumed notes ended with the mysterious phrase, "My family, your family."

To his manifest surprise, Commodore came to depend on his son-in-law, Simon, during the course of all this. On the unlikely terrain of a bicontinental and bicultural romance, the son-in-law Commodore had always regarded as a prig in a stuffed shirt, if not a fool and a blowhard without a sound idea to his name, seemed to anticipate every nuance of the unexpected gift exchange with Miss Loo.

Every time Commodore turned around, Simon was there with pertinent and sensible suggestions about how he should proceed.

The very portentous sixth gift from Miss Loo arrived in the middle of the workday. Barely knocking, Simon hurried into Commodore's office and sat a gilded cage on his desk. Commodore was surprised. A platinum blonde monkey was inside. Of course, he knew immediately it was another gift from Miss Loo. But the old billionaire did not particularly like animals. The shipping container smelled like a pet shop, and the monkey itself seemed heavily sedated if not asleep.

"It's a Golden Weeha!" Simon exclaimed. It was in fact a rare Golden Weeha monkey, one of the rarest and most notorious species in all of China.

The yellow-haired little monkey groaned, grabbed the bars of the cage, and tried to stand up. It smiled a drugged-out transcontinental baggage compartment smile.

Simon buzzed in one of the old university professors. The old professor approached the cage, bent at the waist, and peered intently at the money, stroking his beard.

"Golden Weeha important signal from aristocratic lady," the professor said. "All hexagram align, heaven and earth."

"What are you talking about?" Simon asked.

"Golden Weeha traditional romantic signal," the professor explained. "Predate I-Ching. Legend of Sixth Gift."

"What is the Legend of Sixth Gift?" Simon demanded.

Commodore leaned forward to listen. Even the doped-up little monkey trying to hold himself upright seemed to be listening to the slowly pacing and pointing old professor, who launched into a sort of extended lecture.

"Four thousand year ago in China, Prince and Princess from different kingdoms fall in love, exchange five rounds of gifts. So many presents in castle grumpy Old King say no more gifts allowed for Prince. Prince broken-hearted," he said. "But young Princess clever. When she hear this, send sixth gift—Golden Weeha—directly to Old King. Old King very confused, think she make mistake, order Weeha released into the forest. Soon Old King fall asleep, have strange dream. In dream Old King pick up favorite hand mirror. In mirror see face of Weeha, not face of King. Monkey in mirror make strange prophecy—old King die horrible death if Princess never see Prince again. Old King wake up frightened. Golden Weeha climb in window, singing very happy enchanted song of love, make Old King and all palace servants dance. That night, Old King order young Prince to visit Princess. Prince and Princess marry, live happily ever after in rich new kingdom."

The Weeha fell over in the cage and rolled his eyes.

"Chinese tradition, first five gifts only friendship," continued the professor, his eyes sparkling. "Five gifts give aristocratic lady chance to judge character of aristocratic man. When lady send Golden Weeha, sixth gift, strong signal to man. When Weeha sing, happiness on way!"

As the professor made his exit, Commodore reached into the cage to try to help the struggling little monkey rise to its feet. But the Golden Weeha grabbed his finger and held on with four surprisingly strong paws.

"You've got to see Miss Loo again," Simon said.

Commodore focused on getting his hand out of the cage. However, the drugged-out little monkey held on fiercely, baring its teeth while also feigning sleep.

"Did you hear what the professor *said?*" Simon asked, lifting his eyebrows. "This could be historic. Miss Loo is a national hero in China. China is a major training partner with the United States. Miss Loo wants to get to know you. She sent a Golden Weeha. Six gifts! You haven't had a vacation in more than three years. You don't want to insult the lady. This could be good for business. What else can I say?"

When the monkey let go, Commodore pulled his hand out of the cage and examined his scratched-up index finger.

"Bring me a few ideas," Commodore snapped. "And have someone take this animal to Commodora."

Lying lazily on its back in the gilded cage, the little monkey bared its teeth at Commodore as Simon hurriedly spirited the beast away.

Over the next few days, Simon presented sensible ideas for a proper friendly rendezvous somewhere between China and California. Paris was the best possible choice of places to get to know a woman, Simon suggested. Along with travel brochures from Paris, Simon left a note with Miss Loo's personal telephone number on Commodore's desk.

Behind closed doors, Commodore made a decision. Since he received the portentous sixth gift, it would be the decent thing to call Miss Loo. The beautiful pro golfer had blown in and out of his life like a red tornado, leaving him holding the trophy. She also left a haunting vapor trail of mysterious comments and gifts. Being nothing if not a man, the old sailor pressed forward.

"Miss Loo," Commodore blurted the minute she answered the phone. "This is Commodore Commode, your golf partner in California. What are you doing next week?"

"Tuesday, Wednesday, Thursday, Friday free for Long Drive," she whispered.

"Let's spend some time together—platonically of course. I'll pay for everything. We'll get to know each other—properly. We'll meet in Paris next week, what do you say?"

"Yes," she whispered. "Paris nice city."

"I'll arrange everything," the old billionaire said. "My secretary will call you tomorrow with the flight arrangements."

Miss Loo whispered something he could barely hear.

"Okay?" Commodore demanded.

"Yes. Paris, me, you, next week," Miss Loo whispered with a note of urgency in her voice. This time the old capitalist heard her quite clearly. The exuberant little golfer seemed ready to go.

10. A Fly In The Ointment

Philip **Commode the interior decorator** quietly leaned over a computer screen in his design studio, intent on working out the final details for Mrs. Quinn Rockefeller's recently-remodeled family vacation house in Maine. Philip absentmindedly fingered a stack of fabric samples without really looking at them. He ran his fingers through his bright red dishevelled hair. Perhaps, he thought, some deep magenta drapery on two of the first floor walls would soften the overly rough look of the old-growth hardwood floors he had salvaged from an abandoned Shaker church in the backwoods of New England. Philip looked out his office window, searching for inspiration, but found nothing. He was feeling stressed out, and he desperately needed to dance.

A Pisces with Gemini rising, Philip was usually regarded as cutting edge, always just a bit ahead of the pack, a trend-setting hummingbird of good taste. Philip reveled in the shifting mysteries of style, the way fashions changed with the winds, and there was always something new.

Philip's clients were mostly fussy matrons and divorcees with big houses and lots of money and time on their hands. It was hardly necessary to let his clients know that he came from lots and lots of money.

Philip met his fashion-conscious ladies as an equal, a co-conspirator of sorts. He had a natural ability to make women feel as if they were participating in something new and wonderful, a quest that did involve serious money, but a quest which was also mysterious and fun.

Philip and his assistants came sweeping into mansion after mansion, taking notes, making witty remarks, adoring this and criticizing that, the whole pack of them literally bursting with ideas. As Philip strode dramatically through the houses of the rich and famous, sometimes with Diego at his side, the stylishly-dressed interior decorator tossed off ideas like a maestro conducting the Cleveland Philharmonic. Rich women adored Filly Commode.

Philip frankly didn't give a damn that certain members of his family thought he was an eccentric fop who put on airs.

When he put on his tuxedo, Philip Commode resembled a more muscular Fred Astaire. He had Astaire's dancing eyes and broad forehead, and of course he personally loved to dance. Filly Commode had shaken his booty in the dance clubs of West Hollywood, the French Quarter, the Village, Castro Street, and any number of discos and dance halls in other parts of the world.

As was necessary in his line of business, Philip dressed with impeccable taste. But if close male friends were present and the occasion was very private, Philip might put on one of his vintage dresses and perhaps the heels.

On these special occasions, after having his hair and nails done, Philip might ask Diego to highlight his best features with tastefully-applied makeup. Lipstick to slightly enhance the fullness of his lips. Mascara to enlarge his intelligent brown eyes. A spot of rouge to bring out his emphatic Austrian cheekbones, and so forth.

It wasn't easy, growing older and keeping up your look. Philip was neutral on plastic surgery for the time being, but he had done a great deal of very targeted weight work to minimize the somewhat squat body type he surely inherited from his father's side of the family. In West Hollywood, he had worked for months with Madonna's personal trainer to re-sculpt his entire upper body. He continued to tone himself religiously at the gym. His newly-sculpted arms and legs were as lithe and impressive as he could make them, and they looked good with a good shirt, shorts, and the right shoes.

Since his return to Montecito, Filly had become more tolerant of his somewhat fashion-challenged family. He had however almost given up on his sisters, especially Petunia. The girls were buying their own clothes now, and it showed.

❧

Only when he met Diego did Philip realize he had been searching for love his entire life. He and Diego (who never used his second name) met cute in Barcelona. They became a couple before they finished art school.

Diego was the most strikingly handsome man Philip had ever seen. He was almost too slender, with a head of perfect, straight, shoulder-length black hair. Beneath Diego's perfectly tweezed eyebrows were two large expressive Moorish eyes that smoldered in his face like burning beans.

The first thing he had noticed was Diego's habit of flipping his beautiful long hair back and forth over his shoulders when he was assessing a situation, a gesture Filly still adored.

After art school they moved to West Hollywood with the idea of breaking into movies. Filly worked for a couple of years as a set designer on low-budget movies and Diego worked as a makeup artist. Several times they split up, under the stress of 15-hour work days alternating with weeks of non employment.

Before they got back together for the last time, Philip had developed a taste for poppers and meth amphetamine. And Diego had begun to quietly shoot cocaine.

Drug addicted darkness descended on the lovers, bathhouses and other boyfriends, but their relationship staggered with difficulty through the storm. They both got sober after Philip checked Diego into the best psychiatric hospital in Beverly Hills. Philip had been aghast to come home early one morning and find Diego smack in the middle of a drug-induced psychosis. Diego had actually been sitting on the sidewalk outside their apartment building, urinating on himself and babbling incoherently in Spanish. To get Diego admitted to the best hospital he could find, and in his condition, Philip had to pay $50,000 in advance. Of course, this was the exact moment when several of Philip's credit cards happened to be maxed out and his father had already refused to send any more money. It humiliated Philip that he had to call his sister Petunia, and ask her to wire him the money which of course he paid back as soon as possible.

Before long, fashionably sober Philip and Diego became an item in certain Hollywood circles, the subject of bitchy gossip and snide remarks from many of their jealous gay male allegedly sober friends. On the plus side, Philip found that for the first time in his life, he could trust his intuition.

Philip Commode was thirty-six years old when he returned to Montecito, but it was a very old thirty-six. Like most gay men who lived through the 1990s in a big city, he'd attended far too many funerals and cried away far too many tears. He returned to Montecito to brighten up his mother's last years. Without Commodore's knowledge, Milly had come to Los Angeles and actually begged Philip to return home.

So Filly and Diego moved into their simple, stylish little castle. Before she died, his mother loved to drop in for a visit and have tea on one of the patios overlooking the moat. Of course, Milly adored Diego like a son.

⁊⁅

Philip Commode had long before fallen in love with the shifting tides of the fashion world, where trends grew and fell like ocean waves, or like good gossip.

Philip had seen his friends cycle in and out of the coral and gray iridescent palate, into that awful white period, through New Age linen and biker leather, through the flat earth tones of the Southwest style, through high tech chrome and black and industrial gray, through the faded plaids of thrift shop grunge, to baggy butt primary color hip-hop and serious hipster funeral black, and now, Filly was convinced, the pendulum was poised to swing decisively to red.

American red was a concept Philip was working out in his head, his home, and in the homes of his clients. American red was actually a blend of several shades of red that worked together in a sort of counterpoint. Shortly after September 11, 2001, Filly awoke in the middle of the night. He had dreamed of a world where everything in America was red, and he intuitively felt his dream's significance. Red was after all the color of anger, vengeance, torture, mutilation, and murder. Red was sports injuries, valentines, bleeding hearts, and fire helmets. American red was the grandiosity of blunt aggression itself, the passion of American bodies splashing like exclamation points against the sidewalks outside the World Trade Center on 9/11. At that moment, both blindness and passion were on the ascent with the interminable presidency of the arrogant Christian blowhard, George W. Bush. American red seemed to define the historical moment, from the collective fright of 9/11, to the torturous witch hunts which followed.

Philip talked up American red to his friends on the color board and to several of the fashion journalists he knew. American Red had to be the color of the year. But working out the details had become an obsession. Philip had impulsively posted color charts on every wall of every room in the design studio, each containing a hundred and twenty different shades of red. In a sort of statement to the world, Filly had gone to his hairdresser and demanded that his hair color be changed from its Fred Astaire sandy brown with tasteful platinum highlights to American Red. Philip's latest hair was styled to spurt out in all directions in the loopy, bewigged style of the late Andy Warhol, in a sort of tasteful hair explosion.

Making a bold distinctive statement at the perfect moment was of course how the design game was played, and Filly instinctively understood how to play at the highest levels. He'd already asked a couple of photographers he knew to stop by and take some Polaroid's of the castle's red exterior where he and Diego were trying out a few things with American red.

⁂

Philip looked up from the computer the moment L. Armed Robbbry Rantt strutted into his office. The slender, strikingly handsome young black man immediately smiled and stopped in his tracks. L. Armed Robbbry froze in a gangster pose with a piece of paper between his fingers, held out like a rose.

"This be too chilly, that same lawyer he be calling out Mr. Filly," said Armed Robbbry.

The best dancer in the office, L. Armed Robbbry wore a baggy red jump suit and flowing red scarf. He had an MFA from the Rhode Island Institute of Design, but he was fluent in the edgy black vernacular of the day. Armed Robbbry had some sort of note in his hand, Philip presumed a telephone message since he was not taking calls from anyone but Mrs. Rockefeller.

The message was from Petunia's husband Simon, again demanding that Philip confirm his attendance at the board meeting. Philip did not like the overtone of Simon's message. Philip's neck warmed up. He felt a ball of anger rise up between his ears. As far as Philip was concerned, Simon Butterknut could kiss his ass.

Philip Commode had already received his invitation to the family board meeting in the mail, thank you very much. He had dutifully punched the date into his phone, and of course he would attend since his father expected it. But Philip churlishly refused to RSVP to Simon, who seemed to think he was owed a personal response. Simon's irritating phone calls were a little like receiving an invitation to that same boring party you were obligated to attend every year, and then being chased down in the street over and over again by the chief bore who demanded that you personally promise him that you would attend with a smile on your face.

Crumpling Simon's message, Filly blithely tossed it away.

Sensing an opportunity, Armed Robbbry turned on the CD player. With a toss of his head and dancing eyes, he looked suggestively at Philip. Filly clapped his hands two times. Armed Robbbry kicked up the volume, and the music he selected was hypnotic.

Filly tossed his sports coat onto the light table, clapped his hands over his head, and they began dancing. Philip loved to dance, any time of the day or night. He encouraged his associates to dance at work whenever they felt like it to relieve the pressures of the office. Clapping and turning with the music, Philip tried to dance his fast-talking brother-in-law out of his mind.

Why *had* Petunia married the pompous ass? Filly wondered, dancing furiously. Pompous, fast-talking boys had always fascinated Petunia, and she married the fastest-talking student at Stanford. Where was the plump, gentle older sister he adored, forever running in the mansion with squawking baby sparrows which had fallen out of their nests, or half-dead grasshoppers picked off the windshields of one of the town cars, rear legs still pathetically kicking?

"You be doing it!" Armed Robbbry shouted, changing the music.

He and Filly froze on the beat. Then they continued dancing, employer and employee, stepping left in unison.

During those dreadful family board meetings, Filly remembered, stepping high and stepping left, Simon would talk as long as possible to keep all the attention on himself … Simon would go on and on and on. Philip would get so nauseatingly bored he would search frantically for excuses to leave the room. He'd step out to the rest room as often as he could get away with it. He'd step out for a double latte. He'd step out to check his messages, or take calls. He'd step out to make obtuse tweets on the nature of corporate boredom. He'd step out to meditate and do his deep breathing exercises in the courtyard behind the headquarters building. But every time Filly stepped back into the meeting, he woefully recalled, the family stuffed shirt would just be getting started. Every now and then Philip would make an honest remark or two about being bored, but nothing deterred Simon.

Even his father, one of the most patient people on the face of the earth, would be frowning and shifting politely in his chair as the meeting wore on, quietly pretending not to pass gas.

As each dreary board meeting wore on, Filly remembered, now stepping right and clapping his hands, his father would pass larger and larger amounts of gas, looking innocently from side to side, while everybody in the room struggled to ignore the stout, masculine aroma that flooded the room like the smell of a cantankerous old cigar. Through some quirk of nature, his father's flatulence actually seemed to stimulate Simon, giving his pompous brother-in-law a sort of second wind. As each meeting ground on and on and finally ended, Filly would leave the room with both hands shaking, ready to pull out his hair by the roots and scream. It took Filly three weeks on Fire Island to get his wits back after the meeting last year.

The music slowed to a sort of waltzing dirge. Armed Robbbry took one of Filly's hands, the two of them doing little hip-swaying steps together, Fred Astaire and Ginger Rogers moving gracefully backwards across the floor of Filly's large office until the office intercom crackled and the music abruptly stopped.

"Mrs. Delores Morgan Rockefeller of New York calling for Philip, says it's urgent," came a high-pitched male voice.

"Tell Delores I'll be calling her back in five," Filly replied.

L. Armed Robbbry disappeared.

Philip Commode took a deep breath and cranked open the double French windows overlooking the Pacific Ocean. Inhaling the dusky sea air, he did a quick set of breathing exercises, said his affirmations, sat down at his desk, and quietly picked up the phone.

11. One Hour Later

One hour later Philip Commode glided like a gull down the Pacific Coast Highway in his black Prius convertible, wind streaming through his hair. He was forced to slow down as he approached the rear end of a military convoy.

Nearly a dozen drab sand-colored Hummers festooned with American flags crawled along the Pacific Coast Highway, slowing traffic. Soldiers in battle gear stared glumly out of the back of their trucks, holding their weapons like so many life-sized GI Joes.

It was a good time to speed-dial his father. Philip loved the role of the dutiful son, a role he had played well since his mother's death. Their chats were punctual and pleasant, never too long, and always on the mark. In matters of business, Philip had come to value his father's common sense advice. Since it was Tuesday morning, the son knew just where to find the father. Commodore had become a creature of extremely regular habits since his mother passed away, taking the dreaded family vacations with her.

Philip knew his father would have just come off the golf course. He would be sitting on the patio off the rear entrance enjoying the last of his lunch, and nursing a cup of Earl Grey tea.

To Philip's surprise, R.G. Spartan picked up the phone.

"I'm sorry, sir, but Mr. Commode isn't here and I'm not at liberty to reveal his, whereabouts, you might say," whispered the old valet, who was politely grunting under his breath.

"Dad should be home today. It's Tuesday morning," Philip said.

"I'm flying out of town myself in about an hour and twenty minutes, and very unfortunately, I've been sworn to secrecy regarding Mr. Commode's somewhat mysterious current whereabouts, you might say," grunted the old valet, who was in fact packing a travel bag as he spoke.

"R.G., It's *Philip Commode*," Filly said.

"Mr. Commode's very talented and creative young son, yes," said the old valet, pausing for a moment to catch his breath. "I don't mean to seem impertinent, Philip. I'm just not at liberty to comment on the whereabouts of your father to anyone, not even to you. However, you might ring your father's office," the old valet suggested. "Perhaps the vice president of legal affairs?"

Instead, Filly speed-dialed his father's office on the direct line. He was determined to avoid getting into a conversation with Simon. Filly was not in the mood for his bilious brother-in-law.

"Mr. Commode isn't in today, Philip, sorry," Miss Gander chirped. "I've been asked to transfer all calls regarding Mr. Commode's whereabouts to legal affairs. Hold just a moment, and I'll connect you with Mr. Butterknut."

"Don't bother," Philip said. He hung up.

Filly speed-dialed Clementine, but her answering service picked up. That completely frosted Filly, who knew very well Clementine was in town and always checked her caller ID. He speed-dialed Petunia's cell phone as the traffic crawled toward town behind the military convoy.

"Piggy!" Petunia exclaimed, probably pushing her pink pith helmet back over her brow as she answered the phone.

Philip immediately pictured his sister in pigging clothes by Wallace Velcro, the South African big game hunter turned clothing designer. Velcro wanted to take the animal-loving world on some campy rococo African safari. The crafty old South African designer serviced the exotic animal-loving rich with an expensive line of animal tending clothing. Velcro favored soft pink pith helmets and cashmere jodhpurs for the ladies, with matching chartreuse and accessories for the men. Velcro's work was not to Philip's taste, although Petunia spent her every waking hour in Velcro.

Petunia stood on the shore of her lake, facing Pig Island. A half dozen dripping wet, coal black Chinese pot-bellied pigs stepped gingerly out of the lake. and fastidiously shook water off their hooves. Petunia's landscape architects had opened up a new feeding area close to the mansion, which was not yet completely ringed in double security fence.

As she took the call, Petunia ripped open a bag of premium pig feed, and out came a few loose pellets of yellow corn. At the sound of the open feed bag, pink snouts rose expectantly. If you ignored their grunting, Petunia long ago realized, her Chinese pot-bellied pigs were as mannerly and polite as four-legged little children.

"Piggy, where's Dad?" Filly demanded. "And what's the big secret?"

Feeding time was Petunia's favorite time of the day. and she was lost in it. Her pigs literally ate out of her hand. The pigs rubbed and swirled against her legs, like a school of hairy black fish. It was practically erotic.

"Hold just a moment, little brother," Petunia said.

From the far shore, a second wave of little pigs jumped into the water and swam across the pond toward her, their snouts in the air like so many little snorkels. As parrots squawked in the palm trees, Petunia felt herself the mistress of some small enchanted animal kingdom. She felt responsible for her beautiful animals, every one of them. She especially loved the way the well-groomed little boars brushed hungrily against her legs, politely rubbing and grunting for love.

Petunia filled her free hand with corn, and sprinkled it over the flat, twitching snouts of the sniffing pigs. The pigs opened their mouths, snorting and sneezing, as if trying to drink the rain.

"Petunia, *hello*," Philip snorted. "It's your brother, Philip Commode, and we're *talking*. Have you fallen down and died in your little pig sty?"

"Little brother, talented Philip, talented Philip Commode, little brother, darling, darling little brother," Petunia cooed, as pigs snapped at the corn. "That wonderful old beach chalet! I saw you featured in *Architectural Digest*!"

"Thanks, but that's not why I called, Piggy."

"Surely you don't need a *loan*, little brother?" Petunia said.

In her distracted way, Petunia dropped a live grenade into their conversation. It had been years, but Petunia couldn't stop reminding him over and over again of her midnight wire transfer of fifty thousand dollars. Hallucinating and paranoid, with Diego picking hair out of his arms and threatening to burn down the admitting room, Filly didn't dare ask his mother and especially his father for money. Petunia dutifully wired the cash, and Filly paid the loan back in less than two months. But Petunia never let him forget her life-saving gesture.

"Why did you bring that up? I paid you that money back, Piggy—*years* ago! Remember?"

"Of course you did."

"Years! Can we finally just drop it?"

"If only I knew in my heart that you were actually grateful."

"I'm less grateful every time you mention it, Petunia. But what's with Dad?" Filly said, refusing to be thrown off the scent. "Where is he?"

"My husband Simon, being vice president of the legal department of the Commode Company, has been kept fully apprised and is indeed aware of the pertinent details."

"Perhaps you should ring Simon and allow him to explain the entire situation," Petunia suggested archly.

"So it's a business trip?"

"Darling, Philip, no, no, no," Petunia said, again dipping her free hand deep into the bag of pig feed. "The truth is our father seems to be deeply, deeply entranced with a member of the opposite sex, a lady he met, in short, of course, a woman."

"Dad?" Philip croaked.

"Hold on just a moment."

In the pocket over her left breast, Petunia's other cell phone was vibrating softly against her nipple, to the ring tone of the Johnny Mathis classic, "Misty." It was her darling Simon calling, with some late morning baby-talk for her and the pigs. Sweet, considerate Simon called home twice a day now, during both the morning and afternoon feedings, and even came home every day for lunch despite his enormous workload. Her husband was the only other person in the world who really loved the little pigs, Petunia thought. He was certainly the only one in the family to ask about the pigs by name every time he called.

"I absolutely must take this call," Petunia cried. "Hold on."

"Petunia!" Filly shouted as Petunia put him on hold. "Why am I being excluded from learning what everybody else on the planet seems to know?"

If it were anyone but Simon, of course, Petunia would not have put her temperamental little brother on hold. She sensed her sensitive little brother was getting upset. Petunia recognized the familiar heavy breathing and the raised voice, and she knew it signaled a possible outburst of anger. Philip had always been excitable. As a boy he would blow up like a volcano at some small or imagined criticism, sputtering and spitting and waving his arms, and she and Clementine would tell the servants to please take him away to another part of the mansion until dinner. But brother was better at controlling his temper since he began going to those meetings and attending anger management classes.

Petunia let little brother wait, but Simon talked a few minutes longer than usual.

Philip Commode was still on hold and fuming when he gave the keys to the Prius to a very attractive young Mexican valet parking attendant at Hernando's. Philip angrily folded up the phone. He didn't mind hanging up on Petunia, who probably took some sort of ditzy sadistic pleasure in stringing him along. Besides, he knew Petunia would feel guilty when she realized she'd lost him, and frantically call back.

Hernando's Hideaway was the gay bar of the hour, with its funky Pacific Island décor. Fat, lei-wearing Hernando had decorated his hideaway as a cross between a Hawaiian beach hut and a 1940s Southern California trysting place. It was the kind of place the ghost of Raymond Chandler might have staggered into on a foggy night with lipstick on his collar and a couple of suspicious-looking hickeys on his neck.

Philip moved past the chest-high illuminated tank of blue and yellow salt water fish in the middle of the room as if passing through dark water. Hernando's neon pineapples and oversized neon martini glasses popped out of the darkness. He felt his way to his favorite booth, located under an overhanging thatch of dried palm fronds.

As Hernando waddled over with the usual, a glass of Alaskan glacier mineral water, Philip's cell phone played the "Misty" ring tone and Philip knew immediately who was calling.

"Petunia Butterknut has returned, calling you back, and I'm just very, very, very sorry to have lost you, little brother, I actually am, sorry that is," Petunia warbled. "Please don't be angry. Of course I didn't mean to slight you, and you notice I apologized. I'm just very, very, very sorry because you must grant me it was simply an unintentional accident, Philip."

Philip noted sadly that his sister was slowly absorbing her husband's long-winded style of talking. Every time he and Petunia spoke, it seemed to take her longer and longer to get to the point.

"So where's Dad?" Philip demanded.

"As I was trying to explain, our father is a man, and certainly a mature male of the human species, *homo sapiens*, in some ways a typical human male, a typical man, with all a man's desires, you might say, that is, being a man as are most men drawn toward the human female," Petunia began, in that condescending, long-winded way of speaking she'd developed since she married Simon. It was her own father she was talking about, but she could have been describing an exotic animal she'd seen on *Animal Planet*.

"It's perfectly innocent I presume but our father has all the perfectly normal desires shared by the prepondering majority of normal heterosexual men, and of course like all normal heterosexual men he can be impressed by the female, by a bewitching smile, a trim figure, or even by superior athletic ability if there is that how shall I say that animal *compatibility*," Petunia explained, pausing for breath.

Philip took a slow deep breath and confronted his sister assertively, as he had been taught to do.

"Exactly what are you trying to tell me about Dad, Petunia?"

"I'm told he's riding through the streets of Paris at this very minute with an attractive lady from China."

"Are you *kidding*? Dad never looked at other women when he was married to Mom. I don't think he's looked at another woman in his life."

"Little brother, consider. It is possible that father has met the appealing stranger, an athletic stranger, a compatible stranger, perhaps a beautiful stranger. Imagine father and this stranger developed a meeting of the minds over some mutual interest, say, perhaps, even, for instance, in our father's case, the game of golf. Perhaps a certain attraction grew as one sent a small gift, and the other responded?"

"Okay and so?"

"Perhaps an exchange of gifts bespoke an enchanted language, the language of the heart that brings lonely people together like moths to a flame, in the twilight of their lives. Imagine the oldest flame of love burning higher," Petunia said.

Philip waited impatiently for Petunia to get to the point.

"What you're saying is very out of character for Dad," Philip said. "I just do not believe this."

"Philip, I have very good reasons to believe, on information and belief, and you might assume that Simon has confided this to me, indirectly, you might say, but confided that our father may well be beginning ... a sort of romance."

"Dad?" Philip gasped. "You're kidding."

"Our selfsame father Commodore Commode, whom we call Dad, yes, father, our father, being a man, as I stated. Our father is a normal man, a perfectly normal heterosexual man with normal sexual instincts, instincts toward women, I mean."

"Okay, Piggy," Philip said, ignoring what was probably another dig. How man times could she use heterosexual in the same conversation with a gay man? "Who's Dad with?"

"You recall that our father recently won the Montecito Celebrity Pro-Am."

"The old fart golf tournament at the country club?" Filly demanded. "He entered that crappy tournament again?"

"Philip, Philip, Philip, don't bore me with your street talk and that horrible unnecessary profanity," Petunia said. "It's simply not proper speech, especially for one of your good breeding little brother."

"Are you being condescending to me *again*, Piggy? With these inane little *digs*?" Philip said, raising his voice so he could be heard over the grunting in the background. "Stop it! When's Dad coming back?"

"Contact Simon at the office for additional information," Petunia said, just before she hung up. "I'm sorry but I've said too much. I simply cannot breathe another word."

Beautiful Diego slipped into the booth at that moment, taking the phone out of Philip's hand, folding it up, and putting it back into his pocket with a sweet motherly gesture. Diego pulled his designer sunglasses to the end of his nose, staring over the tops of his sunglasses as if to ask "What's up?"

"Something's going on with Dad," Phillip announced. "And right after lunch, we're going to find out what it is."

❧

Back at the office, Diego rummaged through the recycling bin and found the newspaper with the photograph of Commodore and the Asian woman. Diego handed the newspaper to Filly, lifting one judgemental eyebrow. Neither of them had seen that particular picture before.

The Asian woman was beautiful, of course, although no spring chicken. Philip distrusted her immediately. There was a little too much Genghis Kahn in the way she had her mouth open in that victorious yowl, gloved fist pumping the air like some doped-up professional athlete. Next to her was Philip's befuddled father, trophy in hand. Of course his father would wear that awful red Scotch plaid cap with the tassel and matching wool kilts that Milly had given him for his sixtieth birthday that he would never give away.

"*Her* with *Dad?*" Filly said, pointing to the picture. "This man? And *this* particular woman?"

"She has cruel lips," Diego said.

"And doesn't Dad look a little *too* bewildered?"

"She aggressively dominates all of the space around her," Diego observed. "A warrior personality, perhaps."

"How does someone like *that* wind up in Paris, with *my Dad?*" Filly asked, giving Diego a significant look. "She's nothing at all like my mother."

"It seems impossible," Diego agreed.

"Something is definitely wrong," said Philip Commode, standing up and tossing away the newspaper. He slapped his stomach two times. "I can feel it here. And I don't like it."

12. An American in Paris

Commodore Commode hopped eagerly off the jet and checked into the best hotel in Paris, as giddy as a schoolboy. Miss Loo was to meet him at eight o'clock for dinner.

Simon helpfully suggested Paris's most talked about restaurant, Le Petite Derriere de Morocco, the most expensive restaurant in Paris. and a favorite of American travel agents. Not many Frenchmen dined at Le Petite Derriere but wide-bottomed Americans tourists flocked to its booths and tables. Under dramatic Moroccan tile ceilings and hanging lanterns they sought to capture the romance of Paris as they struggled to read their menus and order dinner in French.

Commodore Commode entered Le Petite Derriere at the stroke of eight. The old capitalist wore his tuxedo. The exotic aroma of Moroccan incense and North African spices drifted languidly through the scented air. Commodore was immediately recognized and seated by the solicitous, cooing, elaborately turbaned maitre d'.

Twenty minutes later, Miss Loo made her extraordinary entrance into Le Petite Derriere. Apparently unaffected by jet lag, she wore a flowing, modestly-revealing red silk gown. Under Moroccan lanterns, the tourists from Omaha and El Paso craned their necks, speculating on her identity. Miss Loo could have been the Empress of Ancient China for the attention she received.

The snooty, smiling maitre d' slowly and majestically led Miss Loo to le Petite Derriere's most private booth in a far corner of the restaurant, where Commodore Commode impatiently awaited.

The old billionaire loosened his cummerbund as Miss Loo approached. He had passed a certain amount of gas in the curtained booth before she arrived and he hoped to appear comfortable and to make a good impression.

The vision in red let out a little squeal when the curtains of the booth were swept back. She sucked in her breath between her teeth and leaned forward to clasp both of Commodore's hands. Shaking her head back and forth, she inhaled as deeply as if she was savoring the scent one of the world's rarest and most exotic flowers.

"You here!" she said, happily wiggling into the booth next to Commodore. "American businessman, you big man, very important man."

"Please," the old billionaire said, waving languidly to the maitre d' for a bottle of wine. "Call me Commodore."

"Commodore," Miss Loo said, savoring the difficult syllables and wrinkling her nose.

A beautiful young French schoolboy in a starched white shirt and tie sheepishly pushed a wine cart to their booth. The maitre d' appeared, moving aside the schoolboy and elegantly uncorking the wine, vintage 1932, the most expensive wine in Paris. The wine had been Simon's idea, a little something to make Miss Loo comfortable before dinner. So far, Commodore observed, all of Simon's ideas appeared to be on the money. Miss Loo was chattering and rocking back and forth in front of her wine glass with apparent delight.

After a clumsy display of cork-popping and cork-sniffing, and a swish and a taste, the sleek French maitre d' poured them both a glass. The maitre d' smiled at them both in that sly Parisian way and left the bottle in its cart, on a bed of ice and swaddled in a monogrammed towel.

This left the two of them alone in the booth under fizzling Moroccan lanterns, examining menus.

Looking up from the menu, Miss Loo cooed, "I have good time, airplane. Your pilot good time, hotel room good time, your limousine, all good time."

"I certainly hope so," Commodore laughed.

So the little lady appreciated punctuality.

"American jet fly fast, drink many cocktail," Miss Loo laughed.

"Yes," Commodore laughed. "American jet fly fast indeed."

Shifting his full attention to Miss Loo, the old billionaire again observed that his dinner companion favored short, punchy sentences.

Putting two or three English words together in a row seemed to make her happy, whether the words made perfect sense or not. Commodore had noticed her distinctive manner of speaking on the golf course, and after a sip or two of wine it became even more quaintly charming.

Suddenly Miss Loo lifted her wineglass toward the Moroccan lantern over their booth. She clumsily proposed a toast.

"To your family, my family, to your family, my family," she cried.

"My family, your family," Commodore said, still puzzled by the expression. They touched glasses.

Miss Loo smiled a happy, sly, knowing little female smile over the rim of her glass.

After a few more sips of wine, Commodore began to wonder if he was a character in some exotic fairy tale. He had a bit of jet lag, and he was enraptured by the exotic sights and smells of Le Petite Derriere not to mention his charming, chattering dinner companion. A piano and violin played American show tunes as Commodore reached for the bottle to pour himself another sip of wine. But Miss Loo had beat him to the last of the bottle, and happily topped off her glass.

Miss Loo quickly opened the curtains and loudly cried out for another bottle. Her shouts caught the attention of a tall, distinguished-looking gentleman in a floppy hat and sunglasses on the other side of the room. The man, whispering into a cell phone, quickly pulled his hat down over his eyes and glanced away, a gesture noticed only by Miss Loo.

Miss Loo looked suspiciously around the room with just a trace of a snarl. She angrily pulled shut the red velvet curtains and kept them closed for the remainder of the meal.

She and Commodore clinked glasses again and again under the flickering lanterns. Commodore knew he should slow down, but he was enjoying himself too much to stop.

Outside was now drizzling rain. Commodore and Miss Loo hurried out of the La Petite Derriere under the solicitous black umbrellas of four slipping and sliding be-turbaned employees who helped them into a waiting horse-drawn carriage. Six perfectly-groomed white horses whinnied and stamped impatiently in front of their coach, snorting and exhaling puffs of steam.

As soon as they were inside the coach, the driver threw his cape over his shoulder, cracked a long whip over the wet butts of the horses, and shouted something in French.

Six white horses jumped forward in unison.

The quaint old canvas-enclosed carriage bounced down the back streets of Paris through steadily drizzling rain.

Feeling the wine, Commodore made vigorous small talk to the steady clatter of the horse's hooves, which seemed to slow to a trot as soon as he began talking. Miss Loo laughed approvingly, occasionally slapping her knee in an oddly masculine gesture. Miss Loo's cute, clumsy questions and laughter brought Commodore out, and out again. The beautiful lady from China seemed to hang on every word he said. All this attention had a magical effect on the old billionaire.

The lady from China actually made him want to talk about himself, something that was out of character for Commodore, or any of his modest, hard-working, self-effacing Austrian ancestors. Eventually the old capitalist began practically bragging of his company's line of sturdy bathroom products to Miss Loo, reciting how many units his each factory produced, how the parts operation was coordinated with new products, and so on. At one point, chuckling to himself about some marketing statistic, the old billionaire quietly passed gas.

A moment later Miss Loo's nostrils flared, and she looked suspiciously from side to side.

"Something dead, I think," she said, pulling back the curtains to the coach. She peered suspiciously out the window into the rain-swept Parisian night. "Maybe dog or skunk dead."

Commodore smiled lamely, uncertain of how to respond.

Miss Loo threw open the carriage windows, and in came the drizzle. She leaned out of Commodore's coach window and shook her fist at the hooded Parisian driver. The driver appeared to be trying to talk on a cell phone. The mysterious Frenchman would not look Miss Loo in the face even after she crawled halfway out of the carriage, shouting at the top of her lungs, and shaking her fist at his averted eyes and dark billowing cape.

"Driver!" Miss Loo cried. "Go faster now, dog dead!"

A short gust of drizzling rain fizzled into the coach as Miss Loo finally returned inside and drew the curtains. Outside, hoof beats quickened for a moment, then slowed down again. Miss Loo wiped her brow and Commodore's brow with a brusque masculine gesture.

She then turned her full attention back to the old billionaire.

"You tell more stories now," Miss Loo smiled.

Commodore soon recovered his composure in the romantic intimacy of the carriage. Commodore's children and many of his employees had long since stopped listening to his stories of what his great grandfather told his grandfather, and which ancestor lived by which particular business homily. But Miss Loo seemed enchanted by the early American mercantile folk wisdom, and by the strange Austrian-American names. Miss Loo laughed brightly at everything Commodore said, even things that he didn't intend to be funny. She had a wonderful infectious laugh.

"You entertaining man," she said, looking up as the coach rounded a corner, and she was thrown against him, chest first. "Why you not marry?"

"My former wife Milly passed away in her sleep almost three years ago," Commodore said, avoiding her question. "Now, every time I wake up, the bed is empty."

Miss Loo took Commodore's hands in her own, which were cold and wet from the rain, but strong from a lifetime of gripping golf clubs. She rubbed Commodore's hands as if wiping the scum off a golf ball.

"Tank run over husband six year ago," Miss Loo said forlornly, batting her eyes. "Long Drive single now. Husband family, my family, Chinese depend on Long Drive. No vacation for me now, only work."

She began kissing his hands.

"Miss Loo, please," Commodore said, gently pushing her away. She had moved much too fast for the old billionaire. Commodore was determined to take his time and keep things proper.

Miss Loo petulantly slumped back in the surrey on the far side of the carriage, staring out the window as rain pattered on the canvas roof of the carriage.

Just before they arrived back at the hotel, the old billionaire noticed a vaguely familiar odor. One moment Miss Loo had been looking out the window with a sort of grimace on her face, the next moment the cab was filled with the aroma of crushed flowers.

Uniformed Frenchmen with umbrellas ushered them out of the carriage and into their grand Parisian hotel, where Simon had booked them separate suites. A picturesque old clock was striking twelve in the distance as uniformed hotel employees lined up like so many tin soldiers in the rain.

The familiar notes of George Gershwin's "American in Paris" rang forth from a rain-drenched little street orchestra under black umbrellas across the street from the hotel. Meanwhile, hotel employees threw planks across the standing rainwater. They unrolled a red carpet which extended across the planks and cobblestones to the brass and glass front door. As Commodore and Miss Loo entered the hotel, two more hotel employees, cooing in French, unrolled a ribbon of plush red carpet all the way to the elevator.

The hotel manager personally accompanied them upstairs. He respectfully unlocked and flung open the door to Miss Loo's suite of rooms, which smelled like a flower shop. Miss

Loo took Commodore's arm, and Commodore escorted her into the foyer. While they were at dinner, her entire suite had been filled with bouquets of pink and white peonies, another of Simon's ideas.

"So many Peony! Long Drive favorite flower!" Miss Loo cried, her voice rising into the high register of a child. "How you know this?" Miss Loo asked in a childlike voice, dropping Commodore's arm. "How you know?"

"A little bird told me," Commodore said.

Pulling the nearest bouquet out of its vase, Miss Loo laughed wildly. She spun around the carpet in her beautiful red dress, looking at the ceiling and holding the oversized bouquet tightly to her breast. That was practically the last thing Commodore Commode remembered.

The next morning, the old billionaire woke up in bed alone, with something of a headache. His tuxedo had magically disappeared. He wore his gray silk pajamas which he thought he had left in the United States. He noticed that his matching gray silk slippers had also been set in place next to the bed.

And here was his faithful valet, R.G. Spartan, bent over the side of the bed, holding his wrist. For a moment Commodore thought the old valet was actually taking his pulse. But Spartan simply patted his wrist and bid him a cheerful good morning, sir. A beautiful young French girl in a black and white linen dress slipped in and out of the room with hot towels, singing a French lullaby. After a decent interval and more hot towels, his old valet brought Commodore a change of clothing.

"Didn't I give you the week off?" Commodore asked.

"Mr. Butterknut, sir, wished that I attend to your needs," R.G. explained. The old valet held out the old billionaire's morning pants, and Commodore stepped into them.

"Oh?"

"Mr. Butterknut thought it might be a good idea for me to accompany you for the rest of your trip, that is, of course, with your permission," R.G. said, buttoning Commodore's pants and fastening his belt. "Of course I'll do my best to be useful."

"Of course," Commodore said.

"You do look quite dapper, sir," R.G. said, as Commodore examined himself in the full-length mirror in the foyer. "You look very dashing, if I may say so, in a Continental sort of way."

Commodore met Miss Loo for brunch in the hotel's cozy little restaurant. A small fireplace illuminated much of the room. The minute they sat down, a bouquet of peonies appeared on their table and Miss Loo squealed with uninhibited delight. Another of Simon's ideas.

They enjoyed a wonderful little French breakfast. Suddenly, Commodore passed gas more loudly than he would have liked, and he looked from side to side as if searching for the source of the noise.

Miss Loo smiled expectantly.

"Goat cheese," Commodore explained, forcing a smile.

"You like more goat cheese now?" Miss Loo laughed brightly, slapping her knee and signaling the waiter.

Commodore laughingly waved the waiter away.

Soon they were flying over the English Channel. Their chartered jet landed near the Old Course at St. Andrews, the world's oldest golf course. Scenic old fairways steeped in history and tradition awaited them, flanked by clumps of heather and gorse.

Commodore quickly fell behind the brilliantly energetic, slashing and aggressive Miss Loo, who always seemed to play golf as if she were 10 strokes behind. Commodore tried gamely to keep up, but he flubbed several shots on the long undulating fairways as Miss Loo waited for him to catch up with a forced smile. All morning, Commodore could not keep his ball out of the heather and gorse, not to mention the course's many deep pot bunkers. As Commodore struggled to hold his own, not quite sure about this particular idea of Simon's, the two Chinese caddies stared glumly ahead, avoiding Commodore's eyes. From time to time, Commodore noticed, Miss Loo's Chinese caddy backed off the green and slipped a cell phone out of his golf bag.

To Commodore's complete surprise, he managed to finish the game in a tie with Miss Loo. She took fourteen shots to pitch out of the notorious "Valley of Sin," a difficult area near the 18th green.

"You happy man, tie game now," Miss Loo said a little gruffly as she finally finished the last hole.

The upbeat lady from China sunk into an uncharacteristic funk as the jet roared back across the channel toward Germany. Commodore tried to figure out how he had managed to play a former world champion professional golfer like Miss Loo to a tie. Something had happened to Miss Loo's game on the last hole. Indeed, her game completely fell apart. She began slashing like a whirling dervish in the belly of the "Valley of Sin." Several times she hit the ball almost straight up in the air. He had never seen anything quite like it.

Noticing the uncharacteristic scowl on her face before they landed, Commodore thought it best not to ask inquire about what happened to her game.

҉

Their jet landed at a private airstrip in the middle of the Black Forest. Until Simon pointed it out, the old billionaire had forgotten that the family held title to a romantic old castle which was once owned by Kaiser Wilhelm. The squat gray castle sat atop a rugged hilltop in rural Germany. Commodore's grandfather had purchased it for a song after the German defeat in World War I.

With polka music coming from somewhere deep inside the castle, Commodore and Miss Loo enjoyed a candlelight dinner on a huge stone table under a wall of rustic stag and boar heads. Miss Loo's good humor returned as soon as they were brought small cold pewter mugs of foaming beer to wash down the meal. They were served some kind of exotic local sausages which unfortunately gave Commodore even more gas than usual for the balance of the night.

The next morning, Commodore was awakened by the sound of noisily migrating birds squawking past the roof of the castle. As he stepped onto the wide granite balcony, Commodore saw the largest flock of ducks he had ever seen, dutifully flapping north. The old billionaire looked out over the misty gray and green countryside where tree-covered hilltops protruded through of a skirt of thin white fog. For a moment, he felt like the king of a very old, enchanted country.

After breakfast they jetted to Vienna, to visit Commodore's ancestral home. Loose gray clouds hung low over Vienna like so much silk drapery as they stepped out of the plane. A limousine whisked them to the birthplace of Commodore's Austrian ancestors. The homeplace had been re-purchased more than a hundred years ago, during a triumphant return to Vienna by Nicholas Commode. It had been years since Commodore laid eyes on the trim, modest little cottage near the center of the RhumPlatz. The last time Commodore visited had been for his European honeymoon with Milly. When he showed Milly the little house, Commodore remembered, she was delighted by the neat little window boxes overflowing with bright red and orange flowers. But this time, as the scowling old Austrian caretaker unlocked the little house, Commodore noticed that the flower boxes were conspicuously empty.

Ominous thunder rumbled throughout the afternoon. R.G. lit a fire in the fireplace, and made toddies. Commodore and Miss Loo sat near the crackling fire, eating a small lunch and then Viennese pastries from a silver tray. A hard sudden shower of rain slapped angrily at the roof as Commodore reminisced about his most colorful ancestor, company founder Nicolas Commode. Nicholas V. "Red Nick" Commode was a fire-breathing socialist when he came to America. In the Vienna of his day, where only the very richest Viennese could afford indoor toilets, Red Nick was a malcontent master pipe and cistern maker, forever reaming out the complicated indoor plumbing systems of the snooty upper crust.

Red Nick knew he was not respected for his dirty work under the mansions of the idle rich. A born entrepreneur, he could not get along with anyone in his family either.

One day, Red Nick packed up his tools and stalked out of Vienna in a huff. Fed up with the calcified class system that oppressed them all, Red Nick hopped a steamer to the United States with the double dream of finding a better life for himself, and helping the downtrodden workers of the world.

Shortly after Red Nick left Vienna, his relatives began dropping dead from a deadly typhoid fever epidemic that swept through the low-rent hovels of the RhumPlatz. When Nicholas Commode returned to Vienna three decades later, with his beautiful American wife and their short, beefy children, he was wealthy and sentimental enough to buy the little house back, and smart enough to pressure the snooty Austrian bankers for a substantial discount for cash.

"Smart relative!" Miss Loo said, clapping her hands and waving to R.G. for another toddy.

She clutched Commodore's arm with both hands, and squeezed it desperately. "Tell more old story."

Although the old billionaire feared that he was beginning to repeat himself, Commodore complied.

Miss Loo sipped toddy after toddy, hanging on his every word and constantly crying out for more stories. Lightning flashes flickered against the drapery. The afternoon disappeared in the twinkling of an eye.

❧

A limousine spirited them to the family villa on the Grand Canal in Venice. After dinner, carrying a lantern, the old valet led them down a cobblestone path to the water, where a large specially-built gondola festooned with flaming torches awaited.

R.G. helped the old capitalist and Miss Loo onto the gondola, but held onto Commodore's wrist for a moment too long while glancing at his watch. But before Commodore could ask, R.G. slipped into the servant's seat just behind them, and busied himself with the snacks and the champagne.

A full moon leapt into the sky as Miss Loo quietly snuggled up next to Commodore. A muscular Italian in a striped shirt and a wide black hat pushed the big gondola off the bank and they were off. For a few minutes they glided quietly through the fragrant Venetian canals, between the crumbling buildings of the ancient city.

As they rounded a corner, the Venice Pops Orchestra magically appeared behind them, in several gondolas, playing an Italianate version of "Moon River." This was another of Simon's ideas, and it went over well.

Looking over her shoulder and clasping her hands, Miss Loo appeared delighted by the sight of the Venice Pops, which was beloved by American tourists. The floating middlebrow orchestra doggedly followed the old billionaire's gondola through the winding canals.

At one point, however, Commodore exuberantly knocked the bottle of champagne overboard as R.G. was attempting to refill Miss Loo's glass. It was their only bottle of champagne, and Commodore experienced a moment of befuddled embarrassment. But before Commodore could open his mouth, the fully-corked bottle shot triumphantly up out of the murky water on the end of a muscular golden arm. R.G. nonchalantly retrieved the bottle from a smiling middle-aged Asian man in a wet suit, who was apparently out for a moonlight swim in the murky canal.

Miss Loo cooed her approval in every possible way. She leaned against him, she laughed, she stroked his arm, she grabbed his shoulder in her strong grip and looked longingly into his eyes. As she finished her final glass of champagne, her eyes began to sparkle like diamonds. She grandly flung the plastic glass over her shoulder for good luck, she told him, just missing R.G. and the patiently smiling gondolier. Back at the villa, on a patio overlooking the canal, Miss Loo took Commodore's hand in the moonlight.

"You nice, rich, big, important businessman," Miss Loo said, squeezing his hand. "Why you not marry?"

"Why you not marry?" Commodore shot back, enjoying the friendly joust.

"You all business man now?" she asked, bowing and squeezing his hand again under the torches. "Never pleasure with woman? Why?"

Commodore managed a crafty smile, which masked the twinge of fear and anticipation he felt inside as Miss Loo longingly released his hand.

That night, before Commodore fell asleep, he happily thought of Miss Loo in the next room, surrounded by peonies. The old billionaire fancied they had begun to get acquainted now, in an entirely proper way.

❧

Rain had come and gone in Shanghai before they landed. Thick white clouds elbowed their way across a somewhat polluted sky. A black limousine with tinted windows and Chinese government flags on the rear aerials drove right out to the plane to meet them. Inside, R. G. Spartan poured Miss Loo a bit of champagne, then discreetly scooted to a far corner of the moving limousine.

The limousine shot across the Yangtze River, and into downtown Shanghai. The narrow streets of Shanghai were tangled with pedestrians, policemen, dogs, street vendors, soldiers, beggars, rickshaws, new model American and Japanese cars, and more bicycles and motorbikes than Commodore had ever seen in his life.

Somehow they sped through the congestion as if on wings.

A forest of unimaginably tall, American-style office buildings was popping up all around them. From the tops of towering cranes fluttered large red Chinese government flags. You could almost hear the sound of money being minted, to the siren song of conspicuous consumption.

When the limousine turned a corner and slowed down, Miss Loo pointed out the window at a large, unoccupied building.

"Look!" Miss Loo said, tapping on the side window. "One empty, my family factory. One million square feet, strong floors for tanks, maybe suit for bathroom products."

Commodore politely leaned over to look outside. He saw what appeared to be a huge empty concrete fortress. In front of the building, several dozen men in matching gray jackets stood shoulder to shoulder on the sidewalk. As if on cue, the men held up identical signs written in English.

WE WORK 25 CENT AN HOUR, read the group's neatly-lettered signs.

"People come here, all over China. Millions workers want work, want more work, always cheap wage," Miss Loo said. "Two dollar day good salary here."

She barked something to the driver in Chinese and the limousine sped away. They squealed to a stop in front of another empty three-story concrete building, with a million boarded-up windows. A group of Chinamen stood outside carrying signs that said:

WORKER VERY CHEAP HERE – NO UNION ALLOW

"My family second factory," Miss Loo said, tapping on the limousine window. "Same size one your factory, maybe buy factory cheap or easy lease."

Miss Loo clapped her hands and they squealed away.

Out the window Commodore noticed two gray-jacketed Chinamen furiously peddling bicycles alongside the limousine, one on either side. Each held out a hand-lettered sign with one hand. The chuffing rider on the left held out a sign that said:

SHANGHAI BEST LOCATION, GOODBYE AMERICA TAX

The uncomfortable-looking rider on the other side, sweating like a pig, struggled to hold up a sign that said:

POLLUTE AIR AND WATER, NO PROBLEM

A minute later, the limousine screeched to a stop in front of still another gray concrete fortress, an empty warren of interlocking concrete buildings with some of the industrial windows broken out. If you used your imagination, the sad gray factory looked a little like the Pentagon in Washington,

D.C. In the foreground, four large Chinese tanks sat on a drab concrete pedestal outside the building, facing all four directions like military sentinels rusting in the rain.

"Number five factory here, same square foot your," Miss Loo said, tapping the window. "Business move in cheap, work cheap, ship cheap, make money for family."

She barked at the driver, and they sped away.

"What a coincidence that your family would have five empty factories right here in Shanghai, with the same square footage as our factories," Commodore said, fumbling for just the right words as they sped away.

Miss Loo smiled enigmatically.

"In China we have old saying," she said as she stared dreamily out the window. "Old fortune meet old fortune, brand new fortune grow."

At that moment Commodore was surprised to see a rickshaw pull abreast of their limousine. The rotund bald-headed man pulling the rickshaw looked like Mao Tse-tung in an old Communist Party uniform. Dodging in and out of traffic, Mao's look-alike was pulling the rickshaw at an almost unbelievable speed, and smiling a curiously forced smile.

From just behind the rickshaw, a smiling bucktoothed Asian woman unfurled a flowing silk banner that read:

HAPPY CHINESE WHEN AMERICAN BUSINESS COME

"Shanghai like big fortune cookie," Miss Loo laughed, waving away the rickshaw. "American open factory, find good fortune every time."

She clapped her hands, then demurely closed her eyes. "We go my place now."

❧

They got out of the limousine under a round orange moon brushed with exotic clouds. Obviously, Miss Loo lived in a former palace. Fragile brass wind chimes tinkled quietly deep inside the enormous stone building, adding a few grace notes of mystery and romance.

"Magnificent little home," Commodore said as they strolled under a series of arches toward Miss Loo's large heavily lacquered front door. Large, perpetually snarling teakwood gargoyles protected the rather grand front entrance.

"Family palace home to Ming Emperor's favorite girl, mistress Tsu Tsi. Emperor build big palace for favorite girl one thousand year ago," Miss Loo said, batting her eyes and pausing near the front door. "Chairman third wife give my family."

In the moonlight, Miss Loo took Commodore's hand.

"I go to U.S., play golf, bring home big prize. Chairman, wife give many gift. Five factory make tank, good money," she said wistfully. "China different now."

An elderly white-haired Chinese woman slowly opened the door, holding a candle. Miss Loo hissed something in Chinese, and the woman blushed and quickly closed the door.

Moving closer, Miss Loo placed both her hands on Commodore's shoulders. She raised her trembling red lips to be kissed. When he realized what she wanted, Commodore responded like a man entirely aflame. Mad under the light of the moon, the old capitalist impulsively swept the lady from China into his arms. The old sailor gave Miss Loo what he believed was the kiss of her life, a real American kiss, he told himself, a sailor's last departing kiss, a kiss ripe with loneliness and longing, the kind of kiss women always say they want when they see it in the movies. The inspired old billionaire held Miss Loo in a backbreaking embrace for several minutes. As he crushed and recrushed the lips of the pliant Asian golfer, firecrackers of desire seemed to explode in his head and possibly in her head, too. Finally, the old sailor was finished As he began to pull Miss Loo up, arms dangling at her side like a rag doll, an entire spectacular sky full of Chinese fireworks popped and exploded over the roof of the old palace. For Commodore, it had been the kiss that united past with future, man with woman, etcetera. For a single luminous moment, blinking and looking up at the sky in popping and exploding riot, time stood still for the old billionaire.

Commodore had been swept away by the enchantment of the moment, by the teasing foreplay and excitement of the gift exchange, the Parisian wine, the travel, by the business confidences he shared with Miss Loo over romantic meals the past few days, by her acceptance and laughter, by the beauty of Europe, the hungry energy of China, by the scent of the peonies and new rain and the high adventure, by the beautiful and mysterious Chinese palace, by the thrill of the chase, by the scent and proximity of a woman, by the torchlight, by American red desire itself.

Commodore sensed a sort of implied promise for the eventual fulfillment of all his fantasies about a female on every level of his life in the hard, warm, wet, lips and muscular arms of Miss Loo. It was almost too magical for words.

"My family, your family," Miss Loo gasped, reeling backwards toward the door like a feather in a gust of wind. She staggered back between the gargoyles and threw out both arms across the face of the door.

As fireworks exploded overhead, Miss Loo paused with a red handkerchief to her cheek for a final comment. She was breathing hard and blinking like a woman whose bodice had been ripped off her breast by gusts of unimaginable passion.

"Together, now, yesterday, today, me, you, my family, your family, five factory, have breakfast, drink tea, tie score, more peony, play golf, happy you, me, champagne, kissing, business, always!" she cried as the palace door opened and she hurried inside. "Always!"

The older woman blew out the candle, bowed to Commodore, and quietly closed the palace door.

The sky was alive with spectacular fireworks along his route back to the airport, as if all of China was announcing the appointment of an emperor. Despite his years, the old billionaire felt as romantic and virile as some modern-day Rhett Butler. Being an American, of course, his less discreet fantasies cried out for more—more wooing, more kisses, more hotels, more travel, more gifts, more amusing laughter, more crushed flowers, perhaps even at some point more marriage, capped by a spectacular honeymoon conquest. Miss Loo, whom he presumed to be chaste as she was obviously the sort to wait for just the right man, would be the second Asian conquest of Commodore's modest love life. At that moment, the old capitalist had every reason to believe that she would be just as thrilled and grateful as his first conquest had seemed to be, and perhaps even more so.

Overloaded with excitement, Commodore went to sleep as soon as they climbed into the plane. R.G. Spartan took his boss's wrist in his hand, quietly counted heartbeats, and reached in his pocket for a cell phone.

13. The Dominoes Fall

The very minute the old billionaire left town Commodore's loyal valet R.G Spartan received an urgent phone call. Mr. Commode's fast-talking son-in-law, Simon Butterknut, the vice president of legal affairs for Mr. Commode's company, summoned him to Commode Company headquarters for an emergency meeting.

Taking off his hat, the old valet walked diffidently past the impressively saluting doormen. He rode the picturesque old elevator to the second floor. He worked his way through a gauntlet of pretty young secretaries in very short skirts, and into the enormous second floor office of the fast-talking vice president of legal affairs.

Mr. Commode's son-in-law sat behind the largest oak desk the old valet had ever seen, with his cowboy boots on the desk in a casual manner. His muscular body was nestled into an enormous padded swivel chair. On the wall were several large pictures of Mr. Commode's oldest daughter nuzzling what appeared to be small, black pigs.

Behind the vice president's desk was a complete wall of ornately-bound law books that looked so new the old valet wondered if they'd ever been opened. The vice president of legal affairs took several minutes to finish what he indicated was an extremely important business call before turning to the old valet.

Mr. Butterknut bluntly announced that he wanted the old valet on the next plane to Paris. His longtime employer's family apparently wanted him to phone in reports about the progress of Mr. Commodore's romance with a certain lady. On the face of it, it smacked of spying to the skeptical valet.

"I'm afraid I don't understand, sir," said the old valet, crossing his hands over his lap.

The old valet had understood only that his employer was going out of town for a few days, and would not require his services. Although he didn't mention it to Mr. Butterknut, the old valet had already planned a modest vacation.

"You see, Spartan, here in the legal affairs department, we all want to do everything possible to make sure Commodore is safe." Mr. Commode's son-in-law gestured broadly, as if he spoke for all the employees in the company.

"My staff is concerned about Commodore's safety and especially about his health. Commodore's companion is younger than Commodore. She's in top physical shape, and she's malignantly attractive. And frankly, Spartan, I've asked you here because I personally am concerned about a particular health problem."

"Oh?"

"As you may know, it's been a long time since Commodore has even looked at a woman."

"Very true, sir. Mr. Commode was quite devoted to Mrs. Commode."

"It's extremely important for you to get close to Commodore and to report everything that occurs to me. We want Commodore to enjoy himself, but not to overdo it in a dangerous way, if you catch my drift."

"Frankly, no, I don't understand, sir."

With flashing eyes, the Prince leaned across his desk and placed his finger on the nose of the old valet.

"Put it together, Spartan," he said. "Your employer is taking a beautiful woman to Paris, Scotland, Germany, Vienna, Venice, and China—in less than a week's time. That's a ferocious schedule even for a man my age, and I work out six times a week under expert supervision in my personal gymnasium. Commodore hardly works out. He's trying to keep pace with a professional athlete. This level of activity could strain his heart. If there's a problem, we'll need to be alerted and we'll have to immediately fly him home. That's why I need somebody trustworthy to keep tabs on him, and I mean you."

"I wasn't aware that Mr. Commode had a heart condition, sir."

"Trust me, Spartan," the Prince said, slamming his boots to the floor with a loud *smack*. "My brother-in-law's a doctor. He's already reviewed Commodore's medical records. Doctor Clipster is extremely concerned about the stress of this trip."

"If that's the case, of course I'll help you, sir," said the old valet, rising to his feet, and extending his hand. "I've had a bit of medical training. When do you wish me to leave?"

The old valet deferentially accepted an envelope containing some highly detailed instructions to be opened on the plane, and several thousand dollars in traveling money. He accepted a special cell phone on which he was expected to call in periodic reports.

One of the company's brusque young cigar-smoking second vice presidents drove him to the airport. As he boarded the plane, the old valet contemplated the strange and somewhat alluring sudden assignment. The whole adventure seemed positively shot through with mystery, romance, and intrigue. Like any decent Englishman, the old valet was madly excited by the idea of little cloak and dagger work.

Over the Atlantic he opened the envelope and looked over his secret instructions. As a young man, he'd served as a medic in the British Army, and memories of his medical training came back to him as he flew. The thought crossed his mind that he had not been back to London in forty years, and he wouldn't go back now, either, since he'd cancelled his vacation. The old valet felt a murmur of homesickness as he watched the southern tip of England pass beneath the wing of the plane as it roared toward Paris.

The moment he arrived, a mysterious Frenchman with a cape drove the old valet to Le Petite Derriere, where he was shown to a special table. In the floppy hat and large false moustache that the Frenchman insisted he wear, the old valet discreetly watched his employer from the far side of the room through opera glasses.

The old valet could not help but notice the enamored, almost childlike look on Mr. Commode's face as Miss Loo made a spectacular entrance. From what the old valet could see, the beautiful Asian lady was quite bold, even openly flirtatious with Mr. Commode.

More than once, he observed, the lady boldly cried out for additional wine. When their eyes met over a sea of American tourists for just a moment, the lady from China's smile changed into a sneer that chilled him to the bone from all the way across the room. As she angrily yanked the curtains of the booth shut, the old valet understood immediately why Mr. Butterknut feared there might be some potential problem with Mr. Commode's heart.

The trusting old valet did not imagine that the Prince had peppered the entire route of Commodore's journey with additional spies. Overdoing it as usual, Simon had planted spies to check and cross-check each other so that no detail of the meticulously-planned trip would possibly go awry.

The day after Commodore departed, the Prince slipped into the secret taping room in his office closet to monitor the first recorded message. It was the Chinese female informant with a thick Asian accent, a trusted member of Miss Loo's household who had been handsomely paid off by legal affairs.

"Limousine pick up Chinese lady, take lady to airport, everything on time," said the voice. "Fireworks crew come tomorrow."

A second message had been left by R.G. Spartan, whose crisp diction was at least easy to understand, although there were long dramatic pauses.

The old valet was whispering into the phone, much like a commentator at a televised golf match.

"Mr. Commode has waited somewhat impatiently in a private booth for the mysterious lady, who now makes a regal entrance," R.G. whispered. "One thinks of the funeral march from *Aida*... Ah, wine is quickly served ... dinner is progressing... the excellent Moroccan soup is borne to their table ... The lady cranes her neck to look out... Egad, the curtains to their booth are pulled tightly shut by nimble fingers of the mysterious lady... who shot me a look which froze me to the bone...fortunately the main course of my own splendid meal arrives. Keeping one eye fixed on Mr. Commode's sealed booth, where privacy reigns supreme, but with nothing further to report at this precise moment, R.G. Spartan, foreign correspondent, signing off, La Petite Derriere Paris, France."

The carriage driver was the notorious Napoleon de la Creppe, the most famous private detective in France. A renowned horseman, Le Creppe came highly recommended. Le Creppe called Simon from the top of the carriage at the stroke of midnight. Simon monitored the call on the treadmill in his home gymnasium, as Petunia slept.

"Here ez lub, ez romantic, ez rain," whispered le Creppe over the clopping of the horses. "But *mon Dieu*, no! Suddenly ez problem—what, *no! mademoiselle!*"

Walking faster on the treadmill, Simon thought he heard Miss Loo's strident cry from all the way across the Atlantic.

"Driver—faster now!" Simon heard Miss Loo's plaintive cry. "Dog or skunk dead!"

"Ze Chinese shriek!" le Creppe exclaimed. "Very frightened of zee dogz! Es emergency, no? *Mademoiselle? Mademoiselle?* In ze carriage, *s'il vous plait?* You calm down please?"

"Perhaps I return to ze hotel early, *monsieur?*" le Creppe whispered anxiously.

"Keep driving, Napoleon!" the Prince hissed. "Our little girl needs more face time. She's got to sink in the hook tonight. For God's sake, think like an American!"

"*Oui, certainment,*" le Creppe whispered, furiously cracking his whip over the butts of the frightened horses. "*Allons!*"

The Prince kicked up the speed on his treadmill. With a wicked smile frozen onto his face, he slowly and deliberately strode in place in his darkened home gymnasium until he broke into a malicious sweat.

The next morning brought the old valet's second message.

"Mr. Commode had a bit of an accident, but I've cleaned him up. He's in his pajamas, and comfortably in bed. Mr. Commode unfortunately consumed several glasses of wine at dinner, and as you know he is not a vigorous drinker. There is some labored breathing, of course, perhaps from the excitement of the night, and a bit of flatulence, perhaps from the spicy Moroccan cuisine. Happily, pulse appears perfectly normal. With all that can discreetly be said from Mr. Commode's bedside this is R.G. Spartan, at 3 a.m., Paris, reporting."

The Prince experienced three days of giddy joy as every one of his carefully-arranged dominoes fell into place. More than once, he was able to take a call in the office closet where the secret telephone taping equipment had been installed.

"Old man, Number One lady on golf course now, big problem here, answer please," came the singsong voice of one of Miss Loo's Chinese caddies, apparently calling from the Old Course at St. Andrews. "Mister pick up please. Chinese lady have question."

"What's the problem, Chinaman?" the Prince snarled.

"Old man down ten, twelve stroke," reported the caddy. "Hole 17 now. Old man look unhappy. Chinese lady worry old man look very unhappy."

Not far away, on a picturesque stone bridge built in Roman times, Miss Loo gestured impatiently to the caddy while Commodore adjusted his beret and addressed the ball.

"For God's sake, she's got to *blow the match*!" hissed the Prince. "American men can't *stand* to lose! We Americans *all* have to win! He's an American, remember? Tell Long Drive to give him at least a tie!"

"Twelve stroke down."

"For God's sake, Chinaman! Just do it!"

"I tell boss lady now."

As Commodore watched his rather pathetic drive bounce into the heather at the right of the fairway, the caddy gave the secret thumb down sign to Miss Loo twelve times in a row.

Long Drive nodded, tried to swallow her pride, sucked in her gut, and bared her competitor's teeth. Taking a deep breath, Miss Loo stepped up to the tee and placed her own shot directly into the center of the "Valley of Sin."

"Mr. Commode and the lady from China enjoy a pleasant afternoon here in Vienna at the family's ancestral home. Mr. Commode has been extraordinarily animated all day, with his reminisces of the business. Ah, and toddies do animate the lady. Happily, pulse strong and entirely normal. This is R.G. Spartan, reporting, from a rain-swept cottage in the heart of the distant RhumPlatz, Vienna, Austria."

The next message was almost impossible to understand with the Venice Pops orchestra blaring in the background. One of the Asian detectives huffed and puffed as he spoke, apparently treading water with a cell phone. Simon presumed it was one of the Chinese frogmen who had been hired to swim behind the gondola and keep tabs on Commodore.

"Beautiful Chinese lady make toast, throw third glass in canal," reported the Chinese spy, who was treading water and puffing for breath as he followed the gondola. "Oop! Old man knock bottle into water. I pick up now, swim fast, take back bottle to old man," said the frogman, breathing hard.

And the highly orchestrated caravan of love rolled on.

Every domino that fell into place sent a thrill up the spine of the calculating Prince. Like some villain in a silent movie, the Bastard Prince rubbed his hands together as he listened to the recorded messages over and over again, in his private tape room. The rogue military psychiatrists, the travel consultants, the wine connoisseurs, the romantic advisors, the meteorologists, the astrologers, the fireworks experts and other professionals he'd quietly hired were all coming through. They had all assured the Prince that the carefully-plotted whirlwind romance with its explosive ending would have a profound romantic effect on the old billionaire and effectively neutralize his usually sober business judgment. The Prince was sure he and Miss Loo, working together as a team, could tilt the old capitalist towards a swift move of all the company's factories to China. At last, every single domino had fallen into place and success seemed to be within the Prince's grasp.

At the exact minute Commodore's plane was taking off from Shanghai, Simon looked at his Rolex Oyster and decided to wait until the next day to savor the falling of the final domino. At 4 a.m. California time, the Prince stepped onto the treadmill in his home gymnasium.

Simon turned his machine to the highest possible setting and began treading at warp speed, as if to overtake the universe in seven league boots. The Bastard Prince began to sweat profusely. Megalomania opened in his brain like a hothouse flower as a line of Machiavelli suddenly popped into his perspiring head.

In those states that are governed by an absolute Prince and slaves, the Prince has far more power and authority; for no one recognizes any other superior but him.

– Machiavelli, The Prince

14. An Uninvited Guest

The next morning the Prince slipped into his private office tape room. He was listening listen to the final recorded message from the old valet, who let a note of poetic nostalgia creep into his voice near the end of what he believed had been a potentially life-saving spy mission.

"With the lights of metropolitan Shanghai burning like torches below us, our small entourage embarks for America. Our jet gracefully lifts its nose into the air and Mr. Commode's long, eventful voyage is over. Once again, Mr. Commode sleeps, and I'm happy to report, pulse normal. Rising like a finch over the bright towers of Shanghai..."

Without warning, Philip Commode burst into Simon's office. The Prince turned to see the mop-headed interior designer trailed by Miss Van Bunkle who was valiantly trying to follow orders and not let anyone in.

"Where *is* my Dad?" Filly demanded, putting his hands on his hips, and shaking his mop of bright red hair.

Simon closed the door to the secret tape room and waved Miss Van Bunkle away.

"What can I say? Commodore met a lady."

"That Chinese chippie from the over-the-hill golf tournament?" Filly demanded. "How old is *she?*"

"Philip, please, let's sit down," Simon said.

Simon sat down and put his cowboy boots up on the desk. His wickedly smiling face peeped out at Philip from behind the pointed soles of his Tony Lamas.

"Do you realize my secretary has been trying to reach you all week to confirm your attendance at the board meeting?" Simon asked.

"What does that have to do with my Father's whereabouts?" Filly asked, feeling his stomach begin to tremble. "Tell me when Dad is coming home, or I'm going to get pissed."

"He's on his way home right now. Are you worried?"

"Let's just say I have a need to know."

Philip walked to the door and gestured to Diego. Beautiful Diego slunk in, as graceful as running water. Diego gazed intently at the Prince from under his bangs. He'd just had his hair done and it looked great.

"What the hell is *he* doing here?" Simon stood up

"Diego supports me emotionally at crucial moments," Philip said. Diego dramatically flipped his hair to one side and glared at Simon, as if to ask, "What?"

"Ask your emotional support to leave, will you? One of you in my office at a time is enough."

"I won't, sorry, ever, ask, my emotional support to do any, such, thing," Philip gasped, suddenly short of breath.

Becoming mindful, Philip tried to breathe down the festering ball of anger in his stomach. He focused to work it down with rhythmic deep breathing, as he had been taught to do in anger management classes. He did not want to offend his sister's husband, although he had a mind to slap Simon silly. Diego put his arm around Philip's shoulder, a gesture of support. For a moment, Philip teared up.

The Prince had such contempt for the two skinny little faggots hugging each other in his office, and he was so certain of success, that he let his guard down for just a moment and revealed his plans.

"OK, *boys*," he growled. "Here's the deal. At the board meeting two days from now, this company is going to move its manufacturing plants to China. We make an additional two billion dollars in profit the first two years. You'll support us, Philip, of course, and so will your sisters. And of course we'll all participate in the profits," the Prince said.

"I'm talking big wampum, boys," Simon winked, smiling his wicked smile.

Philip and Diego looked at each other. Diego made a face.

"Big *wampum*?" Philip said. "Give me a break."

"In Shanghai they work for peanuts."

"So?" Diego asked, arching one eyebrow.

"And that Chinese *chippie*, as you referred to her, Philip, represents a distinguished Chinese family which just happens to have factories that are exactly the right size for our company's operations," the Prince hissed.

"China is not the way we've traditionally done business at the Commode Company," Philip said, breathing it down." We're an American company and we have union contracts"

"So what the fuck?"

Diego looked at Filly.

"*Pardon* me?" Philip asked.

"What the *fuck*, Filly," Simon said. "Your Dad's already taken a look at this. Petunia and Clementine are both aboard. That leaves you, Philip. So you'll vote to move the plants, too. Your sisters will expect you to support the interests of your family, and so will Commodore. Believe me, we'll all be far, far richer in the end because of this."

"*We?*" Diego asked. "*We*'ll all be rich?"

"But isn't this all just a little *too* greedy?" Philip demanded.

Philip mindfully directed his entire breath to his solar plexus chakra. He was struggling to center his feelings with the deep breathing technique, before responding calmly and assertively.

"So it's a business decision," the Prince said. "And for Christ's sakes! Will you stop panting like a puppy and just *deal with it*, Philip?"

Simon made a face and glanced at his diamond-studded Rolex Daytona. Then he pressed a buzzer, summoning the security guards.

"If you sweet little fellows will excuse me—it's our busy time of year in legal affairs."

"But what if Philip Commode *doesn't* vote for it?" Diego asked, tossing his hair. He stamped one of his small Italian shoes on the floor for emphasis, like an angry goat.

"If he has a brain left in his head after snorting all that cocaine, Philip Commode will see the *light*," the Prince said. "The light at the end of this tunnel is *green*."

Security guards burst into the room. Two of them took Diego's arms. But Philip stopped them with an operatic gesture.

"*Stop*! That's my *partner* you're mishandling," Filly said. "Who do you think you *are*, Simon Butterknut? You won't get away with this ... arrogant scheming mendacity."

The security guards released Diego. Philip lifted his chin, and linked arms with Diego. At the door, Diego turned, flipped his hair, and bared his perfect teeth at Simon.

"See you at the board meeting, *Simon*," Philip hissed over his shoulder.

15. GHOST IN THE MACHINE

The next afternoon **Philip and Diego** stepped out of a Learjet under a dark Cleveland sky. Although the weather was cold, they were perfectly put together. Under his overcoat, Filly wore a stylishly-tailored Gucci suit, with an off-white shirt and an American red tie and matching handkerchief. In his hand was a stylish leather briefcase. Diego was perfectly put together in Valentino, with his long hair pulled back into a perfect corporate ponytail. They could have been two visiting corporate executives from Holland.

"You must be Philip Commode," Don Dumper said, as they shook hands. "I'm Don Dumper, plants manager. Your travel coordinator Mr. Armon Robby called this morning and asked me to pick you up in a limousine."

The plant manager wore a plain cloth overcoat, a perfectly horrible clip-on tie, and some kind of plastic thing in his shirt pocket that was full of leaking ballpoint pens and pencils. However, the first thing Philip noticed about him was the man's large, completely honest face.

"It's nice to meet you," Filly said. "This is my good friend Diego."

Diego smiled treacherously as they shook hands.

"I don't think I've seen you since you were a young boy, Mr. Commode, back in the days," Dumper said, walking them toward the limousine they requested, which he had rented from the "Make Cleveland Beautiful" Foundation.

The two guys looked a little sweet to Dumper, frankly, the way they got into the car holding their pants cuffs. But who was he to judge, scrambling into the limousine?

"How is old Mr. Commode?"

"Dad's fine," Philip replied. "But I had a hunch I should come out and sound out the employees about a few things."

"We're getting popular out here in at the plants for a change, I guess," Dumper said "Couple guys came out from headquarters a couple weeks ago. One very important man in your company, lawyer, I guess, in a hurry with everything, even brought his own doctor."

"They're only the in-laws," Philip said, making a dismissive gesture. "And they're not really that important."

"You might say they're from the Machiavellian branch of the family," Diego whispered archly.

"Let's go, Bobby," Dumper said to the driver, dabbing some perspiration off his forehead with a handkerchief.

The driver touched his hat, started the limo, and pulled away. The limousine sped past an subdivision peppered with

For Sale signs, a couple of seedy-looking shopping centers, and what seemed like an endless string of bleak, boarded-up factories that could have been anywhere in the United States.

"We haven't seen much of old Mr. Commode since he moved to California," Dumper ventured. "We get his phone calls, of course. Sort of miss him popping up on the plant floor and keeping an eye on things."

"Dad's been traveling," Philip said, patting Dumper's arm. The plant manager had a slightly lost, pained expression on his face as they crossed the Cuyahoga River.

"Mr. Commode, I may be talking out of turn, but you're Mr. Commode's son and I'm going to lay my cards on the table," Dumper began clumsily. "That short-haired fella with the doctor promised me some big money when you fellows relocate the factory to China, and I signed his confidentiality agreement and all that. But frankly, I just don't feel good about taking all your money."

"Oh?" Philip asked.

"Since you're family, let me just tell you the truth to your face," Dumper said. "My wife and kids don't want to move to China. Golly, and I couldn't face the guys and tell them that, even with that million dollars your lawyer offered me."

"I need to speak to the workers today," Philip said.

"Are you shutting down the plant, today? Are you getting ready to move us all out?" Dumper fearfully asked. "Is that what you came out here to do?"

"No! Of course not. There's a dispute. We brought petitions. I can explain this to all the workers," Philip snapped.

Although he had no idea where this was going, Philip was following his instincts. His instincts nudged him to call his lawyer, to get petitions. His instincts screamed at him to go to Cleveland. Although he didn't have any particular plan, he was improvising and things seemed to be working out.

"Do those other fellows know all about this...talking with the guys?" Dumper asked, tentatively. "Old Mr. Commode, especially, the lawyer with his doctor, I mean, they all understand you're going to do this?"

"My name is *Philip Commode*! I'm an *officer* of this company! I'm *certain* that I'm acting in my family's best interests!" Philip blurted out without thinking.

"But you got to understand the guys don't all work at one time, sir," Dumper said. "We run three shifts a day at this plant."

"Don't even go there," Diego hissed.

"Get the workers together as soon as possible, Don."

"Mr. Robby didn't mention any meeting on the phone."

"Well, *poop*," Filly said.

Diego handed his cell phone to Dumper, and flipped his hair to one side. Dumper dabbed again at the sweat rolling off his forehead as the limo passed the Rock and Roll Hall of Fame.

"Long live Rock 'n Roll," said the driver, who was trained to point out Cleveland's high points to potential contributors. "Let's give it up to Make Cleveland Beautiful."

"We're not damned tourists back here!" Dumper called to the driver. "Turn left up at the second light and take us back to the plant through Shaker Heights."

Lost in thought, Philip Commode stared out the limousine window as late winter Cleveland swept past. The frozen ground was thawing. Trees were beginning to form leaves and the earliest flowers were popping up from bulbs in the yards of the historic old mansions whizzing past the limousine window.

Philip remembered the big house in Cleveland where he grew up, the Linden trees in the back yard, the sudden exciting shifts in weather. He remembered the snowgirls he and his sisters built with their gruff old Austrian nanny and their good-humored Austrian chauffeur. He had been an innocent young Midwestern boy, with an innocent young Midwestern life, before the move to California so many long years ago and the shock of puberty that changed his perspective forever....

Philip Commode was overwhelmed with sudden emotion. California had corrupted his family, he thought, putting his head against Diego's shoulder. His nanny remained in Cleveland and died in her sleep! The old chauffeur shuffled off to a rest home and died! His mother came to California and died! His sisters grew up and married morons! His father was apparently having some kind of second childhood! Had they all, every one, somehow been punished for leaving the home place and betraying the family's long and distinguished Cleveland tradition?

A thought flitted crossed Philip's mind like a mosquito, hinting that he had come to Cleveland to find something greater than himself.

Cleveland was after all the promised land where "Red Nick" Commode ended his personal trek almost one hundred forty years ago, sensing an opportunity in the lack of decent bathroom facilities in the houses of Cleveland's many industrial tycoons. And now, years later, Red Nick's last direct descendant Philip Commode himself was returning to his roots in Cleveland to try to change the course of company history. For the first time, Philip felt the weight of this on his shoulders.

"Is that the old house?" Philip asked.

He had instantly recognized the home place. Red Nick Commode's huge Victorian mansion towered as grandly as the day it was built, half-hidden behind a bank of enormous Linden trees. It was the same stately old three-story Victorian Philip grew up in, all turrets and gingerbread and gables, majestic as ever, still set back a considerable distance off the road.

"That's the homeplace," Dumper said. "You want to stop? I've got a key to the front door."

"Let's stop," Filly said, sensing something. "I think I need to look around."

Philip Commode walked alone through dusty rooms full of family furniture still under white linen dust covers. He wandered up the wide mahogany staircase with his hand on the well-worn banister, looking through the eyes of a child at the narrow hallways and high-ceilinged rooms of the old mansion. The drafty old Victorian was alive with the spirits of his ancestors who had lived there, he suddenly felt, generation after generation after generation.

On the second floor, Philip went immediately to his old suite of rooms, the rooms where he had such vivid memories. He peeped into the functional little Victorian cast iron fireplace on the east wall which faced the leaded glass double windows that opened over the flower garden. He tried to push open the old windows, to let in some fresh air, but he found all the windows had been nailed shut.

One afternoon not unlike this one, Philip suddenly remembered, after an electrical storm that blew in off the lake, he threw open these very windows and saw the first tornado he'd ever seen in his life. It appeared just above the roof of the greenhouse, an undulating apparition which swiveled down like a dangling penis from a bank of black clouds, then twisted like a slow solitary erotic dancer across the red sky before it was gone.

Carefully removing the dust cover, and nearly overcome with emotion, Philip Commode sat down on his old nanny's wide, overstuffed armchair which smelled exactly the same way he remembered.

"Philip Commode!" a strong little voice shouted.

It could have been a thunderclap echoing across the Great Plains. Philip looked around. Not one person was around. But Philip noticed something glowing in the belly of the fireplace where he had seen only a small neat pile of gray ashes before.

"I beg your pardon," Philip said, his voice echoing through the empty house.

Out of the ashes in the fireplace rose a small, curious object which threw off light. The thing moved and glowed an interesting shade of red.

As Filly's eyes widened, a tiny almost transparent red tornado appeared in the center of the hearth. It was a spinning little funnel of iridescent red dust hardly six inches high. The little tornado began to undulate, steam, and glow brighter.

"Philip Commode!" it cried out again.

Entranced and curious, Philip moved closer to the hearth. The tornado appeared to be kicking up a skirt of ashes around itself. Suddenly the thing pulsated with an unearthly brilliance. In a flash Filly saw the profile of a tiny little figure inside the tornado. It appeared to be a tiny little gentleman with a long, red, two-pronged beard. The face looked strangely familiar even though the man was smaller than a Barbie doll and proportioned more or less like a fire hydrant.

Philip drew closer. The shimmering figure was sitting on what appeared to be an old-style, handcrafted wooden toilet, one of the company's earliest models. The tiny bearded man turned to Philip. He angrily shook his fist in the air. He seemed to be attempting to speak.

"Who are you?" Philip whispered, falling to his hands and knees. "What do you want?"

"I'm Red Nick Commode! Turn off your cell phone, this is important! I came back to earth to give you advice, but they only gave me a couple of damned minutes!" boomed the voice.

"What?" Philip said, trembling, switching off his phone.

"I'm Red Nick Commode! I say you rally the workers!" Red Nick said, lifting his fist in the air. "It's time for the workers to rise! Stir them up, boy! Trust me! Trust the workers! And most of all, trust your own heart!"

Whirling away quickly, the wooden toilet caught fire and began disintegrating. The scowling little man also began disintegrating, flailing his arms as the burning red tornado twisted and whipped up the chimney like a glowing snake, shedding iridescent dust, and then it was gone.

Back at the limousine, the driver was grabbing a smoke. A somewhat shaken Philip Commode found Don Dumper in the back seat momentarily placing a hand over the cell phone.

"I'm trying to get the entire bunch together after lunch today, Mr. Commode," Dumper explained, then turned back to his call. "Well, Bill, yes of course it's unusual but we've got a situation here and we need to get the guys together right away," Dumper said, lifting one finger for silence. "I know it's short notice, but you'll have to bend shop rules, because we've got some very important fellows out here from headquarters, Mr. Commode's son! He's flown out here and wants to talk to all the guys right away," he said, winking at Filly.

A little before two o'clock, the Commode Company's assembly lines ground to a halt. The main plant's floor was crowded with restless working men and women, some of whom had been rousted from their sleep. The workers looked up at a podium raised about fifteen feet from the plant floor, inscribed with the seal of the Make Cleveland Beautiful Foundation. Diego puttered around on the podium, fussing with the microphone. Finally he gave Dumper the high sign.

Without much fanfare, Dumper got up and introduced Philip Commode.

After some polite applause at the mention of his name Philip Commode began talking in a surprisingly assured voice.

Although his knees were jelly, Philip looked great in the business suit. His reedy voice became surprisingly clear and firm, like one of those great black Irish orators, improvising and pounding his fist slowly for emphasis, building momentum and intensity as he went along. It could have been the voice of his fire-breathing socialist ancestor, the old socialist "Red Nick" Commode.

"Workers of the Commode Company, throw off your cloak of ignorance! Corporate rats in California want to eat your lunch! There's a conspiracy underway to take every one of your jobs to China and leave you unemployed! This is not Commode Company tradition! This is not the tradition of America! Therefore! Therefore! You must unite! Do you understand me? You must protest this *now*!" Filly said, his voice trembling, pounding his fist on the podium to stuff down his fear, breathing slowly, finding his true voice as the applause began, a little at first, and then louder.

Workers banged wrenches and pieces of plastic pipe on the sides of toilet bowls and fork lifts all along the assembly line to signal their approval.

Filly went on to tell the workers of a plot to take their jobs away, of secret plans by scheming lawyers, of a mysterious figure from China, and finally he hinted at machinations deep within the Commode Company that wanted to put profits, profits, profits over the greater good, over Commode Company tradition, over the company's unions, and even over the people of America.

"Do you want your jobs exported?" Filly demanded, his voice ringing majestically. "Will you stand for this, will you let all this happen?"

"No," the workers answered, not quite in unison, caught off balance a little by the rhetorical question.

"Will we let corporate rats dismantle our factories, and take good American workers away from their good American jobs?" Filly demanded, shaking his fist in the air.

"No!" the workers answered, more enthusiastically.

"Are we going to put our feet down together and just *stop this*?" Filly asked, stamping his foot.

The workers stamped their feet together, as if on cue.

"Yes!" they screamed.

Filly backed away, wiping his brow with a handkerchief. He had never spoken to a group like this before. He was as surprised as anyone else by the words that had just come out of his mouth. Diego rose to the podium, lifting what appeared to be a clipboard holding several sheets of paper, the petition.

"We've brought a petition for all the workers to sign," Diego announced. "It's titled *A Plea To Keep Good Jobs in Cleveland*. Who will sign first?"

Don Dumper stepped up, fumbling in his pocket pen protector, but he wasn't able to find a pen that worked. After a few awkward seconds, Diego handed him a pen.

"I'm going to sign this first, because I'm with you guys. I started with this company on the shop floor, right where you are, and I think we're all in this one together," Dumper said into the microphone. "China go to hell. We're going to beat this thing. Whatever it takes, we're going to *do it!*" He turned to Filly. "Right, Mr. Commode?"

"That's absolutely positively right!" Filly said, pounding his fist on the podium.

All three union bosses jumped up, pens in hand, as the plant floor exploded with applause.

16. THE SHOWDOWN

The day of the company board meeting, Philip Commode wore a soft brown silk Salvatore Ferragamo suit, with a hand-painted American red tie and matching handkerchief, plus pigskin tassel loafers by Bill Blass. Inside his soft leather Christian Dior briefcase was a copy of the workers' petition and the company bylaws. Anticipating trouble, Filly had given a heads-up to his longtime personal lawyer, L. Michelangelo Leonardo, with whom he just had coffee.

Philip ignored his father's ridiculous saluting doormen with their white uniforms and those tacky gold epaulets and walked right up the old hotel's spiral stairway to the top floor, ten minutes early for a change.

"Miss Gander, I need to talk with Dad privately before the meeting."

"I think Mr. Butterknut already started the meeting," Miss Gander said, with a wincing little smile and a toss of her head. "They're in the conference room."

Philip felt a little ball of anger form in the pit of his stomach. He wished to show his father the petition privately. He planned to quietly and discreetly kill the move to China. But Simon had already started the meeting. Philip took three deep breaths. He felt like a man beginning to run a long and dreary gauntlet.

The conference room was dark as a movie theater inside. An undulating knife of vertical light between the balcony drapes was the only evidence of the warm, balmy day outside. As Philip entered, some kind of video being projected onto one wall stopped.

"Filly, what a nice surprise!" Simon's falsely happy voice exclaimed. "Since you didn't confirm, we started the meeting without you."

Philip Commode felt his way to the conference table in the dark. Somebody was occupying his customary place to the right of his father. He felt the crew-cut head of his brother-in-law, Simon, and took a deep breath.

"Who's sitting in my chair?" Philip demanded.

"Who's sitting in my *chair?*" Simon mockingly repeated.

"Sit here, Philip, next to me, where you can see this informative film," cooed The Doctor.

"Yes, sit down, Philip," Commodore said.

Squeezing his eyes closed, and sitting down next to the glint of the Doctor's ludicrous monocle, Philip made out the flickering shapes of his father, Simon, and the Doctor emerge in a soft bath of reflected light. Philip had been seated at the far end of the table from his father. Since the video had resumed the instant he sat down, it was difficult to make an issue of this treatment.

Across the east wall of the conference room, life-sized Chinese men and women in drab gray uniforms hurried past the camera on their way to work. Some kind of tacky march music played in the background.

NARRATOR (VOICE OVER)
"Three billion people live and work in the People's Republic of China, where the average wage is less than $2 per day..."

"*What* are we watching?" Filly asked.

"An educational video," the Prince replied.

The wall was alive with pictures of sweating, toiling Chinese workers assembling car alarms in a huge gray factory. The film had been speeded up, so it looked like the Chinese were working much faster than American workers, which, in truth, they probably were.

NARRATOR (VOICE OVER)
"Living and working hard as they have for centuries, the men and women of the People's Republic of China have been trained under their highly disciplined government to work hard, and then to bear down when the going get tough, and work even harder!"

Trying to stop the obvious con job, Philip assertively fumbled his way to the video console and found the pause button. The video froze on a shot of a short female worker straining to pick up a pickup truck bumper.

"Wrong!" Philip turned on the lights.

Commodore and the others turned toward Philip, who had his finger on the light switch. They were blinking like a cage full of awakened birds.

"Philip," Simon hissed and blinked. "Okay, in the first place, you didn't confirm and in the second place you're late to the meeting. Aren't you the one who always complains the meetings always run too long? Don't slow us down. Turn the lights off and let's get on with it, please."

"Really, Philip," Commodore said. "Don't be rude.'

"For God's sake, turn those lights down and roll tape!" the Doctor shouted, fingering his stethoscope. "I haven't got all day! I'm going to have an office full of patients!"

"Dad, you're being set up, big time," Philip pleaded with his father. "Don't you get it?"

"Philip! Just turn off the lights and sit down!"

Philip slunk back to his chair, breathing rapidly.

"Thank you very much," the Prince re-started the video.

The wall flickered alive with thousands of identically-dressed Chinese workers in some kind of immense public area, doing Chi Gong exercises together. The workers all wore McDonald's paper hats, lifting their arms simultaneously, in perfect military formation.

NARRATOR (VOICE OVER)
"Chinese workers like to work so much, they even bust a move on their coffee breaks. Take a look at these McDonald's employees at a new McDonald's restaurant in Peking, one of the biggest and most profitable McDonald's outlets in the world...."

"Dad," Philip whispered. "This is complete and utter bullshit."

Simon and the Doctor put their index fingers to their lips as the wall brightened to a long line of polite-looking Chinese men and women who quietly looked longingly at a sign which read "Help Wanted."

NARRATOR (VOICE OVER)
"Ready to snap up any manufacturing job they can find, the hard-working men and women of Shanghai line up to apply for work at a brand new washing machine factory, just relocated from the United States. The people of China want to work. God Bless Free Enterprise! And God Bless America!"

After an image of an American flag undulating in the wind, and the closing bars of 'The Star Spangled Banner', the presentation quietly began to rewind. Miss Gander slipped in to raise the lights.

"Blatant propaganda, Simon?" Philip said. "Where did you find that tacky video?"

"It's from the American Chamber of Commerce!" Simon shouted. "It's totally legitimate. Okay?"

"You fellows be quiet," Commodore interrupted. "Philip, I've just been to China and I've seen a little of what they do over there. Philip, just take a look at your agenda. Simon, get on with this."

The Prince rose to his feet, frightfully full of himself, harrumphing and straightening his tie for much longer than necessary.

"Let me open by saying I'd like to make this quick, because I know you're all busy, especially you, Commodore," Simon began. "And of course the Doctor is always busy and even Philip probably has a little something to do. Let me begin with just a few prepared remarks."

Philip looked pointedly at his watch.

"Let me call your attention to the copies of the letters in your folder from our upper management personnel who support this move. And I've distributed the report from legal affairs which I think you've all seen," he said, lifting a copy of a thick report entitled, *Financial Advantages of Moving Commode Company Factories to China.*

"That report has better supportive data than I see for most of our wonderful new medications," said the Doctor.

"I've never seen that report before," Philip said. "Have you, Dad?"

"I fell asleep trying to finish it last night," Commodore grunted.

"Take my copy, Philip," the Prince said.

"You expect me to read this now? This big old fat four hundred page snow job?"

Philip Commode stood up.

"I don't like this. Is this a business meeting or the rubber stamp club?" Philip Commode demanded. "Why didn't I get this report prior to coming into the meeting? Under whose authority did you solicit those letters? Why did this meeting begin without me? I'm a director of this company, remember? And why didn't anybody tell me about the video, which Simon very rudely started before I arrived, by the way?"

Philip Commode opened his briefcase, extracted the petition, and placed it in front of Commodore.

"Dad, I'm sorry, I had hoped to discuss this with you privately. I brought a petition signed by our Cleveland workers, almost every person who works for us. Even the plant manager signed it. Our workers don't want us to move."

"Is this some sort of propaganda from your *unions?*" the Doctor sneered. "If it's generated by unions, it's suspicious."

Filly held up the petition with one hand, and dramatically thumped his chest with the other. "My name is Philip Commode, Doctor Clipster! I'm descended from Nicholas Commode, who had a vision for this company and all our employees. I think you are all betraying our company's mission!"

"Philip that's quite enough grandstanding," Commodore said. "I already asked you to sit down."

"Dad, we have responsibility here! We've got thousands of people who work for us, people who depend on us for a living. Remember your *employees*, Dad?" Philip shouted, pushing the petition across the table to Commodore. "Dad! Read this!"

The Prince angrily stamped both boots against the floor and stood up. His eyes sparkled as he spread his arms in full courtroom battle position, like an eagle flying in to take control of the meeting.

"Philip, sit down, you've had your say," The Prince said. "Do you want to make a motion, Doctor Clipster?"

The Doctor stood up, adjusting his monocle as he looked down at some notes. "Let me say that the video was enlightening. The excellent Department of Legal Affairs report identifies the reasons why we must move the factories and the sooner the better. I see even our Cleveland managers enthusiastically support the move. For the best interest of all, and of course additional profits, I move we relocate the Commode Company plants to China immediately, within the next year."

"Within the next year?" Philip asked, incredulous. "Are you *crazy?*"

The Doctor nodded curtly and sat down.

"I explained all this to you in my office two days ago, Philip," Simon purred. "Surely you haven't forgotten our little conversation. This is a business decision. Off shoring plants right away allows us to take advantage of substantial tax breaks which expire at the end of the year. Basically, the bottom line will nearly double. Therefore, I second Doctor Clipster's motion."

"So we have a motion before the board, properly moved and seconded," Commodore said, nodding politely.

"I say let's make this unanimous," the Doctor said, glancing at his watch. "I have to get back to the office."

"I vote no! No! No! No! No!" Philip Commode shouted, pounding the conference table. "Over my dead body!"

Commodore was rather taken back. He glanced at the worn old oak gavel which had been handed down through the family, purchased by Nicholas Commode's for the first family board meeting. There was a long tradition of unanimous family voting. It just wouldn't do to break tradition.

"And what about your workers, Dad? Shouldn't they have a voice in this?"

"Sit down, Philip," Commodore said, bringing down his gavel. "There's a motion on the floor. Discussion."

"Don't act like a spoiled petulant child, Philip. Look at the bottom line and use your head."

Philip had already speed-dialed his lawyer. Almost immediately there was knock on the conference room door.

"Who is it?" Commodore asked.

A tall, slender black man in a beautifully-tailored three-piece business suit strode through the door, pulling Miss Gander on his arm like a puzzled dance partner. A whisper of musk followed the tall black barrister into the room.

The Afro-American gentleman had very small ears set far back on his bare, brightly-polished head. In one ear was a large diamond earring. With a twinkle in his eye, the devilishly dapper black man drank in the suspense. He then smiled the slightly ironic smile of a well-seasoned snake-killing legal mongoose.

"Doesn't look like the beautiful little secretary here has ever seen a black man in a business suit before," Leonardo boomed in a full courtroom voice. He winked at Miss Gander. Miss Gander immediately let go of his arm and blushed.

"Who are *you*?" Simon demanded.

Leonardo made conspicuous eye contact with Simon.

"My name is Lawrence Michaengelo Leonardo. I'm Mr. Philip Commode's personal attorney. Mr. Philip Commode has asked me to represent him this afternoon since he anticipates some troublesome legal issues which could arise."

Leonardo laid out business cards before them. The Prince sneered at his card, glanced from side to side, then stood up. He slammed both boots on the floor and rose elbows out, a legal toad in full courtroom battle position.

"Going legal on the family, are you, Filly?" the Prince snarled out of the corner of his mouth. " I thought this was all in the family."

"And for your information, counselor," said the Prince to Leonardo, "This is a closed family board meeting. You'll have to leave now."

"You're technically correct but legally incorrect in this particular instance," Leonardo said, turning to face Simon. "Perhaps I should elaborate?"

Leonardo bopped forward to face the glaring Prince.

"As I read the bylaws of the Commode Corporation, here, paragraph five, they do include all direct line family members in each board meeting, but do not necessarily include husbands or spouses. The bylaws also do not specifically exclude counsel for individual board members, such as my client, Philip Commode, at any particular board meeting. Also, as vice president of legal affairs, Mr. Butterknut, it is my understanding that you, too, are an attorney at law. As such, I notice you're not specifically banned from the board meeting, although perhaps you should be," said Leonardo, smiling.

Leonardo firmly placed one hand on the back of Philip Commode's high-backed chair, and held up his copy of the bylaws with the other. He made solid eye contact with every person in the room, as if winding up a closing argument to a jury.

"That's how I interpret these bylaws, gentlemen. I'm afraid you'll need a restraining order signed by everyone here, including my client, to get me out of the building."

"This is ridiculous!" said the Doctor, reaching for his cell phone. "I'll get a restraining order! I've done work for every trial attorney in California. Michael Jackson's trial attorneys! Larry King's divorce attorneys! Joan Rivers liability attorneys! And *more!*" the Doctor hissed, angrily flipping open his phone.

"Clippy, no," Simon said, waving down the Doctor. "No celebrity attorneys—the media follows those guys everywhere they go. Commodore doesn't ever want any publicity."

"That's right," Commodore agreed. "We don't want anything about this company on TV or in the newspapers."

"Shall we now move to binding arbitration?" Leonardo asked, with a graceful gesture, as if asking Simon to dance. "Shall I give you the number of my good friend Mr. Winthrop J. Peabody, chief of corporate arbitration at the American Arbitration Association, who's expecting my call?"

Commodore stood up with a pained look on his face. The old billionaire surveyed the room. It was a look of neither hatred nor anger, but of something even more primitive and basic. Almost instaneously, Philip detected the stout, masculine smell of flatulence in the air.

"I'm going out to lunch, and I'd suggest the rest of you do the same, Philip," Commodore said. "We need a unanimous vote, and we don't have all day. This meeting is recessed until one o'clock."

❧

Filly and Leonardo took lunch with Diego at Tsunami, a Japanese restaurant with a nice outdoor patio and rock garden. Under colorful Japanese banners, the three men fussed with their food, sipped green tea, and asked the cute little Japanese waiter in Bermuda shorts a great many witty questions about the sushi.

Leonardo daintily held up a California roll on the end of his chopsticks and examined it like it was a strange species of exotic insect before he spoke.

"Without your vote, Philip, they're frozen," Leonardo said. "As long as you hold out, it's stalemate."

"How exciting," Diego smiled, tossing his hair.

"Just hold your ground," Leonardo said, turning to Philip.

Leonardo made quick work of the California roll, then removed the tips of the chopsticks from his mouth.

"They won't like this," Diego predicted.

❧

Commodore and Simon dined at The Embassy Hotel. The Prince had already called Melvin Belli's office in San Francisco and told them to fly down two of their best legal bulldogs.

❧

As soon as they all arrived at company headquarters, the two grey-suited San Francisco attorneys began jousting with Leonardo, who was always game for a fight. Commodore insisted that the lawyers try to talk out their differences in the reception area. Meanwhile, the board meeting reconvened without them in the conference room.

Miss Gander had rolled back the drapes. The afternoon sun streamed through the ivy-covered balcony railing. This glimpse of the sun made Philip yearn for the meeting to conclude. But the minute he saw Simon, he began breathing deeply and vowed not to give in. By four o'clock, all four men were exhausted.

"I move we move the plants to China right away," the Doctor said, lifting his hand as if in a repeating dream.

"Moving immediately allows us to take advantage of tax breaks which expire at the end of the year. It's billions in profit, after taxes. Therefore, I second the motion," said Simon, reciting his lines like a robot on a loop.

"Motion on the floor," Commodore said, pounding the gavel. "Discussion."

"I don't think so," Filly said. "Why don't we put it off until next year?"

"All in favor?" Commodore asked, pounding the gavel.

The Doctor and the Prince raised their hands.

"All opposed?"

"Over my dead body," Philip said, crossing his arms. Every time he spoke, Philip imagined he felt the warm, reassuring hand of Nicolas Commode on his shoulder.

"I temporarily withdraw my motion," said The Doctor, once again avoiding a formal vote count and continuing the stalemate.

"Philip," Commodore pleaded several times, turning to his son. "Be reasonable. You're making a mockery of this process."

"I'd like to speak to my lawyer before I answer any questions or make any statement about this *process*," Philip said.

"Oh for God's sakes!" Simon cawed, flapping his arms like a crow. "Little fairy got to speak to his *lawyer*?"

"Simon, please," Commodore cautioned.

Simon glowered at Philip. Miss Gander hurried into the room with another pot of coffee and a pained expression.

"Let's just not kill the goose that laid the golden egg," Filly whispered.

"Kill the goose?" the Prince said. "We're making omelets!"

"My office girls don't have a union, and they're all happy," said the Doctor. "It's not a union kind of world anymore, Philip. I move we move the plants to China right away."

"Second," the Prince said.

Filly crossed his arms.

"Withdraw the motion."

And on it went, a clumsy corporate two-step, with Philip stubbornly holding his ground. The motion was withdrawn and introduced several more times before Commodore mercifully adjourned the meeting shortly before 10:30, his bedtime.

"We're all going to take this weekend off, and we're going to think this through," Commodore announced.

"Philip, you and your lawyer take a copy of that report and read it. Simon, have your staff look over that petition. On Monday morning, we're coming back here at exactly 10 o'clock and we're going to finish this up immediately, and I mean immediately," Commodore stated. "Okay?"

It was not really a question.

The richest family in America filed dejectedly out of the conference room into the arms of their lawyers, with no resolution in sight.

17. Cleveland Calling

Cold spring snow fell down on Cleveland. Gusts of light spring snow scampered across the highway. Cars and trucks sloshed past the old Commode Company factories with their headlights on, scattering slush. The old factories themselves were preparing to go dark, for the first time in more than one hundred and thirty years.

Don Dumper stood fidgeting next to the plant gate, which was wide open. Dumper was simultaneously looking over his shoulder, making an emergency long distance call, and trying to smoke a damp cigarette. The shoulders of the plant manager's plain winter overcoat were already covered with epaulets of snow.

As if on cue, a tall, steaming Commode Company delivery truck sloshed to a stop at the gate with its lights and windshield wipers on and honked loudly. The truck was filled with workers in heavy winter coats. Beneath their coats, a few of them wore short-sleeved Hawaiian shirts and Bermuda shorts, since they were headed for the legendary land of California.

Another big Commode Company truck immediately sloshed to a stop and honked behind them, filled with more workers, and behind that another and another, creating a long string of double headlights that disappeared into the drifting snow. The drivers of the trucks were union stewards. Beneath their baseball caps, many had Poncho Villa moustaches and long, wavy, blue collar hair chopped off flat just above the collar, biker style. The union drivers impatiently revved their engines as Dumper waved his damp cigarette for quiet.

"It's an organizational miracle but we got all the boys ready to roll right now, Mr. Philip," Dumper shouted into the cell phone, wiping a bit of snow off his cheek. He took a quick suck of his wet cigarette, made a face, and then flipped the wet cigarette away.

Dumper put his finger in his other ear so he could hear over the honking. He nodded his head yes two or three times in rapid succession.

"Hell, yes. We're even bringing a couple of the old guys worked on the line with old Mr. Commode," Dumper shouted.

Pete and Dewey, a pair of white-haired old timers about Commodore's age, stood a few feet behind Dumper bundled up in the blowing snow, nodding their assent.

"Boy, do we remember Commodore," Pete croaked.

"Called him one-beer Commie," Dewey added. "Of course, that was a long time ago."

Pete lit a cigarette with a Zippo lighter, and handed the cigarette to Dumper. Dumper absentmindedly took the cigarette, inhaled, and squatted and squinted to hear.

The snowstorm intensified, softening and muffling the sound of the impatiently honking horns. Airy batches of snowflakes swirled in strange patterns past the three men, clustering in the air, rising up from their feet, borne by the wind, depositing snowflakes onto what was left of their hair.

"By God, yes, we'll drive all night and day if we have to or we'll die trying, yes sir, yes sir, yes sir, Mr. Commode," Dumper said, nodding and shutting up the cell phone.

A meandering snowflake swiveled down onto the lit end of Dumper's cigarette, and put it out. Dumper looked at his wet cigarette, made a face, and flung it dramatically down onto the snow.

White snowflakes stuck to his eyebrows, giving him the look of some kind of operatic character. A scowl of determination hardened his features for a decisive moment as he appeared to think. Then Dumper stood up and waved his arm in a big half circle over his head, as if leading his troops forward into a battle as old as time itself.

"We're *all* going to California!" he said.

Dumper jumped into his green Ford Taurus, where a small American flag haad been fastened with duct tape to the aerial. Pete and Dewey jumped in the back seat. Dumper fish-tailed away in the snow and the slush, headed west, and the plastic flag unfurled above him.

The trucks groaned into first gear, spun their tires in the slush, then rumbled and splashed and banged out onto the old highway.

They headed west two hundred and forty headlights strong, their windshield wipers laboring hard to fling off the wet, rapidly-falling snow.

⁂

Halfway around the world, Long Drive Loo stood on the high stone bridge that arched across her palace's largest fishpond. Looking over the still water in her fashionable antique red and gold silk smoking jacket.

Miss Loo's black hair was ornately done up with what looked like porcelain chopsticks whose polished whiteness matched the white of her heavily powdered face, and the bright red of her lipstick. Holding a long lacquered porcelain cigarette holder in one hand, the beautiful Miss Loo enjoyed an imported American cigarette. Exhaling dreamily over the still water, she could have been a Ming Dynasty princess at leisure.

A white and gold Manchurian carp almost 6-feet long swam in the pool below her feet, in graceful circles. Favorite fish finally lifted its head out of the water, opened big mouth.

In her free hand, the beautiful Miss Loo held up a nugget of warm rice and live shrimp, the size of a golf ball, which she waved over the water, teasing the fish. When Miss Loo dropped the rice ball, the huge fish flashed through the pond and took it like a trout the moment it hit the water. Miss Loo smiled as the big fish hungrily thrashed and splashed its way to the deepest part of the pond, to greedily devour her gift.

Miss Loo had a woman's intuitive feel for the situation far away in California. She was certain that the old billionaire would move his plants to Shanghai, and after that, probably even ask her to marry him. He was foolish old man, she thought, probably die soon. There would be a fight with his children over the money. Before she agreed to marry, she would find good American lawyer... she would refuse to marry the old capitalist unless he put aside the foolish American custom of pre-nuptial agreements....

Miss Loo's No. 1 Aunt hurried out onto the patio and up the bridge, taking small polite steps with the vibrating American lawyer cell phone on a lacquered tray. Long Drive unfolded up the little American phone and listened.

"Long Drive?" the Prince's voice crackled.

To make the call in utmost secrecy, the Prince had called on a recently-purchased thousand dollar cell phone, but it wasn't any better than his old one. The Bastard Prince was cursed with poor cell phone reception almost everywhere he went. The new phone's sweet spot seemed to shift by the minute, and the Prince had to feel his way to one side or another to follow the elusive signal out of his home gymnasium and all the way across the back lawn.

Like a fish on the end of a line, the Prince had followed the meandering sweet spot across the bridge to the sties of Pig Island, the only place at his mansion where the cell phone reception seemed to be any good at 3:20 a.m. California time.

Above the Prince, a waxing moon showered Pig Island with pale yellow moonlight. A sleeping pig rolled and grunted in the straw at his feet, apparently having a bad dream. A few other pigs slept here and there, rooting in the hay and snoring loudly.

The pigs had been fed shortly before dark, Simon knew. What Petunia called her Poop Patrol didn't pick up until first thing in the morning. The entire feeding area already reeked of ammonia. Simon had twice put his immaculately-shined Tony Lamas into fresh pig patties.

The Prince was dodging and weaving to keep the signal clear to China. On the way out to Pig Island, he'd already been through several international operators who didn't speak much English and almost lost connections to finally get connected to Miss Loo in what was supposed to be a secret phone call.

"Who call Long Drive?" Miss Loo sang dreamily.

"Simon Butterknut, vice president of legal affairs with the Commode Company in Santa Barbara, California, as if you didn't know," the Prince hissed. "I gave you the phone, remember?"

"Yes," she sang, "Hello."

"You better get out here right away and make a personal appeal to the old man. We got a problem with the approvals."

"No approvals, no bonus for you," Miss Loo sang. "Empty plants for Long Drive, empty bonus check for you and Number 1 brother-in-law."

Extracting a second ball of rice from her feeding pouch and holding it over the water, she added, "Very sorry, I think, because maybe more company want plants now."

Like all Chinese, Miss Loo knew that the way to throw any American off balance was to tell them the situation had become competitive. The heady smell of competition aroused American businessmen to great heights, she knew.

Businessmen went after profits like dogs in heat—a hint of competition quickly destroyed the vaunted American common sense. The idea that somebody else wanted what they were after led the Americans to blindly up the ante and offer concessions that Chinese businessmen would never dream of requesting.

"No! Long Drive!" Simon said. "We can pull it off but I need help. You've got to get out here and work on Commodore. The problem is Philip, Commodore's son. The little faggot's hanging onto his veto like—" but the Prince's heart sank as he realized his voice was fading away in a puff of crackling international static.

"I no understand ... your voice too weak now," said Miss Loo's voice, also crackling with static.

Chasing the sweet spot, Simon quickly stepped to one side. Sadly, he stepped between the legs of a male pig that had been sleeping spread-eagled on its back. The surprised little boar kicked out all four legs and squealed with anger.

The sound itself was amazing. Simon had never heard a pig squeal like that before.

The little pig stood up, hobbling angrily toward the lake, emitting a high-pitched wounded squeal of pain all the way into the water. Simon stood frozen for a moment, mesmerized by the horrible, haunting, high-pitched sound which would probably wake Petunia.

"I hang up now," Miss Loo crackled. "Call back tomorrow."

"No!" Simon hissed. "No! Wait!"

But Miss Loo hung up.

In a panic, Simon suddenly forgot how to redial his new phone. They'd given him a lesson at the phone store, but his mind was now completely blank. Fortunately he still had his instruction booklet, and a small flashlight. The little instruction booklet was smaller than a book of matches, and tightly folded, of course.

The Prince tried to unfold the tiny paper-thin little booklet full of nearly indecipherable little charts and writing with his clumsy fingers, while also hunched over trying to prevent the glare of his tiny flashlight from being seen from Petunia's bedroom.

"Does a thief in the night dare to disturb even peacefully sleeping animals who have harmed no man?" wafted the befuddled voice of Petunia, who had come downstairs and thrown open the back door.

Simon saw his wife shining a flashlight through the trees out toward Pig Island. One of the Mexican maids stood next to Petunia, with a second flashlight.

"What man dares trespass on Pig Island? " Petunia cried. "Answer immediately or I shall have my husband, the vice president of legal affairs at the Commode Company, call the police!"

"It's me, honey," Simon whispered loudly, trying to read the instructions while holding the tiny phone between his ear and his shoulder.

The Prince wanted to shout to his wife, to tell her there was no problem, but he had to finish the vitally important business call. Petunia didn't know the details of his secret arrangement with Miss Loo.

Petunia triggered the alarm system. A loud, ominous siren began wailing. Flares fizzled up into the air over Simon like burning rubies. High in the palm fronds, security floodlights began flashing. The parrots woke up angrily flapping their wings against the fronds of the palm trees, and squawking and relieving themselves on the restless pigs below. All around Simon, sleeping little pigs began waking up and grunting to their feet.

"Honey it's *me*!" Simon shouted, but his call was lost in the wail of the sirens, and could not be heard from the house.

Miraculously he found the tiny redial button, and re-dialed Miss Loo. Miraculously, an immediate connection.

"It's Simon Butterknut. For God's sake don't hang up!"

"You hang up! American hang up!"

"Long Drive! Listen! I need you here!"

"Where?" she asked.

"You've got to come to California, right away," the Prince hissed.

"Flight take one day," Miss Loo said, pausing to inhale. "Very expensive."

Simon didn't immediately identify the new sound, the crashing sound of military boots through brush. He didn't immediately realize that what he heard was the approach of a squadron of buffed-up Pig Island security people, ex-Green Berets and professional wrestlers who all could pick up a hundred-pound boar with one hand.

"Go to the airport right now!" Simon cried. "We've taken care of everything!"

When he glanced over his shoulder, Simon suddenly recognized the flying Pig Island Security Guards. They seemed to be suspended in the air for a moment, like beefed-up cartoon characters over the suddenly frozen, panic-stricken pigs.

Before Simon could open his mouth they fell on him, wrestled him roughly and rudely to the straw, and twisted one leg behind his back. Just before they covered his mouth with their muddy hands, the Prince tried to shout for Petunia. In the primitive struggle for domination that took place on the floor of the sty, one of the security guards bit him on the ear.

※

Commodore Commode was having a bad night. The old billionaire was worried. After dinner, Commodore had turned off all the phones and poured himself half a glass of brandy. He didn't drink much of it, but it did relax him a little to slosh the brandy around the bottom of the big bell-shaped crystal brandy snifter, and quietly inhale the thick rich fumes.

He paced through his suite of bedrooms in a blue satin bathrobe, occasionally farting. The moment the old capitalist heard the familiar cry of the Golden Weeha, however, his entire body froze. He immediately rang for his faithful valet.

It was more than irritating that the Chinese monkey Miss Loo gave him as a love gift chattered up a storm every night. The hairy little angel of love had caused nothing but trouble at Commodora.

The Japanese gardeners put together a nice little bamboo tree house for the monkey as soon as it arrived, and artfully hung the bamboo cage from the limb of one of the Eucalyptus trees near the golf course. But the first night the Weeha chewed its way out of the cage and had to be recaptured near the ninth hole. The monkey chewed through the bars of the swinging cage three times when Commodore was in Europe with Miss Loo. Each escape triggered a frantic search of the grounds and sent the Japanese gardeners into still another panic.

After recapturing the monkey for the third time, the gardeners abandoned the outdoor cage. Fearing they'd lose the Weeha, which they understood was a special gift to their employer, the Japanese gardeners pushed aside the other servants and locked the howling beast and its shipping cage into a suite of unused bedrooms at the far end of the mansion, where it more or less remained until Commodore and R.G. returned.

Commodore had learned for himself that the Golden Weeha had a supremely irritating way of crying out a few hours after the sun went down.

The young Chinese veterinarian called to assess the situation shook his head sadly when he peeped into the bedroom at the sullen Weeha, who again had an erection. As the veterinarian explained, during the long mating season in the mountains of China, the Golden Weehas become very sexually active at night. The males were programmed to let out a series of ear-splitting mating calls, trying to wake up the notoriously drowsy Weeha females, as a prelude to sex in the trees. If no females Weehas responded, the love-starved male Weehas often cried out plaintively for love all night long.

"Shut that damned monkey up!" Commodore shouted as R.G. glided past him in the hallway, already hurrying toward the sound.

Commodore presumed the old valet was carrying one of the pricey imported Chinese coconuts the vet recommended, which cost nearly seven hundred dollars apiece. The coconuts had to be warmed in a sort of Tandoori oven they'd moved into one of the bedrooms until their odor was irresistible. The sad, shriveled-up red coconuts, whose smell was identical to a female Weeha in heat, silenced the horny Weeha for the three or four hours it took him to crack and eat them. After that, the high tryptophan coconut meat helped the Weeha fall sleep.

R.G. would be carefully opening the door to the corner bedroom at that moment, Commodore knew. The old valet would carefully roll the hairy little coconut into the room toward the howling beast, and close the door. Before the coconut rolled to a stop, the little monkey would pounce on it with all four paws—snapping, slobbering, and slashing. Unable to bite through the thick coconut skin right away, the Weeha would eventually stop crying out and begin trying to figure out how to open it.

The muscular little monkey would smash and smash the hard-shelled coconut against the marble floor, the walls, even against some piece of Louis XIV furniture or other, desperately, then methodically, until the tough little red coconut shell broke into pieces, spilling its fragrant elixir. The greedy little monkey would slurp up as much milk as possible and carry coconut chunks back into its cage, one piece at a time. When all the coconut pieces were piled into a corner of the cage, the beast would lock itself inside the cage, turn its back to the wall, and cautiously commence eating.

As the Golden Weeha fell silent, Commodore recounted the troubling events of the day. He could not believe the level of bunk at the board meeting. Philip! Simon! Bylaws! Two sets of lawyers! The old billionaire had a headache just thinking about it. On Monday morning, he resolved, after he had time to think the matter through, he would put his foot down and get it all resolved.

As he restlessly paced his chambers, sniffing brandy and passing gas in his bathrobe, the old billionaire fretted for the future of his family.

At the bustling Shanghai airport, Long Drive Loo got out of the limousine and walked toward an enormous China Airways Concorde jet. Several frazzled-looking family members, following behind, carried her luggage and golf clubs.

In the middle of the night, working behind the scenes, Commode Company lawyers had bribed several key officials in the Communist government, which owned the airlines. Later the lawyers would comment that the Chinese officials were amazingly anxious to be brought into the plot.

The Concorde was the only aircraft in Shanghai that was big enough to make the trip to California quickly, in one hop, on short notice. The plane seated several hundred people, but they'd all been given government vouchers and formal apologies after government officials cancelled their flight.

As smaller jets took off and landed in the distance, several hundred bumped Asian passengers glumly watched Miss Loo and her entourage hurry toward the Concord, and exchanged significant glances.

Miss Loo selected a seat in the middle of the big airplane, on an aisle near the wing. There were no other passengers except for her faithful government escort caddy who sat quietly in the back of the plane. As the Concorde rumbled up the runway, well-trained stewards and stewardesses stood respectfully at their stations near the front of the aisles, showing the oxygen masks and life vests to a plane full of imaginary Chinese passengers, explaining everything along with the video that was subtitled in three Chinese dialects, as well as English, Russian, and Japanese.

After the plane took off with a roar, three neat young Chinese stewardesses pushed a stainless steel cart full of sodas and refreshments toward their only passenger. The chattering young girls were trim and white as matching China dolls.

"You very important lady," one said, bowing slightly.

"Whole plane for you, very important lady," the first smiled, bowing respectfully. "You very special passenger."

"You like peanut bag now?" another asked.

The third stewardess lifted a porcelain teapot. "You like fresh tea now?" she asked. When Miss Loo nodded yes, she poured and asked, "We show you moofy now?"

"What movie?"

"It's Wonderful Lie American moofy," the fourth stewardess responded, bowing slightly. "American moofy classic, three dialect subtitle."

"No moofy," Miss Loo said, leaning back like a queen and dreamily sipping her tea. "Bring rice wine now."

Somewhere over the Pacific, after she woke up and asked for more rice wine, a stewardess put a small perfumed pillow under Miss Loo's weary head. As she carefully plumped the pillow, the girl smiled a smile of innocence itself, the smile of a beautiful young girl who wanted only to make an older woman happy, and show proper respect.

The girl reminded Miss Loo of herself many years ago, before Mao's fourth wife discovered her on a government golf course in the middle of the night, a small girl obsessively whacking a rock around the golf course with a bamboo stick under the half light of the moon.

"Life easier when I young," Miss Loo drowsily confided to the stewardess. "Now big family, many problem. Factories empty, family want factory full. Americans call me, I go right away America."

The young stewardess nodded sympathetically, pouring the renowned golfer another small glass of rice wine.

Miss Loo downed the glass in one quick flick of her head, then handed the surprised girl the empty glass, indicating that she wanted another.

"No more pro golf, no more pleasure me," Miss Loo said, her eyelids closing. "All life big business now."

Nuzzling the scented pillow, Miss Loo dreamed she was flying through the night on the back of a dark muscular bird. The bird circled down onto an island containing a strange golf course covered with pale, shimmering snow and tall, ice-covered trees. A cold silver moon appeared, lighting up the golf course with cool blue moonlight.

Stepping onto what she instinctively knew was the final tee, Miss Loo realized with a start that she was on a different sort of golf course. The long winding fairway rose in graceful curves into the sky at the end of which was the luminous moon itself. It was an impossibly long drive, but Long Drive Loo had always been a competitor who could rise to the occasion.

Red-faced comrades in uniforms of gray ice lined the fairway, frozen respectfully in place. Long Drive did not look into their faces, but she knew they were all very important people who wanted Long Drive to succeed.

A monkey swung down on an ice-covered vine with a strangely glowing pouch in its paw. It dropped the pouch at her feet, bared its teeth, and disappeared in a puff of smoke.

Miss Loo's black hair blew romantically back and forth in the cold, unearthly wind as she stooped to open the pouch. The golf ball inside was soft and curiously fluid, a bit larger than normal, and it appeared to be made of rice and water. Placing the quivering ball on the tee, Miss Loo took a deep breath, carefully focused her thoughts on the far end of the fairway, and hit the longest shot she'd ever hit in her life.

Her drive whipped past her impassive comrades like the irradiated hammer of Thor, rising up and over the long curves of the fairway, bouncing end over end up and toward the shimmering silver platter of the moon as if it would never stop. Then, to her surprise, she heard a small distant "clink." The moon had cracked like a pane of thin glass. The moon's slim broken fragments began a slow spinning descent to earth. All down the fairway, shards of moon glass as big as Redwood trees struck the earth. The implacable faces of her comrades slowly turned away, with looks of supreme disgust.

Miss Loo awoke with a start, gasping for breath as the Concorde began its descent to California.

❧

Lifting her perfect chin a bit, Clementine Commode-Clipster paused on the landing of her mansion and smiled expectantly, like a model holding for applause. Then she tinkled down the stairs toward the Doctor in a hundred and fifty thousand dollar outfit.

Clementine's little Jack Russell terriers followed her, a tiny fan club at her feet. Sensitive to her every move, the dogs shifted and turned as she posed expectantly before her husband. However, the Doctor appeared to have fallen asleep at the foot of the stairs, with his long nose in a book.

"How does the Doctor like *this*?" Clementine asked loudly, holding her pose for effect.

After fashion week in Milan, Clementine came back with several million dollars in expensive dresses. This one, by a hot new Croatian designer who was deconstrucing the ghetto cool popular in the United States, was artfully studded with mattress padding and pictures of cigarette butts. The dress was cut up very high to the crotch, but the sides of the dress draped down to Clementine's shapely ankles. Her ankles were attached to the end of the skirt with two anklets of small brass gypsy bells. To the tinkle of Clementine's bells, the Doctor awoke with a gasp in his lounge chair near the foot of the stairs, somewhat disoriented.

It was Saturday night. The Doctor had been trying to simultaneously read Simon's tedious report and answer two important new e-mail memos from his advertising firm.

Overwhelmed by the work load, the Doctor had fallen asleep. As his imaginary daughters danced away in his dreams, the Doctor adjusted his monocle and focused on Clementine. Clutching his stethoscope, and pretending to be awake, he squinted happily at his wife on the landing. Clemmie was obviously holding for applause.

"It's just beautiful, darling," the Doctor said. The Doctor was not unaware that he was lying between his teeth. Long ago he learned that he had to compliment Clementine several times, because it took a while for even the most over-the-top flattery to penetrate her thick skull. Or perhaps she just preferred multiple compliments. The Doctor didn't truly consider this lying, since his celebrity clients demanded to be treated in exactly the same fashion.

"You don't really like it."

"Oh yes, I certainly do. It's stunning. It's gorgeous."

"Does the Doctor really and truly like it?"

"The Doctor thinks it's beautiful, marvelous, stunning, absolutely, a straight up and down yes. Any surgeon could see the way that fabric clings to your body is breathtaking."

"But does Baron Barrie Clipster like it, too?"

"Let Baron Clipster assure you that your gown is perfect," said the Doctor, snorting and adjusting his monocle for effect. "You wear that gown like a queen!"

Clemmie's eyes lit up. She tried to smile.

"Let me show you another one," she said, hurrying back up the stairs. The dogs danced up the stairs behind her.

The Doctor opened Simon's report, and sighed again. The report was crammed with mind-numbing statistics. The Doctor had a feeling he should call Michael Jackson's lawyer, fax him the report, pay him to read it, and put him on standby just in case. But it was late in the game, and Nutty was calling the shots. Despite appearances, the Doctor was sure his fast-talking old fraternity brother had things entirely under control.

Saturday night was Rhinestone Cowboy Night at Hernando's Hideaway. The sign over the front door said "Welcome, Rhinestone Cowboys!" The bartenders and waiters all wore short neckerchiefs and paper cowboy hats, as did most of the customers.

Filly, Diego, and Leonardo had finished dinner. After two air kisses, Leonardo picked up his briefcase and bopped away under his paper cowboy hat, like a dark, well-dressed wrangler into the heart of Saturday night.

On the far side of the bar, several balding gay men in little cowboy hats huddled around a television set, watching the National Basketball Association playoffs. When one team made a basket, the couple in purple Cowboy hats stood up and cheered. Each time the two in yellow hats stood up, flailing the air with their hats, one of them managed to knock over a pitcher of beer. Each time, Hernando looked up from the bar like a startled hippopotamus. His jowls twitched under his pencil thin moustache.

"Clean it up, *cowboys!*" Hernando hissed. He pushed his cowboy hat back on his head and ominously fingered his lei.

Suddenly the television set began smoking, an ominous portent of things to come. Outside the front door, adjusting his cowboy hat, Simon Butterknut prepared to burst into Hernando's, a big man looking for trouble. Flanked by his San Francisco lawyers in matching gray business suits, the vice president of legal affairs wore a western outfit of fringed leather that clung tightly to his body, like Alan Ladd in "Shane." The Prince's big cowboy hat was a little too large for his head and could not quite conceal the band-aid on one ear.

Simon kicked open the bar door, holding onto his hat. The two gray-haired lawyers entered first, glaring from side to side and baring their expensive teeth as if expecting a sudden attack from either side. The suited-up lawyers made a bizarre accompaniment to the Prince, who at least had gone country western.

Simon strutted toward the bar, swinging his hips in the manner of a Western gunslinger. He paused beside the fish tank, blinked, and searched the darkness.

"I'm a-looking for Philip Commode," Simon barked from the other side of the fish tank.

Filly looked up. Diego looked up, too.

"What do you want from Philip Commode, cowboy?" Diego lisped, tossing his hair to one side as he stood up. "Haven't you done enough already?"

"Me and my boys want a do a little confidential talkin' with young Mr. Philip," Simon barked, turning toward Diego's voice on the other side of the fish tank, and pushing back his hat. "Outside."

"Our client's in a hurry and he's fully represented, pal," the shorter of the two lawyers, Feinstein, hissed across the bubbling water. Simon and his lawyers were ominously lit from below, giving them a shimmering otherworldly look.

"Young Mr. Philip, as you maliciously call him, is currently indisposed," Diego lisped, in a loud but quavering voice. "I'm sorry. Mr. Philip has a headache."

"Shall I call Leonardo?" Diego whispered, bending down.

Philip shook his head no. Slowly, Philip Commode stood up next to his partner.

Philip was rather flagrantly dressed. He adjusted the floppy wide-brimmed black felt hat that most Americans associate with the French artist, Toulouse Le Trec. Then he threw one end of his black cape lined with red satin back over his shoulder, a gesture of supreme contempt. As an artist, he was not ashamed to be caught in drag. The hat was not quite cowboy, but Philip knew his makeup was perfect.

"Lose the lawyers, Simon," Filly hissed, stepping carefully out of the booth.

Across the room Simon's high-hatted head and shoulders of the appeared to be floating over the fish tank.

Philip put his hand on his phone, prepared to speed dial Leonardo if necessary. It was so quiet you could hear the bubbler in the fish tank, and the heavy breathing sports fans. Both Simon and Filly looked ominous and warlike to each other. Both seemed to frighten the rapidly-swimming fish.

"I'll get rid-a my boys, if'n you gettin' ridda your'n," Simon said. His lawyers pressed forward against his extended arm.

"Diego is *not* my lawyer," Filly said.

"Why I get ridda of my boys, your boy stayin'?" Simon grunted. Philip could almost hear Simon's imaginary horse outside, stamping its feet and snorting. It was almost a little too much Rhinestone Cowboy.

Filly turned to Diego, and raised one eyebrow. Diego read his intent immediately.

Diego danced elegantly around the fish tank toward the two lawyers, shooing them away with a sweeping motion of his hands, like a fishwife chasing away flies. Diego linked arms with the two lawyers and pulled them toward the door.

"We're *all* out of here now," Diego said.

The lawyers cringed and shied away as they moved toward the door, unaccustomed to physical contact. Looking from side to side, adjusting their ties and grimacing nervously, the lawyers looked at each other, then at Simon, then at Diego, then at Filly. With their backs to the front door, recovering their composure, they bared their teeth like vicious dogs. Even in San Francisco, the two lawyers had never encountered clients like this before.

Simon smiled a wicked smile, placed a toothpick in his mouth, pushed back his hat, and put his elbows on the rim of the fish tank. As the copious fringe on his sleeve slipped into the water, fish began to circle the fringe, snapping nervously.

At that moment Filly smelled a strange animal odor wafting across the water from Simon. He did not immediately recognize the smell of pig manure.

"And by the way, *where* did you get that after shave?" Filly asked.

Philip defiantly lifted his chin, staring down his nose at his brother-in-law. Although he appeared flippant, he was trembling inside. Among other things, Philip wondered what the water vapor was doing to his mascara.

"Why not join this here posse, little fella?" Simon asked. "We galloping off to China tonight."

"Because it's my family's company," Philip Commode replied, acknowledging the ball of fear in his stomach, but breathing slowly and gathering courage as he spoke. "We don't belong in China. Besides, what you're trying to do is against Commode Company principles. You will rob thousands of good-hearted, loyal American workers of their jobs. If all our workers get fired, how will they buy our products? Besides, I don't trust that Chinese woman. I don't like the way she's throwing herself at Dad."

"Whatsa little China doll got to do with this here billion dollar wagon train rolling off to Eldorado?" Simon said, working the toothpick between his teeth.

"She's working hand in hand with *you*, isn't she?" Filly hissed.

Filly's instinctive shot for the jugular connected. Simon rocked back on his heels and took the toothpick out of his mouth, as if shaking off a punch.

The blue and gold fish let go of his fringe and some of them splashed back into the water.

"Old Mr. Commode he do fancy that little China lady," Simon said.

"Old Mr. Commode fancied my mother, too, even after he was married to her for thirty-seven years, *cowboy*," Filly spat back. " My mother didn't ask Dad to abandon the country that adopted us and made us all rich. No, *cowboy*, Milly Rockefeller Commode loved her children, she loved her husband, she loved her husband's company, and she loved this country, too," Philip Commode said. "It's my country, and Simon, by the way, it's your country, too. Don't betray it."

Simon turned an odd shade of red. Despite his legal training, his meticulous preparation, and his naturally argumentative nature, Simon could not think of a good comeback to what his half-baked brother-in-law had just said. The Prince turned on his boot heels and walked out of the bar, his big jingle-jangle hat following him out the door.

"Turn the god damn television set back on!" somebody shouted from the back room.

Sports fans in paper cowboy hats began pounding loudly on their tables with empty plastic pitchers of beer.

18. A Warm Spring Day

Monday was a warm spring day in Santa Barbara, the kind of day when it seemed all the problems of the world could amicably be resolved with a little heart-to-heart conversation under the shade of an old Sycamore tree.

At the entrance to Commode Company headquarters, Philip Commode casually tossed his crème-colored cashmere jacket over his shoulders, in the manner of an Italian businessman. At his side, in a chartreuse Zoot suit, Leonardo could have stepped out of the pages of a hip-hop fashion magazine. Leonardo pointed out the camera crew he had hired, filming their entrance. The crew at that moment included Diego, who sat on his Vespa just behind the cameraman, watching their arrival broadcast on his cell phone. The cameraman gave Leonardo the high sign.

"In law school, we call this the Mike Wallace defense," Leonardo chuckled, alluding to a famous muckraking television reporter of the day. Ignoring the saluting doorman, lawyer and client walked inside.

A short time later, Old Commodore Commode walked into the conference room with a determined look on his face.

"Hello," Commodore grunted, and sat down.

Simon waved hello with a little too much bravado. The Doctor glanced meaningfully at his watch. Philip sat next to The Doctor with his arms crossed, glumly staring straight ahead. Miss Gander quietly slipped past the lawyers in the reception area and into the reception room with a pot of coffee and an array of mints on a silver tray.

"Now let's get this show underway," said Commodore, after he had sipped his coffee. "We've all had two days to think about it, and I would like this finished up today," Commodore said, rapping the gavel. "Simon."

"Thank you, Commodore. My staff informs me that these so-called petitions have no legal standing with the board. Several signatures, perhaps hundreds, are probably forged. Since the petitions aren't valid or even relevant, I say button it up and let's look at moving the plants," said Simon. "We've identified locations in China, we've negotiated excellent terms. The tax climate is favorable. And Petunia likes the idea of vacationing in China, too, Commodore, by the way."

"I happily second the motion," the Doctor said, turning to Commodore and smiling. "Clementine thinks a trip to the developing fashion centers of the Orient every now and then would be a good idea, too."

"I think it's a *hideous* idea," Philip said, rising to his feet. Simon and the Doctor rolled their eyes. "Dirty old ocean tankers polluting the air and ocean, shipping our products back to where they should have been made in the first place?"

"Our products are made in America," Philip said, somewhat desperately. "Additional *profit*, Dad? It's only money."

"Only *money?*" The Doctor made a sour face.

"Two billion a year is *only money?*" Simon asked.

"How much more does our company need? What's the point? We're profitable now."

"Didn't you read the research report?" the Doctor asked.

"Oh, poop. Did you?"

The Doctor angrily fingered his stethoscope. Commodore banged the gavel, and stood up, pointing with the gavel.

"No, no, no, Philip! Simon! No more talk! We've got to come to an agreement. I'm not letting you out of here until we all agree on this."

"It's now or never, and damn the torpedoes!" the Prince slammed both boots onto the ground and stood up. "Philip, didn't you hear me explain the tax breaks we can get? Those tax breaks run *out* at the end of the year?"

"Pee on your little tax breaks," Filly said.

"Philip!" Commodore said. "What would your mother think of that unseemly language?"

Philip's face softened at the mention of his beloved mother. He sat down, crestfallen. For a moment, Simon thought the little fairy was going to cry.

"Let's put it this way, Philip," the Prince cooed, pressing his advantage.

"Dr. Clipster and I will support whatever your father wishes to do. We support any good business decision that will support our bottom line, and in this particular case I think Commodore knows what that business decision is."

"I'll support any decision Commodore and Simon believe is correct," The Doctor said. "But will you, Philip, support the rest of the family and just make it unanimous?"

Miss Gander knocked twice and scurried into the room. She leaned over Commodore's shoulder and whispered discreetly, "There's a Miss Loo waiting for you in a limousine downstairs. She's asking for you and she says it's an emergency"

"Miss Loo? Here? Now?" Commodore stood up, suddenly puzzled and energized, and lumbered out of the room.

"Where's Dad going?" Philip asked Miss Gander.

❧

Miss Loo smiled stiffly as the old billionaire got into the limousine, looking somewhat surprised. Her beefy Asian driver in the chauffeur's hat stared straight ahead.

"Must talk, private, you, me, important," Miss Loo said, tapping on the limousine window. "Camera watching everything, taping now," she said, pointing outside. "Look."

Out the window, Commodore saw the camera crew crouching and approaching the limousine, as if stalking a bear. The publicity-shy old billionaire reacted with a look of abject horror. His face turned white.

"Driver, big house, go, now!" Miss Loo barked.

Miss Loo pulled down the limousine's white plastic shade as her limousine sped away at the speed of light.

❧

A mud-spattered Ford Taurus led a caravan of company trucks west across the Mojave Desert. The black desert highway cut a perfectly straight black line through the barren otherworldly desert landscape. On either side of the highway were the remains of unidentifiable animals, sickly-looking cactus, and half-dead Joshua trees.

Seen from above, the caravan crept up the long straight asphalt highway like a thin line of ants. At the head of the procession, Don Dumper talked on his cell phone to Philip Commode.

"They had to check every damned truck we had for fruit before they let us across the border, held us up looking for bananas and beans, I can't tell you," Dumper said, mopping his brow with a big white handkerchief and looking outside. "Still checking trucks but we're coming without them."

"For God's sake, hurry up," Filly whispered. "Dad just stepped out for a minute. And you're three hours away."

❧

To play golf was Miss Loo's idea. Commodore supposed it was some sort of ice-breaker to relax her before she spoke of whatever business she had flown in to discuss. The day was gone except for the board business and that wasn't going well.

"Reporting for golf duty, sir," R.G. Spartan said. The old valet had a bag of Commodore's golf clubs over his shoulder.

Miss Loo's beefy-looking Asian caddy stood respectfully at attention, a Sumo wrestler in a red golf shirt and tan slacks, quietly holding her clubs.

While the lady was changing into her golf clothes, the old billionaire took a look at Miss Loo's beautiful golf clubs. They were so exquisitely made they could have been pieces of jewelry. The heads of her golf clubs appeared to be made of some sort of gold alloy, and inlaid with copper dragons and exotic Chinese characters. The old capitalist had never seen quite such a beautiful set of golf clubs. The shanks were so highly polished, they literally seemed to glow.

"Long Drive first," Miss Loo sang, appearing and extracting a driver from under his nose.

"Of course," Commodore said.

He indulgently gestured for her to take the tee. The ingrained habits of a married man led him to quickly agree to anything a woman proposed.

As Miss Loo addressed the ball, Commodore tried to pretend he did not hear the distant cry of the Golden Weeha from deep inside the bowels of Commodora.

Wiggling her rear as she dug in her spikes, Miss Loo stared up the fairway, which was lined on both sides with tall Eucalyptus trees. Miss Loo mentally went over her strategy for the day. Golf first soften up old man, she thought. During game, when he relax, I bring him around.

Miss Loo smacked a magnificent ringing shot that seemed to rise over the tops of the Eucalyptus trees and freeze in the sky.

"My God!" Commodore exclaimed as her ball dropped onto the distant green. Her golfing prowess continued to astound him.

"We play together, we win all time," she said. "Your family, my family."

Commodore smiled coyly. "Indeed."

"Golf we play together, win more tournament, win business together, bed, house, fishpond, dog, factory, together everything," she said, gesturing for Commodore to hurry up and tee off. "You play golf now."

R.G. held out Commodore's No. 4 driver. The old billionaire teed off somewhat self-consciously. It was not a spectacular shot, knocking a low-hanging bird nest off an Eucalyptus branch about halfway down, then ricocheting weakly back across the fairway in a spray of yellow feathers.

The old billionaire felt it wouldn't be proper to ask Miss Loo for a Mulligan, as he often asked his valet. R.G. was already holding out another golf ball, but the old billionaire, floridly blushing, waved the mulligan away.

The smell of new-mown grass was in the air, a smell Commodore loved. Squirrels were chasing each other through trees where unseen songbirds burst into song. Commodore noticed a lonely gray sea gull gliding lazily over the tops of the trees. Miss Loo muffed a shot every now and then, aiming to not get too far ahead of Commodore, but when she was on automatic pilot many of her shots impressed him.

On the sixth tee, Miss Loo waved away the caddies, took off her golf gloves, then moved closer to the old capitalist.

She grasped Commodore's arm, and then took his hand. "You like Long Drive, maybe you *like* Long Drive," she said.

As R.G. and the Chinese caddy both looked discreetly away, Miss Loo guided Commodore's hand between the buttons of her red silk blouse, and placed it for an instant on her swelling sports bra.

"You move factories now, you very happy man, maybe you want marry Long Drive," she smiled, pulling his hand out of her blouse and squeezing it.

The scent of crushed flowers magically filled the air, triggering memories. At that moment Commodore vividly remembered little Isi-fung-flower, his Chinese love of long ago, the object of the only real fling he had ever had in his life.

Commodore was barely nineteen years old at the time. The USS *Felicity* had docked for shore leave near the middle of a long tour of duty in the Pacific. In Hong Kong, Commodore had been a just another naive young sailor on shore leave in a noisy Asian metropolis. Separated from his companions after one beer, he noticed a strikingly beautiful young girl walk out of a musky bar somewhere near the center of town. Commodore had not seen a girl for months. He was immediately struck by her youthful beauty. The girl was walking shyly through a crowd of boisterous French sailors, in a short skirt and high heels with a small brown silk purse over one shoulder.

The girl shyly glanced for a moment into his eyes, like a modest urban damsel in distress, then looked down. Struck by her modesty, the young sailor had impulsively and clumsily overcome the language barrier and invited her to dinner, not realizing she was a prostitute, and barely sixteen years old.

After a lavish dinner and a couple of hours of communicating with raised eyebrows and hand gestures, the young gentleman sailor walked the girl back to the Flying Goose Hotel. He gallantly kissed her hand under the neon sign. His lonely heart rose into his throat at the vaguely floral smell of her hand, the smell of crushed poppy petals, a scent the heartsick young sailor found almost unbearably erotic.

Using only hand signals, young Commodore clumsily and impulsively asked Isi-fung-flower to dinner again the following night. Before she slipped into the Flying Goose, the girl stared at him, her lovely brown eyes blinking in a beautiful round expressionless face. Then she suddenly smiled, revealing small white teeth.

As gently as the wind, she guided his hand beneath her silk blouse for a moment and held it there.

"American come tomorrow, maybe bring Isi fifty dollar," she said, smiling and squeezing his hand.

The young sailor danced back to the ship with a song in his heart. Commodore had been so sheltered from the realities of the world, he didn't realize that the pretty young girl was working. He assumed it was some kind of local custom, to pay the young ladies a small fee for the pleasure of their company, something like bringing a bouquet of expensive flowers or a box of fine chocolate for a first date with an American girl. He spoke about his dinner engagement to no one on the ship.

The next night, Commodore showed up to take the young lady to dinner again. When she met him at the door, the young sailor quietly slipped a fifty-dollar bill into her hand to show her he understood the local custom.

To his surprise, before they'd even had dinner, little Isi gently took his hand and pulled him backwards through the small lobby of the Flying Goose Hotel. Like two characters in a dream, Isi led the young sailor by the hand up the winding stairs to a small room at the back of the hotel. She shyly closed the cloth curtains over the entrance to her modest room which contained only a single bed, a towel, a washbasin, a burning candle, and a small sitting Buddha from whose perforated nostrils rose two shimmering white ribbons of incense.

Glancing shyly over her shoulder, Isi-fung-flower took off her garments one piece at a time, revealing her perfectly formed young body. She was white as a porcelain statue and hairless as a China doll.

Then she bowed to the astounded young sailor, and sat down on the bed. In a businesslike motion, she loosened the sticks which held up her long black hair. That was what Commodore would remember for the rest of his life, that moment when she let down her long, perfectly straight black hair. The sight of the girl's black silken hair falling over her shoulders took his breath away.

As if in some opium dream of flowers and flesh, she extended one hand, and tenderly pulled the young sailor down on the bed with her, into a world of grunting biracial passion that felt like the sweet, quivering mouth of the world.

Afterwards, little Isi quietly pulled open the beaded curtains. She bowed modestly as Commodore left, looking at him as if he were the king of the entire world. Commodore assumed it was her first sexual experience, since it was his. When he got back to the ship, he remembered with some embarrassment that he hadn't taken the young lady to dinner.

He made a pledge to himself that he would return to the Flying Goose the very next night with another fifty dollars and complete their dinner engagement.

"Mr. Commode, sir," said R.G., touching his shoulder. "Your Earl Grey tea, sir," he said again.

Snapping awake from his daydream, Commodore realized he and Miss Loo were having tea on the patio overlooking Milly's English garden. The golf game was over. To his immediate left, R.G. was politely holding Milly's silver Paul Revere teapot, awaiting permission to pour the tea.

"Please," Commodore said.

The old valet poured the tea elegantly, in the English manner. Spartan's elegance was lost on Miss Loo, who seemed bored by the niceties of British style.

Commodore sipped the fragrant Earl Gray, and looked out over Milly's English garden.

"I like you house. I like golf course. I happy live here," Miss Loo said, gesturing with her free hand. "Maybe next week we get marry."

"Are you proposing marriage to me?" Commodore was surprised.

As if to respond, Miss Loo bent over Commodore, took his hand in hers, and guided it inside her silk blouse. She had removed the sports bra, he noticed. He could feel her strong athlete's heart beating aggressively behind her breast. After she kissed his ear, she positioned her mouth near his ear to speak, breathing heavily. The nipples of her muscular breasts became hard as bing cherries and her skin positively electric.

"Move five factories, maybe good term, marry right away, Long Drive promise you happy happy big businessman," she said, gently licking his ear and squeezing his hand tightly around her breast with both hands.

Frowning a bit, R.G. Spartan gazed discreetly away, silver teapot in hand. Miss Loo's caddy was not around. From the servants' quarters came the sound of a toilet flushing.

Miss Loo pulled Commodore's tingling hand away from her breast with a glum expression, and pinched his cheek hard.

"No move factory, Long Drive sad, go home, say goodbye, never see nice businessman again, no happy happy time, nothing, go home, forever goodbye, sorry," she said, slipping back into her chair and patting his hand.

This erotic bait and switch took the old billionaire's breath away. He felt as if he were again standing on the rear deck of the USS *Felicity*, in his dress white Navy uniform, white sailor's hat in hand, frantically waving goodbye to little Isi all over again. That fateful Monday afternoon, Isi had come down to the dock with the other girls from the Flying Goose to wave goodbye to the big grey American destroyer. Commodore thought he saw her bow her head sadly and begin to cry as his ship pulled away. The heartsick sailor knew in his heart he would never see Isi-fung-flower again. He had lost his first and only love! Painful tears of romantic yearning welled up into his eyes. The heartbroken young sailor was so distraught that he could have flung himself into the Pacific Ocean, which seemed to overflow with his tears.

As Commodore opened his mouth to reply to Miss Loo, Commodore realized he could not speak.

In the swamp of his emotions, he was flinging himself into the South China Sea, trying to swim back through time to the warm arms and succulent young arms of his first love.

"More tea now," Miss Loo said to R.G., tapping the side of the teapot with a teaspoon. "Old servant pour, new mistress thirsty."

R.G. turned to face her, lifting one eyebrow. The old valet glanced at Mr. Commode, but when he saw the helpless and unsettled expression on his master's face, and that his master appeared to be crying, he quietly complied.

"We go back to meeting now," said Miss Loo.

❦

Philip's cell phone vibrated violently. He hurried out the door to take the call. Diego whispered into his ear that the camera crew had located the missing limousine parked at Commodora.

They hurried away on the red Vespa, Filly holding onto Diego's waist. Filly's American red hair red blew madly in the wind. They found Miss Loo's limousine parked with its rear end thrust into a bank of Milly's gardenias. Not wishing to ring the doorbell, the boys headed around the corner toward the rear patio and the golf course.

The camera crew waiting behind the limousine saw them get off the Vespa. The crew followed them around the corner of the house—three scruffy men in sweat suits and Birkenstocks, trotting quickly, checking their focus and sound, ready to record the confrontation.

When he heard a piercing animal cry, Philip halted for a moment in front of his old suite of bedrooms on the first floor. Across the English garden and up in the surrounding Jacaranda trees he saw nothing. But when he turned to the center window of his old master bedroom he saw a frightening, grotesque sight.

Some kind of hairy creature that looked like a five-legged spider was shredding the Louis XIV drapery his mother had flown all the way to Paris to acquire. The shrieking little Weeha had twisted itself into a grotesque shape, all four legs and tail extended. As the little monkey struggled to free its nails from the drapery, its short erect penis slapped and bent sideways against the glass. The shrieking five-legged spider-like creature surrounding the small magenta penis appeared to be trying to relieve itself on them right through the glass.

"My bedroom!" Filly cried. "My mother's drapes!"

As the camera crew turned its attention to the window, the long tail of the Weeha slowly curled around its erection.

Philip spun around twice, away from the window like a spinning scarecrow, knocking cameramen awry as he disjointedly fainted.

Diego looked up at the sitting cameraman, his handsome face distraught, in a panic, afraid Philip had had some kind of seizure. The cameraman zoomed in for a dramatic close-up of Diego's anxious face.

"For God's sake," Diego lisped, looking up and flipping his hair to one side. "Don't film *us! They're getting away!*"

In the distance, Diego heard the muscular Chinese driver slam the limousine door firmly shut. Commodore and Miss Loo were leaving.

The camera crew arrived in time to get a good long shot of R.G. Spartan cupping the silver teapot in his hand, gazing wistfully at the departing limousine. Diego watched the footage on his cell phone until his phone went blank.

Still a step behind, the camera crew clamored into their van. They roared down the moss-covered driveway, trying vainly to catch the limousine before it lost them for good on the long majestic curves of Swizzle Stick Road.

19. Out in the Garden

Commode Company headquarters baked quietly in the California sun. Ivy clung to the walls of the white three-story Mission style omelet topped by a red tile roof and flanked by buildings, a bit of traffic, and palm trees.

Miss Loo blew kisses out the limousine window until Commodore disappeared from sight. As the uniformed doormen threw open the doors and saluted, she slyly noticed that Commodore walked into the building like a man who had made up his mind to act decisively.

The old capitalist told her the meeting wouldn't take long, and that in just a few minutes he would rejoin her in the limousine. Miss Loo felt like a patient fisherman who had finally set her hook into the mouth of a very large, soft, succulent fish.

In the elevator, the old billionaire released some pent-up flatulence. The stout, manly aroma seemed to add a note of urgency to the situation.

Memories of Miss Loo's firm, warm breast, combined with her businesslike kiss, a kiss with a point, filled Commodore's brain. His nostrils flared at the memory of the muscular breasts Miss Loo practically thrust into his hand on the golf course, and then later on the patio, too. The old billionaire believed that Miss Loo's suggestive gesture was in fact a romantic commitment, even a sexual promise of sorts, hinting at a glorious future he had already begun to imagine.

After they moved the plants, Commodore had fantasies of happily flying back to China to meet Miss Loo's family. He yearned to pay a visit to the lovely Miss Loo inside her large and beautiful palace, a palace she shared with what he was sure was an equally large and well-mannered family.

Commodore imagined her family lined up in traditional silk costumes and ornamental hats, ready to meet their respected guest. Commodore imagined a row of China dolls respectfully bowing in unison as he walked inside, the revered guest and potential respected family member from the country of dreams, the United States of America.

The old billionaire breezed out of the elevator and into the penthouse. The lawyers froze into silence as he passed through the reception area without a glance and strode into the conference room. The old capitalist was ready to take quick, forceful action and get back to business with Miss Loo.

Clementine and Petunia sat up at the table, blinking like two courtesans awakened from an afternoon nap. Commodore was surprised to see his daughters, who were holding places for their husbands. Clementine waved politely and suppressed a yawn.

"I'm the doctor," Clementine explained. "Piggy's holding her place for Simon."

Petunia nodded briskly. She rolled up the soft pink sleeves of her safari outfit. Commodore knew his animal-loving oldest daughter had already taken her pigs for their noontime walk around the estate. Petunia enjoyed the breezy chaos of those walks, which she had occasionally shared with Milly when Milly was alive. On one of these walks, Milly confided later, she had been horrified to see what she was sure was a pig turd floating in the lake. Milly didn't dare mention this, of course, because Petunia had absolutely no sense of humor when it came to her animals.

"*Bon Jour*, oh my papa," said Petunia, lifting her pith helmet.

"When the boys arrive we're outta here," Clementine observed, glancing at her amethyst-studded watch and scowling disapproval. For a moment, Clementine reminded Commodore of her scowling, impatient husband.

Commodore noticed that his youngest daughter had become a platinum blonde. Clementine's skin was dark as shoe leather, but she was dressed entirely in white. She wore white vintage sunglasses, an amethyst and crystal necklace and earrings, white tennis shoes, and some kind of short white designer garment over her dark, leathery skin.

Commodore did love his youngest daughter, but he sometimes didn't recognize her, she'd had so much plastic surgery. Clementine was strikingly beautiful now, of course, in the Hollywood fashion. She had the nose of one actress and the cheekbones of another. But each time his daughter had more work done, it got more and more difficult to see the pretty, insecure, self-centered little girl he and Milly had brought into the world. These days, even when Clementine forced a smile, it hardly looked like a smile at all.

As Clementine glared at her watch, a diesel truck horn blasted outside the building. It was a sound you didn't hear much in the genteel little beach town. Commodore didn't give it a second thought.

❧

The Prince had hurried up the sidewalk toward Miss Loo's limousine, briefcase in hand. He rapped on the front driver's side window. The Asian driver recognized him and rolled down the window.

"Take a walk, Chinaman," the Prince hissed.

The big driver got out, put on his hat, and lumbered away. The Prince clenched his teeth, walked around the limo, jerked open the rear door, grabbed Miss Loo's arm, jerked her out of the car, and made an aggressive motion with his head.

"Let's *talk*, Long Drive," hissed the Prince.

Simon pulled her toward the courtyard behind the building. Miss Loo looked anxiously from side to side.

The idyllic little courtyard behind the old hotel, surrounded by undulating palm trees, was always empty. At the moment it was bedecked with the smell of lavender and jasmine. Simon sat Miss Loo down under the gazebo.

"Did you give the old fart the pitch?" the Prince asked.

"Yes, but I worry a little," Miss Loo said, again looking from side to side. "When I was secret agent for the Chinese government—I learn sometimes walls have ears."

"We're completely safe here," Simon said impatiently, in a booming voice. "No walls, no ears. Trust me. I'm a lawyer."

"Ah," Miss Loo said, and visibly relaxed.

Simon paused a moment, digesting her previous comments somewhat like a robin struggling to swallow a rather large worm.

"You were a secret agent?" the Prince coughed.

Miss Loo grinned like a little girl caught with her hand in the cookie jar. She shook her head yes.

"Communist government help Long Drive win golf, give me special drugs, make me great golfer. Win China tournament, send to United States, win big lady golf tournament. Steal atomic secrets from U.S. government. Carry atomic secrets to my country. In golf bag!" she said, clutching her purse and sniggering a little at the recollection.

"Nobody suspect famous golfer!" she added. "Family get contract to build tank."

The Prince lifted his eyebrows, a little taken back by this unsolicited information. He suddenly realized that he was not in complete control of the lively Miss Loo, as he had previously imagined. Miss Loo had a dark dialectic past, the Prince realized, as murky as Communist economic theory itself. He felt a feathering away ... for some reason he thought of the disoriented pelican that had smacked clumsily into the bow of Commodore's yacht off the Cayman Islands, haplessly flailing its wings against the water as it sank into the sea.

"So did you talk to the old fart, like I told you?" the Prince anxiously asked, automatically pressing ahead to the next item on his personal agenda.

"Long Drive talk, golf, rub, laugh, old fart feel and listen," she sang matter-of-factly. "Old fart like Long Drive."

Miss Loo pulled two large cheques out of her brassiere and waved them under his nose.

"No more talk! I do my part, lawyer, you do your. Have big check for you, have big check for Number One brother-in-law. Company move plants now, government pay you."

Miss Loo smiled a little, wiggling her tongue between her teeth, teasing the anxious lawyer. The Prince instinctively reached for the check, but she pulled it out of reach with a coy, feminine gesture, like a beautiful snake whipping itself lazily back into a coil.

Miss Loo noticed what appeared to be teeth marks in Simon's right ear. Without thinking, she touched his ear. The thought crossed her mind that, despite his clumsy, buttoned-down facade, the fast-talking American lawyer might actually be good in bed.

The Prince's cell phone chimed. After a moment, he turned to Miss Loo and hissed: "It's show time. The little faggot's back. Get back to the limo. This won't take five minutes."

And away he hustled, a hustler in Armani.

❧

Philip Commode's eyes widened when he hurried past the lawyers, entered the conference room, and saw his two big sisters sitting next to his father. Neither of the girls met his eyes.

"Come in, Philip. Sit down," Commodore said heartily.

Commodore didn't expect the knives to come out between the kids, but out they came. It started when Philip motioned for Diego to follow him inside and sit down. It was not easy being the youngest in the family, and bucking the trend, a role that was suddenly thrust on him now. And at that moment, Philip felt like he sorely needed a friend.

"Little brother, I don't believe any *non* family member is welcome in here just now," Petunia said, her lips curling into a porcine sneer. "Unless Simon misinformed me, only family members are allowed in this room. Your companion may wait outside in the reception area, with … the others."

"Yeh," Clementine snarled. "Out."

"Well aren't we a happy little family?" Philip snapped, sitting down and motioning for Diego to take a chair. "Here's the way it is, girls. Diego's my best friend and I need a friend, so he can stay."

"Did you call him your best *friend*, little brother?" Petunia snorted, her nostrils flaring like an angry sow. "Isn't he the reason someone borrowed fifty thousand dollars from his sister a few years ago to check into a *mental* hospital?"

"That's totally unnecessary and unfair and also old news, Piggy," Filly said.

"Don't be catty, Piggy," Clementine sniffed. "Silly little Filly might be a tad bitchy today, but he's the sweetest little brother we'll ever have."

"But little Brother wouldn't have any clients if it wasn't for Momma and Daddy's friends," Petunia haughtily observed. taking off her pith helmet. "And speaking of your *friend*— what kind of *work* does your little Spanish fruitcake do?"

Out of the corner of his eye, Philip saw Diego's sensitive eyes fill with tears. It infuriated him that his sisters would speak about Diego like that, Diego who was so extraordinarily intuitive and sensitive, creative from the word go, and so gentle and loving that he would never hurt an ant even if an entire ant colony crawled up his leg and attacked him.

Trembling Diego quickly stood up, biting his knuckles, a handsome Spaniard in tight jeans and a $500 T-shirt, silently weeping as he hurried from the room.

It was time to assert himself, Philip thought. He ignored his vibrating cell phone and stood to face his big sisters.

"Piggy, your husband wouldn't even have a *job* if it weren't for Dad," Filly snapped at Petunia. "Do you really think that industrial strength blowhard could get a job at any other company in America?"

"Blow*hard*, sweetie?" Clementine asked, batting her eyes. "Blow *what?*"

"Your boob-butchering celebrity ass-kissing husband with the cornball commercials wouldn't have any business if it wasn't for Mom and Dad either, Clementine."

"*Butcher??*" Clementine shrieked, unfolding her arms from over her own surgically-enhanced breasts. "The Doctor makes men and women *beautiful!*"

"Don't pick on my little sister, Philip," Petunia snorted.

"Having a little more work redone, Clementine?" Filly sneered. "Are you related to the rest of us? You're starting to look like Michael Jackson's oldest sister."

"Don't you *dare* bring up Michael Jackson again to me again!" Clementine shouted, turning to Commodore. "Daddy!"

Commodore held out his hands and stood up.

"Children!" he said. "That's enough."

Commodore hadn't heard a word they said, but he was taken back by the sudden display of emotional hostility. The old billionaire made a firm, somewhat conciliatory gesture.

"Children," Commodore said. "Stop squabbling. This is serious business!"

Simon sauntered in at that moment, swinging his monogrammed briefcase. Petunia got up, put her hands on Simon's shoulders, and obediently pecked her buffed-up husband on the cheek.

"Little brother's extremely—argumentative today," Petunia explained.

Pausing for effect, Petunia lifted herself to her full height, glared for an eternal moment at Philip, placed her pith helmet on her head, and then majestically walked out the door. His big sister could be cold as ice, Philip noticed admiringly. Automobile and truck horns honked softly outside the building, as if applauding her exit.

"Let's get this over, shall we?" Clementine said.

"All right," Commodore said, rapping his gavel. "This meeting has come to order. We know what we've got to do. By the way, I've just discussed the move with a very dear friend of mine and I want you all to get to know her better."

"Not that *Chinese* woman?" Philip snapped, standing up dramatically. "Do you think we want you spending more time with a woman who can't even speak English?"

"Oh please no more *drama*, Philip," Clementine said in her best whisky voice. "Let Dad have some fun. I want to vote yes."

Philip's cell phone vibrated wildly. Without thinking, he unfolded the phone and snapped, "Philip Commode."

As Philip listened, he began smiling, and swaying from side to side as to an unheard music.

Instantly the boardroom became his ballroom. Philip rose and began dancing to a mysterious music. Still smiling, and listening to the cell phone, Filly Commode danced over to the window and dramatically pulled back the drapes to the ivy-covered balcony. With his free hand he threw open the French doors and danced out to grab the long wrought iron rail of the balcony, gesturing toward the setting sun.

"Dad!" Philip cried on the way out the door. "Before you vote, come out here! I've got to show you something!"

Philip Commode's bright red hair fluttered in the breeze as he led Commodore down the balcony, his father like a dance partner in some mysterious corporate rumba. Simon and Clementine followed, but they were not dancing.

A caravan of Commode Company trucks had completely blocked State Street, every horn honking. Angry commuters caught in the impromptu demonstration were also honking and shaking their fists. The symphony of truck horns was overwhelming.

Clementine covered her ears and looked for guidance to Simon. The vice president of legal affairs now resembled a sad old bear who had squatted to relieve himself between two railroad tracks, a bit too preoccupied with what he was doing to hear the rumble of a rapidly approaching train.

Commodore saw hundreds of workers standing on top of their trucks, shaking their fists, waving American flags and picket signs. Commodore recognized Don Dumper on the roof of his Ford, holding an American flag, flanked by two skinny older workers. Commodore stared at the two older men next to Dumper, who both looked familiar. Two old guys in Rock n' Roll Museum T-shirts were waving up toward the balcony. Imperfectly, Commodore remembered them.

"Those are your employees, Dad," Filly said. "American workers, willing and able to work to support their families. They're showing you they don't want you to send their jobs to China."

"Where did these horn-blowing hooligans come from?" Simon croaked, recovering his composure.

"Cleveland," Philip said.

"Cleveland, Ohio?" Clementine asked.

"These workers drove more than two thousand miles to show Dad that they want to keep their jobs," Philip said. "They want to keep working for you, Dad!"

The honking intensified below them as a couple of police motorcycles with flashing amber and red lights wormed their way between the stopped cars and trucks, searching for the source of the impermeable traffic jam.

"Before you vote, Clemmie, Simon, but especially *Dad*," Philip said, gesturing at the street. "Think of these workers. Think of their American families, with little American children to feed. And you, Dad, you're so good to pay them a decent wage that allows them to work and prosper, in the tradition of Henry Ford and Nicholas Commode. More than a hundred and forty years of tradition are on the line today."

Simon rolled his eyes, shook his head, and put his arm on Commodore's shoulder. As the honking continued, Simon walked Commodore back into the conference room, leading the way and shaking his head.

"Before we get this over with, let me just say that all your mutinous employees abandoned our plant and walked off the job, and that is costing your company a lot of money," said the Prince, as if addressing a jury.

"They all ought to be immediately fired. They abandoned our plant. They violated employment contracts. By the way, Commodore, employees in China don't walk off the job, steal company vehicles, and use company equipment to drive across the country to embarrass you like this!"

"Dad, one thought. This all might become news," Philip said, glancing at Commodore as he sat down. "You know what I mean?"

"We don't want any publicity," Commodore croaked. He blanched at the thought of his family's company becoming a public spectacle.

"So let's finish up," Simon said, opening his briefcase. "Legal affairs has prepared the contracts. As soon as the full board approves, Commodore can sign off on them and get back to his lady. We'll do what you want, Commodore, all of us, right, Clementine?"

"That's right," Clemmie said. "I vote yes."

Commodore thought he imagined Miss Loo drifting gracefully into the room, looking stunningly beautiful in a low-cut red silk ball gown, which was monogrammed with thousands of tiny golden golf clubs. Miss Loo positively glowed as she sailed around the room, chopsticks in her hair, surrounded by an aura of soft yellow light, as graceful as a scarlet fish in still blue water.

"My family, your family," she whispered to Commodore, holding out her arms like a yearning virgin in a dream.

Commodore cleared his throat. He wasn't sure anybody else in the room could see what he thought he saw. He assumed the beautiful vision in red was a figment of his imagination, although in truth, he didn't have much imagination.

The beautiful pro golfer drifted gently as the breeze through the room, bent over, and took the old billionaire's head in her hands and bent over to kiss him.

"Oh *please*," Philip said. "Isn't this a *business* meeting?"

Miss Loo circled the conference table like a ballerina circling center stage on point, holding out her golden glowing arms to Commodore in a gesture of stark operatic yearning. At that moment, Philip heard a scuffle in the reception area. He heard the San Francisco lawyers raising their voices in unison, the booming shouts of Leonardo, and the shrill plaintive cry of Miss Gander.

"I move we take the plants to China, right away," Simon said.

"Second!" Clementine cried.

The conference room door burst wide open. With blocking by Leonardo, Diego burst into the room like some kind of crazy halfback, dragging Miss Gander after him. His expensive T-shirt was completely torn off his right shoulder. Diego was gasping, one arm high in the air.

"I beg your pardon," Commodore said.

Diego held something over his head like a football. Gasping for breath, Diego waved his cell phone in the air.

"Philip!" Diego cried as he staggered forward. "This is so important! Just show them!"

Diego's stylish little phone flew across the conference table to Philip, who instinctively wired it to the projector.

"For the love of *Jesus*!" Diego gasped. "Dim the lights!"

Miss Gander quietly complied.

In the shady darkness of the conference room, the Prince's final humiliation materialized against the wall. The footage on Diego's phone began with a long shot of the old valet looking up the driveway with the Paul Revere teapot in his hand, followed by an exterior of a limousine sitting in front of Commode Company headquarters, and Simon limping away from the limousine and into the garden with Miss Loo.

Next, panning in as if from above the garden wall, Simon saw a shot of himself and Miss Loo half-hidden in the gazebo behind a lavender bush covered with half-dead purple blossoms. As the clip progressed, and his face grew larger, the Prince sunk lower and lower into his chair.

"Did you give the old fart the *pitch*?" the Prince asked Miss Loo, as the camera moved closer. The sound was so loud, it made him sound like he was shouting. The close-up on his face made him look positively Machiavellian. As Simon watched in horror, his nose actually appeared to grow.

"Old fart very happy, old fart *like* Long Drive," Miss Loo whispered loudly, her dark eyes darting from side to side in a positively paranoid fashion. "But I know from my days as a secret agent for the Chinese government—walls have ears."

"Did she say *secret agent*?" Philip asked, hitting the pause button for an instant. "Dad? For the *Chinese government*?"

Diego nodded yes, looking around the table for approval. Commodore looked surprised. Clementine tried to smile.

Into the dark room walked the Doctor. Before his eyes adjusted to the light, the Doctor stuck out his arms and walked toward the table like a slender zombie in scrubs feeling its way into the belly of a cave.

"The little walls *do* have ears, Simon," Clementine sneered, glancing at the Doctor. "And little eyes, too."

"We're completely safe here! Trust me, I'm a *lawyer*!" Simon's image barked. He nodded affirmatively, but his face slowly registered a sort of mild bewilderment as the camera zoomed in closer.

Simon's nose appeared to lengthen again as he croaked: "You were a secret agent?"

"Of course," Miss Loo laughed. Miss Loo then smiled. She looked like a squirrel with its cheeks full of nuts. "Secret Agent trained by Communist government."

"Did that woman say she was trained by the *Communist government*, Dad?" Filly asked, pausing the tape again. "To steal atomic secrets from *the United States of America*?"

Diego grabbed Philip's hands, shaking his head yes.

"Did she say trained by the *Communists*, Dad?" Filly asked. "Weren't you at all *surprised* by that remark, Simon? Oh Mr. Vice President of Legal Affairs. Yoo hoo!"

The Prince appeared to be shrinking into the chair before their eyes. The blushing barrister was frozen into a perspiring block of ice that was slowly melting into a puzzle beneath his chair.

Commodore stood up, white as a sheet, and grave now, very grave and serious, as serious as Philip had ever seen him in his entire life. The old warrior against Communism straightened completely up, like a soldier at perfect attention. Nicholas Commode's gavel fell from his hands. Commodore's lips parted to speak but he said nothing as the clip continued.

"I Communist government golfer. I take special drugs, steroids, special training make me best golfer in China. Come to tournaments in U.S., big golfer. Steal atomic secrets from U.S. government, bring them to my country. In *golf bag*!" Miss Loo snickered, hugging her purse with twinkling eyes. "Nobody suspect pro golfer. Family get government contract for tank."

"Good God!" Commodore said, holding his heart. He sat down again. The Doctor slipped toward him in the darkness, stethoscope in hand.

"Stop that damned video!" the Prince managed to scream. "We've got to vote now! Commodore?"

But the Doctor was squinting and listening to Commodore's heart. He wouldn't let Simon near him.

The camera zoomed in on Miss Loo, whose tongue appeared to be flickering rapidly, like the tongue of a snake. With an expression of extreme contempt, Miss Loo pulled two large cashier's cheques out of her blouse and waved them under the Prince's nose which was now monumental. The Prince could not believe his own idiotic expression as he gawked at the checks.

"Have big check for you and Number One brother-in-law. One hundred fifty million U.S. dollar. You move company now, government pay."

'Number one brother-in-law?" Filly sniffed, turning to Clementine. "Is The *Doctor* getting *paid off*, too?"

The Doctor looked up from his work, and nodded curtly. He took the ends of the stethoscope out of his ears.

"Have we voted yet, Nutty?" The Doctor asked. "If not, I vote yes! For God's sake, move the plants to China now."

The Prince's long nose stuck out like the beak like a predatory bird as he clumsily reached for the check. Was his nose really that long? Simon could not believe the greedy look on his own face as Miss Loo pulled the checks out of reach with a coy, feminine gesture. She rubbed the cheques across his face, like a pair of panties across the nose of a bloodhound, then pulled the checks back, teasing him. Big numbers on the checks were clearly visible. Miss Loo smiled a little. Then her mouth dropped open as she lovingly touched Simon's ear and examined the unhealed tooth marks.

Simon's cell phone chimed, his personal line.

At the same time, in the conference room, the Simon's cell phone also chimed away, the first few notes of "Misty." Simon was so deep into his own humiliation he didn't know where he was or who might call him. He paused for a moment before he took the call.

"I think I've seen enough," Commodore gasped, standing up, and pushing the Doctor out of his way. "Turn that damned thing off. This year's board meeting is over!"

In the outer office, Commodore barked at the huddling lawyers, "Pack up your briefcases. Send your bills to Simon."

"Oh Dad," Clementine cried, following her father to the elevator. "That woman made a complete fool of you!"

From the belly of the elevator, standing alone, Commodore glared at his daughter for a moment. When Clementine realized what she'd said, a small part of her face blushed.

The Doctor automatically put his arm around her shoulder, a supportive gesture.

"Clementime and I vote yes!" the Doctor cried. "Let's move those factories now!"

As the elevator door ricketed shut Commodore bellowed, "Over my dead body!"

Simon took the call. It was Petunia. The minute she got home, Petunia excitedly told him, several younger pigs had stampeded. The pigs had worked their way off the island and under the security fence on the west side of their house. She couldn't have her animals picked up by Animal Control! Simon barely understood that Petunia was at that moment following a herd of galloping pigs around the estate, chasing them in her Range Rover, crying to Simon for help over her cell phone.

The elevator door opened again. Commodore staggered back into the conference room, a changed man. He was white as a bed sheet, ashen, crestfallen, shaking, and visibly upset.

"I'll call you back," Simon said.

The old capitalist locked the door to the conference room and turned to face them.

Suddenly, horribly, definitely, Commodore had realized with a gasp, he was on the crest of becoming a ridiculous public figure. The old billionaire's cherished privacy was collapsing around his ankles, like a pair of old boxer shorts.

The old capitalist felt naked and exposed before the prying eyes of the world. He wanted to run but at the moment that was impossible. Commodore was also unable to talk.

"What's the matter, Dad?" Philip asked.

Commodore could not reply.

"Are there reporters in the lobby?" Philip asked.

Commodore nodded yes.

"They're not *our* cameras," Diego whispered.

"It's the media!" Philip turned to Simon. "I told you, Dad."

Thinking on his feet, and ignoring another incoming call, Simon quickly speed-dialed his second vice president of public relations and ordered her to bring some press information into the office right away.

"Where did the TV cameras come from?" Commodore gasped, in a voice not unlike the voice of a small child. "They're all over the lobby. When the elevator doors opened, reporters mobbed me. I had to fight my way back into the elevator."

Commodore blurted, "This is not right! We're a private company. We don't want publicity."

"Maybe Filly and his little friend called the *media*," Clementine hissed.

"Maybe the media saw all the trucks outside and decided to *investigate*," Philip retorted.

Miss Gander's voice floated into the room over the intercom, interrupting and trumping everything.

"Mr. Commode," she said." There's a Mr. Mike Wallace from *60 Minutes* in the waiting room. He says he wants to speak to you right away."

Shuddering with horror, and holding his fist over his heart, Commodore Commode collapsed into the arms of his only son.

20. Simon is Famous

Philip Commode crept down the old spiral staircase at Commode Company headquarters. Just below him, in the lobby of the old hotel, reporters shifted back and forth across the entire length of the floor like a flock of agitated chickens.

All the networks seemed to be there, as if by magic, along with local TV luminaries. Handsome television news people with bright orange make-up on their faces and less attractive radio and print reporters with tape recorders, notepads, and laptops drifted like flotsam around the foot of the staircase. Near the bottom of the stairs, some of the guys from Cleveland stood on the landing nervously preparing to talk into a solid wall of blazing white klieg lights.

For the Prince, on a raised platform at the opposite end of the room, it was a corporate nightmare. Only by default was he speaking for the company. Simon felt himself on the cusp of instant notoriety in the business community, but it was the not the sort of fame he had hoped to achieve.

The Prince wanted to hide. He had just been humiliated and vanquished from the board room. He was surely going to be fired. Yet here he was, a corporate trooper of sorts, trying to manage an impossible situation for the company. The Prince knew with certainty that Old Commodore didn't want the media or anybody else to know anything about him, his family, or anything connected with his company. And yet here the reporters came, aggressively sniffing into every corner of the lobby for information like a pack of insatiable hungry dogs.

On the other side of the lobby, Simon could see several dozen Commode Company workers with their arms folded like implacable iron men, holding American flags. He saw Don Dumper approach the microphones, the armpits of his long-sleeved shirt florid with sweat.

"Like I told you, the boys here, all they're saying is they're going to wait here until they get to talk personally with their boss, well, that is, our boss, Mr. Commodore Commode," Dumper began, gesturing at the men behind him

"What's with all these trucks?"

"We came out from Cleveland, Ohio," Dumper said. "Sorry about the double park."

"You drove those trucks all the way across the United States?"

"I didn't drive them all, no, the guys up here drove them after they voted to come out to try to get their voices heard."

"Is this a strike?" another one asked.

"Heck no," Dumper said, looking over his shoulder at heads shaking no. "Not exactly."

"Who is Commodore Commode?"

"Mr. Commodore Commode is the boss of the Commode Company, and the boys would like to know where he is right now. He a real good boss, his family's been good to us, all of us, but we'd like to speak with him today. As for why we did it, the boys don't want that fella in the nice suit over there to take all their jobs to China," Dumper said, pointing at Simon.

"China no!" the workers shouted, raising their fists.

Almost immediately, the flock of reporters scrabbled toward the Prince and his vice president of public relations, Sue Spooking. Dressed for success as usual, Spooking was a slender, grimacing woman in a yellow pantsuit who was thin as a pencil. Spooking gamely tried to signal the press that the company was not yet quite ready to make a statement yet.

Spooking's boss was in trouble. The Prince didn't have a statement prepared. He didn't seem to have the faintest idea what he should say. His mind appeared to be entirely blank. As reporters approached, Spooking began to fear that on top of everything else her fast-talking boss was about to wet his pants.

"He's wired," somebody shouted, tapping one of the microphones to make sure they had sound. "Who wants first shot at the flacks?"

Simon kept shaking his head "no," and looking at his Rolex Oyster as if time itself would save him.

Next to the Prince, Spooking stood quietly at attention, her arms full of press kits advertising the Commode Company's bathroom products. It was a damage control situation, the most sensitive task in PR.

Spooking had a law degree, but she was not prepared for this. Her job up to that point had been to smile and greet customers at the Commode Company booth at Kitchen & Bath trade conventions, and field softball questions from clueless reporters from this or that trade magazine.

The slender, bespectacled publicist winced at the writhing sea of aggressively shouting reporters, almost as many as she saw on TV during the search of Michael Jackson's house a few weeks before. Spooking's immediate boss, the vice president of legal affairs, she saw with a glance, was already dripping with sweat and didn't seem prepared to answer questions either.

A heavy-set female reporter waddled aggressively forward and shouted out a question into the Prince's face.

"Candy Rollins, *Los Angeles Times*, when can I talk to Commodore Commode?"

The Prince shook his head no, without replying, and backed away from the microphones. He pushed Spooking forward. Spooking quickly bent down and handed the reporter a press kit.

"Pictures of *toilets*?" the outraged reporter said, turning angrily to her colleagues and holding up the press kit. "I ask for an interview and she gives me pictures of *toilets*?"

"Bring Commodore Commode down here!"

⁂

Outside Commodore's upstairs office, Leonardo and the San Francisco lawyers watched respectfully as a slender old man in an expensive suit pinned on his microphone, wearing orange TV makeup. The orange-faced reporter, whose angular face was known all over the world, waited for the red light, and then began talking into the camera.

"This is Mike Wallace, in Santa Barbara, California. Today thousands of angry workers drove all the way from Cleveland,

Ohio, to protest the planned relocation of a giant industrial company's factories to China. But the corporate big shots and bosses cower behind their desks in this plush office building, which today has taken on the feeling of an embattled military stockade. Let's get to the bottom of this right now," he said, nodding at the camera.

Mike Wallace turned on his heels, walked across the room with a theatrical flourish, and pulled opened the door to Commodore's conference room, where the old billionaire and Miss Gander had been hiding. Mike Wallace walked inside, followed by a cameraman, a grip, a makeup artist, and a couple of sound men.

Commodore looked up when they entered the conference room. His mouth dropped open as he recognized Mike Wallace. He turned white as a porcelain toilet.

"Get out!" Miss Gander shrieked.

Like a drowning rhinoceros fighting for air, shaking his head no, the old capitalist blundered clumsily past Mike Wallace and into the reception area of his office. The three lawyers looked up in unison and smiled, all instantly aware that they might be on national television.

Commodore turned to the lawyers.

"You're all hired," he said, pointing to Mike Wallace.

The lawyers jumped into action as Mike Wallace angrily burst out of the conference room, just ahead of the cameras. Leonardo stood up and spoke first, blocking Wallace's pursuit with one slender arm.

"I beg your *pardon*, Mr. Wallace," Leonardo hissed.

Leonardo threw his slender body between Commodore and the famous TV reporter.

Puffing out his chest as the camera turned toward him, Leonardo boomed, "I'm representing both Mr. Philip Commode and Mr. Commodore Commode, owners of this privately-held company, and I don't believe you have obtained the permissions necessary to film in this office."

The San Francisco lawyers stood up and nodded in unison, like two angry silver-haired bulldogs. The two lawyers momentarily linked arms, scowled, and bared their teeth.

"Telephone the authorities, sweetie," the short one hissed to Miss Gander. "All these fine gentlemen are trespassing."

The taller of the two stepped forward:

"Mike, we love your show, we respect your reputation, and we know your viewers are interested in this. But you're on private property, as you well know, Mike. My client certainly wants to cooperate fully, but at some later time. Right now, he has asked me to get a restraining order on you and every member of your crew," Feinstein said, gracefully handing the famous reporter a business card.

"It's not personal, Mike. Come to my office tomorrow and I'll give you an exclusive interview on this," said the other. "We'll give you all the time you want."

Drawing himself up to his full height, Leonardo advanced menacingly on Mike Wallace, and his crew.

"For your benefit I repeat, Mr. Wallace, *neither* of my clients chooses to answer any questions from the print or broadcast media at this time," Leonardo boomed.

Leonardo was joined by the San Francisco lawyers. They puffed out their chests like tiny peacocks and moved forward too, cell phones in hand.

The flying wedge of well-dressed legal flesh advanced on the glowering celebrity newsman—a phalanx of fast-talking lawyers muttering threats, hinting at lawsuits, calling security, raising objections, and talking shit on their cell phones.

"This is *ridiculous*! Do I have to call our network's lawyers, *myself?*" Mike Wallace shouted, standing his ground in what was sure to be a dramatic showdown in front of the cameras.

At that moment, all of the company's security guards and the two saluting doormen leaped out of the old slow-moving elevator and hurried into Commodore's office.

In the confusion, Miss Gander took Commodore's hand and helped him slip back into the conference room. She quietly locked the door behind them.

Commodore staggered through the French doors onto the ivy-covered balcony which was now bathed in the eerie glow of pristine Southern California moonlight.

⁂

Pete and Dewey stood in the courtyard, below the rear balcony, where they'd gone to light up a smoke. They watched the old billionaire skinny over the balcony railing, grab hold of a stalk of ivy, give it a shake, look over his back, and begin climbing down the ivy-covered wall of the old three-story building.

"Look up there, Pete," said Dewey.

"Ain't that one beer Commie?" Pete asked.

"That's our boy," Dewey said.

Dewey and Pete had worked with Commodore at the main manufacturing plant, the one summer he'd worked on the line, bolting lids onto Commode Company toilets.

The three of them were the No. 34 lid-bolting crew, a proud proletarian work unit that had the second best safety record in the plant. Pete and Dewey remembered that as a youth, Commodore had worked hard to be one of the boys.

When Commodore got his first paycheck, they both recalled, they'd taken their naive young co-worker out for a beer. Their future boss had gotten blind drunk on less than one beer, they remembered fondly, so drunk he couldn't climb up into Dewey's pickup truck without assistance. They'd quietly driven him home.

For a couple of weeks Pete and Dewey called their young co-worker "One beer Commie."

Finally the naive young bathroom fixtures heir exploded. Almost in tears, he strongly protested, "I'm not, repeat, I am not and never have been a Communist."

Commodore's reaction was so strong and heartfelt that they stopped ribbing him. Then he moved upstairs into the big office. Then they heard he'd joined the Navy.

"You think Commie's going to jump?" Dewey asked.

"Are you kidding?" Pete snorted. "Rich guys don't never kill themselves."

It was a perilous climb down from the penthouse for a man in a business suit, they saw, and it looked to be extremely hard on the hands. The old billionaire was slipping and sliding, even hanging perilously on the vines with one hand like a monkey at one point, but he made it down to the ground, where Dewey and Pete had moved to catch him if he fell. Philip's video crew had also noticed the activity, and discreetly began filming everything.

"Ain't this one-beer Commie?" Pete asked Commodore.

'Hey, Commie?" Dewey laughed, touching his arm. "Why not just use the elevator?"

Commodore turned, shaking, dusting off his skinned-up hands, anxious, belligerent, trembling, distraught, fearful, and ready to cry or fight. But he smiled a nostalgic smile when he recognized his old drinking buddies from the lid-bolting crew. Despite his burning hands, Commodore immediately felt younger and more robust. Pete and Dewey impulsively hugged him, a three-way back-slapping hugfest that transcended labor-management politics, if it was perhaps a little corny.

"Old Pete," Commodore said, slapping their backs as they slapped his. "Old Dewey."

"Old Commodore."

"One Beer Commie."

Dewey backed off, his eyes twinkling with sentimental tears.

"After all these years," Dewey said, "Can the big boss himself make time to pick up a brewski with a couple of old clunks from Cleveland?"

Before Commodore could reply, Pete also threw his arm around Commodore from the other side and said: " Come on, Commie. Let's go just have one little beer—just for old time's sake."

They walked off, arm in arm, as if in a dream.

❧

Holding her cell phone, honking her horn, driving her faded olive green Range Rover wildly, Petunia Butterknut-Commode followed a herd of frightened pigs back and forth and down the driveway of her mansion.

The sense of foreboding grew large within her. Petunia was trying to herd the pigs off the road before the approach of the dreaded animal control truck which regularly cruised the streets not far from her property. Petunia had switched on her windshield wipers and fog lights and her hazard lights were flashing. She hoped to honk and scare the frightened animals back into their pens on Pig Island without running over any of them. This was impossible. Petunia could not get ahead of the pigs because the tiny little herd kept spreading out all over the road, scattering this way and that like a flock of frightened animals, forcing her to hit her brakes, honk, wait for them to regroup, and try to head them off again.

It infuriated Petunia that Simon had hung up on her in her hour of need. Her fast-talking husband, usually so solicitous when she talked about the pigs, was nowhere to be found when she so desperately needed him. Petunia had little time to think this through as she swerved frantically to and fro, trying to round up the pigs. When Simon hung up on her, Petunia realized with a gasp of horror that she would not be able to turn the herd around before they reached the main gate on Swizzle Stick Road. The gate automatically rumbled open as the pigs approached.

The galloping pigs turned out of the driveway, a snorting, frightened, thundering herd. The brass bells on their hand-tooled Argentine leather collars jingled wildly as their hooves pounded down Swizzle Stick Road toward downtown Santa Barbara like a pack of thundering wind chimes.

The pigs were followed by a frantically waving and honking Petunia, who feared now that they would be hit by a car or a truck, or worse than that, run away into the wilderness of the surrounding hills and die.

As soon as Petunia was able to catch her breath, she again speed-dialed her husband.

※

Clementine Clipster-Commode parked her white Alfa Romeo in one of the Doctor's reserved parking spaces, next to his surgical steel gray Porsche. Clementine hurried into The Doctor Is in Surgery Center. The red light over the No. 2 operating room was on, so Clementine stood quietly and waited.

Several minutes later, the Doctor burst out of the operating room, and ripped off his surgical mask with a manly scowl. Clemmie caught up with him at the door to the men's room.

"What is it, Clemmie?" hissed the Doctor. "For God's sake, I've got a *celebrity* in there."

Clementine gestured, unable to speak. After a moment she recovered her breath.

"Why," she began, still gasping a little, "Why did you and Simon—deceive Dad—with that—woman?"

"Hold that thought," said the Doctor, who still wore his surgical gloves. The Doctor held up a bloody index finger, like a college professor contemplating just the right words to get across his point. Then he heard the op room bell ringing.

The ageing actress was almost under the anesthetic, was what he wanted to say, and he had to get into the bathroom, pee, and get back into the operating room so as not to waste a minute of her time.

"Baron Barrie Clipster!" Clementine pleaded, "Talk to me! Why did you and Simon—conspire—against Dad?"

But the Doctor had disappeared into the men's room. Clementine waited forlornly for a few minutes until he hurried out and brushed past her with a fresh operating room mask on his face. Clemmie followed him down the hall, still trying to understand.

"Clemmie, for God's sakes, I've got an important breast enhancement redo for a client whose name is confidential in Operating Room 2," he brusquely explained.

Pausing before the double stainless steel doors, the Doctor ripped off his surgical gloves, and threw them in the white plastic wastebasket in front of Operating Room No. 2. Then he adjusted his monocle, and rapidly washed his hands.

"The Doctor is in!" he cried, lifting his surgeon's fingers.

A surgical nurse appeared, with a pair of fresh rubber operating gloves for doctor. She was unusually beautiful, Clementine noticed, with a nearly perfect nose and two very large breasts which she rubbed against the doctor's elbows as she muscled on his tight latex gloves. Clementine felt a twinge of jealously as the two of them hurried into Op Room 2, two strange blue figures from the distant planet of Smock.

"Doctor, you've got a *public relations* problem," Clementine shouted as both stainless steel doors swung closed and automatically locked shut.

❧

"**M**iss Gander, pull yourself together. Think! Where did Dad go?" Filly demanded of an overly stimulated and suddenly speechless Miss Gander.

Miss Gander had taken her customary place at the reception desk but sat there staring blankly as people moved around her like a trembling, well-dressed corporate mummy.

Finally Miss Gander stood up, stumbled forward, and with trembling fingers wordlessly unlocked the conference room. She pointed speechlessly to the balcony door, which she had locked from the inside.

"There's nobody here!" Filly shouted from the balcony.

Below him in the moonlit courtyard, where fortunately there was no dead body, nobody who looked anything like his father was visible. Nobody was visible inside the gazebo. Beyond that he saw only the lights of downtown Santa Barbara, and beyond that the dark lightless expanse of what he knew was the Pacific Ocean.

On the balcony Philip Commode took a moment to breathe deeply, inhaling the healing negative ions of the brisk sea air. It was a deceptively peaceful moment.

Beautiful Diego appeared. Diego threw one arm around Philip, and for an instant they were lost in the gentle flush of victory.

"Philip," Miss Gander urgently whispered as she tiptoed up behind them, breaking the moment of enchantment. "Mr. Butterknut needs you downstairs right away. He says it's very important."

❦

Not far from the old elevator, every reporter in the room was huddled around celebrity TV reporter Mike Wallace, who was talking to his network's lawyers on a cell phone. As Mike Wallace angrily related the graphic details of his confrontation in the penthouse, other reporters took notes of his highly confidential conversation and glanced at each other.

The Prince hurried toward Philip as soon as he stepped out of the elevator.

"You've got to make a statement right away," Simon hissed. The grim-faced publicist nodded dumbly in agreement.

"Just be very upbeat and positive," said Sue Spooking in a high-pitched voice that did not disguise her own fear. "The content isn't important. Once you've made a statement on behalf of the company, they've triangulated. They'll all file their stories, and go home for the night."

"Dad doesn't want *any* publicity," Philip whispered.

"No *shit*," Simon hissed.

"It would be a betrayal of Dad to speak for him in public," Philip said.

"It's a betrayal if you *don't* make a statement and get these guys out of here right away," Simon hissed, pushing him up the stairs toward the bank of microphones. "They all want to talk to Commodore, but Commodore doesn't want to talk to them and besides that, we can't find him."

"It's not my *job*," Philip said.

"Your name is *Commode*," Simon hissed.

Simon's cell phone vibrated and he picked up.

"I can't stop them," Petunia desperately sobbed, from behind the wheel of her Range Rover. "They're almost onto State Street! Simon, for the love of God, help me! I'm afraid they're all going to have heart attacks!"

"I'll get back to you," Simon snapped, folding his plastic phone and turning it off.

"For God's sake, Philip, just get up there and *say something*," Simon said, pointing toward the podium.

The Prince did not want any more attention on himself. He was not enjoying his first fifteen minutes of fame. Although accustomed to the nitpicking give and take of legal argument, the smoke-blowing Prince was unprepared for the open-ended questions lobbed at him by the reporters, one after the other, like ticking hand grenades. The vice president of legal affairs had nothing prepared, he had not planned for this, he had no notes, he was afraid of sticking his foot in his mouth, and at that moment he was not capable of improvisation.

Hugging her press kits to her chest, Sue Spooking looked up at her buffed-up boss. She heard the rumble of more reporter's feet, as Mike Wallace completed his call and led the pack of righteously agitated reporters back across the lobby toward them. A frightened expression spread across her face.

"They're back," she whispered.

The reporters gathered around the base of the podium like a school of hungry fish. Spooking led the shell-shocked Prince back up the stairs to the makeshift podium. Diego squeezed Philip's hand, and kissed him on the cheek.

The Prince found himself before a tottering, jerry-rigged bank of live microphones, which again seemed to shift in the air before him so like the heads of so many black, hooded, poisonous snakes.

"Philip Commode will make a statement for the Commode Company," the Prince eventually managed to say.

"He's the son of the board chairman, he's 47 years old, and he sits on the board of the directors. That's Philip with one L, and Commode with one C and two Ms," Spooking called out to the scribbling reporters.

Philip Commode approached the microphones, impeccably dressed but not exactly sure of what he was going to say.

The TV cameras caught a handsome, well-dressed young man in Salvatore Ferragamo. With his suit jacket tossed casually back across his shoulders, the young man looked every inch the blue-blooded young corporate Turk, except for the slightly discordant note of the sprouting blood red hair. None of the reporters noticed the long-haired young Spaniard with the soulful brown eyes looking adoringly up at Philip, with clasped hands. Nobody at all noticed Philip's beautiful sister Clementine creep shyly in the front entrance, apparently frightened as she looked around and tried to smile.

"Friends, American workers, members of the press," Philip Commode said. "I wish I could tell you that a great industrial tragedy has been already been averted. These men have come here because they love their jobs and our great country, the United States of America," Philip began. "These wonderful men and women drove across the United States because they don't want our family's plants to move to China."

Surprisingly, a cheer rose up from across the room. The workers rushed around a figure near the entrance. A few American flags began waving on the other side of the lobby.

"I'm Commodore Commode, I'm the head of this company, and I don't want our plants to move, period!" shouted Commodore Commode from the other side of the room.

After a few sips of beer, the old billionaire and his two old friends strode manfully through the front door. Nobody noticed him for a minute or two. Commodore had to wave his arms and shout his words a second time to be heard.

"Dad?"

At the microphone, Philip Commode recognized his father's voice. Some of the reporters turned to see Old Commodore Commode walking unsteadily forward, flanked by his old pals from the lid-bolting crew. Philip could tell his father had something to drink because he was already slurring his words. His father could not hold two drops of liquor. The cameras and reporters shifted focus, undulating around in mass to face Commodore Commode.

"That's my father, Commodore Commode, CEO and chairman of the board of directors," Philip Commode said. "Give my father some walking room, please."

Suddenly, the sea of reporters parted. Philip was surprised to see his father stagger across the room, hug him, and take the podium in both hands as if he were an accomplished public speaker. His pals Dewey and Pete hung back, but Commodore motioned for them to come up on the platform beside him. Next to Commodore, Dewey and Pete blushed and blinked shyly as the workers across the room began stamping their feet in unison. There was electricity in the air.

"I'm Mike Wallace!" shouted Mike Wallace, mounting the platform with a microphone which he stuck in Commodore's face. "And the world wants to know why the corporate fat cat owners of this company are planning to send seven hundred and fifty thousand American jobs overseas?"

"We're not moving our plants *anywhere*," Commodore shouted, pumping his fist in the air, to the roar of the crowd. "We're an American company. And by God, we're staying put in the United States of America!"

Commodore impulsively clasped hands with Dewey and Pete. In unison, the three men raised their hands into the air in a sort of triple victory salute.

Strobe lights clicked like castanets. After a moment of confusion, the silence morphed into a roar. The men from Cleveland stomped their feet, jumping and clapping. They began to run across the room with tears in their eyes to hug Commodore and Philip Commode.

"Let's get these men and women back to work!" Commodore shouted.

Another roar welled up from the crowd, which had become an animal with a brain of its own. In the twinkling of an eye, working men and women mixed with reporters, photographers, and TV crews. Commodore, Pete, and Dewey were swept up on broad shoulders, muscular shoulders, big shoulders, and carried out of the lobby, perhaps to Hernando's Hideaway, which was still open and only blocks away.

In the lobby, reporters pecked away on their laptops, dutifully e-mailing away their stories on cell phones. Sue Spooking, more relaxed now, was getting a little turned on by all the cute media guys. Unbuttoning her pale yellow blouse a bit, she circulated around the room, flirting and trying to pass out the last of the press kits to the suddenly disinterested reporters.

The Prince felt faint. The world was not as he imagined it to be.

Gasping for breath, Simon staggered outside the building, and onto the sidewalk for some fresh air.

Simon sat down on the curb next to one of the uniformed doormen and opened his mouth without speaking. Workers and reporters streamed past him into the street without looking at him. Simon actually did not see the herd of miniature pigs gallop by.

The Prince also did not notice the pale green Range Rover, just behind the pigs, whose driver was wildly waving and frantically honking her horn.

And if his successors had remained united, they might also have enjoyed possession at their ease; for no other disturbances occurred in that empire, except such as they created themselves.

—Machiavelli, *The Prince*

21. ABSOLUTION

The boys from Cleveland remained in Montecito for several days. The first night, they carried Commodore around to every bar in Santa Barbara. He had never had his back slapped so often. After trying valiantly to keep pace with the toasts and counter-toasts, the old billionaire passed out. Dewey and Pete took him home in Don Dumper's mud-spattered Taurus. They delivered their drunken boss into the competent hands of R.G. Spartan, the tallest and most distinguished-looking Englishman they'd ever seen.

Following the tall Englishman, they carried Commodore's limp frame down a long hallway, and into his suite of bedrooms. The two workers lay the old billionaire on a very large empty bed, which somehow made him look small and practically frail. After Commodore mumbled something they couldn't understand, the tall Englishman graciously insisted Pete and Dewey spend the night in one of the guest rooms, and told them to invite the other workers from Cleveland to come out to the mansion, too.

Soon Commode Company trucks honked down the driveway of the well-lighted mansion. The line of parked trucks extended past Milly's gardenia bushes almost all the way out to Swizzle Stick Road. The guys and gals from Cleveland were then treated to an incredible feast, the likes of which most of them had never seen.

Commodore's personal chefs had been called in on short notice. The chefs were kept busy for several days, bringing out gourmet dishes one after another to the endless buffet in the Grand Ballroom. In their tall white hats, they worked like so many short-order cooks to serve the tidal wave of workers.

"Damned if old Commie don't know how to eat," said Dewey, helping his plate again. "You ever had grub like this before, Pete?"

"Hell no," Pete snorted approvingly. "But I'm having me some more."

As more workers drifted in, the old valet graciously took them on a stately midnight tour of the mansion.

"You mean to tell me only one person living in this great big house?" one of the guys asked.

"Mr. Commode's beloved wife passed away some time ago. Mrs. Commode dearly loved to entertain," R.G. said in a doleful tone of voice, as he concluded the tour in the Grand Ballroom. The ballroom's high ceilings and crystal chandeliers had some of the workers turning and blinking like so many spinning tops around the dance floor.

The most soulful among them sensed a whiff of loneliness at the top of the material world. The less sensitive simply ate and drank all they could hold, spent the necessary amount of time oogling the mansion's spectacular bathrooms, and then claimed this or that bedroom to catch a few Zs.

When Commodore finally sobered up and wandered through the crowd, he was so happy he immediately broke open his modest wine cellar. The wine and champagne flowed at Commodora for several days, until the bottles of all the best wine he had had been tossed into a pile behind the servants' quarters like so many useless canisters of glass, and all the extra food Commodore's chefs prepared had been eaten, replenished, and eaten again. A few of the men even tried out the golf course, making the rounds with a delighted Commodore, who promised every worker who played golf a complimentary set of golf clubs.

During the week, Filly and Diego and the Commode girls Petunia and Clementine made an appearance here and there. They were all happily embraced and greeted by the celebrating workers. But mindful of their responsibilities at the plant, after a few days the guys from Cleveland began longing for home.

Saturday morning, the men and women of Cleveland bid the old billionaire goodbye. One by one, company trucks lumbered out onto Swizzle Stick Road and rag tag made their way back home to Cleveland. Dewey and Pete were the last to say goodbye to Commodore. All three of them choked up on the porch as they hugged and said goodbye, quite probably, they knew, for the last time.

After the guests departed, R.G. unlocked Mr. Philip Commode's old suite of bedrooms, where closets had been filled with red coconuts and so forth. The rooms had been locked and kept off limits to guests. However, the old valet was mildly surprised to come upon the remains of Mr. Commode's Golden Weeha. The monkey's lifeless eyes were wide open. Its hard purple tongue hung silently out of the side of its mouth. In just a few days the little animal had apparently become hideously overweight and a victim of its own gluttony.

The fat little creature had most likely died when its stomach and small intestine burst, according to a veterinary autopsy which followed. Whatever permanently silenced the sad little monkey left it sitting up like a rag doll in the seat of a coconut milk-stained Louis XIV chair. The old valet remembered that young Mr. Commode once had the 250-year-old chair, his favorite, immaculately upholstered in white satin.

❧

Before the party was over, Petunia filed for divorce. Her husband of many years had disgraced himself in front of her father, of course, but even Simon's shameful plotting and double-dealing wouldn't have been enough for Petunia to divorce him. For Petunia, Simon's unforgivable offense had been to ignore her and her runaway pigs. In her hour of greatest need, on the one night in her life Petunia needed Simon's assistance with the pigs, she told her patiently nodding divorce lawyers, Simon was too busy to take her frantic emergency calls. Her husband actually hung up on her! Twice! He turned his precious cell phone off! Her lawyers nodded sympathetically and took notes as Petunia angrily removed her pith helmet, rolled up her sleeves, and began to recount the night of the lost pigs in copious detail.

When the marshals arrived to forcibly remove Simon from the mansion, the Prince tried to call Petunia one last time on his cell phone. By the time he finally got through to her, the Prince was sitting behind wire mesh in the marshal's truck as it headed out the driveway. Petunia wouldn't listen to the first few words of his long-winded explanation.

It infuriated Petunia that she chased her pigs right past Commode Company headquarters. Furthermore, she caught a glimpse of Simon idly watching them pass with a completely vacant expression on his face. Where was her fast-talking husband when she needed him? Simon had not come to her rescue on what she would always and forever remember as the most traumatic night of her life.

Of course the frightened little pigs had stampeded north through Santa Barbara, though Isla Vista, and continued on out onto the shoulder of the Pacific Coast highway. Then, with a suddenness which surprised her, just after they crossed a bridge, blinded by oncoming headlights perhaps, the horribly exhausted little pigs had galloped off the right side of the road and down a tall embankment toward a dumpy little Santa Barbara County park which was surrounded by chain link fence and locked up for the night.

Screeching to a halt on the road shoulder, Petunia froze to the wheel of the Range Rover, helplessly looking out the window. At the bottom of that dangerous rock-strewn arroyo, the entire frightened pack of hysterical little pigs rooted and rutted at the base of the chain link fence. One after another, the pigs broke under the fence and galloped heedlessly away, tossing their snouts in the air like proud little horses. Petunia did not notice a white-haired old troll under a nearby bridge, passively witnessing the scene.

As her pigs galloped away forever, completely breaking her heart, Petunia experienced a kind of trembling paralysis. In short, she had a brief, intense nervous breakdown.

Petunia's trembling hands froze to the steering wheel. She was unable to scream. She was unable to get out of the vehicle and follow the pigs. She was unable even to take her hands off the steering wheel of her Range Rover until the ambulances arrived at her vehicle, red lights flashing.

When Petunia was released from the mental hospital three days later, of course she blamed Simon for everything. It had been Simon who had slipped onto Pig Island in the middle of the night. It had been Simon whose devious late-night phone call began the long chain of events that had led to the pigs being moved into a temporary pen off the island for security reasons, from which they'd broken loose that fateful night. Thanks to Simon the pigs had been able to crawl through a tiny opening in the temporary fence, eluding the frantic gardeners and security men who immediately radioed Petunia for help.

As Petunia leaped into her Range Rover to head them off, the entire little herd bolted for the driveway like a school of frightened minnows. As she explained over and over to her divorce lawyers, the culprit and the scapegoat for the tragedy which followed was Simon Butterknut, her father's former employee, once the love of her life, a gentleman who could no longer be characterized as The Prince.

As the stone-faced marshals ushered the protesting lawyer out of the mansion and into the truck, Petunia added insult to injury by blocking the marshal's transport vehicle at the gate with her Range Rover.

With burning tears of rage streaming down her cheeks, Petunia got out and flung Simon's expensive leather briefcase toward her disgraced husband, who was gesturing in the back seat with his Rolex and his cell phone. The expensive briefcase came open and spun clumsily in the air, scattering papers as if attempting to take flight on hot air, but it bounced off the hood of the marshal's truck and collapsed limply to the ground.

"Honey," Simon said, rolling down the window as far as he could. "I'm sorry."

Petunia froze for a moment like a woman summoning up all the furies of Hell. She pointed a quivering index finger at Simon, the Angry Avenging Angel herself.

"Honey me no longer, Simon Butterknut," Petunia said. "Not only are you the traitorous snake in the grass who conspired to cheat and humiliate my father. Ultimately, you became a *pig killer*! Three pigs lost, probably *all* dead! And it's all your fault!" Petunia shrieked.

She ripped off her pith helmet and angrily threw it at the truck, too. Simon crouched in the back of the truck, his mouth agape as the pith helmet careened off the roof of the truck. The former vice president of legal affairs was at that moment a lawyer unable to talk.

With a toss of her mane and a gesture to the marshals, Petunia climbed into her Range Rover and pulled away with a powerful finality that cried "goodbye, fool."

A few minutes later, Petunia's lawyers brought up Simon's sad smoking old Corvette. They left it parked just outside the gate, with the keys in the ignition. As Simon watched, Petunia's lawyers quietly locked the driveway gate behind them.

❦

The Doctor tried his best to ignore what had happened to his old fraternity brother. He made no effort to see Nutty at all, even on the day that Clementine snarled over lunch that his no-good fraternity brother was being evicted from his mansion for good.

The Doctor tried his best to throw himself back into his work, and to distance himself from the whole mess. Unfortunately, he wasn't getting along well with Clementine at all.

But fortunately for Doctor, Clementine had done what she always did when faced with an unpleasant situation. She put her dogs in Madam Renoir's private boarding kennel, hopped on a plane, and went shopping.

Filly and Diego took a long vacation, which Commodore and the girls learned about through postcards, postings on Filly's Facebook page, and snapshots and snippets of video they sent back from their phones.

For the first part of their vacation, Diego and Filly were followed and taped by the camera crew. After what happened, Philip felt an enormous debt of gratitude to the crew. The camera crew had been so helpful he just couldn't bear to let them go. Filly and Diego decided to keep them working and traveling with them until it got too boring.

Trailed by the camera crew, Filly and Diego flew to Jamaica, where they spent two days getting mud packs and massages, having their hair braided into cornrows, and drinking expensive bottled water at a picturesque, highly fortified Club Med. The boys and the camera crew frolicked on the beach under the eyes of security guards, and danced to reggae music with each other and with the shapely young wives of aging corporate executives far into the night.

They were on their way to Cannes, changing planes at JFK Airport in New York, when they unexpectedly ran into Clementine. Clementine had just arrived in town for Fashion Week, perhaps to look at a few new things. The three of them said hello and parted without much ado. Philip's intuition told him that something was amiss with Clementine.

At Cannes, they discreetly shopped around the footage, which the camera crew had shaped into a sort of documentary.

Although everybody just loved the story, and they especially liked the old butler character, and all the Hollywood types really enjoyed meeting them for coffee and dinner and having them pick up the tab, the boys concluded that nobody was seriously interested in their project, which after all ended with an uneventful return to the status quo. And all this was probably a good thing, Philip realized afterward, since Commodore abhorred publicity of any kind, and he might have seen even a small tasteful documentary as a violation of his precious privacy. After the fizzle and pop of Cannes, the boys bid an goodbye to the camera crew, and continued on to Rome.

They sped around Rome on two rented little red Vespas like two mad characters out of *La Dolce Vita*. The food was rich and wonderful although the Mediterranean sun was not kind to Filly's red hair, which seemed to turn a different shade of red every day. Still, they both got great tans. They went to several meetings. They puttered through the ancient streets of Rome and wandered lazily through boutiques and open-air markets, releasing pent-up stress. Diego used his rusty Italian to dicker with the street vendors, waving his arms and gesturing wildly like an Italian as he dickered, which amused the natives. Filly learned enough Italian to say "Good morning," and "What is your best price for this item?" The boys sent a few little things home before they were off for the last phase of their vacation in the distant mountains of Nepal.

❧

The Prince had been banished from the richest family in America. Like some sad, Biblical figure, the former Prince drove his smoking Corvette around Santa Barbara in a daze, like a homeless person, which for a while he technically was since for the first few days he slept in his car. What was left of his hair soon grew out on the sides and back, giving him a slight resemblance to the comic figure, Bozo the Clown. The former vice president of legal affairs was not really surprised that no one in the legal affairs department would take his calls.

After he angrily pawned the first of his Rolex watches, the Prince took a room in a Motel 6, on the seedy side of Santa Barbara. Sleeping in the tiny little room felt like sleeping in a can of smoked sardines. With its rickety aluminum window and the heavy plastic drapes, the modest little weekly rental seemed unbelievably small and drab after life among the mansions and millionaires of Swizzle Stick Road.

Somewhat humbled although still not entirely repentant, Simon longed for the soft easy life of the Commodes. He racked his brain for a way to win back the position which had been handed to him in the upper echelons of American society, a position he feared was lost forever as he polished his resume under the small plastic lamp bolted to the fake wood desk.

The former Prince had come to the Motel 6 with all his worldly possessions—his copy of the pre-nuptial agreement, all the Armani suits and accessories he could carry, his Rolexes, his designer edition Mont Blanc pens, half a box of Cuban cigars, half a case of good wine, and his hand-tooled leather briefcase—everything Petunia's lawyers and maids could stuff into the only car he had ever really owned.

It was a sad fact that the only one of the family's many vehicles actually in Simon's name was the vintage red and white Corvette he drove while at Stanford. Petunia had insisted he keep it in the one of the garages after their marriage, for sentimental reasons, he presumed at the time.

The old Corvette smoked like a tank, the rings were nearly gone, but it still ran after sitting in one of the garages for more than a dozen years without even being started. The Prince had gotten so used to his personal fleet of Mercedes, a different colored sedan for every day of the week and one to spare, that he had forgotten about the old Corvette. Now the chuffing and banging old sports car was the former Prince's sole remaining transportation, a bitter reminder of his glory years in law school when all things seemed possible and when he believed he could bullshit his way to the top of the world.

Simon dearly missed his enormous mansion, his home gymnasium, his fleet of Mercedes sedans, his corner office, his secretaries, long lunches, his employees, and his other office perks. He even missed sleeping with Petunia.

The day after he was evicted from the mansion, Simon consulted a cynical old lawyer he had gotten to know while serving on the tournament committee at the country club Perhaps the old lawyer could broker some kind of divorce settlement? Petunia's lawyers had frozen his assets and almost all of his credit cards. All the jointly-held cards were technically in Petunia's name.

The lawyer he consulted, the misnamed "Happy" Finnegan, shook his head with disbelief when he read the agreement.

"You went to in law school, and you *signed* this?" Happy Finnegan asked. He looked at Simon with a sad pair of baggy, doleful eyes.

Simon shook his head yes.

"Your ex-wife had a good attorney."

The old lawyer made a sour face like somebody's dog was crapping in his vegetable garden. He returned the document without looking at Simon, and buzzed his secretary.

As Simon strode out of the office, he thought he heard the old lawyer and his secretary burst into laughter behind him.

Among the other causes of evil that will befall a prince who is destitute of a proper military force is, that it will cause him to be scorned; which is one of those disgraces against which a prince ought specially to guard, as we will demonstrate later on.

– Machiavelli, *The Prince*

When Simon moved into the Motel 6, temporarily, he hoped, he immediately began to speculate on how he could find one of Petunia's three lost pigs. Nothing else would save him. Perhaps one of the pigs wasn't dead. He knew park rangers had recovered two pigs rooting around in the ashes of the park's barbeque pits the next morning, but three of Petunia's favorite pigs remained missing. If he could find even one of his wife's beloved pigs, the desperately scheming lawyer reasoned, he might have a chance to talk his way back into Petunia's cold, unforgiving heart.

With a hope born of desperation, the Prince began driving his smoking Corvette up and down the hills and back roads of Santa Barbara County in an elusive search for any of Petunia's three lost pigs.

It was not easy to find a pig gone native, Simon knew. He didn't believe any of Petunia's pampered darlings could survive for very long in the wild. The clock was on. Simon had heard Petunia babbling on about pigs enough to know the three lost pigs probably wouldn't stay together, unless it was mating season and there was only one boar in the group. A hungry pig eats anything, the former Prince reasoned, and there were enough dumps, garbage cans and dumpsters around the hills of Santa Barbara to keep hundreds of wandering pigs alive for a long time.

Several times, Simon desperately slipped through the rusting barbed wire fence on the far side of the county dump to avoid paying the admission fee.

Ankle-deep in trash, the Prince walked up and down steaming fragrant mountains of rotten food, plastic bottles, crushed refried bean cans and other trash in a vain search for lost pigs. He ruined more than one pair of cowboy boots. However, if he could just find one of Petunia's pigs, he thought, tromping tirelessly up and down trash mountains like a thirsty man lost in the desert, maybe he could find a means to slip into Petunia's king-sized Princess Diana Special Edition English canopy bed, and sweet talk his way back into his former exalted place in Petunia's angry, broken heart.

Unfortunately, many days passed. On the day he found out he didn't qualify for unemployment, Simon reluctantly pawned his second Rolex.

But a few hours after he left the pawn shop, the former Prince experienced a bit of good luck. Simon was eating frequently at McDonald's now, when he could afford to eat, and he had already let out his belt two notches when he overheard rumors of a mysterious Egg McMuffin-eating pig.

This pig had apparently become a regular at the McDonald's right down the road from his motel, a nocturnal cannibal of sorts, rooting through food wrappers and trash for its favorite food, castaway sausage Egg McMuffins. That day, as he waited for his Big Mac and fries, Simon overheard one of the pimple-faced young girls in paper hats gossiping. Her boyfriend, a supervisor on the night shift, told her a little black pig had been coming around the dumpster every night for a week. The pig would only eat thrown-out sausage Egg McMuffins, she said. Her boyfriend made all the new employees try to shoo the little pig away, just like a homeless person, the girl laughed, but it was hard to shoo the Egg McMuffin-loving pig away.

The wild-eyed lawyer in the rumpled Armani suit leaned over the counter to interrogate the girl in the paper hat. The frightened girl, backing away from the fast-talking stranger, swore that every word of the pig story was true. Simon instantly reasoned that the pig was probably one of Petunia's.

Shortly after midnight the same night, Simon scrunched down low in the driver's seat of his car. His suit remained damp. Earlier in the evening, McDonald's Spanish-speaking employees had twice run him away from the trash bins. Macho young Hispanics in paper hats doused the loitering lawyer with a water hose, scornfully cursing at him in Spanish when he shook his fist and threatened to sue them. In broken English they threatened to call the police if they saw him hanging around their dumpster again.

Simon slumped down in the bucket seat of his Corvette in a far corner of the parking lot at McDonald's, out of sight of the drive-through window and his arrogant young tormenters. The night was cool and he had begun to shiver. A half-eaten sausage Egg McMuffin grew cold in his hand.

Simon left his keys in the ignition, in case he had to leave quickly. He had a Motel 6 blanket in the passenger seat along with a couple of white Motel 6 hand towels he'd drenched in 100 proof vodka, in case he had to pacify the pig. His Rolex Daytona read 12:03.

The drive-through lane was full of cars, what seemed like an endless procession of cars full of dopey-looking teenage boys on still another vain search for midnight pussy. The air pulsated with the throbbing bass of their strange aggressive rap music, which unsettled the already shivering lawyer.

A carload of girls wheeled into a parking space not far away. Immediately, two carloads of guys pulled in, one on either side of the girls, music ominously pumping. The two carloads of guys glared at each other while the girls pecked at their phones. As music throbbed, Simon was afraid to look.

The guys competed for the girls' attention by insulting each other in the nastiest possible street language. It was the fashion of the day—middle class kids trying to talk like prison inmates or foul-mouthed professional athletes.

"You baggy ass motherfuckers get the fuck out of here!" one guy shouted to the other car over, cranking up his music. "We be hanging with these hoes!"

Were the kids talking about him? Simon wondered. He thought they said, "That lazy-assed lawyer in the Corvette over there? Homeboys inside just gave him the hose!"

The driver of the second car turned up his sound system and cried, "Homeless lawyer kicked outta that big house! Now he be hanging out here?"

Another voice cried, "Ain't your heart he broke, boy. His woman gone, his pockets empty, he got nothing left but that old car!"

"You're a loser!" cranking up the music.

"You be the loser, fool!" cranking it up again.

Suddenly the girls' car pulled away, followed by both carloads of boys, all pecking on their phones. In the sudden silence Simon's stomach fizzled. Did every person in Santa Barbara know of his fall from grace?

As he stared at his cold Egg McMuffin, trying to blush, the Prince experienced a moment of profound reflection.

Life was a game in which the strong ate the weak, the former Prince believed, but he did not feel particularly strong at that moment and he was not even particularly hungry. The cruel Machiavellian homily which rolled over and over in his brain helped chill the former Prince to the pit of his stomach. Simon glanced at his Rolex. 12:45.

A Santa Barbara police car cruised toward the drive-through, breaking the silence, police radio crackling. The heavy-set female at the wheel seemed to be glaring right at him. Simon held up his half-eaten Egg McMuffin, took a bite of the stone cold sausage, and tried to smile. The portly female cop made a remark to her partner, scowled, and looked away. 1:37.

Finally the McDonald's employees changed shifts. Simon had waited until the last possible minute to hurry inside to use the bathroom. The bathroom door was locked. The night shift employees looked knowingly at each other, and refused to give him a key. A smirking pimple-faced kid in a paper hat who looked about 12 years old swore that the men's room was out of order. Hurrying outside, aware that the kids were lying to him, Simon tried to start his car to go to a gas station. Unfortunately, the little Corvette wouldn't start. Hopping out of his car, holding his pants and ready to burst now, squeezing his crotch, half-peeing on himself, Simon ran into the alley behind the McDonald's dumpster, unzipped his pants under a streetlight, and relieved himself on a pile of empty cardboard croissant boxes. As he shook the last bit of urine off his penis, Simon heard the sound of music. It was a hard, clicking sound, not unlike the sound of flamenco boots on hardwood, or dancing castanets.

Simon recognized the sound of cloven pig feet on pavement, the characteristic starting and stopping. He was hearing the footsteps of a finicky little pig looking for dinner.

Hurriedly zipping up his pants, Simon caught the end of his tender penis in the zipper. Cursing to himself, and stifling a scream, he carefully pulled his flesh out of the zipper, screaming inside but trying to be quiet and freeze since he saw a skinny black Chinese pot-bellied pig waddling heedlessly up the alley toward the dumpster

The pig had managed to survive in the big city. It rooted and runted down dumpster alley, in a leisurely fashion. The pig stopped to sniff some empty McDonalds' bags, then disgustedly tossed one of them away into the air with its snout. The pig froze for a moment with a half-eaten yellow Egg McMuffin wrapper in its mouth as Simon crept forward on all fours.

Lifting its snout, the little pig's eyes narrowed. The hair on its back stood up like the bristles on a hairbrush. This one was a male, Simon realized. The little boar assumed a fighting position, snorting and pawing the earth with one hoof.

Motel 6 blanket in one hand, wet towel in the other, Simon leapt clumsily onto the squealing, snapping pig. He struggled to put the towel soaked in vodka over the pig's snout, but the pig didn't like that and squirmed away. With surprising animal strength, the wiry little animal squirmed out his arms and bit Simon's index finger. Simon howled, shaking his bleeding hand, as the pig lunged away. But the little pig stopped with a snort, momentarily blinded and confused by the yellow Egg McMuffin wrapper over its eyes.

Shaking his bloody hand to stop the bleeding, Simon managed a spectacular dive to land on the pig's back. Using a wrestling hold he had learned in high school, the desperate lawyer rode the squealing little pig down to its knees. With a burst of strength he didn't know he had, he carried the kicking and squealing pig to his car like a cowboy with a calf over his shoulders, wrangled it into the trunk of his Corvette, and with all his remaining strength wrapped the vodka-soaked towel around the snout of the squirming, kicking pig and held it there. The pig kicked and snorted as Simon brought down the lid of the trunk, but after it kicked a couple of dents in his trunk lid the little pig finally relaxed and was quiet.

The next morning, Simon pushed the buzzer on the gate to the driveway of his old mansion on Swizzle Stick Road. He naively expected a bit of gratitude, or at least a thank you, come in and have a cup of coffee, from Petunia.

The Prince wore his dark blue Armani suit, because he knew Petunia always said he looked like a real lawyer in the dark blue suit. It was the suit she always said made him look most like the snarling, portly lawyer on her favorite TV show, *Beverly Hills Law.*

Simon had gained weight on the fast food diet, making the suit tight on his muscular frame, but this only heightened his tired, pathetic look and might work in his favor.

"Petunia, open up, it's Simon," he whispered into the intercom. "I've got little Beaufort in the car. Your lost little Beaufort, still wearing his little name tag."

Before long, the Pig Island security truck arrived at the gate. Out of the truck came a couple of beefy guys and Petunia's Mexican maid. With hand gestures, the little maid wouldn't let Simon come near the gate. She supervised the pig handlers from a safe distance, using hand signals. She motioned Simon away from the gate as the men lifted the groggy pig out of the trunk of Simon's Corvette, and carried it away. Simon watched them carefully place the groggy pig into a cage in the back of the Pig Island pickup, lock the cage, and disappear.

As she slammed and locked the gate, Petunia's Mexican maid raised her chin, defiantly glaring at Simon and whispering into a cell phone.

A few minutes later, Petunia grandly and arrogantly arrived. On the other side of the metal gate, Petunia stepped out of her Range Rover, nose held high in the air. Taking off her pith helmet, Petunia put her hands on her hips and glared at Simon through the gate's reinforced steel bars. Simon put both hands on the bars, then sadly lowered his eyes before his glowering, estranged wife.

"Two missing pigs!" Petunia cried. "Two helpless animals lost, or alone, and probably, dead! Two more missing pigs because of—one attorney's extreme negligence! Negligent stupid heartless pig-killing monster!" Petunia screamed.

She angrily turned on her heels.

Petunia's little maid was already sitting in the Range Rover, two bright brown eyes glaring out the window of the passenger side.

"I'll find another pig!" the former Prince cried in his best courtroom voice. "Honey, I'll find another one, I swear it."

Petunia threw the Range Rover into gear, fishtailed around in a smoking circle of flying grass and dirt, and disappeared.

⁂

Clementine met an exciting man during Fashion Week in New York. She had a VIP invitation to the exclusive Rikki Montana showing, held in a urine-soaked crack house in Harlem. It was a sordid environment chosen to be edgy, exclusive, sexy, and slightly dangerous. Several dozen high rollers like Clementine Commode were escorted from their limousines into the show by beefy black bodybuilders in purple tuxedos and white turbans. This lent a fizzle of racial excitement to Rikki Montana's trashy, overpriced collection.

Inside, cocktail waitresses dressed up like crack whores circulated through the crowd, taking orders for free drinks. As the show began, amazingly skinny biracial models staggered quickly down the makeshift runway, kicking aside crack pipes and jerking this way and that to loud, hostile rap music. To many of the less discriminating, the ambiance disguised the fact that Rikki's exciting new collection was composed mostly of recycled variations of his last trashy urban look collection—a little too much baggy butt red hopsack and plastic mesh covered with crystal buttons, strips of recycled Levis, and accessories studded with pieces of broken CDs.

An unusually wide captain's chair next to Clementine was conspicuously empty. Suddenly, a heavy-set stranger appeared out of nowhere and hurled his bulk down into the chair. The wide-bodied stranger took an expensive Cuban cigar out of his pocket. He threw a nasty glance around the room and wrinkled his rather large, protruding nose.

"Smells like piss in here," the man sniffed, in a heavy New Jersey accent.

The obnoxious stranger was short, big, bald, cynical, about sixty, and impeccably dressed. For a man, he wore a lot of diamonds. Everything about him screamed Big Shot. The mysterious stranger, Clementine would learn later, owned a dozen Rump's department stores, among the most exclusive on the East Coast. His name was Judas Rump, and his manner was as cold and blunt as his name.

Judas Rump arrogantly lit his cigar. Smoking, Clemmie knew, was at the top of the list of this show's prohibited activities she'd been given on the way over, in the limousine. But she found the man's macho swagger strangely exciting.

Judas inhaled deeply, large nostrils flaring. Sniffing just a little, Rump arrogantly flicked cigar ashes on the floor. As he inhaled and turned to face Clementine, Rump's large black eyebrows banged together.

The mysterious stranger appeared to have one long hairy eyebrow which ran from ear to ear.

Judas Rump's stare instantly hypnotized Clementine, who at that moment could not stop herself from staring back at him with her mouth halfway open. Electricity passed between them as Rump exhaled two streams of white cigar smoke from his fleshy nostrils. He stared at Clementine from under the one long eyebrow.

"No smoking allowed?" Clementine suggested.

It embarrassed her that her voice quavered like the voice of a young schoolgirl.

"We're sittin' in a fucking crack house," Rump sneered. "And I'm a buyer here."

With Clementine agog, he arrogantly knocked a cigar ash into her third martini.

"You ever hear the name, Judas Rump?" he asked, pausing for effect before he inhaled again.

When Rump saw Clementine trying to blush and struggling for breath, he leaned over and whispered, "Take off those expensive panties, and I'll give you a little taste of big Judas right here on the table."

Clementine was speechless. She struggled to breathe. All around her, wildly erotic hip hop music pounded the air up and down. Momentarily speechless, in an unexplainable swoon, her mind raced into overdrive, overflowing with wild sexual fantasies. Her moistening vagina seemed to lift and tilt hungrily toward the stranger through the parting sea of her fashionable short skirt. Strangely fascinated and energized, she felt her vagina quiver—a breathless female porpoise wildly kicking toward the surface of the ocean, ready to open its wet mouth for a breath of sweet, fresh, life-giving air.

"I'm in the Abraham Lincoln suite," Clementine gasped. Almost without thinking, she brashly placed a duplicate of her Waldorf Astoria room key on the man's table.

Rump sneered at the key. But he picked it up, dropped it in his pocket, and looked at his oversized diamond-studded Omega watch.

"Maybe I'll peep in on ya' later tonight," he sneered out of the side of his mouth. "If I got a couple minutes."

Clementine's entire body tingled. Why did she love the department store mogul's rough, masculine talk? Why had she always been attracted to tough-talking, self-centered men? And why didn't the Doctor get rough with her anymore? She didn't know what happened to their big neck-biting, back-scratching, hair-pulling romance. Even the last round of butt implants and the vaginal rejuvenation didn't seem to stimulate the Doctor, who lately seemed to be distancing himself from everyone in the family including Clementine herself.

"I like it rough," Clementine blurted.

Rump snorted. He put out his cigar on her bread plate with a sneer. The air reeked of burnt butter as he stood up and turned his formidable body away.

"It's a pleasure to meet you," Clementine warbled, extending her trembling hand.

But the tough-talking stranger arrogantly waddled away.

Not far away, Rikki Montana models staggered down the runway two at a time to the pounding, martial beat of crack house rap music. The song they played over and over again was entitled "The Ruiner."

❧

It was not exactly by chance that the Prince heard there was a pig on top of the mountain. Not knowing what else to do, and having a lot of time on his hands, the disgraced barrister had returned again and again to the little state park where Petunia's pigs ran under the fence, searching for clues to their whereabouts.

On one of these expeditions, Simon ran into an ageing surf bum who lived under a nearby bridge. The old surf bum had the longest head of white, sun-bleached hair Simon had ever seen, like a hippy aged for 50 years in a vat of white wine. The skinny old troll in the cutoff jeans and yellow beach hat claimed to have been there the night Petunia lost her pigs.

Simon was cluelessly pacing the fence when the old bum whistled him over to his shanty under the bridge. The old bum had built himself a sweet little cardboard hut with a roof of palm fronds on the dry rocky streambed under the bridge. Simon was surprised to see a short, well-waxed old surfboard chained to the door of the cardboard house, over which hung an old Beach Boys 45 of "Good Vibrations" on a string. The old surfer lifted the half-empty bottle of Gallo Burgundy and flashed a set of pink teeth as Simon suspiciously approached.

"So you want pigs, dude?" he said, waving Simon over.

Simon obediently squatted down next to the old bum, pulling up the cuffs of his soft brown Armani suit pants to keep them out of the mud. The squatter's packed mud front yard smelled vaguely of grape must and urine.

"That's correct."

"So, dude, we talk. Sweet."

The old surfer stared into the distance. He seemed to be waiting for something. Even though he was getting short of cash, Simon finally figured it all out and handed the smiling bum a twenty.

"Let's hear your story," Simon said.

"It was like a very dark night? Full moon over the bridge? Had a little late night vino? Taking a leak near the fence, right over there?" the old bum was pointing.

"Babe in a Range Rover stops up on the road? Babe honks and flashes her lights? I see scrambling little pigs slipping and sliding right down this hill? Babe in that Range Rover just sits up there, bawling like a baby, watching it happen, dude?" the old surfer began, nodding in agreement with himself.

He could have been the Ancient Mariner risen from a clump of seaweed to tell his tale to the former Prince.

"Babe didn't even get outta the vehicle, honking, you know?"

"I know all that," Simon said impatiently.

The old surfer waited a while, but when Simon didn't volunteer more money, he wiped his mouth with the back of his hand and continued anyway.

"Next thing I see pigs running up to that fence over there? One little pig dude gets caught in the barbed wire, but the other ones leave him there, squealing to high heaven? Deserted their little pig brother, dude? Little pig gets its foot caught in the fence, dude. Other pigs run off? And I see it all, right here, I see it all? Meanwhile the Babe sits up there?"

The old bum was enjoying his story so much, Simon wanted to punch him in the nose. Instead, the former vice president of legal affairs smiled and nodded, trying to be the most interested audience in the world. He hoped the old bum's story was going somewhere. If it didn't, Simon had already decided to physically overpower the old bum and get his twenty back.

The old surfer unscrewed his bottle, chugged down a couple swallows of Hearty Burgundy, and offered the bottle to Simon who politely declined. The old surfer paused another moment or two for effect, waiting for the wine to hit what was left of his stomach. Then he smiled at Simon with seriously bad teeth.

"First Highway Patrol, then ambulance to take the babe? But one little pig stays caught in the fence, hung up the entire night, and I'm the only one who knows? In the morning I wake up? Now it's beach time, hey, surf's bitchin', sun's shining? It's now ten a.m.?" He paused for effect. "Pig starts squealing again? I get my board, I make my way to el bueno beacho, but once again I need to pee?"

"Of course," Simon said, struggling to hide his impatience.

"So I walk over to that same bush, to take a leak?" he said, pointing toward the fence. "You see, I don't pee in the ocean or my house, but I do use that bush, right, dude?" he giggled, rocking to one side. "Because on the beach the code is we do not foul our own nest? Right? Right?"

Simon forced a smile. He was getting more and more disgusted, but he nodded yes.

"So I'm shaking off my lily when over me passes this, like, *shadow of darkness* like I've never seen before, like a *strategic bomber*, dude," the bum said, spreading his arms for emphasis. "But this is no airplane, right? Up there, swooping down from the sky, like, the biggest, blackest bird I ever seen, looking like a huge giant mercenary crow?"

"Yes."

"I think maybe, a Condor? But here? California Condor? Yes, this is true, dude? Ten foot wingspan, at least, this big, big, dude, you got this, from here to there? I have seen this."

"Please go on."

"Bird drops out of the sky? Big wings flapping, I mean *flapping*, dude? Bird sinks claws into pig, pulls pig off the fence, rips the pig's foot off, flies away?" he said. "Sweet."

Pausing for another slug of Hearty Burgundy, the bum smiled suggestively. After a long pause, he offered Simon a drink. Simon desperately needed something. Against his better judgment, the former vice president of legal affairs took the bottle and wiped off the neck with his sleeve, praying that the alcohol would kill whatever germs the bum had left there. Simon was already kicking himself for giving the bum twenty dollars for some bullshit story that probably wouldn't lead anywhere.

"Get to the point, if there is one," Simon grimaced. "Otherwise, I want the twenty back."

"You simply do not believe this, right?" the bum asked.

Before Simon could answer, the bum reached into his back pocket. He tossed Simon an object, which the clumsy lawyer immediately dropped into the cuff of his right pant leg. Simon extracted what appeared to be a small dry, black, hairy object—one cloven hoof, attached to a section of bone and dried ligaments and skin, obviously the real thing.

"And I do know where that bird took that pig, yes, I do certainly know this, because I live here and I *followed* it, dude," he said, looking from side to side. "Like, maybe I could show you where? Like, maybe I could show you more, if you could just help me out with a little more, you know?"

Simon took off his last Rolex, and handed it over.

❧

Clementine Clipster-Commode lay on an ornate bed in the penthouse of the Waldorf Astoria, a heavily-perfumed odalisque in a short Rikki Montana bathrobe she brought home from the show. She had room service bring up an arrangement of gardenias, the flower of romance, her mother taught her. The sweet sticky aroma of gardenias permeated the air as the Civil War era grandfather clock struck twelve in the entryway of the Abraham Lincoln Suite.

A few minutes after twelve, Judas Rump unlocked the door with Clementine's key, and lumbered inside.

"Hey," he shouted. "Rump!"

"I'm in here," Clementine warbled, closing her eyes and crossing her perfect legs.

Rump loosened his tie. The department store mogul sniffed around suspiciously before he opened the door to the darkened Lincoln bedroom. He flicked a light switch.

The crystal chandelier over the Civil War era canopy bed excitedly lit up. Rump looked Clementine up and down as she writhed expectantly, excited by the searing heat of his eyes.

Rump's big nostrils flared. He put a fresh cigar in his mouth, producing a sort of crunching sound as the cigar was still in its cellophane wrapper. Two rows of nicotine-stained teeth appeared around the unsmoked cigar. Rump's eyebrows banged together.

Clementine opened her eyes to the approaching eyebrow and cigar of the diamond-studded department store tycoon, who suddenly reeked of expensive cologne.

"I like it," Rump growled, crunching his cigar.

On the other side of the United States, the former Prince drove his smoking and sputtering Corvette up a dirt-covered fire road, along the precarious ridge of a mountain several miles northeast of Santa Barbara. A few drops of rain had fallen on the Los Padres. Simon was already feeling a little vertigo from the altitude. Arms extended like a mad orchestra conductor, the bum in the passenger seat kept pointing out turns at the very last minute, platinum hair flying. When the narrow fire road suddenly ended, Simon hit the brakes. The bum pointed left, up what looked to be a steep, crooked goat trail.

"Are you absolutely sure that—?"

The bum looked offended, then angry. He pointed again.

Simon gamely headed up the trail. The powerful old Corvette engine strained as the car bounced up a steep incline, over a teeth-shattering run of sharp small granite boulders, and then around a corner past a steep precipice, where the passenger side of the Corvette scraped loudly and achingly against the rocks. The bum held onto his headband as the little Corvette groaned upwards, bouncing into a light drizzle which suddenly changed to drifting patchy fog.

Finally, the bum signaled for Simon to stop. Simon pulled the parking brake on a precariously tilted slab of granite, and locked the car in gear. He had no idea where he was. He could have been at the top of the world. It was eerily quiet as Simon slipped out of the car, trying to keep his leather-soled Tony Lamas from slipping off the damp tilted rock.

Simon now saw that they stood at the base of an even higher mountain peak, way above the tree line at an altitude where only a few sad little Manzanita bushes grew. The old surf bum pointed to the tallest peak, which shot up like a granite knife through the foggy mist.

The bum held his heart, and put the other hand on Simon's shoulder. He was blinking rapidly in the fog and he appeared to be possessed by some kind of blinking, sputtering spirit.

"Go forward, slightly younger dude, for I am not strong enough to make the final leg of this difficult journey," the bum said, pointing somewhat melodramatically at the fog-shrouded peak. "Far up there, on the tallest peak of the highest mountain, if your heart is clean and pure, you will find that thing which you desire most."

Simon rolled down his sleeves, pulled up his tie, and put on the suit jacket he almost left in the Corvette. Then the lawyer took a deep breath and hurried up the last and most challenging part of the difficult, crooked, rock-strewn trail.

The granite rocks were slippery under the Tony Lamas. It was foggy and wet up there in the clouds. The former Prince could hardly breathe.

With a great physical effort, slipping as he went, the desperate lawyer scrambled up the winding trail toward the summit, using both his hands and feet. Then he paused and struggled to catch his breath.

Ahead, nestled in an orifice in the granite, was a huge bird nest, bigger than any bird's nest Simon had ever seen in his life. It was the size of some rich kid's plastic wading pool. Sitting on the bird's nest was the biggest bird Simon had ever seen in his life. It looked like a giant black vulture, only meaner, and much more muscular. The yellow-eyed Condor riffled the edges of its huge wings, which were ominous and black as night. Opening its sharply-hooked beak, the Condor emitted an animal-like cry, a cry unlike any Simon had ever heard from a bird before.

The eerie cry came again.

It took Simon a minute to realize that the sound he heard was a squeal of a pig, trapped under the feathers of the giant bird.

The next few seconds of Simon's life happened in slow motion, as if in a primal dream. The Condor fluffed its wings and slowly rose to the lip of the nest, squealing like a pig. In a flash Simon saw that the bird had the front leg of a squirming, squealing pig in its talons. The Condor spread its great black wings and squatted, preparing to fly off with the squealing pig. At that moment, the desperate lawyer became possessed with unbelievable courage.

Simon flung himself toward the nest and grabbed the kicking pig's hind legs as they rose into the sky.

What happened over the precipice became a Stone Age battle between man and beast. The bird could not fly away with Simon hanging onto the pig.

Simon could not let go because he wanted the pig more than he wanted life itself. Simon tried to kick at the bird, but this was difficult in the leather-soled Tony Lamas because every time he tried to kick the clumsy lawyer lost his footing.

The bird pecked at the desperate lawyer, ripping at the shoulderpads of his blue Armani suit. The bird cried out, beat its huge wings in the lawyer's face. Caught in the middle, the traumatized pig relieved itself over Simon's head and shoulders. Simon began blinking and shouting and trying to strike the bird with one arm. Finally, at the edge of the precipice, just before they were all going over the edge to their deaths together, the bird released the pig, which miraculously was still alive, but quite frightened.

As they fell the pig bit Simon's wrist, and then immediately kicked out of his arms, leaped out of the nest, and tried to hobble away down the rocky path on its three good legs.

The exhausted lawyer tripped and stumbled down after it, finally tackling the hobbling skinny little pig and bringing it to the ground on an oddly-tilting slab of granite as the Condor circled overhead, angrily cawing.

More than three hours after the search began, the scratched-up lawyer backed his smoking, bouncing Corvette down the rocky trail, his suit's shoulder pads loosely flapping. The pig's name tag read Desdemona. The old surf bum held the quivering pig, stroking little Desdemona like a baby. Somewhere down the mountain, the fog partially lifted.

As soon as Simon got rid of the old bum, he drove to Swizzle Stick Road, where the sun immediately broke out of the clouds and began to shine brightly.

"What did you do to her little *foot?*" Petunia shrieked, taking the hobbling pig into her arms.

Simon reached for the pig's missing foot, still in his pocket, but thought better of it as Petunia personally carried the angrily-grunting pig to the back seat of the Range Rover.

The Pig Island security men crossed their arms and glared at Simon after they slammed and locked the gate.

The little Mexican maid hurried toward the gate and shook it to make sure the gate was locked. Then she caught Simon's eyes with her own. The maid's angry eyes were the color of chili beans and her scowl was unbelievably ferocious.

"Es one more porky pig," hissed the little maid. "Senora say you go get last porky now."

※

Flying back to China, Long Drive Loo sat unhappily squeezed into a small seat in coach class on one of the bankrupt international Texas airlines. Her bag of golf clubs was uncomfortably squeezed between her legs because she couldn't afford to pay to check it.

It had taken her family what seemed like an eternity to wire the funds to return to China, and they sent only enough for an economy ticket. The economy ticket was a sign of disrespect, she well knew, an indication that the family was very unhappy because she had promised them many things, and was bringing home only failure, dishonor, and disgrace.

Miss Loo grimaced as she watched the uniformed backs of the stewards in their tight pants and small red cowboy hats disappearing up the aisle, a stainless steel refreshment cart full of sweet American beverages between them. The air was extremely stale in economy class, she noticed, and she could barely move her legs.

Too many of Miss Loo's countrymen were wedged into seats on either side. They smelled like they had spent the previous week washing pots and pans in Chinese restaurants, and then boarded the plane without bothering to wash or change their clothes. Far ahead, in the roomy first class seats, she could see several arrogant Japanese passengers working on desktop computers and happily smoking.

Miss Loo's plane had flown out of San Francisco in pursuit of the setting sun, but the sun disappeared. The crowded plane careened toward Asia in pitch darkness. The Pacific Ocean lay somewhere below them, like a dark, wet mouth.

It would be almost two days more before she arrived in Shanghai, she knew, with an inconvenient stop in Tokyo and a long layover in the hated country of Japan where people were politely rude and even the smallest items were ridiculously expensive. Miss Loo had less than one hundred American dollars in her silk purse, and with the sleeping compartment rental she would be completely broke by the time her fourth plane landed in Shanghai. Her entire family would meet her at the airport, bringing flowers and welcome-home gifts, but not very many.

Long Drive dreaded what she knew was her duty. She didn't want to explain what happened to her in America, and why. She knew she would be politely questioned at length by the oldest members of her family, some of whom had warned her against an alliance with the Americans, and specifically warned against having government cashier's checks drawn for the Americans in advance.

Trying to put these memories out of her mind, Miss Loo ordered more expensive little bottles of pre-mixed Martinis. She opened and drank the little bottles down as quickly as possible, in between extremely small packages of salted American beer nuts. America was big country! Long Drive would find another American company to occupy her family's factories, that was for sure, she would tell the family. She was a competitor and she would try again, and next time she would win, because everyone in China knew that America was full of greedy capitalists eager to sell out their countrymen for even a small increase in profit.

Miss Loo's blood pressure rose every time she remembered the bumbling American vice president of legal affairs who had betrayed her, and in such a public and humiliating way. Thanks to the clumsy lawyer, she told herself, she would return home in complete disgrace. Her ancestors would not be happy, and neither would the elders of her dead husband's family to whom she had foolishly promised success.

Facing her assembled relatives would be the ultimate humiliation. Long Drive could do no more than face their questions bravely, with her athlete's determination and her strong competitor's heart.

"Waiter, little bottle empty now, here, cowboy, hiya!" she shouted, waving one hand and holding the tiny empty plastic bottle in the other.

The young American stewards in small cowboy hats were far ahead on the plane, near the first class passengers. Although she caught the eye of one, the arrogant young American blithely ignored the empty bottle she held up, probably because she hadn't left a tip for the last two bottles. Her cheeks stung with additional humiliation. Miss Loo was even more humiliated because she had to watch her money now, when she had been on the threshold of becoming the richest woman in the world.

Long Drive stood up, furiously angry, tired of being ignored, flinging the tiny bottle up the long aisle at the distant stewards and blowing her professional athlete's cool at last.

"Waiter, hiya, hiya, customer here more drink here!" Miss Loo shouted hysterically, shaking her fist and trying to stand up while squeezing her golf clubs between her legs. "No drink now, American sorry, I hijack American airplane right away, no stop Tokyo, go straight to China!"

At the sound of her cries and the loudly rattling golf clubs, every steward looked up and froze in position. Suddenly the plastic doors to the first class cabin glided shut. The out of focus movie starring Charles Bronson darkened on the big screen ahead, and the air circulation system went off, making the bad air in the cabin stand still and reek even more strongly of cigarettes and Chinese food.

As the Asian passengers looked cluelessly from side to side, a few American military types with buzz-cut hair slowly stood up a few seats behind Miss Loo, crouching here and there, creeping forward, their muscular arms bent to their sides. The airliner became intensely quiet. The reading light over Miss Loo's seat began to flash on and off slowly.

Ahead of her, as if in slow motion, the stewards in their tight pants pulled out cans of pepper spray and assumed defensive positions.

Behind her, the American military types slowly glided quietly forward, like phantoms in a dream. Miss Loo didn't realize what was going to happen until one of the leaping Americans grabbed her around the neck from behind, and with the help of a steward wrestled her roughly down into the aisle, kicking and screaming, spraying her with pepper spray and knocking the golf clubs between her legs askew.

❧

It was not relevant that the odds of finding the third pig were less than zero. The third pig was the missing part of Simon Butterknut's personal grail, and if it hadn't been his only hope for redemption, he would have realized it was impossible.

By the time his phone weakly chimed, Simon had almost run completely out of money. Facing a choice between paying another week's rent at the Motel 6 and paying his cell phone bill, the former vice president of legal affairs began sleeping in his car with his last remaining cell phone at his side.

In a matter of weeks, with a rapidity which surprised him, the disgraced barrister had maxed out his credit cards, and cleaned out the balance of his personal bank accounts in the Cayman Islands. For several days after he returned the first pig, his strategy was to send flowers and candy every few days, to try to soften up Petunia, but all his gifts were refused.

The Prince sensed a slight shift in Petunia's position when he brought in the second pig, but he knew her well enough to realize it was not a genuine change of heart. Only by finding and returning home with the last pig would he actually have a chance to hack through the frozen river of ice over Petunia's heart, and weasel his way back into the mansion on Swizzle Stick Road that he still considered his rightful home.

Although the odds decreased by the day, finding the last pig would give the former Prince his last best chance to worm his way back into the good graces of the richest family in America.

Basically an optimist, and something of a fool, Simon never lost hope that it was possible to find the third pig.

The former Prince was eating Big Whoppers at Burger King on a 2-for-1 coupon when he answered a fateful call. He'd been charging the phone on the cigarette lighter of his Corvette as his batteries were already dangerously low. The voice on the line was difficult to hear, but somebody was apparently responding to his ad in the *Penny Saver*, a free ad and the only advertisement he could still afford to run. Nobody from the family, he knew, not even Clippy, would now call him now on his personal line. The Prince rose from his plastic chair with both Big Whoppers in one hand, and hurried outside for better reception.

"Are you calling about the ad?" Simon asked.

Simon thought he heard some kind of snorting in the background. He hoped it wasn't another giggling teenager, preparing to break out in a high-spirited pig call.

Simon had already gotten too many crank calls about his ad, at all hours of the night. It was kids, of course, mostly high-pitched juvenile voices with what sounded like legitimate information about seeing a pig on this or that street, and asking out how fat the pig was, how long was its tail, and what color were its eyes, what its oink sounded like, and could you show me how a pig call sounds, and finally if its name was Porky, or Babe, or Charlotte, giving themselves away, the kids cracking up, unable to maintain the charade, oinking and grunting at him, making pig calls and shouting obscenities, and finally hanging up on the disappointed lawyer.

"You say you the one looking for a pig?" said a reedy voice, crackling with static.

"I'm having trouble hearing you!" Simon shouted.

"I say I got a little pig farm up near Santa Margarita Canyon!"

Simon wasn't sure he understood, but it didn't sound like a joke. He stepped lightly between the plastic tables and chairs on the patio searching for a sweet spot to improve reception on his cell phone. He put a finger in one ear and stepped backwards, tripping over the curb of the drive-thru lane. He fell down neatly on the seat of his pants, one of his Big Whoppers rolling neatly away.

A passing Labrador Retriever barked at the rolling paper-jacketed hamburger as Simon cradled his precious cell phone in both hands.

"I said I gotta pig out here!" the voice rose and crackled. "You got a reward, I gotta pig!"

"I don't want to buy a pig," Simon groaned. "I'm looking for a particular pig—a beloved family pet."

"Little black sow with some kinda fancy-ass name tag?" came the suddenly clear voice.

"Yes!" Simon said, suddenly excited.

"Yes!" Simon said again. "Hello?"

When he heard the squawk box, and a female voice shouting out an order, Simon realized he was sitting in the middle of the drive-through lane. He waved one hand, not wanting to lose his precious cell phone connection. The woman's huge black Hummer slowly rolled toward him in the drive-through lane, ominously revving its engine.

"How much reward you bringing out?"

"How much reward do you *want?*" Simon asked.

"You come out here tonight, we'll dicker it out."

The Hummer stopped just short of Simon. Simon was pointing to his cell phone to try to explain, but the heavily made-up older woman behind the tinted windshield just gave him the finger and leaned on her air horn.

"Give me directions!" Simon shouted, refusing to move, waving the Hummer off, and fumbling for his last usable Mont Blanc pen.

Simon scribbled directions on the back of his hand and rolled away as the Hummer clunked into first gear.

Night was approaching. Long wet fingers of Pacific Ocean fog crept up the streets and alleyways of Santa Barbara.

Just John, as he identified himself, lived several miles north of Santa Barbara, up Highway 101 toward San Luis Obispo. He said he had a hog farm a couple miles off the road. Simon brought all the cash he had in the world, which was a little more than $41, and hoped for the best.

Turning on his headlights in the fog, windshield wipers flapping, Simon prayed hard for a miracle, just one decent, reasonable, sympathetic man.

Following the directions he scribbled on the back of his hand, Simon turned off Highway 101 onto a country road. He drove down a crunching gravel driveway between two wet fields of freshly-cut alfalfa. For a minute he thought he was lost. Then several large corrugated metal buildings loomed up through the fog. Behind a sad little white shack of a house was what looked like an entire city of twenty foot high corrugated metal Quonset huts sweating quietly in the fog.

Simon parked and headed for the huts. Each shed contained hundreds of squealing, eating, shitting pigs. In the first hut, he saw that each pig was locked in a small pen on a concrete floor half-covered with straw, rice hulls, and piles of wet pig shit. Everywhere the desperate lawyer looked, an enormous pig lifted its snout above the top of the pen and squealed wildly.

It was obviously feeding time. Mexicans in bandanas hurried from pen to pen, sloshing portions of wet slop into each metal feeder.

The trembling lawyer had never smelled so much pig shit. Billowing clouds of ammonia and methane made his eyes water.

As he walked through the enormous shed, the sheer concentrated force of the smell nearly knocked him down. He also noticed that all the pigs he saw were considerably ... bigger ... than Petunia's last lost Chinese Pot-Bellied Pig.

"Beulah!" the former Prince cried, for this was the name of the last pig.

A hundred pigs squealed, and stamped their feet. Simon paused, quietly looking from side to side. He heard the moist, wet sound of two pigs lifting what was left of their tails and relieving themselves behind him. Grimacing Mexicans hurried past him with buckets of slop in both hands, averting their eyes.

Directly outside the open metal barn, Simon suddenly noticed, was a sort of large lighted corral with a dirt floor, ringed by a galvanized metal fence.

In the center of the corral, two black pigs appeared to be mating. For some reason, Simon's eyes fastened on the fat little sow who was squealing frantically, with a high-pitched voice, while carrying the much larger and clumsier male on her back. The clumsy boar struggled to keep its front legs on the shoulders of the squirming little sow. The squealing little sow fought and pawed her way valiantly toward the barn where Simon stood in a sort of trance, helplessly watching.

"That one on the bottom's yours," said a reedy voice. Simon turned to face the voice.

"John," the tall man said, sticking out his hand and giving Simon a bone-crushing handshake. John wore canvas overalls with a tee shirt underneath. His bright blue eyes sparkled behind a pair of very thick, mud-flecked granny glasses.

John quietly pointed into the corral at the still copulating pigs. By this time the little sow had struggled up to the railing where Simon and John were standing. The little sow hurried anxiously back and forth before them, carrying the clumsy male, like a little girl pulling a rickshaw.

John leaned on a metal fence rail overlooking the pigs. He looked up, smiled, and lewdly winked at Simon.

"Your pig's having herself a time," he drawled.

"That's the wrong pig!" Simon hissed. "The pig I want is a lot smaller than that one."

"That's your same little sow, we just fattened her up," John said. "Since she wandered into here, we've been feeding her pig chow. This thing barely fits around her neck anymore."

He tossed Simon a collar with a bell on it, which Simon promptly dropped. When Simon picked up the collar and wiped if off, he saw "Beulah" engraved over the familiar ornamental inscription, "Resident of Pig Island."

"Little bitty slip of a thing came up and sniffed my hand just like a dog. Fattened her up I thought for me," John smiled.

Simon stared at the collar, and then at the stout little sow in the pen. The pig seemed to be three times as wide as Petunia's other pigs. Beulah must have gained a hundred pounds. And her hooves had not been trimmed, Simon noticed. Beulah's front hooves curled up in front of her feet like the slippers of an Arabian fairy princess.

"Expensive little sports car you driving in here," John said. "Must have cost you a bundle."

"I had that old piece of junk since college. Old car hardly even runs anymore," Simon parried, shaking his head.

"Classic car now, I bet," John said. " Worth a lot of money, huh?"

"Try to sell it."

"Forty thousand, fifty thousand, maybe more? Auction it off on EBay?"

"You're dreaming," Simon protested.

"Nice suit, too. Armani, ain't it? Who ripped out your shoulder pads?"

"Listen," Simon said, holding out a twenty dollar bill. "Let me be honest with you. I've only got twenty dollars to my name. This little pig is important to my wife. That pig is my wife's beloved family pet. It would break my wife's heart if I didn't bring back that pig. My wife loves that pig more than she loves me. She threw me outta the house because of that pig, and I'm almost broke, my credit cards are maxed, bill collectors are calling me, I got thrown out of Motel 6 and I can't even qualify for unemployment. I'm living in my car, eating one hamburger a day and I really, really need this pig. Have a little pity on me, please."

"Pity, sure."

"Excuse me?"

"Bring me thousand dollars tonight, you got your pig"

"What?"

"I think you heard me," John said. "You advertised reward for a pig, I said okay. Your ad said big reward, I said okay. Tonight you get your pig for a thousand dollars cash and I gotta have it all by midnight tonight. Truck's loading up for the processors in three hours. I don't get the dough tonight that little pig's pork chops, if you get my drift."

John opened a corral gate Simon hadn't even seen, and whistled Beulah into the shed. Using one foot, John expertly kicked the male off her back and pushed him back into the corral as Beulah entered. Suddenly free, Beulah waddled forward to Simon, rubbing her wet, hairy snout on Simon's pants leg, and then looking up at him with wet brown eyes. Simon imagined the pig had been crying. For an instant, the clumsy lawyer's heart was touched by the pathetic little animal, whose scratched-up flanks were partially covered with semen and pig shit.

Beulah shook herself like a wet dog, scattering shit and semen onto what was left of Simon's Armani suit.

"Little pig maybe loves you," John said behind his hand, as if telling someone else a joke. John shook his head as if he didn't believe what he'd just said but his blue eyes remained cold. "But I got some money in her."

"So bring the dough tonight, Corvette, you got your pig," John said, shaking Simon's hand as they paused beside his car. "Otherwise, stop by the processors with that twenty and buy your little wife five or six pounds of bacon. Be cheaper."

Farmer John smiled enigmatically as he held open the door of the Corvette and Simon got in.

> All things considered, it will be found that some things that seem like virtue will lead you to ruin if you follow them; while others, apparently vices, will, if followed, result in your safety and well being.
>
> —Machiavelli, *The Prince*

All the way back to Santa Barbara, plumes of fog swirled past the former Prince's windshield.

As his windshield wipers flailed frantically back and forth, the desperate lawyer racked his brain. Where on earth could he lay hands on a thousand dollars? Simon had no allies left. He'd stopped speaking to his own family years ago, and he wasn't even sure where any of them lived anymore, although he vaguely remembered receiving an angry letter from his older sister announcing that his parents were going into a rest home in Arizona and never stopped asking for him to call. His parents were probably already dead, Simon reasoned. Then an inspiration struck him: Call The Doctor! Clippy had been fastidiously ignoring him, he realized, but his old fraternity brother was Simon's last best chance to rescue Petunia's beloved third missing pig.

Simon hurried into The Doctor is In Surgery Center, hardly realizing that the pants of his rumpled Armani suit were stained with flecks of pig shit and pig semen. The Doctor's big-breasted receptionist smiled warmly when he straightened his tie and walked inside. But as Simon approached the desk she wrinkled her nose and looked from side to side, as if searching for the source of a sudden gas leak. It was then that Simon realized his ripped-up suit was emitting a powerful, porcine odor, and he took a step back.

"I'm sorry, but the Doctor is out," the beautiful receptionist purred. There were a couple of fresh hickeys just below the collar of her starched white uniform. "Doctor finished up surgery a few hours early today, but he'll be back in the morning if you'd like a professional consultation," she warbled, flipping open her appointment book with a suggestive gesture.

"Eye work?" she suggested.

Simon drove immediately out to his old fraternity brother's mansion—Two Teat Towers, he and Petunia used to joke when they felt so superior, back in the days. The gate to Clippy's driveway opened automatically. The former Prince drove right up to Two Teat Towers and leaped out of his car in what had become quietly drifting fog, hoping against hope that Clementine wasn't home.

A Mexican maid in a bizarre silver uniform led him back through the empty house, and out the back. Simon found the Doctor sitting on a jeweled lounge chair, under a heat lamp near some sort of waterfall.

At first glance, his old fraternity brother looked like some strange African god reclining in the primeval mist. He had a mudpack of green clay on his face. Thick yellow straws extended out from his nostrils. A serious-looking woman with spiked lemon-colored hair made a slashing, shushing gesture as he squatted down quietly next to his oldest friend.

Doctor was focusing his mind on his weekly whole body rejuvenation, she whispered, beginning with a facial and climaxing in a pedicure. A good facial combined with Pacific Ocean fog, she whispered conspiratorially, was a particularly good tonic combination for the Doctor's medium olive skin.

The flaxen-haired consultant handed Simon a business card which identified her as Johanna Handy, Body Artist. The Body Artist had rings on every finger of her right hand, and a fresh hickey between the rather pendulous breasts which nearly fell out of her chartreuse uniform. Just under the hickeys, Simon also noticed the beginning of some kind of exotic upper body tattoo. His old fraternity brother was barefoot, he noticed, and so was the body artist who began briskly rubbing his left foot with both hands.

With her nose in the air and her English accent, the body artist seemed absolutely serious about what she was doing.

"Doctor must be absolutely still for one hour," she said with perfect English diction, enunciating every syllable as she began to shape Clippy's toenails with an oversized emery board. "We absolutely cannot have wrinkles set up shop anywhere in the facial area."

Simon ignored her. He leaned over his old fraternity brother's mud-packed face.

"Clippy, it's Nutty," Simon told the still green mud mask and yellow straws. "I'm in deep shit. I've got to have a thousand bucks tonight. Spot me the cash, for old time's sake, I'll make it up a hundred times soon as I get back in with Petunia."

Clippy shook his head faintly, no.

"Only 45 minutes to go now, doctor," the girl crooned, stroking his right foot with both hands. The doctor faintly nodded, yes.

Simon leaned back toward his friend. But with a surprisingly muscular foot, the body artist pushed Simon away from the reclining doctor, and wagged her finger in his face.

"If you can't refrain from talking, sir, I'll call Doctor's security and have you removed from the premises," she whispered to Simon in a matter-of-fact voice. "What I'm doing is crucially important. Please do be patient. You've got less than forty minutes to wait."

Simon opened his mouth to speak.

"Please be silent," she whispered.

The body artist carefully placed a triangle of cardboard over the Doctor's forehead. Then, with a significant glance at Simon, she bent over the doctor's left foot to resume the rub and pedicure. She lifted the big pink emery board as if conducting a small but important symphony.

As she resumed work, Simon was barely able to contain himself. The waterfall cascading over the plastic boulders behind him was loud as Niagara Falls. The air reeked of chlorine.

Behind the figure of his reclining friend, the brushed aluminum palm trees seemed to sweat anxious tears in the fog. And beyond the crying aluminum palm trees rose the spectacle of Two Teat Towers, a vision in the fog. The mansion's two oddly bent stained glass towers, illuminated from within like lighthouses, seemed at that moment looming portents of impending disaster to the former Prince.

The sounds of the body artist's emery board were followed by the pungent smell of nail polish. Several times Simon glanced at his Rolex which was no longer there. Before long, he thought he saw one of Clementine's little Jack Russell terriers staggering drunkenly through the fog like a tiny phantom, and quietly relieving itself on one of the palm trees.

"Is Mrs. Clipster home?" Simon blurted, suddenly frightened.

The lemon-haired Englishwoman shook her head no, then reflexively buttoned the top button of her uniform.

At that moment a gentle gong tone signaled the end of the Doctor's facial.

The body artist bent over the sleeping doctor, and gently peeled off most of the absorbent clay. Then she carefully cleaned the remaining clay from his face with a cotton pad soaked in lavender and rosewater. Finally, as if rising from the dead, the Doctor slowly sat up.

The Doctor lifted his eyebrows and gently blinked his eyes. He moved his lips and cheeks as if he had never used them before.

The body artist handed him a large oval mirror: the Doctor examined each side of his face carefully and critically.

"You look at least three years younger," said the body artist, as she slipped into her Birkenstocks.

"I like it," the Doctor said.

"How did we do with our foot massage?"

"Better. The right foot feels lighter now."

"Your feet certainly *look* good," the body artist purred, playfully licking her fingertips and rubbing them across his toes.

When the Doctor lowered the mirror, he looked at Simon and smiled blankly. Clippy did look younger, Simon noticed, as well as relaxed and more benign. Simon had the feeling Clippy was waiting for a compliment but somehow it didn't feel right to compliment his old fraternity brother. So Simon nodded and forced his face into an appreciative smile.

The body artist made one last critical check of the doctor's face, nodded briskly, collected her tools, and kissed him on the forehead. Then she walked away, carrying a chrome case full of rejuvenating clays and aromatic facial products. Meanwhile, the Doctor heard his imaginary children approaching, and stood up.

"Nice to see you, Nutty. I'll walk you to the door," the Doctor blurted with false good humor.

"Clippy!" Simon exclaimed, grabbing his old friend's arm. "For God's sake! It's Nutty! We've been through hell together! You've got to help me now, for old time's sake!"

Desperately, disjointedly, falling to his knees twice on the way to the front door, Simon lurched into the story of his fall from grace, the snarling marshals at the door, the cruelly frozen so-called joint assets, the cancelled credit cards, the failed ads, the telephone jokes, the horrible Motel 6, his heroic rescue of the two pigs, Petunia's inexplicable ingratitude, finally to greedy Farmer John who was holding him up for a thousand bucks and it was the last pig, too.

"You think you got problems, Nutty? Clemmie's been gone for two months now," the Doctor said, absentmindedly opening the front door for his friend who had again fallen to his knees. "Clemmie's at the Waldorf Astoria in New York, and I'm not sure when she's coming home...."

Holding his front door open, the Doctor stared off into space, lost in his own thoughts under the Clipster crest.

Simon brusquely pulled the Doctor out the front door and into the Corvette. Simon didn't have time to waste feeling sorry for his old fraternity brother, who was obviously down in the dumps. In a flash they were sailing down Swizzle Stick Road in Simon's Corvette, with the top down, wind in what was left of their hair, pulling into the Montecito branch of the Bank of America.

Simon didn't stop talking until Clippy obediently withdrew a thousand dollars in cash. Simon hastily pocketed the twenty dollar bills as soon as they came out of the ATM machine.

"Just like old times, Nutty, you, me, your beat-up old car, you borrowing money," the Doctor said, putting his hands in the pockets of his scrubs. He fingered his secret cache of business cards and enjoyed a sentimental look into the past.

The two fraternity brothers had loaned each other money when they were courting the Commode girls, Clippy remembered. Before that first fateful double date, the two Omega Pi's made a pact never to have one of the Commode girls pay for anything, ever, even if they had to borrow, beg, or steal money to help each other. This happened more than once during their unusual double courtship. They so wanted to make a good impression on the Commode girls, Clippy remembered. And they succeeded, the Doctor recalled, thrusting his hands deeper into his pockets and grabbing his entire emergency cache of business cards. He and Nutty got the Commode girls, and they got everything else that came with belonging to the richest family in America. In the distance, just around the corner from the ATM machine, the doctor's imaginary children began happily singing.

Rocketing into action, Simon jumped over the back of the little Corvette like a cowboy over the butt of a horse. The former Prince landed neatly in the driver's seat, and started the Corvette without a backward glance.

"Nutty?" the Doctor cried, his sentimental mood broken.

The Doctor's imaginary children began crying out, and his worry wolf began yowling. The Doctor didn't have a way home. The Doctor suddenly noticed a number of surly Mexicans staring at him from an old car parked just across the street. Their banged-up old car was idling ominously in the fog.

With a wet screech of nearly bald tires, Simon left his old fraternity brother stranded at the bank.

The former Prince barreled north up State Street and onto Highway 101. Wet fog smacked his hair back to the side of his head as he desperately speeded north, windshield wipers flapping. It was late when Simon crunched up the gravel driveway to the illuminated pig farm. Hyperventilating without his watch, Simon feared he was already too late.

The former Prince slashed his way through a cloud of strangely damp dust near the sheds, dust that was already turning to mud on his skin. Parking quickly, Simon hurried quickly through the strange wet dust toward the sheds in the unearthly quiet of the fog.

When Simon finally found Shed No. 48, the last place he had seen Beulah, his heart dropped. The large corrugated metal shed was completely empty. The silent concrete floor of the shed was cold and silent as death itself.

Drawn outside by the sound of frantically squealing pigs, Simon saw hundreds of pigs packed into a huge metal corral next to the shed, an unearthly spectacle under bright lights. A long sinister pig truck with metal cages hung on both sides was parked in the center of the corral, its diesel engine idling. Behind the mud-spattered cab, half the long truck's metal cages were already full of squealing, bawling pigs.

Simon could just make out slow-moving Mexicans with red bandanas over their faces. Mexicans moved through the dust like so many phantoms, cutting out pigs. Each Mexican had what appeared to be a willow switch in each hand: they flicked and worked pigs out of the bunch, one squealing pig at a time, and flicked and drove them up narrow metal ramps which led up to the cages. As soon as one Mexican kicked his pig into a cage, locked it, and hopped off the ramp, another Mexican moved the ramp to the next empty cage, and up went another pig.

Some of the pigs had managed to turn themselves partway around in the narrow cages. They all seemed to be squealing anxiously at Simon.

Farmer John approached Simon through the dust, moving his arms as if swimming. He wore a red bandana over his nose and the outline of his mouth was already covered with mud-colored dust.

John pulled down the bandana, revealing a mouth that was much whiter than the rest of his face. His blue eyes were almost invisible behind the thick, dusty lenses of his granny glasses.

"You would come too damn late, of course," John said.

Simon's heart dropped.

"Your little sow's still out there somewhere," John said. "Mexicans didn't separate her out like I told them to. I got that little collar back on her after you left so you can try to find her but we don't have time to help. She's not loaded up yet so you got five or six minutes before the truck fills up and takes off."

Simon took off his suit jacket, rolled up his sleeves, and gamely wandered into the herd of grunting, pushing pigs, squatting down occasionally to try to find one with a collar. There seemed to be a million of them. The animals' muscular shoulders and hocks pushed his knees and thighs in one direction and then another, like powerful ocean riptides. Simon's beat up Tony Lamas mashed through fresh wet pig shit, causing him to often slip off balance. The slipping and sliding lawyer could endure the acrid smell of pig shit for as long as he had to, but the grunting and squealing of the pigs was deafening. Their frightened high-pitched squeals and cries were punctuated by the sharp clackity-clack of little hooves stopping and starting along their final journey up the metal ramps and onto the death truck.

Simon thought he heard Beulah's bell ringing at the far edge of the corral. He desperately tried to push and wade through the thigh-high sea of squealing pigs. The pigs all seemed to be trying to step on his last good pair of boots, step into his pants cuffs, fall onto his ankles, and nip his knees and thighs.

The pigs were shoving him from side to side like a bobbing cork as he walked.

"Beulah!" Simon desperately cried.

One of the pigs actually climbed on the back of another pig to pull on the end of his tie. The pig was trying to pull him down into the herd to his death, he feared. The pig's hostile gesture frightened the desperate lawyer. Simon slapped the nose of the pig; the pig squealed with pain, but frantically leaped for his tie again, and then again. At last, Simon realized that the pig jumping and snapping at his tie, the pig he had just slapped down into the herd for a third time, wore a collar from Pig Island.

"Beulah!" he cried. "Wait!"

But Beulah was already waddling angrily away through the sea of pigs. Pushing her way through the mob, toward the truck itself, with her snout in the air, Beulah wouldn't look at him. Simon realized he had hurt her feelings. He tried to wade through the pigs in pursuit. Finally, as if fighting his way through heavy surf, Simon caught up with Beulah. He stooped down to hug and grab her, but at that moment he was hit hard from behind and pushed down into the herd. For a moment the former Prince foresaw his own death—pounded to death by a thousand sharp hooves. But he pulled himself up by Beulah's collar, and pulled Beulah down instead. The elbows and back of his Egyptian cotton dress shirt were now wet with pig shit, his pants were ripped, his tie was gone, but he had not lost his boots.

"Come on, Beulah," Simon said, pulling her up by her collar. "Let's get outta here."

With two fingers inside her collar, more pulled than pulling, constantly off balance, the former Prince clumsily walked the snorting little pig out of the herd, away from the death truck, and toward a distant gate. John was waiting with Simon's suit coat which Simon removed to reveal the business end of a double-barreled shotgun.

"Suppose you did bring cash," John smiled.

For one horrible second, feeling his pants pockets, Simon thought he'd lost his cash in the pigpen. Then he found some of the bills sloppily folded in his front pants pockets, some in his shirt pockets, and the rest of in the pockets of his suit coat. To his relief, counting out twenty-dollar bills into the hands of John, he counted out exactly a thousand dollars.

"I thought you said two thousand," John snorted. "Maybe let's just call this all off."

Simon's bowels loosened a bit.

"No," he squeaked.

"I'm shitting you," John said, laughing behind his hand.

John whistled over a couple of Mexicans and said something to them in Spanish. He pulled the bandana back over his mouth and turned away as the Mexicans flicked Beulah out of the barn with their switches, whistling and snapping her flanks all the way out to the car.

"Put her in the trunk," Simon said, opening his trunk. The Mexicans looked at him blankly. "Put pig in trunk! In here, *aqui*," Simon gestured.

"Porky too big one, boss," a Mexican said, pulling his bandana down off his mouth. "No fitting car."

"Put the pig in the trunk, god damn it! I want the pig put in the god damned trunk!" Simon shouted.

The Mexicans shrugged helplessly, holding Beulah in place with flicks of their switches.

"You think I'm going to take any shit from you?" Simon shrieked at the shrugging Mexicans.

But when Simon took a second look at Beulah, he realized the Mexicans were right. Beulah had grown much bigger than Petunia's other pigs. Little Beulah would definitely not fit in his Corvette's trunk anymore.

As if he knew what he was doing, Simon angrily slammed the trunk of his Corvette. He jumped in the drivers' seat, and opened the door to the passenger side. Simon knew from dealing with Mexican gardeners and janitors that it was important for him to act like he was in charge at that moment, like a *patron*, and to show the Mexicans that he knew exactly what he was doing. The Prince ratcheted back his passenger seat as far as it would go and angrily pointed.

"Put Porky!" he screamed.

The two Mexicans looked at each other, and then laid down their switches. One obediently picked up the pig's front legs, and the other picked up the hind legs. Working together, they dropped Beulah lightly into the passenger side of the Corvette, head first, knees bent, and somehow closed the car door. Beulah was face down on the floorboard; her big hairy black ass and legs stuck up over the seat. Beulah's squeals were muffled, but she began kicking her hind legs wildly as one of the Mexicans buckled the seat belt around her back and pulled it tight.

"That seat belt's never going to hold!" Simon shouted, turning on his windshield wipers as Beulah kicked him sharply in the ear. "You guys don't know what you're doing!"

The Mexicans were already walking away. Hesitating for only a moment, Simon took off. He headed up the driveway, leaning out of the car window to duck the hooves of the kicking pig. The former Prince turned south on Highway 101 in the fog, windshield wipers flapping.

Commodore spent almost a month on the Cape without a telephone, cut off from the world in the summer house that the family no longer used for family vacations. The old billionaire and his faithful valet spent several days walking along the Atlantic seashore, watching the distant sailboats and sorting things out.

As gentle waves caressed the shore, Commodore and his valet strolled past grand old beachfront mansions and private docks, twisted pine trees, sharp rocks, dead fish, and occasional piles of dog poop. They passed windswept tufts of wild grass waving wildly at them from atop dunes of sand.

The old billionaire and his faithful valet contemplated the ups and downs of life on beach after beach of slowly blowing sand.

When Commodore returned to California, Miss Gander gave him a pile of correspondence. Commodore was surprised to find several telegrams from Miss Loo. He hadn't imagined he'd ever hear from her again. The last time he saw her, out of the corner of his eye, he remembered her strangely twisted smile as she blushed, bowed, and hurried out of company headquarters as quickly as she could go.

Miss Loo had plotted to deceive him, but of course, the old billionaire had already forgiven her. He had made enough mistakes in his own life to keep him humble.

Commodore Commode was also not a vindictive man. As a young man, he had been taught that it was proper to forgive.

From what he could make out from Miss Loo's telegrams, her airliner had made an emergency landing on the island of Guam. She had been arrested. Miss Loo had been taken to some sort of secret American detention camp. The camp was one of several dozen that had been erected for international terrorists although here Miss Loo was the only inhabitant. Miss Loo was unable to leave the island, since the U.S. military would not release her. Apparently she was even forbidden to play golf which for her was probably another form of torture.

Commodore knew he owed Miss Loo nothing. His heady infatuation was gone with the wind. But as a matter of decency and fairness, he felt obligated to call his personal lawyer, and ask him to look into Miss Loo's dilemma.

Commodore's lawyer reported back that Miss Loo was indeed being held on a small island in the Pacific, in a sort of international limbo. A Chinese citizen, she had been flying over international waters on a bankrupt Texas airline financed by a suspicious Middle Eastern arms dealer. Miss Loo had been arrested by off-duty American military intelligence officers in mid-air, as a suspected hijacker. Military intelligence computer programs forced the airliner to make an emergency landing on Guam. When they searched Miss Loo's belongings, they found two very large cashier's cheques issued by the State Bank of China in a secret compartment in her golf bag which she refused to explain. American military intelligence held her for questioning as the airliner departed without her.

Miss Loo sank into a legal quagmire. The Chinese government demanded Miss Loo's release, but claimed it knew nothing of the cheques although they were issued by a Communist government-controlled bank. When contacted by the Department of Homeland Security, both Americans whose names were on the cheques had vehemently denied knowing anything about them. Miss Loo had arrogantly refused to make a statement of any sort until she saw her Chinese government lawyer, but of course she was not allowed to see a lawyer since she was being held in a secret American prison for terrorists where there was no possibility of that. The American military was already filing attempted hijacking charges on her, since two off-duty civilian contractors testified they heard the suspect making verbal threats at the moment they passed over a top secret American military base, an obvious terrorist target. At first, Commodore's lawyer reported, the authorities had found no evidence beyond the mysterious cheques and a surprising number of tiny empty plastic bottles on the floor beneath her passenger seat.

The only thing to do on the barren island prison was to play golf, which Miss Loo as an international prisoner was forbidden to do since only American military officers and civilian contractors were authorized to use the course. Miss Loo had been placed in a cell which overlooked the golf course, where she had nothing else to do than to listen to the sound of golf balls being hit all day long. To watch the clumsy, large-bottomed Americans waddle clumsily around the course—one of them even apparently daring to use her personal golf clubs—was torture itself.

When Miss Loo angrily and insistently demanded the return of her golf clubs to her cell, the strange urgency of her request made several of the private contractors suspicious.

None of the military contractors could read the Chinese characters on the ends of the clubs and Miss Loo refused to make any statement about the clubs or anything else until she saw a lawyer. On a hunch, one of the interrogators sent the clubs back to Maryland for several types of forensic tests. The tests all came up negative except for the radiation survey which found small traces of a suspicious atomic material, Strontium-90, in a secret compartment inside her No. 4 driver. The military contractors immediately placed a permanent hold on Miss Loo's golf clubs as material evidence, and sent all three pair of her golf shoes back to Maryland for nearly a dozen more expensive, time-consuming government tests.

Looking sadly out the window at the golf course, Miss Loo remained the central figure in a minor international scandal. She was caught in a sort of legal limbo, not exactly deserted by her native country, which quietly protested her detention, but not given much assistance either. The situation was extraordinarily complex. Commodore's lawyer said there wasn't really much which could be done.

Commodore explained the situation to his faithful valet the next morning, during his Tuesday morning round of golf.

"What do you think I should do, R.G.?" Commodore asked, stooping down to size up a short putt.

"I believe the Chinese lady can quite take care of herself, sir," R.G. replied. "Don't forget, she's an experienced double agent. And she's extraordinarily clever, sir."

"She is clever," Commodore agreed, pausing for a moment to pass gas before he sank a short putt.

"The lady can surely take care of herself, sir."

"I suppose so," Commodore said, as he retrieved his ball. "It's a different world we live in these days."

And that was that.

❧

Simon Butterknut parked his Corvette across the driveway from the main gate of his former mansion on Swizzle Stick Road. Fog drifted slowly across Santa Barbara County. Simon waited in the car with the upended pig all through the night. Twice he got out and clandestinely peed in the bushes next to the gate hoping the security cameras were not on. Around three o'clock in the morning, he was awakened by a sharp kick in the ear from the struggling pig, but he was able to stroke Beulah's hindquarters, talk to her a bit and quiet her down.

As the sun rose and the fog lifted, Simon looked for the Rolex that was no longer there, and felt a deep material sadness. With the third pig wedged into the passenger seat, his grail complete, the former Prince also felt curiously out of time, as if a major portion of his life's work had finally ended.

Birds began chirping high in the Eucalyptus trees that lined Swizzle Stick Road. The former Prince's heart leaped to his throat as he imagined he heard the cawing and flapping of parrot wings on far away Pig Island, and the distant snorts of awakening pigs. Although he was tired and exhausted, Simon was determined to personally present the last pig to Petunia and make one final inspired try to get back into her good graces before giving up for good.

He then heard Petunia's Range Rover roar toward the gate. Simon knew it was Petunia on her way to her animal husbandry class at the university, which she faithfully attended on Tuesday mornings. He knew his wife was probably listening to her Johnny Mathis CDs, perhaps Johnny's signature hit, "Misty," Petunia's favorite song and ringtone, a song she played over and over again to herself. Simon prayed that the third pig would make a spectacular Tuesday morning surprise.

The front gate automatically opened. Petunia stopped the Range Rover and honked impatiently at Simon's car, which was parked sideways across the driveway, partially blocking her exit.

She angrily gestured for Simon to get out of the way.

Simon got out and gestured that he had something in the car.

Petunia dismissively gestured so what.

Simon gestured to the pig.

Petunia angrily leaned on the horn and motioned for Simon to move.

Simon gestured for Petunia to stop her car, and look.

Petunia furiously killed her engine.

She slapped on her pink pith helmet. Then she got out of the Range Rover and stopped before Simon, hands on hips.

"What?" Petunia demanded.

Simon pointed to the car, toward the upended pig in the passenger seat. Beulah's little tail switched back and forth. Beulah farted a couple of times, and began slowly kicking her right leg.

"That isn't?" Petunia gasped.

"It's Beulah!" Simon sang, dancing toward his estranged wife. "It's your last lost little pig, darling, and I found her. I gave all the money I had for her and brought her back to you because I love you so very, very much and this is only one small token of my love and my affection but it's everything I can possibly give."

"You have not returned my Beulah," Petunia said, pushing Simon away and walking closer. "She's too big."

"She's your Beulah. She only gained a little weight, darling, a few pounds, she'll lose it back, the weight is nothing," Simon sang. "Darling, I found your pig!"

As if on cue, Simon heard the opening strains of "Misty" coming from Petunia's cell phone. His heart rose up into his throat, as helpless as a kitten up a tree.

Simon danced around the Corvette, strangely animated, with a song in his heart. No matter what, the disgraced lawyer was giving it everything he had, and more or less following his heart for the first time in his life.

"Our Beulah was being held captive by an evil man on a pig farm. The mean farmer fattened our Beulah up for market. The mean farmer was going to kill our Beulah, and turn her into bacon. Beulah almost had a final ride on the death truck. But at the last minute I saved Beulah, I saved her, and it wasn't easy," Simon sang. "Darling, you wouldn't believe what I had to do. I struggled and fought for Beulah, I could have been trampled to death, I forked over my last dime, I gave it all I had, just like I'll struggle and fight for you for the rest of my life, Petunia Commode," he sang, falling to his knees for a moment. "Darling!"

"Now look at this," sang the lawyer in the shredded, shit-stained Armani suit, getting up and throwing open the door to the Corvette. "Resident of Pig Island! Proof! Proof!"

Taking the pig's hind legs, Simon twisted her one way and another to get her out of the car. Beulah's front legs were wedged on either side of the bucket seat. Beulah began kicking her hind legs and squealing to high heaven when Simon tried to pull her out since among other things her front legs were asleep.

"For God's sake, Simon," Petunia said. "Be gentle."

In his moment of happiness and triumph, Simon heedlessly ignored his former wife. With a great deal of sweating and effort, Simon tussled and twisted and dragged the squealing, farting pig out of the car. Finally Beulah's two front feet hit the dirt, her knees buckled, and her huge magnificent snout and fattened-up chest thudded against the ground.

Big Beulah blinked her eyes, as if recovering from a bad dream. Taking a step forward and bending down, Petunia clasped her hands under Beulah's corpulent chin, and carefully examined the name tag on her collar.

Beulah slowly rose to her feet, sniffing, limping a little, shaking Petunia off, and falling down once or twice, but glad to be released. She shook herself off like a wet dog a couple of times, and then began to waddle away. Beulah waddled and clattered with deliberate speed through the gate and back up the driveway, her tiny brass collar bell ringing. She had caught the distant aroma of home, the scent of Pig Island.

Before she could stop him, Simon sprinted inside the gate and took off after Beulah, who was waddling quickly away through the tall grass. Simon ran as if his life depended on it, in his stained and shredded Armani suit, what was left of his shoulder pads flapping wildly. He ran right out of his broken-down cowboy boots but it didn't matter anymore. As the pig broke into a trot, Simon broke into a trot too, the two of them lumbering through the grass toward the big slate-roofed mansion at No. 2 Swizzle Stick Road.

❧

The Silent Banner was an exclusive Buddhist retreat in the foothills of the Himalayas. For the last leg of their vacation, Philip and Diego flew to the little-known monastery in the mountains of Nepal.

The moment they arrived, the boys were required to take off their shoes. They walked barefoot down a winding, moss-covered path to the monastery, almost a mile away. They arrived to the exotic sounds of fluttering prayer flags and tinkling brass wind chimes. An bearded old monk silently washed their feet in aromatic oils and issued them sandals and robes.

In one of the small huts flanking the great monastery, the boys joined the renowned silent monks of Nepal in their colorful purple and yellow robes. Silent Banner monks practiced a few sacred silent rituals each morning, and meditated from morning to night. The monks never uttered a word to anyone because they believed talking interfered with the purity of their prayer and blocked communication from God.

The loudest sound the boys heard all month at the monastery was the sound of the brass gong calling them in from meditations by the water garden for breakfast and dinner, the monks' only meals of the day.

Although it was never actually spelled out, the wind chimes that were everywhere were understood to be God's responses to the monk's prayers. Eventually the boys understood that God received and answered prayers in a musical fashion at all hours of day and night, speaking with the voice of the wind through the fluttering yellow and purple silk banners at the top of the monastery tower, speaking in a voice that was mystery itself through the wind chimes.

Diego lost three pounds on the monk's diet, which didn't agree with him, and Philip lost three pounds, too. For several days the boys became very spiritual as they silently meditated all day long, each day blending effortlessly into the next, until they felt like two floating spirits detached from time.

But in the end, of course, they had to take off their purple and yellow robes and wordlessly bid goodbye to their hosts. They walked barefoot up the moss-covered path, put on their comfortable shoes, and quietly climbed back into their small airplane to begin the trip home.

Philip and Diego came home full of love for the world. They had gained what felt like a profound spiritual understanding of the oneness of all the world's diverse talking people—people who were, after all, just like them, separated only by their hopes, their trials, their dreams, their disappointments, and the harsh sounds of their many competing voices.

THE END

ABOUT THE AUTHOR

David Drum is an award-winning journalist and writer based in Los Angeles, California. He has worked as a newspaper reporter, a craps dealer, a funeral director, a stock speculator, a ranch foreman, an encyclopedia salesman, a short order cook, an advertising copywriter, a hot tamale vendor, a construction man, and an inner-city schoolteacher. A native of Wichita, Kansas, he is a graduate of Brevard College, the University of California at Riverside, and the University of Iowa's Writer's Workshop. A member of the AFT and UTLA, Drum is the author of several nonfiction books and one book of poetry. He is also the resident artist at Burning Books Press. This is his first novel.